FULL
CIRCLE

FULL CIRCLE

COLLIN WILCOX

A TOM DOHERTY ASSOCIATES BOOK
NEW YORK

MAR 9 5

This is a work of fic
in this book are ficti
events is purely coincidental.

FULL CIRCLE

This book is printed on acid-free paper.

A Forge Book
Published by Tom Doherty Associates, Inc.
175 Fifth Avenue
New York, N.Y. 10010

Edited by Teresa Nielsen Hayden

Library of Congress Cataloging-in Publication Data

Wilcox, Collin.
   Full circle / Collin Wilcox.
      p.   cm.
   Sequel to the series' first novel: Berhardt's Edge.
   "A Tom Doherty Associates Book."
   ISBN 0-312-85521-4
   1. Bernhardt, Alan (Fictitious character)—Fiction.   2. Private investigators—California—San Francisco—Fiction.
I. Title.
PS3573.I395F85   1994
813'.54.—dc20   9432703
                                                        CIP

First edition: November 1994

Printed in the United States of America

0 9 8 7 6 5 4 3 2 1

*This book is dedicated
to Scott, my very
first grandchild.*

PROLOGUE

As Frazer pushed back his cuff and checked the time, he realized, too late, that he should have included a new watch in the deal: a Patek Philippe, or a Rolex at least. He'd thought of everything else, even the white silk underwear, with his initials embroidered on the boxer shorts. Once, at a gallery party in Paris, he'd heard someone say that there were only two kinds of people: those who responded to the feel of silk against the flesh, and those who didn't.

What would they think, if they knew his underwear was pure silk? His mum and his dad, with their work-callused hands and their dull, defeated eyes, what would they think?

The time was exactly six-thirty. In mid-March, Manhattan was already dark, and there was a hint of snow in the air. Just ahead, at the corner of Park, he saw the small red neon sign: JERRY'S. How long had it been since he'd last walked this way? Nine months? A year?

Feeling the lice on his skin, watching the erratic progress of the cockroaches across the shit-stained concrete floor, hearing the scurry of rats, smelling it all, had he ever believed he would return here, now, feeling silk against his flesh? As he continued his progress, comfortably conscious of the smartly dressed pedestrians with whom he shared the broad, crowded sidewalk, he drew a deep, appreciative breath as, unconsciously, he fingered the fine melton of the overcoat that had been specially tailored for him.

Behind the glass counter at Jerry's, two young women, both strange to him, were waiting on customers. He turned to the glass-doored display cabinet set flush with the wall. Yes, he saw exactly what he was looking for: a dozen small red roses. Behind the counter, one of the clerks turned to him. She was a tall, slim woman with cold gray eyes and long, silky blond hair.

"Yes?" She was polite but unsmiling, remote and haughty, fire and ice. She wore a skintight beige body stocking covered in front by a navy-blue apron with "Jerry's" stitched in white. Her breasts were small, perfectly formed. She wore no makeup. Except for one slim gold ring on the little finger of her left hand, she wore no jewelry. Making love, he imagined, she would at first resist. Then, subdued, finally penetrated, she would turn fierce, wild, and abandoned, taking it all for herself, sharing nothing, giving no quarter and asking none.

"Can I help you?"

He pointed. "A dozen of the small red roses, please."

She turned away, went to the refrigerated showcase, opened the door, bent down. Yes, the shape of her buttocks was perfection. Tomorrow, with more time, he would come back. She would remember him, he was certain of that. His clothes, the way he talked, the way he handled himself— she would remember.

In prison, at night, stroking himself, beginning, she would have been the perfect apparition, his fantasy for the night.

Working deftly, she wrapped the roses, made change for the fifty, thanked him for the five-dollar bill he left on the counter. His answering smile, he could feel, was just right, interested but not fawning, begging for nothing, offering only a little more. Yes, she would remember him.

At the corner of Park and Eighty-fourth, the traffic light

turned red. A knot of pedestrians stood clustered around him, waiting for the light to turn green. He raised the roses, protecting them from jostling. With the green light, he was crossing Park, walking east on Eighty-fourth. Once more, he checked the time: six forty-five. In less than five minutes, he would arrive at her building. She would be displeased. Even to arrive at seven o'clock, precisely on time, might irritate her—just as arriving more than ten minutes late would also be unacceptable.

All of it, he knew, was payback, required penance. A woman scorned, someone had once said, was a woman without mercy. And the more desirable the woman, the stiffer the penalty. Jilt an ugly woman, and she might come back for more. But if a beautiful woman came back, without coaxing, it was probably for revenge, not love. He'd just as soon do his penance and get it over with.

At the next corner, another red light, there were fewer people waiting. As he joined the small cluster at curbside, he became aware of a car beside him, a big Lincoln town car. In the light from streetlamps and passing headlights he could see the driver—a small brown man, perhaps a Filipino, wearing a dark suit, white shirt, and a small black clip-on bow tie. He was staring straight ahead.

The traffic light turned green. Holding the roses clear of a teenager on a skateboard, Frazer began crossing Lexington. Just ahead, the Lincoln was progressing slowly, now stopping at the curb on the far side of Lexington. He was aware that the easy, confident rhythm of his steps had gone out of sync; he was walking more slowly, letting the other pedestrians go ahead. But the "Walk" sign was off now; the "Wait" sign was on. Meaning that he should walk faster— just as, ahead, the smoked rear window of the Lincoln was coming down. Inside, in the uncertain light from the street, he could dimly see a man. The man was bareheaded, and wore a bulky leather jacket. Was it a familiar figure? At this distance, in this light, he told himself, it wasn't possible to know. With the Lincoln on his left, he began angling away to the right. The curb was just ahead; the traffic light had turned red, releasing the traffic streaming down Lexington.

Was discretion the better part of valor? Should he—?

"Ned." The voice came from the back seat of the Lincoln. Instinctively he turned toward the car—and saw the gun barrel. The gun was a large-caliber revolver with a long barrel. The orange flame erupting from the muzzle was prodigious.

He dropped to his knees. As he fell to his left, striking the curb with his shoulder, he was able to hold the roses clear, protecting them as he rolled on his back.

Forty minutes later, taking the required four pictures from each of four different angles, amused by the corpse clutching the bouquet of roses to his chest as he stared with empty eyes into the dark sky, the police photographer smiled. Saying: "Jesus, rest in peace, huh?"

ONE

"There it is—twenty-one forty-six." Haigh braked the Buick to a stop on the steep slope of Vermont Street and pointed to a turn-of-the-century building. The two-flat building was in good repair, newly painted to accent its neo-Victorian gingerbread. "It's the bottom flat. His office is in the front room."

Archer glanced at the building, surveyed his surroundings, shook his head. "Jesus, these hills. San Francisco's got to be paradise for brake shops."

Haigh released the brake and let the Buick climb the hill in low gear. Because of the grade, parking was permitted only on one side of the street, at right angles to the curb. Haigh checked the mirrors, swung the car into a parking slot. He surveyed the angles. Yes, he could see whoever entered Bernhardt's building, which was attached on either side, with no alley behind. He killed the engine, set the brake, checked the time: nine-thirty on a foggy April morning. He was running exactly on schedule, always a source of satisfaction. In his financially secure, conservatively dressed, meticulously groomed early forties, with promotion to agent-in-charge clearly in sight, Haigh had made punctuality one of his trademarks.

Seated on the passenger's side, Archer spoke expectantly: "Are we going to talk to him?"

"I haven't decided." Haigh spoke crisply, decisively.

When dealing with subordinates, especially new additions to the staff, his first priority was always to establish who made the decisions. "Primarily, I want to get a feeling for his operation, his lifestyle." Haigh surveyed the cars parked at the curb. Some were upscale imports, others conventional domestics; most were of recent vintage, though a few were aging gracelessly. Located on the north slope of Potrero Hill, Vermont was typical of the district, originally a working-class neighborhood that had lately become gentrified. Thus the trendy color scheme of Alan Bernhardt's building.

"Nice view," Archer offered cheerfully as he looked out across rooftops to the downtown cityscape of San Francisco.

Haigh pointedly made no response. Then, after a moment of disciplinary silence, part of Archer's indoctrination, Haigh continued speaking in the same clipped voice of command.

"When we get back to the office, I'll have Records cut you a file on Bernhardt. Most of it's hearsay, but there's enough to get us started. He's a private investigator, duly registered and licensed. He's only been licensed as an individual operator for a few months—six months, no more. He originally worked as a part-time investigator for Herbert Dancer. Apart from that, Bernhardt is an actor. Also a director, mostly at the Howell Theater, which is a very highly regarded little theater. Nobody makes a living in little theater, though. They all moonlight, unless they're independently wealthy. So Bernhardt decided to work part-time for Herbert Dancer, who runs the biggest, most profitable, most unprincipled private investigative operation in Northern California. Which is why, I'm told, Bernhardt left him. They had a major blowup, after which Bernhardt went off on his own."

"Did you get all this from Dancer?"

Haigh shook his head. "Bernhardt has two good friends in the SFPD. Frank Hastings and Peter Friedman. They're both lieutenants, and they run Homicide jointly. It's a strange setup, but it apparently works. Friedman got lucky in the stock market, and Hastings likes to work outside. Friedman hates office politics, and Hastings hates red tape. So neither of them is interested in a captaincy."

"How big is the squad?"

"About a dozen detectives, plus Hastings and Friedman."

"So I gather you got most of your information on Bernhardt from Hastings and Friedman."

Once more Haigh decided not to reply. Superiors asked the questions. Underlings responded. When so directed.

"Bernhardt came from New York originally." He continued. "And he once wrote a play that was produced off Broadway."

"Huh . . ." Intrigued, Archer sat up straighter, looked at Bernhardt's building with renewed interest. "Impressive."

"In fact, it looked like he was on his way in the New York theater," Haigh continued. "And he was still in his twenties. But then his wife got killed, and his mother and grandparents had all died a year or two before that. So Bernhardt had to get out of New York. He went to Hollywood, wrote a few scripts, made pretty fair money, I understand. But then, a few years ago—six or eight, maybe—he came to San Francisco. He got into little theater. In fact, he bought into the Howell Theater, with money he'd inherited. Which, according to Friedman, wasn't a very good investment. Which, still according to Friedman, Bernhardt should've known. But, in any case, after a year or two, Bernhardt started working for Dancer. And then, maybe six months ago, after their blowup, Bernhardt opened his own shop. Meanwhile, he found a girlfriend. Her name is Paula

Brett. I don't know a thing about her, except that Hastings says she's beautiful—and Friedman says she has class. Someone also said she was an actress, a bit player down in Hollywood. Both her parents are college professors, whatever that means. Anyhow, regardless of their love life, the past few months Paula Brett has been helping Bernhardt, mostly doing surveillance, things like that."

"Did they work together during the time frame we're looking at?"

This question, respectfully asked and framed in departmental officialese, Haigh decided to answer. Perhaps, after all, Archer was trainable.

"We think Brett knew about Betty Giles, but we don't know whether she actually worked the Giles case. We *do* know that Bernhardt was still working for Dancer when he was assigned to find Betty Giles."

Archer considered, then decided to say, "I suppose the next question is who hired Dancer to find Betty Giles."

"Dancer's client was a high-powered Los Angeles financier. That's all Dancer'll say. He won't give us the financier's name."

"Can't we squeeze Dancer?"

"The one I want to squeeze is Bernhardt. Dancer might be an SOB, but he's our SOB. He plays ball with us, and he's got connections. Bernhardt, though—" Haigh shrugged well-tailored shoulders. "He's expendable."

Archer nodded, but decided to say nothing. He'd arrived in town from Fresno only a month ago. Until now he'd never dealt directly with Haigh, who was known as a tight-ass manipulator who never laughed during office hours. Which, some said, was the reason he was on the fast track to top management.

"Very briefly," Haigh said, "I'll summarize the Giles case for you."

"Ah." Archer nodded again, focused his full attention on the other man. "Good. Thank you."

Haigh acknowledged the tribute with a nod, then said, "About four months ago, the anonymous Los Angeles financier flew up to San Francisco in his corporate jet, and contacted Dancer. The job seemed pretty straightforward. One of the financier's employees had stolen some company secrets, which were unspecified. Betty Giles was the employee's name. She lived in Los Angeles with a boyfriend, whose name was Nick Ames. Dancer's instructions were to find Betty Giles, whose mother lives in San Francisco. Then Dancer was to notify the client. Betty Giles wasn't to be contacted. She was just to be located, then put under surveillance."

"The client didn't want the secrets identified."

Haigh chose to ignore the opinion, saying instead, "Dancer gave the job to Bernhardt, who tracked Giles to Santa Rosa. Bernhardt staked out Betty Giles and Nick Ames in a cheap motel room, then called Dancer, who called his client in Los Angeles. The client wanted the couple kept under surveillance for a couple of days. Whereupon, surprise, Nick Ames was killed. It happened in Santa Rosa. Bernhardt thought he'd been set up. He thought Dancer had hired him to finger Nick Ames for the killer, who could've been a pro. So Bernhardt, who looks like a mild-mannered Abe Lincoln but has a pretty hot temper, decides to go looking for Betty Giles on his own time."

"Why?" Archer asked.

"Because," Haigh answered, "Bernhardt figured Giles was in danger. Which, in fact, she was. Bernhardt didn't want another murder on his conscience."

"And is that what happened? Was she murdered?"

Choosing to ignore the question, another turn of the disciplinary screw, Haigh continued. "Bernhardt tracked her to a place called Borrego Springs, which is a small resort town in the desert about sixty-five miles southwest of Palm Springs. So then, another surprise, a black hit man, a professional named Willis Dodge, showed up in Borrego Springs. He tried to kill Betty Giles. She was in a motel cabin when the attempt was made, and Bernhardt was with her. When the shooting stopped, Willis Dodge was dead."

"So Bernhardt is a tough guy." Once again, speculatively, Archer looked down the hill at the pair of Victorian flats.

"Tough or lucky, take your pick." Haigh shrugged. "I will say, though, that Dodge was very good at what he did. And smart, too. He was never convicted of anything, never did time, except in county jail."

"Was Bernhardt held?"

"No. It was pretty clear that he acted in self-defense."

"So we don't have any leverage with Bernhardt."

"Not really. The weapon he used was a sawed-off shotgun, and the state police investigator on the scene was all set to have him locked up for possession of an illegal weapon. But then someone found a ruler, and it turned out that the barrel was precisely sixteen inches long. Which, as you may know, is exactly the legal limit for sawed-offs."

"Possessing a sawed-off is a federal offense, though. We could've kept him for twenty-four hours, and sweated him."

Deciding on a don't-give-me-a-lecture-on-the-law expression, Haigh stared the younger man down. Then, with elaborate patience: "We aren't about to get involved in a pissing contest with the state police. Is that clear?"

In a dark, brooding silence, Archer shifted his gaze to the San Francisco skyline, diffused by the morning fog. After five frustrating years in Fresno, he'd campaigned long and hard for the opening in the San Francisco office. He'd been warned about Haigh, but had chosen to ignore the warnings. Had he made a mistake? Would private industry be his next career move—his only way out? In the Bureau, from a Class A posting like San Francisco, there were only two possibilities: up or out, Washington or the private sector.

"In fact," Haigh was saying, "Bernhardt and Betty Giles aren't the primary targets of this investigation. They're little fish, really."

Archer nodded. "I figured."

"They're our responsibility—this office's responsibility. But, as of now, the Los Angeles office is calling the plays." Plainly Haigh was experiencing pangs of bureaucratic discomfort, contemplating the prospect of himself in a secondary role. Therefore, he was compelled to add, "That could change, though, once we talk to Bernhardt and Giles. They're little fish, admittedly. But little fish wriggling on a hook can catch the big fish."

"Where's Betty Giles?"

"That's the problem," Haigh admitted. "We can't find her. She's in Europe, we're almost sure of that. But we don't know where."

"What's her mother say?"

"All she knows is that Betty Giles is in Europe. She doesn't have an address. I've talked to her twice, and I'm pretty sure she's telling the truth. But a couple of times the mother let it slip that Bernhardt knows how to locate Betty Giles."

"What's the reason for that?"

"I don't know. But I definitely plan to find out."

TWO

"Yes, sir?" The receptionist's smile was polite but remote. Except for a telephone console and a crystal bud vase that contained one yellow rose, her desk was clear. Both the desk and the receptionist were discreetly high-style.

"I'd like to see Mr. Haigh, please. My name is Bernhardt. Alan Bernhardt."

"Yes . . ." The receptionist nodded. The smile faded; the nod suggested discreet disapproval. "Yes—four o'clock." She gestured to one of two elegantly fashioned couches. "If you'll just have a seat, I'll tell Mr. Haigh you're here." She waited until Bernhardt had seated himself, then spoke briefly into the phone. As she spoke she avoided direct eye contact with Bernhardt.

Bernhardt crossed his legs and checked the time: three fifty-five. It had been noon when Haigh phoned, two o'clock before Bernhardt had retrieved the cryptic message on the answering machine. "This is Preston Haigh," the voice had said. "Call me as soon as possible, please." Followed by a local phone number. To Bernhardt's theater-trained ear, Haigh's voice had projected smooth, smug authority. The guess had been accurate: "Federal Bureau of Investigation" had been the first words he'd heard when he'd returned the call. The four o'clock appointment had come as a command, not a request.

Across the waiting room, on the room's other couch, a

woman in her thirties sat beside a girl in her teens. Neither the woman nor the child spoke or acknowledged the presence of the other. Both sat rigidly, hands clenched. Their faces were expressionless, frozen by something more profound than simple fear.

As if he'd been caught eavesdropping, and therefore felt guilty, Bernhardt looked away from the woman and the child, turned his gaze on the oil paintings that were the reception room's only decoration. The paintings were uniformly framed, and were original oils, certainly painted by the same artist. All four were semiabstract landscapes. The windowless room's softly diffused lighting was indirect, a glow that emanated from a continuous ceiling cove. The walls were covered with mauve grasscloth. The matching end tables beside the matching sofas were as bare as the receptionist's desk. The FBI apparently didn't believe in providing reading material. In Russia, Bernhardt had once read, the KGB provided tea for its waiting victims.

At the thought, Bernhardt smiled. Hot tea from a brass samovar and hard wooden benches at the KGB; the glow of indirect lighting, soft modern sofas, and thick carpeting at the FBI.

He'd been here only once before. Running an errand for Dancer, he'd dropped off papers relevant to an insurance fraud case that had netted Dancer almost a half-million dollars. Bernhardt had talked briefly to two agents, both of whom wore three-piece suits and spoke deadpan Harvardese.

Meaning, therefore, that today Bernhardt had chosen to wear corduroy slacks, scuffed running shoes, a rough tweed jacket, a tattersall checked shirt, and no tie. Years ago, in New York, he'd bought the jacket at a salvage shop for twenty dollars. As soon as he slipped it on, he knew it would be his all-time favorite article of clothing.

Bernhardt yawned, slid down on the sofa until he was sitting on his spine. His legs were outstretched, crossed at the ankles. Like the clothing he'd chosen to wear, his posture expressed his opinion of the FBI, past and present. In his private pantheon of American fascists, J. Edgar Hoover was the archvillain.

Bernhardt yawned again, blinked, felt his eyes grow heavy. He was a tall, lean man, slightly stooped when he stood. Like his body, his face was long and lean, deeply etched. It was a Semitic face: nose long and narrow, slightly hooked; complexion dark; forehead high and broad. His gray-flecked hair was dark and thick, carelessly combed and long enough to curl over the open collar. His chin was prominent, his mouth generously shaped. Beneath dark, thick eyebrows, the brown eyes were both calm and acute. It was the face of a tough-minded aesthete, reflective in repose, uncompromising when challenged. Only the designer glasses, aviator-styled, hinted at the vanity of the intellectual.

At three minutes after four o'clock a buzzer sounded. The receptionist lifted the phone, listened, then nodded to Bernhardt and gestured him to an inner door. As he approached the door it automatically swung slowly open, then swung slowly closed behind him. In the inner hallway, smiling slightly, a conservatively dressed man in his late thirties stepped forward, offered his hand.

"Graham Archer," he said, introducing himself.

"Alan Bernhardt."

"Thanks for coming." Archer led the way down the carpeted, paneled hallway to the end, then pushed open a door to an impressively appointed, discreetly decorated conference room. An older man in his well-tailored middle forties sat at the head of a long surfboard-shaped conference table.

"This is Special Agent Haigh, Mr. Bernhardt."

Without rising, Haigh acknowledged the introduction with a remote nod, at the same time gesturing Bernhardt to a seat on his right. Arrayed before Haigh on the rosewood and walnut table were a leather-bound notebook, open; a file folder, closed; two ballpoint pens, and a microphone. The two pens, the notebook, and the file folder, Bernhardt noticed, were all geometrically aligned. Haigh's mannerisms, too, were geometric.

Bernhardt sat in a leather armchair equipped with casters; Archer took a facing chair on Haigh's left. The FBI's offices were on the ninth floor of the Federal Building; a floor-to-ceiling window offered a close-up view of the downtown skyline, with the Bay Bridge beyond.

Haigh cleared his throat, made an imperceptible adjustment in the alignment of the file folder. Then he gestured to the microphone.

"Do you mind if we record this, Mr. Bernhardt?"

The presence of the microphone displayed so prominently had given Bernhardt the time he needed to decide on a response:

"First, if you'll just tell me what this is all about . . ."

Haigh shifted his gaze to the microphone, let a long, thoughtful moment linger between then. Then he spoke deliberately: "We can forget about the microphone."

Bernhardt decided to make no response, give no hint of his reaction. Was Haigh trying to intimidate him? Or was he feeling his way: probing, evaluating, improvising? Just as, yes, Bernhardt was also improvising.

Now, projecting an executive's air of dispensing with the preliminaries, Haigh raised his head to stare directly into Bernhardt's eyes, saying softly, "I'm going to give you a name, Mr. Bernhardt. When I've given you the name, I think you'll know why I've asked you to come down here."

Bernhardt nodded, then decided to shift his attention to

Archer, seated directly across the table. Archer's expression was unreadable, but, at the corners, his mouth stirred with some faint suggestion of fellowship. Or was this the FBI's pallid version of the good cop? Or, more probably, was Archer suppressing a smirk at the thought of what was about to follow?

"The name," Haigh was saying, "is Raymond DuBois." He pronounced the words with exquisite precision, timed to perfection.

Raymond DuBois . . .

Instantly the searing images flared in Bernhardt's consciousness: he and Betty Giles in the darkened cabin, no phone, no protection. No hope. Never had time moved so slowly, yet also raced inexorably ahead, bringing with it the certainty of death. He could still feel the sawed-off in his hands, slick with sweat. He could still feel the hammering of his heart, and the weakness of his legs, and the incredible dryness of his mouth and throat.

"I take it," Haigh was saying, "that you know the name."

Bernhardt cleared his throat, delivered the only line that came to him: "DuBois. Sure. One of the—" His throat closed momentarily. Then: "One of the world's richest men."

As if he were encouraging a slow student, Haigh nodded as he said, "What else do you know about Raymond DuBois, Mr. Bernhardt?"

Bernhardt shrugged, raised one hand, let it fall, a disclaimer. The gesture had come easily. He was getting into the part; the lines were there as the game came clear: both of them were probing, trying to discover what the other man knew—and didn't know.

"I know what everyone else knows, I suppose. DuBois is old. He's a recluse. In failing health, I think."

"And that's all you know?"

Projecting a casual indifference, Bernhardt nodded, but said nothing. It was a gambit. If another microphone were hidden under the table, Haigh would want him to say something, not simply nod.

Gambit declined.

"Have you ever had any direct contact with Raymond DuBois?" Haigh asked.

The question required a frown that projected puzzled innocence. "I'm afraid I don't understand the purpose of the question."

Now Archer spoke, the junior partner, taking his turn, sharply shifting ground. "How about Betty Giles?" Like Haigh, he spoke easily, conversationally. But his eyes were watchful. "Are you acquainted with Betty Giles?"

Once more the images flashed: in the darkened cabin, Betty, crouching between the bed and the wall as Bernhardt heard the sound of the bathroom screen being cut. With the sawed-off raised, he'd advanced until he stood in the open bathroom door. When the gun fired, as if by its own volition, flame filled the high window over the bathtub.

Then the screams had begun.

Then the figure engulfed in flames, running blindly in the darkness. Finally falling to his knees.

Dying.

Was his puzzled frown still in place? Yes, incredibly, yes. Permitting him to look from one FBI agent to the other before he said, "I think I'm entitled to know what this is all about."

"Just answer the question. Do you know Betty Giles?"

"The answer," Bernhardt said, "is yes, I know Betty Giles. But I'm not going to elaborate until I know where this is going."

"When we want you to know where it's going," Haigh said, "we'll tell you."

"Am I being treated as a suspect? Are we on the same side, or what?"

"Do you know Betty Giles's present whereabouts?" Haigh asked.

Bernhardt sat up straighter in the leather armchair, folded his arms, met Haigh's gaze squarely—and said nothing.

"Listen, Bernhardt . . ." Haigh's voice dropped ominously. His fingers were spread wide on the rosewood conference table, as if he were restraining himself from gouging the wood with his fingernails. The fingernails, Bernhardt noticed, might be manicured.

"You're a very small cog in this investigation," Haigh said. "The only reason you're here is that we're looking for Betty Giles. So if you feel like cooperating—telling us where to find her—" Haigh's bureaucratic mask contrived an ingratiating smile as he gestured down the long conference table to the door. "Then you're free to go—with the Bureau's thanks."

"The problem is," Bernhardt replied, "that I've promised not to reveal her current whereabouts."

Haigh's response came quickly, smoothly. "Who'd you promise? Betty Giles? Or Raymond DuBois?"

Bernhardt made no reply.

"*Why'd* you promise?" Archer asked. "Was it personal? Or professional?"

"The problem with this discussion," Bernhardt said, "is that it isn't a discussion."

"Oh." Haigh's voice was heavy with sarcasm. Repeating: "Oh. You don't feel we're being candid. Is that it?"

Eyes level, mouth firm, Bernhardt made no response. For a long, hostile moment the two men eyed each other.

Then Haigh spoke softly, in a cold, precise voice: "If you've got any smarts at all, you've figured out that this"—he tapped the microphone—"could be just a blind. You probably figured there might be a microphone under the desk that's picking up everything we say. There could even be a hidden camera."

Bernhardt decided to affect a world-weary smile, followed by a world-weary nod.

"Well," Haigh said, "to demonstrate that there's no concealed microphone, I'm going to favor you with a rundown of what I'm thinking about you and your future." His pale, prissy face registered a wintry pleasure, a latent sadism. "Would you appreciate that?"

"Oh, yes." In the words, Bernhardt tried to distill the essence of irony.

"First of all," Haigh said, "you're a gnat. You're of no significance whatever. The Bureau chews up people like you every day. Every hour, maybe—that's how powerful we are. Are you with me so far?"

"Oh, yes. I'm with you." And, in silent counterpoint, his secret self was kicking in: *I'm with you, you pampered, pompous asshole, you puffed-up, slicked-down jerk.*

"We know all about Betty Giles," Haigh said. "We know she and her boyfriend were blackmailing Raymond Dubois. After the boyfriend was killed in Santa Rosa, probably after you fingered him, we know that Betty Giles tried to hide out down in Borrego Springs, in the desert. You followed her. Then, surprise, a professional hit man showed up. He decided to toss a Molotov cocktail in Betty's window. He'd burn her out, then kill her—that was obviously the plan. Instead, though, his Molotov cocktail exploded as it went through the window, and the hit man—his name was Willis Dodge—got turned into an instant human torch. Are you with me so far?"

25

"I'm with you." Bernhardt was satisfied with his own response. His eyes, he could feel, were clear and alert, revealing no fear.

"When the sheriff arrived on the scene, he found you and Betty Giles. He also found a sawed-off shotgun that had been fired. You admitted that the shotgun was yours. You told the sheriff that you fired in self-defense when you saw the Molotov cocktail coming through the window. Correct?"

"It was a reflex. Someone was outside, cutting the screen in the bathroom window. It was dark. When I saw the bottle framed in the window—the wick, flaming—I pulled the trigger automatically. From fifteen feet the shot pattern was probably twelve inches across. I couldn't miss."

"How'd you feel, watching Willis Dodge burn to death?" It was a casual question, a matter of academic interest, nothing more.

"I have nightmares." As again, his inner voice kicked in: *Not that it's any concern of yours, you bloated bureaucrat.*

"Hmmm—yes." It was a perfunctory expression of bogus sympathy followed by a short, speculative silence. This, Bernhardt suspected, was the carefully calculated pause that preceded the final thrust.

"So," Haigh said, speaking with an air of finality, as if he were about to finish the business between them, "what you've got here is a pretty clear choice, Mr. Bernhardt. You can either tell us where to find Betty Giles, in which case you're off the hook, or else you can elect to stonewall us. If you decide to stonewall, in the belief that you're protecting Betty Giles, then I have no choice but to contact the United States Attorney. I'll ask him to prepare two charges against you—one for illegal possession of an outlawed firearm, and one for conspiracy to commit murder. The latter charge would include the murder of Nick Ames and the attempted murder of Betty Giles."

"You're joking."

"Oh, no. Don't make the mistake of thinking that, Mr. Bernhardt. I promise you that you'll be indicted. Whether or not we have a winnable case, that's a matter of conjecture. The point is, though, that you'll go bankrupt long before the trial starts. We took the liberty of running a credit check on you. And it looks like you have a total net worth of about forty thousand dollars. Meaning that, even if the case is thrown out of court, you'll have long since gone broke."

"You must want Betty Giles very badly."

Haigh nodded. "Very."

THREE

"So what'd you *say?*" Paula demanded. "What'd you *do?*"

"I stalled. I told them I'd need time to talk to my lawyer. They bought it. I've got until tomorrow. At least."

"Jesus, the FBI—our tax dollars at work." She lifted her glass of white wine, drank, returned the empty glass to the table. Sitting across from her, Bernhardt smiled. Only when she was agitated did Paula gulp her wine. Otherwise, she sipped. He caught the waiter's eye, signaled for a second glass for each of them, red for him, white for her. At seven-fifteen they'd gotten the last table at Bernardo's, their favorite spot for Italian food. The pasta was made fresh daily, the house wine came from gallon jugs, and the prices came from another era. The waiters at Bernardo's wasted no time in pleasantries, a nostalgic evocation of Bernhardt's past life in New York.

"I think," Paula said, "that it's time you told me the whole story."

The waiter set the fresh glasses of wine before them. Then, frowning, he stood with pencil poised over a pad, ready to take their orders. As she talked to the waiter, discussing the scampi, Paula's face was in profile. It was a multifaceted profile, one of the most compelling Bernhardt had ever seen. It was all there in her face: humor, intelligence, curiosity, even a certain restlessness that could turn reckless. God, had it only been four months since they'd met? He'd been conducting a read-through for *The Buried Child*, at the Howell. Because it was the first read-through, a get-acquainted session, he'd sat on the edge of the stage, legs dangling, facing the dozen-odd hopefuls sitting in the first two rows. He'd talked about himself, described what he'd done in the theater—and what he hadn't done. Since one of the things he hadn't done was support himself by acting, or directing, or playwriting in little theater, he'd admitted that, yes, he moonlighted. It was part of his standard spiel, illustrating the axiom that most actors shouldn't give up their day jobs. Ever.

All during the spiel, intrigued, he'd watched Paula, who was avidly watching him. When the meeting broke up, he'd maneuvered adroitly enough to leave the two of them alone in the darkened theater, after the others had gone. He'd asked her out for beer and pastrami sandwiches. Immediately she'd pointed to the pager clipped to his belt. "Do you moonlight as a brain surgeon?" she'd asked. When he'd told her what he did, told her that he was a duly licensed private investigator, her whole face had come alive. A few weeks later, pillow-talking, she'd announced that she wanted to be a private investigator. She was sure she'd be good at the job—and she was right. A month into the job, she'd faced down a murderer and saved a young woman's life. Afterwards—hours later—in his arms, her whole body shook with the inevitable delayed reaction. But the next day she was back on the job, no problem.

A month ago, when he'd ordered stationery, her name was on the letterhead.

"So?" she prompted.

"You know most of it. A high roller from Los Angeles hired Herbert Dancer to find Betty Giles. I got the job. All I was told was that she was involved in industrial espionage. I was told to find her, then call Dancer, who'd contact the client. I got lucky, and found her at a cheap motel in Santa Rosa. She was with a guy named Nick Ames. I called Dancer, who ordered me to keep them under surveillance until he got back to me, probably in twenty-four hours. The following evening, Giles and Ames had a fight. Nick slammed out of the motel room, got in their car—Betty's car—and drove to a bar. He had a few drinks, then left the bar. He was starting the car when a well-dressed black man walked up and shot him through the glass. The weapon was a twenty-two-caliber automatic pistol firing high-speed hollow points. Which, as it happens, is a favorite weapon of the professional hit man."

"Why?"

"There're three types of twenty-two automatics that can be very effectively silenced. That's because the barrel isn't surrounded by a slide. The Colt Woodsman with a six-inch barrel is a special favorite. The combination of a long barrel and the small powder charge makes a silencer very effective, and the high-speed hollow-point bullet at close range is devastating. Plus, the bullet breaks up when it strikes something, so there's no ballistics. From the hit man's viewpoint, it's the ideal weapon, especially since the gun'll hold ten cartridges. In the Nick Ames homicide, the victim was shot five times, all in the head. That's a typical professional hit."

"Did you see the actual murder?"

"No. My orders were to tail Betty, so I was at the motel when Ames died. I didn't know about the murder until the next morning. By that time, Betty was with the police, answering questions and identifying the body. I decided to get the hell out of there, drive back to San Francisco. About an hour down the road, I figured out that I'd been set up." He sipped his wine, watching her over his raised glass. It was inevitable, he realized, that this moment would come—inevitable that he put his glass down, look into her eyes—

—and tell her the rest of it.

"Ostensibly," he began, "Betty Giles worked for an outfit called Powers Associates in Los Angeles. Actually, it's a front for Raymond DuBois."

"The zillionaire financier."

"Right."

"Based in Los Angeles."

"Right. Powers Associates is an investment firm—real estate, stocks, venture capital, whatever makes money. Justin Powers is the head man. Which makes him DuBois's number-one gofer. A couple of years ago, Justin Powers recruited Betty Giles to go down to Los Angeles and work for his company. Betty majored in art history at Berkeley, and she was Chevron Oil's art curator, based in San Francisco."

Paula frowned. "Chevron has an art curator?"

He nodded. "They're constantly acquiring art for their executive offices and public areas. Paintings, sculpture, everything. It's a huge program. They donate art, too, and they sponsor art scholarships. Betty administered millions of dollars in acquisitions. She also made money for Chevron, buying and selling. In fact, she more than earned her keep."

"And that's what she did for Powers Associates?"

"That's what she did for Raymond DuBois. That's where this all starts—with Raymond DuBois's collection of art, which is worth millions. Tens of millions. Hundreds of millions, for all I know. DuBois is an obsessive collector. He's got no wife, no children, no relatives that he trusts. And his health is failing. Several years ago he had a stroke, and he's confined to a wheelchair. Art is his whole life. Art and money. He's apparently got a great eye, because when he buys and sells art he always turns a handsome profit. He's not married, as I said, and apparently he became very attached to Betty, a daughter substitute. He treated her very well—paid her a damn good salary and gave her a percentage of all the money they made selling art. If she made a profit, she took a percentage. If there was a loss, which almost never happened, DuBois swallowed it. Plus, she got to travel all over the world, acquiring art."

"So she had a great life."

Bernhardt shrugged as the waiter arrived with salads and French bread. When Bernhardt asked for a third round of red and white, almost always their limit, the waiter informed them that they should have ordered two small carafes.

"So what went wrong?" Paula asked. "Did she do business on the side, put some money in her pocket?"

"About a year ago, DuBois told Betty he had something important to show her. He revved up his electric wheelchair and took her to a door at the end of a windowless hallway in a little-used wing of his house, which is in the hills above Hollywood. There was a door at the end of the hallway, and a control panel beside the door. DuBois punched out a code and the door slid open. They were in a smaller hallway, facing a second door. He punched out another code. The first door closed behind them and the second door slid open. It turned out to be a thick steel door, like a goddam bank vault, and—"

"Don't tell me." Dark eyes dancing, her whole body came alive. "A room full of rare paintings."

Teasing her, Bernhardt ate some salad, ate some French bread. Then: "You're half right. Care to try for the second half? I'll give you a hint. The room was only about twelve feet square. But there was a Van Gogh and a Braque and a Reubens, just to name a—"

"Stolen," she breathed. "Stolen art treasures, sure as hell."

"The Van Gogh alone is worth twenty-five million."

"Jesus . . ." Her eyes searched his face; she was trying to guess the rest of it. "He was trusting her with his whole life."

"That's it exactly."

"Why'd he do it? Tell her, I mean."

"He's in his late seventies, and his heart is shot. He's had a stroke, and he's confined to a wheelchair, so he can't take care of the paintings. There're dehumidifiers, for instance, to be serviced. Plus, he wanted someone to know about the paintings if he died. He showed her the combinations that operated the doors, had her memorize them. Then he told her what he wanted done with the stuff. All this was done verbally, nothing written down."

"What *did* he want done with the paintings?"

"He wants them all returned to the original owners, which are mostly museums. In his will he gave her the house, so she'd always have access to the paintings. It'd take time, you see, to dispose of the stuff. Time and money. Lots of money, because she'd need security. Lots of security. He said he'd leave her a million dollars. Cash."

"My God." As the complexities began to multiply in her mind, she spoke in a soft, awed voice. "The responsibility—the danger."

He nodded. "Exactly. Danger for him, danger for her."

"How the hell would you go about contacting a museum and telling them you wanted to return a twenty-five-million-dollar Van Gogh?"

"Good question." Bernhardt finished his salad, began wiping up the dressing with a chunk of French bread.

"So why the sudden urgency? The FBI—what's that all about?"

"There's a man named Ned Frazer whose specialty is fencing stolen art. Apparently he'd done business with DuBois in the past, before DuBois had his stroke. So then, about a year ago, Frazer went to DuBois with something DuBois couldn't pass up. It was a stolen Renoir, one that DuBois was tracking. It was apparently the dream of a life-time for him. Except that, now, he was in a wheelchair. So he needed someone he could trust to get the painting hung in the secret gallery. He also needed someone to carry the money, make the payoff, actually take possession of the painting."

"Betty."

He nodded. "Betty."

"But—what—was she afraid of the deal, afraid of re-ceiving stolen property?"

"That was part of it—at first, anyhow."

"Well? What's the rest of it?" She finished her own salad, began sopping up the dressing with the last of the French bread. Bernhardt raised the empty basket over his head, was rewarded with a curt nod from the waiter.

"Apparently," Bernhardt said, "Betty is one of those women who doesn't think she's attractive to men. Low self-esteem, that's the current buzzword. Result: she was always getting involved with no-good men, one after the other. Maybe she subconsciously craved the way they mistreated her. Apparently her father was a drunk and a bully and a wife beater. Then he left them, after messing with both their heads, permanently."

"So what's the bottom line?"

"Betty started working for DuBois, making damn good money, about two years ago. About six months ago—and about six months after she knew about the stolen art—a guy with slicked-down hair and bench-press muscles and a good tan and no visible means of support moved in with her. It was a classic story. She met him at a bar one Friday night, and they went to her place afterwards. He stayed all night—and the next night, too. And the weekend. After a week, he moved in with two suitcases and a guitar he couldn't play and a set of weights."

"Nick Ames."

"Right."

"And she told Ames about DuBois—about the stolen art."

Ruefully Bernhardt nodded. "It was pillow talk. She didn't mean to tell him; it just came out a bit at a time. She probably felt like she had to tell someone, especially when Ned Frazer showed up. And there was no one else. She certainly couldn't tell her mother."

"Loneliness . . ." Paula sighed. "The heartbreak of loneliness." She smiled at him, discounting the soap-opera cliché.

"Exactly."

"So what happened? Shall I guess?"

"Sure. Guess."

"Nick Ames," she said promptly. "He decided to try a little blackmail."

Impressed, with his mouth full of wine, Bernhardt nodded vigorously. Saying finally, "That's a pretty good guess."

"It was obvious," she answered, "given the way you structured the story."

"Oh, God—I'm obvious. Is that it?"

"Only to me, love." Her smile was mischievously sweet.

"Hmmm."

"So what happened?" As she spoke, their dinners unceremoniously arrived, along with a basket that contained

35

only two hunks of bread. Bernhardt sprinkled Parmesan cheese on his fettucini and white clam sauce, began to eat. "How's the scampi?"

"Perfect." She savored a forkful, then said, "DuBois had Ames killed, to shut him up."

"I'm sure of it. I'm also sure that Justin Powers set the whole thing up. He hired Dancer to find Betty, and then he hired the hit man."

"Powers had Ames killed in Santa Rosa, and he tried to have Betty killed in Borrego Springs?" she said, checking.

"Yes. Except that at the eleventh hour DuBois claims he tried to stop the guy from killing Betty. He claims he sent Powers to Borrego Springs to stop it. But Powers was too late. And, in fact, there's evidence to support the allegation."

"Why'd DuBois change his mind?"

"Sentiment. I already told you, Betty is the daughter DuBois never had. When it came right down to it, he couldn't bear to have her killed." Once more Bernhardt raised the empty bread basket. "Jesus, next they'll be charging extra for bread."

"So DuBois got Betty out of town. Paid her, probably, to disappear."

"This," Bernhardt said, "is the part I'm not sure I should be telling you."

"Why's that?" She asked the question easily, conversationally. Then, with a teasing smile, eyeing him over a forkful of scampi, she said, "Shall I take another guess?"

"Go ahead."

"You're the middleman, the go-between. You know where Betty is, but DuBois doesn't."

His silence was eloquent.

"You're involved."

Once more, no reply was necessary. Yes, he'd gotten involved.

"I didn't have a choice. Christ, Betty was petrified. For all she knew—or I knew—there was another hit man on the way to finish the job, finish both of us, maybe. I figured I had to see DuBois to save my own skin. And I'm still convinced it was the right decision." Once again he waved the empty basket. This time, the waiter narrowly avoided eye contact.

"*Dammit.*" Bernhardt shifted the basket to his left hand, waving it as he ate the fettucini with his right hand.

"You're making a spectacle of yourself." But she was smiling, enjoying the contest.

"Without sopping up, fettucini loses its meaning. You don't come from New York."

"New York?" Teasing him, she repeated, "*New York? Am I missing something?*"

"In New York it's either you or the waiter. Unless you don't tip. Then it's the Italian leg-breakers. Or a safe, mashing you on the sidewalk."

"A *safe?*"

Finally, resigned, the waiter gritted his teeth, minimally inclined his head in a long-suffering nod, snatched a basket of bread from the serving counter, placed it with elaborate ceremony on their table. Without thanks, Bernhardt sopped up the last of the fettucini's sauce.

"*Alan. Tell* me. What *happened*, for God's sake? You talked to DuBois. How'd you manage it?" Now Paula, too, was sopping up her scampi sauce. But it was a pro forma gesture, merely keeping the faith while she urged him to continue: "*Tell* me."

"Betty had his private number. I called him from a pay phone. He knew who I was. Immediately."

"Ah." Avidly she nodded. "Sure, he knew your name. Of course."

"Are you up for dessert?"

Vehemently she shook her head. "You *know* I don't want dessert. Alan—come *on. Tell* me."

"As soon as I identified myself, he told me to come to his house. Of course, I didn't do it. We finally settled on the promenade outside the Huntington Library." As the waiter cleared their table in haughty silence Bernhardt ordered two espresso decafs. Wordlessly the waiter accepted the order and turned away.

"We talked an hour and a half," he said. "And, God, it was incredible the way the conversation went. I mean, there I was, essentially a Jewish kid from New York with a college diploma and a widowed mother who taught modern dance in our loft and marched for whatever left-wing cause was in the news. And there he was—Raymond DuBois, who could probably buy out the Rockefellers in the morning and the Du Ponts in the afternoon."

"Maybe he could buy out the Rockefellers, but you could ruin him. And he knew it. That's why he agreed to meet you. My God, Alan. How could you *keep* this from me?"

"When I finish, you'll understand." He spoke quietly now. Reflectively. Meaningfully.

Picking up on his mood, watching him closely, she made no reply, but waited instead for him to go on.

"DuBois came with three people, a driver and two men in blue suits with shoulder holsters under the suits. The driver stayed in the car, but he was parked so he could see us. The two bodyguards stayed about twenty feet away. DuBois was in his wheelchair. I sat on a marble bench. The first thing he did was ask about Betty. I said that, considering she'd almost been murdered, she was all right. Then, immediately, he asked whether Betty had told me about his 'room,' as he called it.''

"What'd you say?"

"Betty and I had talked about it. I told him that, yes, I knew about the room. 'Then it's possible,' he said, 'that only the three of us know.' His eyes are rheumy, that's the old expression—you know, white at the edges, and watery, a sick old man's eyes. But, Jesus, when he said it, said that only the three of us might know, those eyes bored in like they were lasers, going right through me. And suddenly I thought, my God, what was I *doing* there, risking my life for a woman I'd first seen only a couple of days before.''

"Good question. I've wondered myself." Her expression was inscrutable, her voice remote. Was Paula jealous?

"I felt an obligation to find her and tell her she could be in danger," he explained. "That's how it started. Then I killed a man. Meaning that, God, I was involved even before Betty told me about the paintings."

"And so there you were at the Huntington, chitchatting with one of the richest men in the world. Whose fate, literally, is in your hands."

He sugared his espresso as he said, "Here, talking about it over dinner, it sounds like it could never have happened—like it's a fantasy. But, boy, it was real then. Believe me."

"Did he threaten you?"

"At first he wanted to know about me—*all* about me. Everything, beginning with my parents, even my grandparents. In a half hour, he had my whole story. And, God, it was a surreal experience. There we were, in that beautiful setting, me on the marble bench, him strapped in his space-age wheelchair so he wouldn't fall out, the two of us talking politely on a sunny afternoon, with people strolling past and the two bodyguards in matching three-piece suits and dark glasses, utterly impassive. I felt like I was in some kind of a—a trance, just sitting there meekly answering questions and feeling like those eyes were rearranging my brain.''

"Ah." Paula was nodding appreciatively over the rim of her cup. She was into the story now, hooked. "He was making up his mind about you, whether you could be of use to him.''

He nodded decisively. "That's it exactly. After the question-and-answer session about me, he asked about Betty, about her plans. I said that Betty's plans—her future—depended on him. What he'd like, he said—his best-case scenario—was for Betty to come back to him, everything forgiven. After all, her only sin was telling Nick Ames about the paintings. Of course, he knew it would never happen. Even if Betty believed that he'd tried to call off the hit man assigned to kill her, the fact remained that, originally, DuBois had given the order. I told him he was absolutely right, Betty would never—ever—go back to him. So then he made the proposal that I'm sure he'd intended to make all along. He said that he wanted Betty to go to Europe and disappear. He'd send her money—all the money she'd need. But she had to stay in Europe.''

"Mmm." Intrigued, calculating the variables, she looked thoughtfully away as she sipped her espresso.

"His whole left side is paralyzed," Bernhardt said, "including the left side of his face, so that his mouth sags on the left side, and I don't think he can close his left eye. And, yes, he drools. He's very frail. There was a blanket covering his legs. With his right hand he took a small electronic black box out from under the blanket. He showed it to me, and the right side of his face smiled. It was a scrambler, in case I was wearing a wire. Then he took out a large envelope, which he handed to me.''

"Money. To disappear."

He nodded. "Lots of money. 'Take ten percent,' he said. 'Send the rest to Betty.' "

"So he made you the middleman. The cutout." Awed at the thought, she spoke solemnly. Then, incredulously: "Jesus, Alan. You're on his payroll. You're a goddamn accomplice."

"What else could I do, if I wanted her out of harm's way?"

"You could've told him to get someone else. Her mother, maybe."

Decisively he shook his head. "No. I talked to Betty's mother. It wouldn't work. Ever."

"But look what's happened. It's only been—what—four months, something like that? And already the FBI's on you."

Glumly he finished his espresso, slowly replaced the cup in its saucer, wiped his mouth—and sighed.

"So did you give Betty the money you got at the Huntington?"

He nodded. "Fifty thousand."

"Less five thousand for you."

"That's right, Paula." He spoke in a hard, flat voice, challenging her now: "You don't approve?"

"Jesus . . ." She reached across the table, covered his long, bony hand with hers. She'd always liked his hands, the way they moved, so expressively, so intelligently. "I'm not judging you, Alan. But I'm *worried.* And *you're* worried, too. I can see it in your face."

He smiled bleakly, shrugged.

"You're a soft touch, sweetie." She patted his hand, a gesture of reassurance, of support. "That's why I love you, I guess." She gave his hand a final pat, smiled, took back her hand. The tension between them had passed. And Paula wasn't given to holding hands in public.

"A week after I saw DuBois at the Huntington," he said, "Betty was on her way to Europe. She's in Spain now—she's rented a stone house with a vineyard. Every quarter—three months—DuBois sends me a cashier's check. The first one came last week, for twenty-five thousand. I put the check in my account, then sent a different cashier's check to Betty, at a small-town post office in Spain. There's no phone in her house, but she's made arrangements with a local restaurant to take phone messages for her. She's only called me twice in four months. The first time she sounded terrible. The second time, though, she sounded better. She'd met a guy—a schoolteacher. It sounds like he might be married. Still . . ." He shrugged.

"Another wrong man in her life, it sounds like."

He shrugged again, picked up the dinner check, began counting out money. Bernardo's didn't take credit cards.

"So what're you thinking, Alan? What's the plan?"

He looked at his watch. "It's eight-thirty. There's nine hours' difference between here and Spain. I plan to rent a tape, go home, and watch a movie. Around midnight I'll call the restaurant in Spain. I'll leave an urgent message for Betty to call me. When she calls, I'll tell her the FBI's looking for her. I'll tell her to pack a couple of bags and take a trip, drop out of sight for a month or two, no forwarding address. Then, tomorrow, I'll call the FBI. I'll tell them that the last I heard, Betty was in Spain. If they sweat me for the name of the town, I'll give it to them. Then I'll tell Betty to relocate."

"What about the money—the check you sent? Will you tell the FBI about that?"

"I'd be implicating DuBois if I told them about the check. I'd also be implicating myself."

"Jesus, Alan." She shook her head. Her eyes were dark with concern. "This is dangerous. This is very high-risk behavior."

He dropped his eyes, a mute admission that, yes, he knew.

FOUR

Waiting for the connection, Bernhardt spread out the sheet of paper beside the phone. Moving his lips—learning his lines—he mouthed the words he would say until he heard a man's voice on the line:

"Sí? Café Tosca."

Bernhardt read the message from the sheet of paper, repeated it slowly, waited for an acknowledgment, in Spanish. He conveyed his thanks, returned the phone to its cradle, checked the time: twelve-fifteen. In Marbella, the time was nine-fifteen; a new day had already begun.

"If she doesn't get the message until noon," Paula said, "it could be three A.M. when she calls."

They were in Bernhardt's office, originally the flat's front bedroom. Bernhardt sat behind his desk, Paula on the small sofa they'd just bought at a garage sale for a hundred dollars. Crusher, Bernhardt's Airedale, lay with his muzzle resting on Paula's foot. Bernhardt rose, went to Paula, sat beside her, put his arm around her shoulders, leaned his head against hers.

"All the more reason," he said, "to go to bed."

"Mmmm . . ." She put her hand on his thigh. It began as a companionable gesture, but promised an erotic conclusion.

* * *

Was it thunder, racking the building? Cannons at Gettysburg? The warbling of countless ravens, sitting on a fence that bordered the battlefield? Or robins in chorus?

Or the phone, chirping in his office, down the hallway? Betty, calling from Spain.

He threw back the blankets, tripped over his bedroom slippers, snatched his robe from its hook on the door, went barefooted down the hallway, pulling on his robe as the telephone warbled again. From the bedroom he heard Paula's voice, sleep-blurred. From behind him he heard the click of Crusher's toenails following him down the hallway.

He was standing beside his desk now, finally with the phone to his ear.

"Yes. Hello?"

"Alan. This is Betty."

"Ah." Conscious of a surging sense of relief, he riffled his hair with his free hand as he yawned. "Yeah, I figured. How's it going?"

"Is something wrong, Alan?"

"It's a complication. I didn't want to wait for the mails. I wanted to talk to you."

"A complication?"

"It's the FBI, Betty. They're apparently gathering information on DuBois. They talked to me today. And they want to talk to you."

"Is it—" She let the question fade into an awed silence. Then: "The art? Is that it?"

"I think so. But that's just a guess. All I know—all they really told me—is that they want to talk to you."

"Do they—can they—?" Defeated, she couldn't finish it.

"Do they have some kind of jurisdiction in Spain? Is that the question?"

"Yes."

"They don't, and they can't extradite someone just on suspicion. So I don't think you have anything to seriously worry about. But if I don't tell them where to find you, they can sure as hell make my life miserable. They can put me out of business. Overnight."

"Alan—I trusted you." In her voice he could plainly hear a quaver. He could visualize her face, pinched by uncertainty, tremulous with sudden fear.

"I know. But these guys—the FBI—they've got all the cards. The best I could do was stall them. You'll have a day, probably more. Pack a bag and take off. Become a tourist for a month. Don't give up your house, have someone look after it for you. Don't leave a forwarding address, obviously. And call me once a week, without fail."

"Are you sure they're the FBI? Or someone who wants to find me so they can—" She couldn't finish it.

So they can kill me would have been the rest of it.

"They're the FBI. I went to their office. There's no question. Absolutely none."

Silence.

"Betty. Please. There's nothing to worry about. They don't want you. They want DuBois. So just do what I told you to do. And call me."

"There could be just the three of us that know about the art. You know that."

"Betty. Let's stop talking. Let's hang up."

"I trusted you, Alan."

"It'll be all right, Betty. I promise." He broke the connection, moved the phone console aside on the desk, sat on the edge, head bowed in thought, one bare foot swinging. In the darkened room, lit only by the nighttime glow from a streetlight, he let his eyes stray to his Rolodex. In the D's, there was a phone number for *RDB:* Raymond DuBois's private number. Tomorrow he would recopy the number. Then he would—

"Alan?" Wearing only one of his shirts, Paula stood in the doorway to the office. Her short dark hair was tousled, her voice was sleepy. His shirt draped down from the swell of her breasts to her midthigh. He slid off the desk, went to her, held her at the waist, drew her close. As his hands dropped to her flanks, then to her buttocks, he felt her hands inside his robe, pulling it apart. Her mouth, open on his, was urgent.

She knew, then.

She knew that here, in this shadowy hallway, he must lose himself in her.

Tomorrow, the unknown glowered.

Now, there was only the urgency of lust—and, yes, love.

FIVE

Today the tiny red light at the base of the microphone glowed as Bernhardt told his story. When he finished, Haigh added the date and time to the tape, identified himself, identified Bernhardt, identified himself again, then switched off the microphone. The two men were in the same conference room they'd occupied yesterday. As he'd done yesterday, Haigh sat at the head of the table. Before him on the table was a yellow legal pad, almost completely covered with writing. Predictably, Bernhardt thought, the writing was small and precise, meticulously organized.

Finally, as if he felt a reluctant regret for his victim, Haigh shook his head.

"What you're doing, Bernhardt, is telling me only part of the story. I guess, in your position, I'd do the same. I'd tell the truth, but I wouldn't tell the whole truth."

Bernhardt decided not to reply. He'd decided to wear his only three-piece suit for today's interrogation. And he'd had his hair trimmed. It had been the right decision. Facing off against Haigh, playing the part of the conscientious professional earnestly determined to protect his client while he cooperated with law enforcement, he felt sure he'd held his own.

"You tell me, for instance, that you know where Betty Giles is living—what town, in Spain—but you don't have an address or a phone. I find that very strange."

"Less than a week after Willis Dodge tried to kill her, I put Betty on a plane for Madrid. She was badly shaken. She didn't want anyone to know where she was going. *Nobody.*"

"But she got in touch with you later."

Bernhardt shrugged. "As far as I know, I'm the only one who knows where she is. I'm her go-between."

"Who'd you contact on her behalf?"

"Her mother, for one."

"Who else?"

Bernhardt made no reply.

"Raymond DuBois?"

"I told you yesterday that I don't feel I can—"

Emphatically Haigh tapped the yellow legal pad. Suddenly his voice rose, roughened. "I've been reviewing the notes I took after we talked yesterday. And one thing stands out."

"Oh?" Bernhardt tried for an urbane, aloof projection. "What's that?"

"When I said that Nick Ames was killed because he was blackmailing Raymond DuBois, you seemed to agree."

Bernhardt frowned. "I did?"

"You certainly didn't disagree."

Bernhardt considered, then decided to say, "It doesn't follow that if I didn't disagree then it means I agree. It could just mean that I—"

"Come on, Bernhardt. I don't have time for word games."

Keeping the frown in place but dropping his voice to a note of earnest appeal, Bernhardt said, "Betty Giles was almost killed a few months ago. She was terrified, and she ran. She knew she had to have someone here to act for her, and also to guard her privacy, for security reasons. She retained me, engaged me professionally. Meaning that I have the same rights of privacy conducting her affairs that she would have." He was satisfied with his voice: firm and decisive, not strident, not whining.

"I believe that Raymond DuBois is retaining you."

"Well, sir, you're mistaken." But as he said it he could feel himself losing focus. The lines were slipping away; he'd lost his place in the script. He'd never been good at lying; it was an occupational handicap.

Haigh sighed. "I don't believe you, Bernhardt. I think you're lying to me." As if he were pained by the necessity of making the accusation, Haigh spoke gently, regretfully.

Bernhardt shrugged, said nothing.

"Yesterday when you were asked whether you'd ever talked directly to Raymond DuBois, you refused to answer the question. Is that still your position?"

"I said that until I knew the reasons for—"

"Cut the shit, Bernhardt." It was a harsh bully-boy's retort. "Just answer the fucking question. *Now.*"

The sudden shock of the obscenity produced a flare of anger. "You told me yesterday that if I told you where to find Betty, I could walk out the door and go about my business. And now you're squeezing me. That's bullshit. We had a deal."

"When I say we've got a deal, then that's when we've got a deal. Not before. Have you got that, Bernhardt?"

"If you want to take me into custody and make a charge"—Bernhardt pushed back the leather armchair on its easy-roll casters, rose to his feet—"then you'd better make it. Otherwise, I've got an appointment. Sorry." He contrived a small, insulting smile and walked to the door.

"Don't do it, Bernhardt. I'm warning you. Don't open that door."

"Sorry," he repeated as he turned the knob.

SIX

"Mr. Bernhardt." It was a statement, not a question.

About to twist the key and open the Honda Civic's door, Bernhardt straightened, turned to face a smiling, affably nodding, middle-aged man standing on the sidewalk a few feet from the car.

"Open-faced" and "convincing" were the adjectives that came to mind. "Gregarious" fitted, too, and a quick appraisal of the stranger's tweed sports jacket, flannel trousers, button-down shirt, and soft wool tie suggested "Ivy League."

"John Graham," the newcomer said, extending his hand. Predictably his grip was firm, but not competitive. "If you've got a few minutes, I'd like to talk to you." As he spoke, he took a business card from an inside pocket of the expensively cut houndstooth jacket.

JOHN GRAHAM
Special Accounts
The Consolidated Insurance Group
New York, London, Berne, Tokyo, Frankfurt

"If you've got a few minutes," Graham said, "I'd like to discuss something with you. A business proposition."

Bernhardt reflexively ran a thumb over the card. Predictably, it was engraved. "I've only got a few minutes now. But—" He smiled. "I'm always interested in a business proposition."

Graham consulted a thin gold watch as he said, "I'm staying at the Fairmont. What about four o'clock, in my room?"

"How about four-thirty?"

"Four-thirty is fine."

"Can you give me a general idea of what we'll be talking about?"

"We'll be talking about art, Mr. Bernhardt. Art and insurance. And losses. And settlements. Very large settlements." Graham's manner had become more somber, perhaps out of respect for the magnitude of the sums he meant to discuss.

John Graham's two-room suite was expensively decorated in imitation Italian Renaissance. The antiqued white and gold tables were claw-footed, cupids adorned the living room's cornices, the crystal chandeliers sparkled, the velvet upholstery was luxuriously soft to the touch. The view swept across downtown San Francisco and out over the bay to Berkeley. The daily rate, Bernhardt estimated, would be at least five hundred dollars.

As Graham waved him to an armchair he smiled cordially. "Is it too early for a drink, do you think?"

"Whatever you say." Bernhardt returned the smile.

"I figure you for a white-wine man," Graham said. "Am I right?"

"You're close. Actually I'm a red-wine man."

"Ah, good. Anything in particular? Cabernet?"

"Cabernet is fine."

Graham called room service, then settled back on a small love seat. Although Graham reclined at his ease, it was obvious that his preference wasn't for velvet furniture.

He wore no jacket or tie, and his button-down Oxford shirt was open at the neck. He was robustly built, and moved with the easy confidence of a man who had always been able to take care of himself. His complexion was ruddy, his casually combed hair was ginger, thinning across the top. Beneath thick ginger eyebrows, behind gold-framed designer glasses that resembled the aviator glasses Bernhardt wore, Graham's eyes were a bright, lively blue. This man, Bernhardt decided, had never suffered the pangs of self-doubt. For Graham, life was a pleasure.

"I understand," Graham said, "that you were a playwright—that you had plays produced off Broadway."

"One play. It closed after twelve performances."

"Still." Graham gestured with a freckled hand. "That's a big deal. Did you ever try Hollywood?"

Bernhardt nodded. "Years ago. It didn't work out. When I arrived in Los Angeles the studio sent a limo for me, and put me up at the Beverly Hills Hotel for a week. When I left, I couldn't even find someone to take me to the airport."

Graham studied the other man's face, then said softly, "That's a sad little story."

Bernhardt shrugged. "The arts. It's survival of the fittest. A lot of people don't realize that."

"So now you're a PI."

"Now I'm a PI."

"And you've got Raymond DuBois for a client."

Bernhardt nodded to himself. Yes, this was about the moment the other man would choose for his opening move. Graham had played this game before. Many times.

"I think," Bernhardt said, "that you'd better tell me why you're asking."

"It's like I said at the Federal Building. I'm in the insurance business. We're a reinsurance company. In fact, we're one of the biggest reinsurers in the world. Let's say one of

the major insurance companies insures a work of art for—
pick a number—ten million dollars. Which, these days, is
modest. The client would probably be an art museum. But it
could be a rich collector—an American, probably, or a Japanese. In any case, it would be prudent for the primary carrier to lay off some of the risk. That's where we come in. If
it's a measly million-dollar deal, we probably wouldn't be
interested. Ten million, that's different. So then let's say the
painting, if that's what it is, gets stolen. We pay the primary
carrier ten million, and he pays off the client. And then—"
For emphasis, Graham let a beat pass before he said, "And
then we start looking for the painting."

"And that's where you come in."

As Bernhardt spoke, a uniformed youth arrived with a
glass of cabernet sauvignon and a double Scotch on the
rocks. Graham signed the chit, waited for the room service
waiter to leave. Then, after a silent toast and a deeply appreciative sip of Scotch, he nodded. "Precisely. That's where I
come in. And the truth is, I'm a man who loves his work. I
just turned fifty. Most of my life I was a pretty conventional
product of old New England money. You know—Choate
for prep school, then Yale. Then it was the canyons of New
York, dressed in the mandatory Brooks Brothers suit and
carrying the mandatory attaché case. Christ." Ruefully Graham shook his head. "I think I might at least have worn a
derby, except that I didn't quite have the nerve. But, anyhow, I spent the first forty years of my life exactly as pro-
grammed. I married a girl from Smith who, in fact, majored
in art history. We bought a house in Connecticut, and we
raised two well-behaved little girls. Meanwhile, I was positioning myself for a vice president's slot at Prudential. But
then—" Graham broke off, sipped more Scotch. He smiled
reflectively, fondly. "Then, the week after I turned forty—
the very week—it all turned around for me. It was incred-

ible, really. The first part of the week—it was a Tuesday—I had lunch with one of my ex-roomates. He'd already made VP, at Consolidated. His name was Charlie Lucke, and he was a man in a hurry. He'd called me for the lunch, so I knew he had something on his mind. He never did anything that wouldn't turn him a profit eventually. So, after the first martini, he told me about an opening at Consolidated. It was a brand-new department, he said, and he knew I'd be right for the job. His real purpose, of course, was to fill high-level slots at Consolidated with Charlie Lucke loyalists, so that when he made his move for CEO, he'd have a cheering section already in place."

"And is that what happened?"

Graham's wide, slightly freckled face broke into a cheerful grin. "That's the way it was going, no question. But a couple of years later, on the tennis courts, Charlie dropped dead. He'd been warned not to play singles."

"So did you take the job?"

"I had a week to decide. At first, I wasn't going to take it. Even Charlie wasn't smooth enough to gloss over the potential pitfalls. I mean, Christ, the job represented the exact antithesis of every professional guideline I'd set for myself. I wanted predictability in my life, and especially in my work. And what Charlie was offering, by its nature, was off the reservation. But then—" Now Graham's smile turned wry, ruefully philosophical. "But then, three days later—it was on Friday night, at the country club—I discovered that, for Christ's sake, my wife had been screwing the goddam *golf* pro. And everyone—*everyone*—knew about it. Except me."

"So you decided to take the job."

"That's right." Graham finished his drink, and looked reflectively at the empty glass. "I drove home from the club, packed a couple of suitcases, and drove to New York that same night. Monday I called Charlie and told him I'd take the job."

"And you've still got the job," Bernhardt said, then drained his own glass.

"I've still got the job. And I love it. I am to Consolidated what the CIA is to the government: a spook. Except for the woman who's my personal assistant and secretary"—his smile became even broader for a split second—"nobody besides the president of the company and three directors have any idea what I do. I have complete freedom, and an expense account to match. Heaven on earth, in other words. Hell, I even carry a gun sometimes. Personally, I think carrying a gun is a bad idea. But the truth is"—Graham's grin turned sly—"the gun turns my secretary on. She's twenty-seven, and she's got—ah—an inventive imagination."

Tongue in cheek, Bernhardt returned the grin. He decided he was going to enjoy bantering with John Graham.

"By this time," Graham said, "I'm sure you know where I'm going with this. There are a couple of stolen paintings—Renoir's *The Three Sisters* is one—that we have reason to believe are in a secret collection belonging to Raymond DuBois. They were stolen from the National Gallery. I'm sure you remember the theft." Graham looked expectantly at Bernhardt, who nodded on cue. At the time the theft had been billed the biggest art theft ever. And yet, almost immediately, the story had died in the press.

"The Three Sisters was appraised for twenty-five million," Graham said, "and the other one—a Rembrandt study that was only given a studio number—was also appraised for twenty-five million. Prudential was the primary insurer, but they only wanted to keep ten million. We reinsured the two paintings for everything left—forty million dollars." Graham spoke evenly, almost casually. "Obvi-

ously, the chances of recovering a stolen painting—or anything that's stolen—diminishes with the passage of time, and it began to look like the two paintings might not be recoverable. At that point Prudential offered us their claim on the paintings for fifty percent of their end—five million, in other words. Mostly to preserve good customer relations, we took the deal. So now we own the paintings. Or, more precisely, we have clear title."

Bernhardt put his empty glass on a small, round, marble-topped table. The base of the table was two entwined amoretti, male and female. A second look at them revealed that the male had one hand cupped artfully around the female's breast.

"Have you talked to Raymond DuBois?" Bernhardt asked.

"DuBois is totally inaccessible. At least—" Graham looked meaningfully at Bernhardt. "At least for the likes of me he's inaccessible."

Bernhardt made no response.

"More wine?"

"No, thanks."

"What about you, Mr. Bernhardt? Do you have access to DuBois?"

"If you didn't think I had access, we wouldn't be having this little talk, would we?"

Graham chuckled appreciatively. "Touché."

"I'll tell you the same thing I told the FBI. If you're willing to put everything on the table, then I'll decide what I'm willing to tell. But not otherwise."

Graham smiled. "I'd be interested to know how Haigh reacted to that kind of talk."

"No comment."

Reflectively Graham allowed his eyes to wander across

the room. Then he glanced at his watch, saying: "I have a feeling we can do business together. So if you've got a half hour or so, I'll be happy to fill you in."

"In that case . . ." Bernhardt gestured to the empty wine glass. Graham ordered two more drinks, then began:

"In almost two years, I've done little else but try to recover these paintings. Especially since, surprise, the market value of the Renoir, in particular, has soared. I've spent thousands on bribes, and thousands more picking up the checks at four-star restaurants. 'Enhancing my credibility' is the operative phrase. These art thieves, you see, are high rollers."

"What about the police?" Bernhardt asked. "How do they fit in?"

"In this business you've got to choose. Do business with the police, and the crooks won't talk to you."

"What happens if the police find out you're doing business with the crooks?"

"That," Graham said, "depends on how surefooted you are. It also depends on geography. In most countries, all it takes is a little judicious bribery to keep the police happy. In general, everyone knows what everyone else is doing, so everyone's calculating the odds. The crooks have only two interests—getting as much for a painting as possible, and then getting away clean, staying out of jail. The police, of course, want to look as good as possible, by catching the crooks. However, the police lack finesse. Their first priority is to arrest someone, get their names in the papers. They don't give a shit whether the artwork survives undamaged. I, on the other hand, am concerned solely with keeping the art intact. So, in general, I've found the police don't suit my purposes. Also, if a painting is stolen in one country—one jurisdiction—the first thing the crook does is take it to another country. That's assuming the crook is smart. Which, generally, they are. *Very* smart. Which, in fact, keeps the game interesting."

After signing for the second round of drinks and toasting Bernhardt with a long, appreciative swallow of Scotch, Graham said, "Stealing a painting is no mean feat, as I'm sure you know. Jewel thieves can stick their haul in a vest pocket and get lost in a crowd. Art thieves have got to be logistical geniuses, especially since their best move is to get the stuff out of the country immediately. That makes them vulnerable to customs searches, you see. Then they've got to let the art cool off. They've got to have patience. They've also got to have capital—lots of financial backing."

"Why's waiting so important?"

"First, because the police lose interest. And second, because the art collectors get *more* interested. Don't forget, fine art usually increases in value over time. But finally, of course, there's a ransom demand. If he's smart, the crook makes the demand on the insurance company, not on the original owner. That's why it's so important that I get the word out that I'm in the game."

"Why wouldn't the crooks contact the owner?"

"Because," Graham answered, "if it's a museum, the director always has to contact the police. If he didn't, his board of directors would have his head on a platter. But, the police don't have credibility. A lieutenant will make a deal in good faith, but then his captain will make another deal on his own. And so on, up the line."

"So what about the Renoir and the Rembrandt?"

"In some ways," Graham said, "it started out following the standard script. A highly disciplined gang of smart-as-hell, high-tech thieves, probably five of them, disabled the multiple electronic alarm systems and got into the museum through a common wall to the parking garage. It took three hours minimum, the experts said, to get through the wall.

There were three guards. They were disarmed and gagged and bound with duct tape. Then each guard was taken to a different part of the museum and handcuffed to a water pipe. And then, surprise, two wires were attached to each guard. There was a hand grenade at the end of each wire. The grenades were placed at twelve o'clock and six o'clock, if you visualize the face of a clock, and were rigged so that, if a wire was pulled, the pin would come out of one of the grenades. It turned out that the grenades were dummies, but the guards didn't know that."

"Jesus . . ." Imagining the guards' night of terror, and the toll it must have taken, Bernhardt shook his head. Then, reflectively: "Very ingenious."

"Art thieves are very inventive, no question, though your average eighteen-year-old car booster from the ghetto probably has about as much imagination as a large mollusk."

"So these guys got away clean, I gather."

"Oh, yeah." Graham finished the Scotch and water, fondly clinking the ice cubes in his empty glass. He glanced at Bernhardt's wine glass, still half full. "They got away clean," he repeated. "Which is all the more remarkable because both paintings were taken intact, still on the stretcher bars. Most paintings, sad to say, are cut out of their frames and rolled up. What's more, the hole in the wall was just large enough to take the Renoir, which was the larger of the two. With exactly an inch clearance." Graham shook his head appreciatively. "You've got to admire good workmanship."

"So what happened next?"

"For the mandatory year," Graham answered as he reluctantly set his empty glass aside, "absolutely nothing happened. No phone calls, no ransom notes, nothing. Of course, I kept one finger on the cobweb, bought a lot of four-star lunches, did a lot of theorizing. Inevitably I wondered whether the paintings had been stolen on order and went right into someone's secret collection."

"That actually happens?"

"It makes sense. Let's say DuBois has an absolutely unquenchable passion for the Renoir and the Rembrandt. And let's say he hires someone to steal them. Let's say he pays a crook five million to do the job. He'd get merchandise worth maybe fifty million. That's a pretty good deal, wouldn't you say?"

"But he'd be guilty of receiving stolen property. And if he ever sold them, the penalty would be even worse. He'd go to jail."

Graham shrugged. "Guys like DuBois, they don't turn up in holding cells. Not unless they go soft in the head. Which, of course, happens."

"What if he tried to sell the paintings? He'd put himself in jeopardy."

"You're assuming he'd sell them legally. To a museum, or a legitimate collector. Or you're assuming he'd consign them to Sotheby's. But he'd never do that." Graham leaned forward, dropped his voice, brought his clear blue eyes into sharp focus beneath their spiky ginger eyebrows. "Don't forget, Raymond DuBois is a member in good standing of the world's most exclusive club."

This, Bernhardt knew, was a test. He considered, then guessed: "Black market art collectors, you mean."

Graham looked pained. "That's not a very elegant way of putting it. Especially since two members of the club own their own castles."

"How many members are in this club?"

"Four, now. DuBois and three others. The fifth member died several months ago. And DuBois, as you know, isn't in the best of health."

"And these men are known to have collections of stolen art?"

"They're known to people like me. But they obviously aren't known to the general public."

"What about the police? Interpol?"

"Now," Graham said, "you're talking about blindman's buff. Because if Interpol admits to knowing about the club, then politicians are going to ask the police to start making arrests. Except that other politicians—a *lot* of other politicians—are in hock to these guys. They are, in fact, *owned* by these guys. Therefore, arresting someone like Raymond DuBois gets very, very complicated."

"So what about the Renoir and the Rembrandt?"

"I believe," Graham said, "that they were held somewhere in the Middle East for the first year. At the end of that time the leader of the gang contacted Ned Frazer."

Caught by surprise, Bernhardt blinked, dropped his eyes.

Ned Frazer . . .

Betty Giles had dealt with a man named Frazer, who brokered stolen art. Was it Ned Frazer? Yes, almost certainly.

"I can see," Graham observed dryly, "that the name rings a bell."

Struggling to keep his expression noncommittal, Bernhardt made no reply.

"Ned Frazer," Graham said, "was the world's smoothest, smartest, slipperiest dealer in illicit art. He grew up dirt poor in Ireland, but he was rich by the time he turned twenty-five. He was never seen wearing anything but Savile Row suits. Unless, of course, he was sunning himself on the Riviera, stretched out beside a beautiful woman. Ned had an absolutely unassailable reputation for complete integrity. A handshake from Ned was better than a bearer bond, and just as bankable. But we all have a fatal flaw, and Ned's flaw was women. He simply couldn't manage his women, and eventually it cost him. I won't go into the sordid details, but he made the mistake of jilting an incredibly beautiful woman named Andrea Lange. She was born in Argentina. She was just as smart as Ned was—and not nearly so ethical. She set him up—stung him—and he got caught fencing a set of four Cellini gold goblets. That was eight, nine months ago. He was arrested in Mexico, where Andrea knew the ropes. He was arrested and, in effect, held for ransom, which is what Mexican justice is all about." Graham shook his head sympathetically. "Poor Ned. He'd never been locked up, and the experience devastated him. There he was, wearing denims, eating slop, and brooding about the gorgeous women being screwed by others. Finally he couldn't take it anymore. He got word to the FBI that if they'd spring him, he'd talk to them about some very, very big numbers involving some very, very big fish. A deal, in other words. The FBI jumped at it. But, as always, Ned had an angle, a way to stay ahead of the game. First, he told the state's attorney, and later the FBI, that he would testify that he'd brokered the sale of two stolen art treasures that ultimately ended up in the secret collection of an enormously wealthy man—an American. He would, of course, identify the paintings. He would also identify the person with whom he'd done business. The cutout, in other words. But, predictably, there was a condition. Before he named names, Ned wanted to talk to me in an environment that I could guarantee was bug-free. After a lot of negotiating, it was agreed that Ned would be allowed to dress in newly purchased Savile Row clothes that were custom-made according to the measurements his tailor already had. Then, accompanied by four FBI agents, who kept their distance, he was taken to Manhattan, where he called me on a pay phone. I'd made reservations at the Four Seasons, and while we lunched the four FBI guys stayed out in the lobby, a fact that did wonders for Ned's morale. Then we cabbed it to Central Park, where we found a bench. I had a pocket radio, of course, and we played Mozart while Ned gave me the deal. First he would name names, for the FBI. Then, when he was cut loose, he would tell me where to find a stolen Picasso sketch that we'd insured for ten million and which had been stolen two years previously. Of course, I knew about the Picasso. It was stolen on order for a Japanese real estate tycoon, but the tycoon died during the year's cooling-off period that Ned always demanded. Then, for God's sake, the thief got his throat slit when he was caught cheating in a game of cards. Result: only Ned knew where to find the Picasso. The standard deal is fifty percent, and that's what we agreed on. With the proceeds, Ned said, he could retire, live on the interest."

"And is that what happened?"

Morosely Graham shook his head. "Unhappily, no, that's not what happened. As always, Ned kept to his word. He told the feds that Raymond DuBois was the collector, and he named Betty Giles as the cutout who gave him the money—ten million, he said—in exchange for the Renoir and the Rembrandt. And, for once, the feds kept their word. About a month ago, they turned Ned loose. He gave me a call as soon as he got settled, and we started working on the Picasso deal. But then, Jesus, he got killed, shot on the street in Manhattan. Almost certainly it was a professional job. Rumor has it that he was on his way to meet Andrea when he was killed."

"So he didn't know she'd set him up in Mexico."

Graham shrugged. "We'll never know."

"When was Frazer killed?"

"Three weeks ago. In Manhattan."

"What about Andrea?"

"She was questioned and released. The story was that when she arrived in Manhattan South for questioning, it was as if the whole squad room was rendered helpless. She even had her shih tzu with her, for God's sake. Plus, of course, three lawyers. It was the grandest, sexiest entrance in squad room memory."

"What about the Picasso?"

"I'm still working on it."

"When did Frazer tell you about DuBois?"

"He never actually *told* me about DuBois. That wasn't part of our deal. But he dropped a few hints. And, of course, the underworld has a fantastic intelligence network. A lot of people—art thieves and their minions—suspected that DuBois had a secret collection. They also suspected that he had the missing Renoir and the Rembrandt."

"Do these people know Betty Giles? By name?"

"I don't think so. Ned told me, but only to take out a little insurance, I think. He was contemplating retirement; that's probably why he did it. Also, he didn't trust the FBI to do the right thing."

"So why're you telling me all this?" Bernhardt asked.

"Have you ever done business with DuBois? Face to face?"

Bernhardt considered, then decided to nod. "Once."

"When was that?"

"A few months ago."

"Does he trust you?"

"I think so."

"All right—good." Once more, Graham dropped his voice, all business now. "What I want," he said, "is to get in touch with DuBois, face to face. Of course—" He paused, for emphasis. "Of course, it'd be worth something to me if you could set it up."

"Why do you want to see him?"

Graham countered with another question: "Do you think DuBois knows the feds are on his trail?"

"I have no idea. Why?"

"If I can convince DuBois that the FBI is about to get a warrant to search his premises for contraband art, then he might take a few million to divest himself of whatever he's got—including the Renoir and the Rembrandt."

"Is that what you think will happen? Will the feds try for a warrant?"

"Not as matters stand now. I have sources in the state attorney's office. And, in fact, I have a mole or two inside the FBI. And the word is that the state's attorney won't take action against someone as powerful as DuBois on the secondhand information from a deceased art fence. However, if the feds find Betty Giles . . ." He let it go meaningfully unfinished.

"Ah." Looking away, Bernhardt nodded. "Yes, I see."

"Which is why," Graham said, "I'm willing to offer you ten thousand dollars if you arrange matters so that I can meet with DuBois face to face, in a suitable environment. I'll pay five thousand now, and five thousand once I've had the meeting, no matter how it turns out."

"You're kidding."

Gently, Graham shook his head. "No, Mr. Bernhardt, I'm not kidding."

SEVEN

"Is he kidding?"

"No," Bernhardt answered, "I don't think he's kidding. Whatever else he's doing, he's not kidding."

"He'll pay ten thousand," Paula said, "just to set up a meeting for him with DuBois?"

"The way Graham operates, ten thousand is pocket money."

"Alan . . ." She put down her fork, reached across the table to touch his hand. "There's something wrong. You've got to be careful."

Lying on the floor beside the dining room table, reacting to the new note of concern in Paula's voice, Crusher raised his head, frowned as he looked at her. Then, sighing, the Airedale lowered his head again to the floor, allowed his eyes to slowly close.

"This Ned Frazer," she said. "How long has he been dead?"

"Not long. A month, maybe." Bernhardt took a second helping of rice pilaf, and helped himself to the salad. Tonight they'd had swordfish steak broiled with lemon sauce on a hibachi.

"The way you tell it—this Graham, with all the money he throws around—it all sounds very civilized, very urbane. But the truth is, he deals in stolen art. And there're two people dead. The FBI is threatening to throw you into bankruptcy. You're taking money for services rendered to DuBois, who could be arrested at any time. Then someone named Graham suddenly appears, and offers you a lot of money to make a phone call." Exasperated, she sharply shook her head. "My God, can't you see the red flags flying?"

Once more Crusher raised his head, this time whining anxiously.

"Listen, Paula, all I'm doing is—"

"It's the money. Isn't it? All the money, it's blinding you to the danger."

"Well, of *course* it's the money. You'd like to take a trip to Europe. Airline tickets cost money, you know."

Placed on a nearby chair, the portable phone warbled. It was the office number, ringing in the flat's front room, the office. Bernhardt glanced at his watch. Eight o'clock.

"Go ahead." Paula pushed back her chair, rose from the table. "Answer it. I'll uncork another bottle of wine."

Watching the rhythm of her walk as she strode into the kitchen, aware of the stiffened tilt of her head and the particular set of her jaw, he realized that Paula was exasperated.

Exasperated and, yes, worried.

He answered the phone on the third ring.

"Mr. Bernhardt? Alan Bernhardt?" It was a man's voice, a voice that, even in just two words, conveyed an aura of aloof command.

"That's correct." Reacting to the peremptory note in the caller's voice, Bernhardt clipped his reply.

"This is Justin Powers. Can you talk?"

Justin Powers—the front man who'd hired Willis Dodge.

Again, the desperate images flared: the figure engulfed

in orange flames, so ghastly in the blackness of the desert night.

The flames, and the shrieks: animal screams, finally gurgling into silence. And then, in the darkness, the thin, shrill sound of the siren, coming closer. All of it juxtaposed on the other obscenity: Justin Powers, presiding behind his huge desk at Powers Associates. Justin Powers, the ultimate executive, smiling, smooth-talking, infinitely secure, granting Bernhardt a few minutes of his precious time, ostensibly to help Bernhardt find Betty Giles, once a Powers employee.

"Yes," Bernhardt said. "I can talk." His eyes were on the doorway to the kitchen, where Paula was struggling with a stubborn wine cork. Crusher, ever optimistic whenever anyone was at work in the kitchen, was sitting attentively beside Paula, hoping for the best.

Bernhardt turned his back on the kitchen. "Why're you calling?"

"I want to meet with you. Tomorrow. Preferably down here, in Los Angeles."

"Why?" As he spoke, it was as if he were two characters in tandem, his outer self and his inner self. The inner self spoke next: *Why do you want to see me? So you can hire someone else to kill me, you son of a bitch?*

"I'll have five thousand dollars for you, and I'll meet you in the terminal at LAX. I'll be wearing blue jeans, running shoes, a Dodgers warm-up jacket, and a Dodgers baseball cap. I'll be wearing sunglasses, and I'll be carrying a copy of a car magazine, probably *Motor Trend*. I'll be in Concourse C, gate forty-two. That's four-two. I'll arrive there at three P.M., and I'll remain there until four-thirty. I'll be sitting down, either reading the magazine or looking out the window. Is that clear?"

Bernhardt decided to pitch his response to a patronizing

note distilled in pure, savage hatred. "You sound like you're doing a very bad imitation of a third-rate spy, Powers."

"Tomorrow. Three o'clock. Concourse C. Gate forty-two." The line clicked, went dead.

EIGHT

Even in the warm-up jacket and Dodgers cap, Powers was unconvincing as a sports fan waiting for his flight. Perhaps, Bernhardt decided, it was the razor-cut hair showing beneath the cap. Or perhaps it was body language: the well-paid, infinitely secure executive, accustomed to regarding the masses with disdainful tolerance.

Bernhardt slid into the empty chair beside Powers—and waited. His eyes were focused on the floor-to-ceiling window of Concourse C that offered a view of one of the busiest airports in the world. Seen at this distance, the taxiing airliners looked like battery-powered toys. Only on takeoff, roaring down the runway and climbing into the sky, undercarriage dangling, flaps extended, whorls of exhaust trailing the engines, did the airplanes acquire scale and substance.

Finally, also looking straight ahead at the airport view, Powers spoke: "Mr. Bernhardt."

"Powers."

"Let's get a cup of coffee." Without waiting for a reply, Powers rose, walked rapidly down the concourse in the direction of the main terminal. Soon the two men were sipping coffee from Styrofoam cups as they looked at each other across a tiny Formica table that hadn't quite been wiped clean. Powers dropped his copy of *Motor Trend* on the floor beside Bernhardt's flight bag.

"In the magazine," Powers said, "there's an envelope with the money inside. I'll leave first. When you leave, pick up the magazine."

"Fine."

"My, ah, employer told me to do this, meet you here."

"Mr. DuBois."

Plainly fearing that Bernhardt wore a wire, Powers looked pained as he nodded.

"DuBois told you to hire the man who tried to kill Betty and me in Borrego Springs."

"Mr. Bernhardt—" Powers' voice was no more than a whisper, his meager mouth pursed. Behind dark designer sunglasses his eyes were mercifully invisible. "Please."

"I could have died, you son of a bitch, and you're asking me to spare your feelings." As he said it, Bernhardt experienced a sudden surge of rage, a vestige of the fury that had engulfed him that night in the desert. "I should strangle you."

"I'm here to do business, Mr. Bernhardt. If you'd rather call me names . . ." Powers let it go unfinished. Watching him, Bernhardt realized that at some deep, primitive level, himself surprised, caught utterly unaware, he must abuse this man until he saw fear in his face. There was no other way.

"You should be in jail, you bastard. Dead—you should be dead, lying in the desert, rotting. You should—"

"I brought you five thousand dollars, to show good faith." Powers pointed to the magazine lying on the floor. Was his forefinger trembling? Inside, in his guts, was this craven satrap cringing? Was it enough? Probing the depths of his own anger, Bernhardt drew a deep, tremulous breath—one breath, and another. Finally he spoke:

"Take off those goddam glasses."

After a moment's hesitation, Powers used both hands to remove the dark glasses.

Yes, there was the proof of surrender: the furtive movement of the eyes, the uncertainty around the mouth.

It was enough. For now, it was enough.

"All right." Bernhardt gestured, a rough flick of his hand. "Go ahead. Tell me what it's all about."

"My—my employer. He wants to see you. Talk to you."

"I thought that might be it."

"Tomorrow morning. Ten-thirty."

"Where?"

"At the same place you met before. Mr.—my employer—said you'd know where." With an effort, Powers raised his head, looked inquiringly at Bernhardt, who merely nodded, a slight, contemptuous inclination of the head.

"I've got you a hotel room and a car. A Lincoln." Powers spoke indistinctly, without inflection. On the tiny round table between them, he still gripped the sunglasses with both hands. Now his naked gaze was fixed on the table.

"What's DuBois want to talk about?"

Eyes still downcast, Powers shook his head. "I don't know. I was just told to contact you, make the arrangements."

"You're a fucking errand boy."

No reply. Yes, the surrender was complete.

"When you put Willis Dodge on Betty's trail, told him to kill her, were you just following orders then?"

"Mr. Bernhardt—" Once more the frightened eyes begged. "Please. Let's not—"

"You don't have to worry about me, Powers." Bernhardt spoke bitterly. "I'm not wearing a wire. Because, you see, I'm on DuBois's payroll, too. You didn't know that, did you? You didn't know we're both infected by the same virus. It's called greed."

"If you knew what really happened in the desert, you'd realize that I went there to stop it. Those were my orders. But I couldn't locate Dodge in time," Powers said.

"First DuBois told you to have Betty killed. Then he changed his mind, and told you to stop it. Is that your story?"

"I was there, that night in Borrego Springs. Would I have been there, if I hadn't wanted to stop it? Would I—"

"All right, forget about Borrego Springs. What's this all about—this meeting tomorrow? What's the purpose, errand boy?"

"It—" In futility, perhaps desperation, the husk of a hollowed-out man, Powers slowly shook his head as he said, "It's what I said. I don't know why Mr.—my employer wants to see you. I only know he does."

"How much money did you make last year, Powers?"

"I don't see what—"

"How much?"

"Almost—almost a million. Maybe a little more."

"Are you happy in your work?" Bernhardt laced the question with all the contempt he could command.

"You're—you're trying to humiliate me."

"That's right, Justin. That's exactly what I'm trying to do. See, this is the first time I've ever faced someone who ordered my death. It's a new experience for me. I'm amazed at the anger I'm feeling. I'm absolutely awed. If we were somewhere else—an alley—I'm sure I'd try to kill you with my bare hands. All this despite the fact that, since grammar school, I've never struck anyone in anger. And I—"

"You killed Willis Dodge."

"No. Willis Dodge was tossing a Molotov cocktail through the window of that cottage in the desert. I had a shotgun, and I fired instinctively as the bottle came through the window. It was a lucky shot. Dodge wasn't so lucky."

Eyes once more downcast, submissively, Powers nodded agreement, but made no reply. Bernhardt finished his cup of coffee and checked the time: almost four o'clock on a smoggy April afternoon in Los Angeles.

"Where's the car?" Bernhardt asked.

"I'll show you. It's in the short-term parking garage."

As if he were exasperated at some petty inconvenience, Bernhardt sighed impatiently. "If I'm ever alone with you in a parking garage, asshole, I'll punch out your lights. Haven't you figured that out yet?"

Helplessly shaking his head again, the other man made no reply.

"You're disgusting. You're unbelievably disgusting. There are no words to describe how disgusting you are."

Still no reply.

NINE

Braced in the custom-contoured seat that held him erect in the car, Du Bois allowed his eyes to close, allowed his head to lean slowly back against the leather headrest. Recently the gardener's eight-year-old daughter had watched while DuBois was being lifted into the seat, then strapped in. "Hey, look," she'd said, calling to her father. "Look, it's like a baby seat."

Raphael's mortification had been monumental. Therefore it had been a particular pleasure to instruct a secretary that a comic card be sent to the child, with a ten-dollar bill inside.

DuBois opened his eyes as the driver and the bodyguard began talking in low voices. Now James, the principal bodyguard and chief of security, was studying the side-view mirror on his side while Ferdinand, the Chicano driver, slowed the Mercedes. Probable significance: the two bodyguards following in a second Mercedes had fallen behind, either caught by a red light or clogged in traffic. DuBois touched a button on the console built into his chair's arm, an identical console to the one in his wheelchair. In response, the window between the front and the rear began to close. Whenever he was in the decision-making mode any distraction, especially conversation, was unacceptable.

Time: ten o'clock. The Friday morning traffic was light. They would arrive at the Huntington in twenty minutes, allowing James and Ferdinand to get him out of the car and into the wheelchair with a comfortable time margin. As he'd done before, Ferdinand would park so that, remaining in the car, monitoring two radios, he could see the marble bench where DuBois and Bernhardt had first met, almost six months ago. Ferdinand would take a small submachine gun from the compartment beneath the Mercedes's dash. James and the other two guards would assume their positions, two on the pathway that connected the marble bench to the main building of the Huntington. Holding a tiny surveillance radio concealed in his hand, James, the leader, would take up a position beside the car. An intelligent, impassive, quick-thinking South American in his middle thirties, almost improbably handsome, James was built like a linebacker and moved like a quarterback. Of all his domestic employees, James was the only one in whom DuBois reposed any real trust, the only one who'd demonstrated mettle. The test had come only three months after James began work. In downtown Los Angeles, at noon, three black men in ski masks had tried to kidnap DuBois as his limousine stopped for a red light. With incredible coolness under fire, James had taken careful aim at each of the three kidnappers, dropping them with three shots from the Browning nine-millimeter he carried in an elaborately tooled leather shoulder holster. That evening DuBois had written out a bonus check for ten thousand dollars. A month later, James was given his own rent-free bungalow on the DuBois estate. Earning thirty thousand a year, James prospered.

Sometimes DuBois estimated the expense, hour by hour, day to day, of his own personal maintenance. Here, now, there were three bodyguards and two drivers who doubled as guards. At his home, high above the sprawl of Los Angeles, there was a valet. A nurse lived on the grounds. Two day women cleaned. There was a cook, two gardeners, and a secretary. Grand personnel total, thirteen. Grand total yearly outlay for salaries, almost two hundred thousand, give or take.

Like James, the spinster secretary—Grace Campbell—enjoyed a particular measure of DuBois's trust, and was rewarded accordingly. It was Grace Campbell who took responsibility for running the house. She did the accounts, paid the staff, paid the taxes, contracted for needed repairs and maintenance. She'd been with him for ten years, and was the only employee who lived on the premises in the main house, in an apartment with a separate entrance and its own garage. For the first five years, she'd been scrupulously honest. Then, when she turned fifty, still unmarried, without prospects, Grace had begun systematically skimming from the household accounts. On principle, DuBois reviewed the accounts quarterly. When he'd first discovered Grace's lapse, five years ago, he had considered firing her, even considered having her prosecuted. But he'd already had his first heart attack and one small stroke. He needed Grace more than she needed him. Therefore, if she were intelligent enough to keep her graft to a minimum, which she did, DuBois would ignore her lapse, charging it to "retirement."

Justin Powers could profitably learn from Grace Campbell, because he had lost his way, somehow slipped his moorings. During eight of the past nine years, he had made himself indispensable. Powers had been, in fact, the perfect second-in-command, the ultimate functionary. He ran complicated, far-flung financial operations with precision and, yes, a certain imagination, a certain creativity. But like all bred-in-the-bone assistants, Powers had no appetite for risk.

All this DuBois could abide. Could, in fact, turn to his own advantage.

But Powers was a coward.

And cowards, DuBois had learned, couldn't be trusted.

As he once more allowed his eyes to close, he realized that, in the next several minutes, he must make his decision. At age seventy-eight, doubtless with less than a year to live, he'd come to the last crossroads. Would he turn toward the battle? Or, for the first time—the last time—would he turn away?

The Mercedes was slowing. He opened his eyes. It was a traffic jam, doubtless an accident. Would Bernhardt wait? Unless he could be contacted by phone, a remote possibility, the question was unanswerable, therefore must be dismissed in the interest of efficiency. Dominion over other, lesser men, DuBois had learned, was essentially a question of who could think most effectively. And the secret of efficient thought was not to allow trivialities to intrude. While lesser men fretted as a hurricane approached, DuBois would sell insurance stocks short.

Now the car was inching forward, inexorably impacted in traffic until they reached the next freeway off-ramp. Once more, DuBois allowed his eyes to close.

Seventy-eight years . . .

In financial histories still unwritten, his name would figure prominently. But to what end? He'd gratified uncounted whims. He'd ruined a succession of adversaries, and rewarded a like number of allies. He'd demolished whole city blocks and built skyscrapers in the rubble. He'd once cornered the copper market, a coup that would never be equaled. He'd dined with heads of state, and turned down Cabinet posts. He'd married twice, both times because he wanted children—sons to carry on his name, daughters to cherish.

But there'd never been children. And the wives had taken the millions he'd given them and left the country.

In the next moment, his heart could falter. But there was no doctor with him, no nurse. No help could reach him in time.

Billionaire Dies in Freeway Traffic Jam.

At the thought, the right side of his mouth twisted in a grotesquerie of a smile. It was, after all, a news bulletin with a Los Angeles twist. In the whole world, there was nothing to equal the role of the freeway in the lives and the loves—and, yes, the deaths—of Angelenos.

Then, weeks later, perhaps months later, there would be another headline:

Stolen Masterpieces Discovered.

And under that a subhead: *Billionaire's Secret Gallery Contained Priceless Art.*

Alive or dead, his seventy-eight years were coming down to the last headlines. The jackals were beginning to circle, beginning to take his measure. Ned Frazer, the weakest link, had snapped. The DuBois case file, he'd been warned, was on the United States Attorney's desk. Meaning that his options were narrowing. If he didn't move his collection, he would be vulnerable. But, strapped to a wheelchair, he could hardly lift his right hand to push the chair's control buttons, much less lift a painting. Meaning, therefore, that he must have help, someone he trusted.

But who?

Betty was in Europe, fearful that he would have her killed.

Powers? No. During the months since Nick Ames had died, Powers had been disintegrating, no more than a husk now.

Leaving, incredibly, only one possibility: Alan Bernhardt, the failed actor-cum-playwright who now supported himself as a private investigator.

Because, yes, Bernhardt was an honest man. Whatever his shortcomings, he was probably trustworthy. Meaning that he could be DuBois's only hope.

He felt the car changing directions. Opening his eyes, he saw that they'd finally reached the off-ramp.

Soon he would know.

TEN

"First of all, Mr. Bernhardt, I hope to gain your trust. So if you'll permit me, I'd like to address the matter of Nick Ames and Betty Giles. I'm going to be completely honest with you. Usually, especially in matters of business, it's unwise to be completely honest. In fact, it's usually stupid, at least in the opening game. However, I find myself in an unusual position. That's to say, I find myself in a situation I can't control."

Bernhardt's response was a slight, noncommittal smile. He was biding his time.

"The problem, basically," DuBois was saying, "is time. Or, more precisely, infirmity. Without assistance, as you know, I can't get out of this chair. Which means that I'm incapable of dealing with the problems that began when Nick Ames started blackmailing me, several months ago."

"The problems began when you bought your first stolen painting," Bernhardt said. His manner, his inflection, everything suggested that Bernhardt had come to collect his pound of flesh.

"If that's your conclusion, Mr. Bernhardt, I can but agree."

Grimly Bernhardt nodded. "Thank you."

"I suppose," DuBois said, "a writer of another era might have described me as a mighty stag at bay, surrounded by a slavering pack of wolves. It's an image that used to stir my boyhood imagination: a huge, majestic stag, wild-eyed, rearing and bucking in the blood-flecked snow while the wolves, desperate for food because of the snow, are lunging at the stag."

Bernhardt made no response. He was sitting on a marble bench beside a pedestrian path that led through a small grove of olive trees and up a slope to the Huntington Library. DuBois had positioned his chair on the grass beside the path. From where Bernhardt sat he could see two of DuBois's bodyguards. Dressed in identical dark blue suits, white shirts, and regimental ties, they might have been IBM salesmen from an earlier era. Each man wore a shoulder holster so bulky that the amply cut suit jackets failed to conceal the bulges. Each man wore sunglasses. Each carried a walkie-talkie small enough to be concealed in the palm of his hand. Doubtless by prearrangement, one guard kept his gaze on Bernhardt while the other continually scanned the surrounding terrain. Since DuBois had arrived, fifteen minutes ago, perhaps a dozen sightseers had come down the path.

"In my case," DuBois went on, "the wolf pack includes law enforcement, various members of the insurance industry, several politicians, and perhaps the underworld."

"I know."

"That implies that they've contacted you."

Bernhardt made no response.

"I instructed Powers to give you five thousand dollars, plus expenses," DuBois said. "You accepted it, I assume."

"That's why I'm here. Because I accepted it."

"Have others offered you money in connection with my, ah, problems?"

Impassive, Bernhardt made no reply as he studied the small, frail man strapped in his high-tech wheelchair. Like his bodyguards, DuBois was impeccably dressed in a dark blue suit, white shirt, and tie. A blanket covered his shrunken legs. After they'd gotten him out of the Mercedes and into his wheelchair, one of the guards had put a small electrical device in his lap, then covered it with the blanket. If Bernhardt were wearing a wire, the device would blank out reception.

"Will you answer the question?" DuBois asked. Then, obviously with great effort, he added, "Please?"

"Money has been offered." Bernhardt spoke cautiously.

"But you haven't accepted."

"Not yet."

With an effort DuBois inclined his head as he said, "You might accept later, though. Is that correct?"

"No comment."

Now DuBois spoke softly, from the depth of what was certainly a weariness that penetrated his very being: "My strength is usually limited, Mr. Bernhardt. After an hour or two, especially if there's stress, I must rest. So, if you'll allow me, I'm going to put my proposition to you as concisely as possible. Do you understand?"

Bernhardt realized that, in spite of himself, he was drawn into the web of DuBois's confidences. Because he believed they *were* confidences: the gift of truth, offered by one of the most powerful men in the world. Never during his lifetime, Bernhardt realized, would the drama of this moment be surpassed.

"I'm aware," DuBois began, "that the FBI has questioned you. I'm also aware that you've been approached by a man—a civilian—as you were leaving the Federal Building on Wednesday. I know this—" As Bernhardt moved as if to interrupt, DuBois slightly shook his head, a mute request for permission to continue without interruption. "I know this because I ordered Powers to contact Herbert Dancer, the man for whom you were working when this all began, about seven months ago. I contacted Dancer because I'd learned that the FBI might be about to question you, and I wanted to verify that possibility. They did question you, twice. Their purpose was to get to Betty Giles through you. They'll charge her with receiving stolen goods, then offer to drop the charges if she testifies against me. As for the civilian who contacted you, and who you later visited at the Fairmont, I assume he—" Suddenly DuBois broke off. Startled, Bernhardt saw the frail head fall back against the wheelchair's contoured cushions, saw DuBois's eyes close, saw his right index finger touch buttons on the chair's arm. Moments later the bodyguard who'd stayed with the car was coming fast down the walkway. Beside his employer now, the bodyguard, obviously the man in charge, took a medicine vial from his pocket and shook out two pills, one white, one red. Now he touched DuBois's flaccid cheek. In response, DuBois's eyelids fluttered, and the pale purple lips parted. The bodyguard put the two pills on the old man's tongue while one of the two drivers arrived with a glass of water. Three spasmodic gulps, a cough, a momentary convulsion of the rattled cords of the throat, and the pills were swallowed. Moments later, DuBois's eyes opened, then came into focus, fixed on Bernhardt. DuBois coughed again, then began speaking in a low, clogged voice:

"I don't trust Dancer, and I've instructed Powers to terminate him. And, in fact, I no longer trust Powers. He's greedy, and he's lost his nerve. So—" His misshapen mouth stirred in the pale shadow of a smile. "So I'm left with you, Mr. Bernhardt. You and Betty Giles. I have no wife, I've had no children. There are no close relatives. There's only you and Betty." The gargoyle's smile widened, revealing tightly clenched teeth. The teeth looked false.

"It's ironic, isn't it," DuBois murmured, "that of all the

hundreds who would leap to do my bidding, there's no one I trust enough to save me. There's only you, a stranger, someone I've only seen once, a few months ago." He broke off as he seemed to nod over what he'd just said. Then, softly: "By my standards, Mr. Bernhardt, you're nobody. I've had you checked out. You're in your middle forties, and you've got a net worth of less than a hundred thousand dollars. But I think you're an honest man. Therefore, I propose to make you rich. In return, you will save me from possible arrest and public disgrace."

"How?"

"You'll contact Betty, and tell her to come back. Then, together—with suitable security—the two of you will dispose of my art collection. There are fourteen paintings and three ceramic pieces. I want them all returned to their rightful owners, in most cases major museums."

"You're out of your mind. You tried to have Betty killed for what she knew. And now you expect me to tell her to come *back*?" As if he were baffled, Bernhardt shook his head. "It'll never happen."

"You're not acquainted with the dynamics of the problem, Mr. Bernhardt. You see, during the previous two administrations in Washington, I enjoyed considerable influence. But in politics nothing is forever, and now there's a new administration. The current administration, naturally, will do anything to punish people like me for our previous allegiance. That's the background situation. Then come the players. Some months ago, a man named Ned Frazer was arrested in Mexico." As he said it, DuBois saw the flicker of recognition in Bernhardt's face. Yes, Bernhardt recognized the name. "To save himself, anything to get out of the Mexican jail, Frazer offered to testify for the authorities that he'd sold a stolen Renoir painting to Betty Giles, who worked for me. The deal was struck, and the gears began to turn. However, the United States Attorney was reluctant to ask for an indictment based solely on the unsupported word of a felon. The solution, of course, was to find Betty, and that's what the FBI is desperately trying to do. If they can get a confession from her, they'll certainly proceed against me. Meanwhile, they still had Ned. But then Ned was killed, in Manhattan. It happened just last month, and the authorities believe the killing was done by a professional. They—"

"A professional you hired," Bernhardt interrupted. "You had Nick Ames killed when he threatened you. And you tried to have Betty killed. Why wouldn't you have Frazer killed?"

DuBois answered calmly. "Because I would have to tell Powers to handle it, as he handled the Ames matter. But Powers is no longer reliable. He sees the possibility that he could be indicted for conspiracy to commit murder, and he's terrified."

"You had Ned Frazer killed," Bernhardt repeated doggedly.

"No."

"You *did* have Ames murdered, though. You admit that." The statement came in a flat, uncompromising voice. Bernhardt would not be denied.

"Mr. Bernhardt . . ." DuBois considered, then drew a long, weary breath. "I told you I meant to tell you the truth. And the truth is that, for someone in my position, it's sometimes necessary to have people killed. At the highest echelons, murder for gain is a lot more common than most people realize. Sometimes murder is the only possible resolution of a problem. When Nick Ames threatened me, I had no choice. He couldn't be trusted with a secret that could ruin me, so he had to be killed. It's as simple as that. But then Betty became distraught at the murder of her lover—

the only lover she'd had in years, I suspect. She called, and threatened to betray me. Probably she wouldn't have done it, but I couldn't be sure. So I ordered her killed. Then, on reflection, I changed my mind. I simply couldn't order Betty killed. But by that time it was too late to recall Dodge. And you know the rest."

"I don't believe you tried to recall Dodge. I don't think that's why Powers was in Borrego Springs that night."

For a moment DuBois focused all his faculties on Bernhardt. Then: "It's a hackneyed phrase, but Betty was the daughter I'd never had. Additionally, as I said, upon reflection, I decided that she wouldn't really betray me, not when she became more rational. And I think I was right. I *still* think I'm right. Which is one reason I want you to bring her home."

"What about Ned Frazer? Did you have him killed?"

"I've already answered that question. I suspect Ned informed on others besides me to get out of his Mexican prison. One of the people he betrayed probably had him murdered. He was, after all, a member of the underworld. And the underworld has its own code. He'd just agreed to work with the United States Attorney. When word of that circulated, I imagine his fate was sealed." As he spoke, DuBois's voice began to fade again. "I don't have time for quibbling, Mr. Bernhardt. Neither the time nor the strength. So I'll come directly to the point. I want you to get in touch with Betty, and I want you to bring her back to Los Angeles. Then, as I said, I want the two of you to make disposition of the paintings. It must be the two of you. Alone, Betty isn't tough enough for the job. And you, alone, don't have the expertise, even with my guidance." He broke off, then spoke softly, reflectively, his voice softened by memories. "For years—decades—those paintings were the entire focus of my life. It's a passion that only a collector can truly understand. To own something of great beauty that, in the whole world, is absolutely unique is, well, indescribable. And to share that pleasure with tourists in a museum . . ." Eloquently he shook his head.

"You're a very rich man. Why didn't you simply buy the paintings? Why have them stolen?"

"I've never ordered anything stolen. Others did, but not I. Never."

"If we do business, though—if I accept your offer—the art goes back to the museums."

"True. And I'll regret that. But I'll do anything—*any-thing*—to avoid getting hauled into court. I simply won't allow that to happen."

"If Betty comes back, and she's killed, then you'd be safe."

"No, Mr. Bernhardt, I wouldn't be safe."

"Why not?"

"Because there's you, Mr. Bernhardt. There'd still be you."

ELEVEN

Andrea set the hand brake, switched off the BMW's engine, glanced in the mirror, then carefully scanned the immediate area. Yes, Harry was safely out of sight. From her leather tote bag she took a surveillance radio. She put the transparent earpiece in place, switched on the radio, and verified the channel. Then she palmed the tiny microphone, lifted her hand, spoke into the microphone: "What's happening?"

"Still talking," Harry answered. "There're two guards on the path, one guard with the car. Two drivers."

"Five people. Plus DuBois and the other one."

"Right."

"I'm going to have a look. You go back to your car. If they leave, you follow DuBois. I'll follow the other one."

"Yes."

Moments later she saw Harry leaving a small grove of olive trees. He was dressed perfectly to imitate the typical tourist. Harry was a tall, good-looking, muscular man, but the slouch he was affecting made him less conspicuous. Despite his arresting good looks, Harry had a gift for surveillance, which required protective coloration, blending into his surroundings.

Name the part, and Harry played it to perfection.

Even if the role meant murder.

Years earlier, when they'd first met, Harry had been diagnosed a sociopath. In later years, "psychopath" had been added to the diagnosis. Most men went wild when they committed murder. Harry merely smiled.

She got out of the car, locked the door, slung the leather tote over her shoulder, dropped the earpiece and microphone into the bag. She, too, had dressed for the job. But while Harry was doing a polyester imitation of a tourist on Easter holiday, she was dressed for a more compatible role: one of the beautiful people, perfectly at ease with her own desirability, a with-it urban Californian, courtesy of Calvin Klein, Coach, and—the common touch—Christian Dior.

On the asphalt walkway, no skateboards allowed, she stood still, waited while one family group passed, then another. Next came an older couple in their cheerful, energetic middle sixties. She let them pass, then followed them, not too closely. As she walked, she took a small battery-operated camera from the bag, checked it, slung it around her neck. Ahead, standing on the grass beside the walkway, she saw a short, thick-necked Chicano, one of DuBois's bodyguards. He was dressed in a formal blue suit and black shoes, wearing the bodyguard's mandatory dark sunglasses. She smiled, shook her head. Was it a hint of senility, that DuBois would trust his safety to this caricature?

Or was DuBois, as always, thinking ahead, setting the agenda? Often it was advantageous that a bodyguard be conspicuous.

As she drew even with the guard, ignoring him, she was aware that, yes, he was turning his head, running his eyes over her. The male animal—how predictable, therefore banal, therefore contemptible.

And, likewise, the contemptible women who led them on, each doing their pitifully shallow numbers on the other, both existing at life's lowest level, wallowing in a morass of sensation, companions to beasts.

Ahead, the path was curving toward the grove of olive

trees, evocative of the sunny slopes of Tuscany under a topaz sky. DuBois was sagging in his wheelchair. The newcomer was sitting on an imitation Grecian marble bench. As soon as she'd seen the two Mercedeses draw to a stop, she'd driven past, searching for a parking spot; this would be her first glimpse of the newcomer. Now the elderly couple was drawing even with DuBois and the other man. The white-haired woman looked with compassion on DuBois, slightly shaking her head as she murmured something to her companion. Now the couple was beyond the bench. Allowing Andrea, for the first time, an unobstructed look at the stranger. He was a tall, lean man in his middle forties, was casually dressed. Like his body, his face was long and lean, deeply lined in an arresting pattern that suggested an intriguing depth of experience and perception. "Lincolnesque" was the cliché that fit. Or, factoring in the dark, lively eyes behind designer glasses and the thick, carelessly combed hair, "professorial" could equally apply.

Bernhardt, the private investigator. Certainly it was Alan Bernhardt, in avid conversation with DuBois. Just beyond the bench she stopped, as if to check the camera, adjust it. Then she took a picture of the Huntington. Behind her, she could hear their voices: DuBois's thin quaver, Bernhardt's cryptic reply.

She took one more picture, then continued up the grassy slope to the library. As she passed the second bodyguard, she smiled politely. He did not return the smile.

TWELVE

"So how'd you leave it with him?" Paula asked.

With the phone propped against his shoulder, sitting on the edge of the bed, Bernhardt was unlacing his shoes as he talked. "I said I wanted to think about it—wanted to talk to you. By that time, he was fading. James—his head body-guard, apparently—gave him another pill and loaded him back into his limo. DuBois had revived a little, and we talked for another fifteen minutes. He gave me a phone number. I have to call him by ten o'clock tonight." Bern-hardt glanced at his watch. The time was seven-thirty; they'd been talking for more than an hour. Would Powers pay for the phone calls, as well as the hotel suite? The an-swer, Bernhardt knew, was yes. For now, at least, they were serving the same master.

"DuBois sounds like an electric car. He needs recharg-ing, or he'll run down." She let a moment pass, then said, "Poor guy. It must be terrible, knowing death's so close."

Shoes off, Bernhardt leaned back against the king-size bed's headboard. "If he didn't have state-of-the-art medical care, he probably would've died years ago. Maybe with less pain."

"Did you tell him about the FBI? About John Graham? Any of it?"

"No, I didn't. I just listened. DuBois doesn't need me to advise him."

"When you call him, what're you going to say?"

"I figured I'd call you, and we'd figure out a game plan."

"Mmm." She was deciding whether he really meant it.

"I'm serious. After I came back from the Huntington, I sat here for two hours, trying to sort it all out. I even wrote it down, the pros on one side, the cons on the other. And, Jesus, they're about even."

"*Even?* Here's a guy with a secret collection of priceless art, all of it stolen. Here's someone who admits he's had people killed, admits he hired the hit man who almost killed you. And you say the pros and cons are *even?*"

"What he wants me to do—me and Betty Giles—is to return all the art to their rightful owners. And he—"

"Sure," she interrupted. "When he knows he's about to get busted because his buddies in Washington lost the election, now he wants to return the art. He's doing it to save his ass."

"If that were his only concern—saving his ass—he could call up another Ned Frazer, and sell the stuff overnight for millions. But he doesn't want to do that. He doesn't want the art to go back on the underground market, because art can get damaged that way, hauling it around in pickup trucks, whatever. He wants the art back in the museums, or in legitimate private collections. He's taking a chance doing that. But he's willing to give it a shot. Someone like him, as sick as he is, you've got to admire him. He loves that art collection. For a long time it's all he's had. Maybe it's all he *ever* had."

"Have you considered the possibility that all this is a trick to get Betty back here where she can be killed?"

"That couldn't happen. Not now."

"Why?"

"Because if DuBois wanted her dead, he'd need a middleman, someone to contact a killer, like Powers contacted Willis Dodge. But DuBois doesn't have a reliable middleman, not anymore. Powers has lost his nerve. He's out of it. Incidentally, before you pass judgment on DuBois, remember that Nick Ames started it all. He's the one who decided to blackmail DuBois. Ames broke the law first. Not DuBois."

"Aside from being a receiver of stolen property. You're making excuses for him, Alan. You want to take the job. Admit it."

For a moment Bernhardt made no reply. Then he began speaking slowly, seriously. "My father died in World War Two. My mother raised me in a loft in Manhattan, where she gave modern dance lessons. Whatever extra money she had, she gave to causes—all kinds of causes, mostly women and whales and minorities. Her father manufactured clothing for little girls. He was a wonderful man, and he took care of me and my mother. There were no frills, but I always had books and records, and I went to first-class schools. But then my grandfather's heart went bad, and in a few years his business failed. Two years later he and my grandmother died in a one-car auto accident. They said he had a heart attack. A year later my mother died of cancer. My grandparents left my mother everything they had, and she left me everything *she* had—about fifty thousand dollars, which I promptly lost backing a play off Broadway." He paused. Why had he begun this? How should he end it? When he realized that Paula meant to say nothing until this unintentional confession had ended, he said, "When that play failed, I felt as if I'd betrayed my whole family, my whole heritage. That fifty thousand represented my grandfather's whole lifetime. And I blew it in a few months."

"Alan . . ." Her voice was low, warm with compassion.

"If we can get rid of those paintings," he said, "there'll be a million dollars for us. At least."

" 'Us,' you say."

"That's right, Paula. Us."

"Jesus. This . . ." Bemused, she broke off. Then, ruefully: "Jesus, I can feel it infecting me. All that money . . ." Once more her voice died.

"Listen, I've got a great room—a suite, really. And a Lincoln town car, no less. It still smells new. Why don't you see whether Mrs. Bonfigli'll take Crusher for the weekend?"

"What about business? Holding down the fort."

"That's what answering machines are for. Besides, we'll be *doing* business."

"Alan, there's too much happening here to just take off. That fraud case for Patterson and Sayers—the trial starts Wednesday, and we're getting close. I *know* we're getting close. If we can find the handle before the case goes to trial, we'll be in at Patterson and Sayers."

For months he'd been romancing Patterson and Sayers, one of the fastest-moving law firms in California.

"There's something else, too." In her voice he could plainly hear bad news coming.

"What?" He spoke grudgingly.

"Haigh called at one-thirty today. I told him you were out of town, I wasn't sure where. He didn't believe me. God, he sounds like an officious bastard."

"What's he want?"

"He wants you to get in touch with him. He gave me three numbers. Do you want them?"

"No. I want you to fly down here tomorrow. As far as he's concerned, I'm unreachable."

"If he calls the United States Attorney . . ." She let it go ominously unfinished.

"There's nothing he can charge me with that'll stick, Paula. Nothing."

"But you'll have to defend yourself against the charges. We'd go broke, Alan."

"That's assuming the United States Attorney would indict. I don't think he would. And if he did, it wouldn't get past the grand jury, which would make the U.S. Attorney look bad, not to mention the FBI. Haigh knows that."

"So you aren't going to call him."

"Not until Monday. Not until we've had a great weekend. Jeff Sheppard's got a play running here, at the Trident. It's in its second month. I'll get tickets tomorrow. We'll arrive at the theater in our fancy car, and we'll have a valet park it. And after the play we'll eat at Musso's and Frank's."

"What about DuBois? What'll you tell him when you call?"

"I'll stall. I'll tell him, truthfully, that I won't be able to contact Betty with his proposition until she calls me. And if Betty follows my instructions, which she will, she won't call until next Tuesday. So I'll let DuBois sweat until then, hopefully to soften him up. Same for Haigh. This is Friday evening. I'll call Haigh Monday or Tuesday."

"I have the feeling," she said, "that you're in a very high-stakes poker game with some very, very good players."

"Maybe I'll have beginner's luck."

"Maybe."

"Is there anything else besides Haigh?"

"As a matter of fact, yes. John Graham called, too."

"The only thing I have going with Graham is his offer of ten thousand dollars for access to DuBois. Which, come to think of it, I could sell him right now, since I've got DuBois's private number."

"Mr. High Roller."

"I'm not saying I will. I'm saying I could. But if I don't make a deal with DuBois, then Graham's offer will be a consolation prize. Which—" Struck by a sudden thought, he broke off, testing the validity of the new thought. Then, speaking slowly as he searched for the words that fitted the thought, he said, "Which, come to think of it, might be the best resolution of the whole thing. I put Graham and DuBois together, and collect fees from both of them. They make a quick deal. Graham writes out a check to DuBois for, say, twenty-five million dollars. He gives the check to DuBois, and hires a Brinks truck and a dozen gun-toting guards. Once the paintings are out of DuBois's house, he can die in peace. And the paintings will stay in the legitimate art market, won't be taken underground. In fact—" Aware of a rising tide of excitement, perhaps his shekel-smart heritage, he broke off again, considered more carefully. Then: "In fact, this might really work out. What if—" He took a moment, recalculating. "What if I got Graham to go twenty-five thousand for the introduction? He's already offered ten thousand, so I'll bet he'd go twenty-five, no problem. And if DuBois saw a chance to divest himself of the paintings and still be assured they'd be properly treated, I'll bet he'd go a hundred thousand to me, for a finder's fee. So Graham gives DuBois, say, twenty-five million for the paintings, which is a small fraction of what they're worth. Graham would get the paintings at bargain prices, and DuBois would be safe from prosecution—and twenty-five million richer than he'd be if the government impounded the paintings. I, meanwhile, would be in the very big bucks. And best of all, the FBI would be screwed."

For a full minute, only a static-sizzling silence came from San Francisco. Finally, tentatively, Paula ventured, "It could work."

"Of course, if I went along with DuBois, get Betty here, help her dispose of the paintings, get them back to the museums, wherever, my end would come to more. Plus, that way—"

"Alan . . ." The misgivings were back in her voice.

"That way," he went on, "Betty would get a slice of the pie, too. Which she wouldn't if DuBois and Graham made a separate deal. She'd also be back with her mother, which would mean a lot to both of them. All they have is each other."

"Unless Betty's dead."

"DuBois won't have her killed. He needs her now more than ever. Besides, he *did* relent after he ordered her killed. He tried to stop Dodge in Borrego Springs."

"Are you sure of that?"

"I'm sure. Also—" As another thought surfaced, he tested the logic, then said, "Also, if DuBois acts without Betty's help, unloads the paintings to either Graham or the underground—or if the FBI gets a search warrant, and confiscates the paintings—then Betty's screwed. For life. As long as DuBois has the paintings, he's got to keep Betty pensioned off, out of the country. But once those paintings are off his premises, Betty's got no more leverage. So sure as hell, DuBois would cut her off."

"Jesus." It was a reflexive response that nevertheless suggested vexation. Paula had no interest in complexities. Beyond two-dimensional speculation, she became impatient.

"I feel like I've got to do my best for Betty. I saved her life a few months ago. We're—" Uncertain how the thought would end itself, he broke off, then said quietly, "We're connected. Betty and me."

"Ah, Alan." He could imagine her as she said it: the resignation, the essential approval—and the exasperation. "I agree. You *are* connected, and more power to you, darling. But I don't want you to go to jail. And I—" She interrupted herself, then said, "I just remembered: Mrs. Bonfigli said something about visiting her son in Sebastopol this weekend."

"Ah." It was a rueful, frustrated monosyllable. Then: "There's that kennel up in Marin County."

"In the first place, it's not Marin County. It's *Sonoma* County. And in the second place I'm not going to put Crusher in a kennel. He's your dog. If you want to personally take him to a kennel, fine. But I'm not going to do it. I'm just not. All weekend I'd remember the reproach in his eyes when they closed the cage."

"Well, Jesus, the point is that I'm *not* there. And a weekend in a kennel isn't going to—"

"I'm not going to do it. You *know* I'm not going to do it."

"You're a very stubborn lady."

Now her voice turned soft, intimate. "It's not that I don't *want* to see you. You know that."

"Well, see what Mrs. Bonfigli says. Her son, you know, is pretty erratic."

"I've been working my buns off on that Patterson and Sayers case. What you're doing, this high-stakes game, it's a turn-on. But Patterson and Sayers could be bread and butter. For years. Decades."

"Let's get back to your buns. See, after the play, tomorrow night, we have a late dinner, and we get in our fancy car and come back here, then we—" On Paula's end he heard the warble of the office's other line.

"Why don't I get that?" Her voice was husky now, an evocation of other weekends, other nights, remembered with sensuous pleasure. "Time out?"

His reply was resigned. "Time out."

Her conversation was short, and when she came back on the line her voice was crisp, no longer sensual.

"That," she said, "is John Graham. Again. He wants you to call him."

"Hmmm."

"The way he said it," she offered, "it sounded like he knew you were out of town."

"Does he sound anxious?"

"He sounds like if he wasn't so cool, so Ivy League, he'd probably be anxious."

He chuckled appreciatively. "That's Graham. You've got him exactly. Is he holding?"

"Yes. But he doesn't know you're on the other line."

"Then tell him you'll try to reach me."

"Right."

"I'll call you later. Meanwhile, check with Mrs. Bonfigli. And I'll keep thinking about your buns."

"Love you." The line clicked; she was talking to Graham. Bernhardt cradled the phone on the nightstand, laced his fingers behind his neck, leaned back against the headboard.

Patterson and Sayers . . . a bird in the hand. Security. Predictability. Probity. Modest profitability.

Raymond DuBois . . .

How many times in the past months had DuBois dominated his thoughts like some cancerous temptation that fed upon itself, endlessly burgeoning? In those months, as if it were unintended, in random reading, he'd discovered more and more about Raymond DuBois. Like Daniel Ludwig and J. Paul Getty, DuBois was a virtual recluse, neurotically secretive. Opportunistic, utterly ruthless, a genius at predicting trends, DuBois had begun working as a boy of sixteen, a runner for a major brokerage house in New York. In less than ten years he had bought the business outright. Married twice, divorced for decades, he'd never had children. If he gave to charity, the gifts were secret. His net worth was at least three billion dollars, probably much more. Pictures of DuBois were almost nonexistent, leaving Bernhardt to imagine how he must have looked as a young man. Somehow the images closely resembled Franz Kafka: a slight, frail, dark-haired man with a pale face, large, lustrous, feverish eyes, and a small, tight mouth, vivid against the pallor of his skin. The mouth never smiled, the enormous eyes never wavered, pathologically intent, constantly probing, never smiling, never shifting focus. Bernhardt imagined the younger DuBois sitting behind a huge, austere desk. There might be a glass-domed stock ticker behind the desk. He would be impeccably dressed; he was the kind who in an earlier era would have worn a morning coat, striped trousers, dove-colored spats, and a black silk top hat when he left the office, perhaps strolling down Fifth Avenue from his office to his mansion.

Then cut to the Raymond DuBois he'd left only hours ago: a frail, shrunken man, totally bald, utterly helpless. Only the right arm and the right side of the face were functional. But like so many others confined to wheelchairs, the force of DuBois's intellect was almost palpable, so that, sometimes, Bernhardt imagined a surrealistic Raymond DuBois: only a brain that resembled the distended head of an octopus. But instead of eight tentacles, there was only one member attached to the pulsating brain. It was a single forefinger, poised over the electronic console that was always just beneath his right hand. A touch of the forefinger on the console in a certain sequence, and the world of finance trembled.

Another touch, and a murderer would begin packing the tools of his trade.

THIRTEEN

As if from a lengthening distance, Powers was aware that the surrounding voices were receding until the separate words and phrases were no longer distinguishable, merely meaningless blurs that diminished as the urgency of his own thoughts blanked out the babble.

Friday night on the Beverly Hills dinner-party circuit—twelve of the beautiful people, the collar-and-tie crowd, not the bomber-jacket crowd. They were gathered together to celebrate themselves while they sipped chardonnay that lacked distinction and murmured polite approval of a tomato and fennel bisque that was too thin and too flat.

The Levys' cook, it was reported, had received a better job offer, and the bisque would seem to confirm the rumor.

Once more he sipped the chardonnay, and swallowed another spoonful of the bisque. Then, as he pressed a napkin to his lips, the desolate refrain returned: Today, April ninth, might mark the beginning of the end: farewell Powers Associates. For hours now—ten hours, at least—the certainty had been growing. At ten-thirty that morning, at the Huntington, DuBois and Bernhardt had met. Powers had waited until two o'clock to call. DuBois, the nurse had said, was resting. She would see that DuBois knew Powers had called. As he thanked her and hung up, Powers could plainly sense the coolness in her voice, the distancing.

The first hints came, he knew, from the invisible people—the servants, the ordinary staffers. Keeping their eyes and ears open, they could predict the future, who was in the ascendancy, who was falling out of favor. Inevitably, then, they would join the winner's retinue, distance themselves from a loser.

Was blindman's buff the operative metaphor?

No, the metaphor was Machiavelli—or de Sade.

Raymond DuBois, the master manipulator, the consummate tactician. For years he'd worked through Powers, the puppeteer and the puppet. Pick up the phone, buy a million shares of copper, watch the market rise, see the suckers flock into the tent, buying. Then sell, pocket the profit, do the same with other commodities, other corporations. Sell lira short, go long on the mark. Lose a million one day, make two million the next. The buy or sell orders always originated with a phone order from DuBois and were routed to Powers, then to the traders—a hundred traders for a major transaction, protecting DuBois's sacred anonymity.

And then had come the stroke, a burst artery in the brain, a microevent that had undermined a hundred deals, ruined a thousand careers when Powers had put his ear close to the pale purplish lips and heard two words: "Freeze everything."

The stroke, and then the heart attack. Followed by the period of convalescence. The brain, that incredibly complex, infinitely inventive ganglia of neurons that constituted the particular genius of Raymond DuBois, had restored itself. But the body would be forever withered, henceforth a burden—the burden that had precipitated the unprecedented thirty-minute face-to-face meeting. Previously, their business had been conducted by phone: buy a given stock at a certain price, option a certain tract of forest at a given price per acre, sell a billion yen. Terminated, invariably, by the three words: "Thank you, Justin."

But in the matter of Nick Ames, a face-to-face meeting had been required: DuBois in his motorized chair, dressed, as always, in a conservative suit, white collar, and tie, legs wrapped in a blanket even though the night was warm. The place was the deck off DuBois's study, both of them staring out on the wondrous panorama of a clear night in Los Angeles, a miracle of a million lights. Betty Giles, DuBois said, had discovered a vital corporate secret. Nick Ames, Betty's larcenous boyfriend, had learned of the secret, and was threatening blackmail. It was necessary, therefore, that Ames be silenced—permanently. Could Powers handle the job?

There'd been no question of refusal. Even though—

"—if the Japanese control the entertainment industry, then they control our culture." It was Bart Estes, across the table. Estes was a dedicated Japan basher. Powers nodded, shrugged, sipped his chardonnay, exchanged a fragmentary glance with Marge. Also sitting across the table, she was frowning slightly as she looked at him. As always, Marge had guessed that he was troubled. During the hour's drive to the party, he'd felt her watching him. Her expression had been pensive; she'd said very little. She was conducting a running review of her options. Like perfect gems, women like Marge required a suitable setting; no other possibility existed.

Perfect gems . . .

Utter perfection . . .

Always, DuBois required utter perfection. Nothing else was tolerated.

Almost two years ago, on DuBois's order, he'd searched for a curator to oversee DuBois's extensive art collection, most of it modern. Many of the paintings were done by fledgling painters. Inevitably, then, responding to an even deeper instinct than his passion for collecting art, DuBois began trading, buying and selling. And, also inevitably, the enterprise had prospered. After his first heart attack, but before his stroke, DuBois had decided to employ a curator. His activities in the art market, after all, yielded considerable profit. But to buy low at the auctions, it was essential that he be invisible. Thus, a curator.

Betty had worked in San Francisco as a curator for Chevron, and when DuBois approved of her, it was a simple matter to lure her to Los Angeles at a very generous salary, plus a percentage of trading profits. The arrangement worked perfectly, and a close bond developed between DuBois and Betty Giles. As DuBois's health deteriorated, Betty had acted with more authority, once selling a painting for almost a half-million dollars. Never, in almost two years, had there been a hint of acrimony.

Not until DuBois's stroke.

Conclusion: Something fundamental had changed with DuBois's stroke.

Something so dire, so dangerous, that it had precipitated the murder of Nick Ames. Something that Betty knew.

Something that Nick Ames had discovered.

Something, certainly, that concerned DuBois's art collection.

Something that—

"—twenty-first century," Estes was pronouncing, "will be the yellow man's century."

Marge smiled, chiding Estes: "Don't I remember the Yellow Peril from History Two-oh-three, Bart?"

Estes answered the smile, then drank deeply of the wine. In an expansive mood tonight, with good reviews in the trades on his new movie, Estes would doubtless drink too much.

As Powers sipped his own wine, his thoughts once more turned to DuBois and Betty Giles—and Alan Bernhardt.

If I ever had you alone in a parking garage, Bernhardt had threatened.

Followed, today, by the private meeting at the Huntington.

Followed by silence.

Signifying, certainly, that the encircling action had begun. Betty Giles had told Bernhardt that DuBois had ordered the death of Nick Ames. Bernhardt, who had almost died at Borrego Springs, was determined to expose DuBois for the murder. DuBois had discovered that Bernhardt was on the trail. DuBois's next move was obvious: summon Bernhardt, make a deal, betray Powers. Conceivably the bargain could have been outlined during DuBois's first meeting with Bernhardt, months ago, and was now being implemented. Soon the police would call.

Powers placed his crab fork on his empty plate, and glanced at the menu, clipped in its silver holder. The next course was sautéed scallops Provençale, followed by duck a l'orange.

The condemned man would eat a hearty meal.

FOURTEEN

Bernhardt opened the leather-bound address book Paula had given him for his birthday and turned to the last page, where he'd written DuBois's phone number. He placed the open notebook on the desk beside the phone, placed a ball-point pen beside the notebook, drew up a chair. For this conversation, it was not appropriate to lie on the bed, shoes off, pillows propped against the elaborately quilted head-board.

Picasso, so the mythology went, had once found himself with no money in his pocket after he'd invited several friends for lunch at a Parisian restaurant. He'd called for a pencil and a paper napkin. In moments he drew a dove, then signed the sketch. "Here," Picasso had said, handing the sketch to the waiter. "It's worth thousands of francs."

Just as the phone number written in Bernhardt's note-book had currency: Graham's ten thousand dollars, per-haps more.

Clearing his throat, he touch-toned the number. The connection was made on the second ring. A man's voice said only, "This is eight-two-four-oh-seven-six-nine."

"Yes. This is Alan Bernhardt. I, ah, have an appointment to call Mr. DuBois before ten tonight."

"Just a moment, please." The line clicked, went dead. Seconds passed, perhaps a full minute. Then came DuBois's unmistakable husk-dry rattle: "Yes, Mr. Bernhardt. Have you come to a decision?"

"I have an idea. A way out, maybe—a solution."

"Is it something that can be implemented quickly? My sources tell me that time could be of the essence."

"I think it could be done in a few days. I'd need assurances, though. And you and I haven't discussed terms."

There was a silence. Then the voice said, "Tomorrow I would like you to come here. I'll send a car for you. James—my security man—will be in front of your hotel at nine o'clock. He'll be driving a gray car, a Lincoln."

"James—he's the one who helped you today. With the, ah, pills."

"That's correct. Is nine o'clock tomorrow satisfactory?"

"Yes, that's satisfactory." As he said it, the sense of unease he experienced was almost palpable. It was as if, in some mysterious way, he'd surrendered his free will. There was, he knew, a word for what he was experiencing: "temptation."

FIFTEEN

At two minutes to nine, Bernhardt rose, crossed the hotel lobby, went out through the automatic glass doors. A uniformed doorman smiled as he asked, "Is your car in the garage, sir?"

"No." Bernhardt gestured to the gray Lincoln just drawing to a stop at the curb. "I think that's for me." As, yes, the driver got out and went to the rear door, holding it open. He was the big, broad-shouldered man who had remained with the cars yesterday at the Huntington, the one who gave the other two guards their orders. He moved smoothly and confidently, with a grace and economy that hinted at great physical strength balanced by an equable nature. His knuckles, Bernhardt saw, were scarred white. His name, Bernhardt remembered, was James.

Yesterday James had worn a somber blue suit and striped tie. Today he wore a blue blazer, gray flannel trousers, a soft white shirt, no tie. His broad, blandly oval face and obsidian black eyes were expressionless. His black hair and olive-brown skin suggested Latin descent. Or, a more imaginative guess, Samoan.

As Bernhardt covered the few yards to the car he considered his options; never had he been driven alone in the back seat of a limo. Was this the time for a new experience, a delayed ego sop, a unique page in his life story? Or were there philosophical considerations that transcended mere ego gratification?

With only a few feet separating him from the driver, Bernhardt shook his head. "I'll ride in front, thanks." He opened the right front door and slipped into the glove-leather seat. Impassively James closed the rear door, rounded the car, slid under the steering wheel. Bernhardt extended his hand, introduced himself. Predictably, James's grip conveyed a sensation of restrained power. He nodded politely, but did not offer his name in return. Moments later the big car moved smoothly away from the curb and joined the light Saturday morning traffic.

"Where does Mr. DuBois live?"

"He lives above Benedict Canyon, in the Hollywood Hills."

"Do you live with him? On the premises?"

"I live near him. I have a bungalow." James spoke softly. His voice was flat, yet somehow melodic. They were traveling east on Santa Monica, about to intersect Wilshire. Beyond Wilshire, the improbable affluence of Beverly Hills began. During his two years of frustration, living in Los Angeles, Bernhardt had come to avoid driving through Beverly Hills. Others, he knew, enjoyed basking in the reflected glow of great wealth. His reaction was a complex mix of derision and, he suspected, envy.

"Does Mr. DuBois live in a compound? Several buildings?"

"Yes, sir." The two words were spoken with admirable equilibrium, a perfect evocation of servant-speak.

"Mr. DuBois and I are discussing a business transaction. Did he tell you that?"

No response. On a Saturday morning, traffic was light

and fast. James drove smoothly, effortlessly. He never exceeded the speed limit. He kept his eyes on the road.

"The reason I mentioned our, ah, arrangements is that it would save time if you could give me a rundown. You know—a description of Mr. DuBois, how he lives, what he does in a typical day. What you do. Things like that."

For the first time James took his eyes from the road, looked appraisingly at Bernhardt. Then, returning his eyes to the road, he said, "I know that you must be a very important person, Mr. Bernhardt. I tell you that because it has been a long time—six months, at least—since Mr. DuBois has left his home to meet someone, as he met you yesterday. But the truth is that I do not talk about Mr. DuBois. I never have."

Bernhardt let a silence pass, then said, "Your name is James, that much I know. Mr. DuBois places great trust in you, which I can understand."

Once more James looked at Bernhardt. Then, gravely, he nodded. "Thank you. I appreciate that." They were turning north on Canyon Drive, beginning to travel steadily uphill. The road ahead, Bernhardt knew, would become narrower, more winding.

"How long have you worked for Mr. DuBois?"

"Almost three years."

"How many staff are there besides you?"

"That's hard to say. Only the cook and the nurse and Miss Campbell and Roger live on the premises—besides me. But then people come during the day. Gardeners and cleaning people. And Raul, too. He drives, takes care of the cars."

"Who's Miss Campbell? Who's Roger?"

"Miss Campbell is the secretary. She runs things, really—pays us all, takes care of Mr. DuBois's appointments, decides who Mr. DuBois might want to see."

"And Roger? What's he do?"

"He takes care of Mr. DuBois, gets him dressed, gets him bathed, things like that. He and Miss Gross, the nurse, they work together."

"So Roger is Mr. DuBois's valet."

A faint suggestion of a smile touched James's mouth at the corners. "Mr. DuBois doesn't like that word."

" 'Valet,' you mean?"

"Yes, sir. Valet. Mr. DuBois, you see, he's proud that he started from nothing, running errands in New York City for stockbrokers."

"Ah." Bernhardt nodded approval—and surprise. "Does Miss Campbell screen Mr. DuBois's phone calls?"

"Yes."

"Does Mr. DuBois have many visitors?"

"Not many. Mr. Powers comes sometimes. And Mr. Robbins, too. But that's about all."

"Who's Mr. Robbins?"

"He's Mr. DuBois's lawyer. He comes every few days."

"What about other visitors? Friends?"

James hesitated, then discreetly shook his head. The message: one of the world's richest, most powerful men had no friends.

"Betty Giles," Bernhardt said. "She was a friend."

James nodded gravely. "Yes. She was a friend. But then—" He broke off. Climbing more sharply now, they were winding through forested hills. Here, Bernhardt knew, back among the trees, estates were measured in acres; homes were valued in the millions. Occasionally there was a private gate, usually flanked by stone pillars.

"But then Betty left," Bernhardt said. "Is that what you were going to say?"

"Yes."

"Did she live on the grounds?"

"No, sir. She had her own place in Santa Monica."

Testing the other man, Bernhardt asked, "What did Betty Giles do for Mr. DuBois? What kind of work?"

"She took care of his art—the paintings. They were always talking about the paintings, buying and selling. You know—" James was searching for a phrase. "Like stamp collectors."

"Did Betty report to work every day?"

"Mostly, yes. Sometimes, though, she traveled, buying paintings, or selling."

"Mr. DuBois's collection of art must be very valuable."

"Yes."

"You're in charge of security for Mr. DuBois. Do you also guard the house—the paintings?"

"Yes, certainly."

"You and the other two guards I saw yesterday—is one of you on duty all the time? Is that how it works?"

"It depends. There's an alarm system."

"A very elaborate system, I imagine."

"Oh, yes." James almost smiled. "It takes a lot to keep up with that system. Once a week, people from the alarm company are here."

"I can imagine." Bernhardt decided to chuckle, an effort at camaraderie. Then, shifting ground: "Why did Betty leave, do you think? Was there an argument? Disagreements about the art?"

James turned to look briefly at Bernhardt. How much, he was plainly wondering, should a trusted employee reveal? Finally: "No, sir, they never argued."

"Why do you think she left, then? Money?"

"Please, sir, I'd rather not—" James broke off. Almost immediately, the car slowed. With one broad, knuckle-scarred hand James unclipped an electronic wand from the dashboard as he nodded ahead. "Here we are." He guided the Lincoln into a short driveway that ended in a massive wood and iron gate. James aimed the wand; moments later the double gates swung ponderously inward. Beyond the gate, the driveway was graveled. The extensive grounds were so heavily wooded that no buildings were visible until they'd driven through a long, gentle half-circle. Then, among the trees, Bernhardt saw a group of low one-story outbuildings. They were "Malibu modern," natural wood and extensive glass combined with rock masonry, each one built to integrate with its surroundings, an evocation of Frank Lloyd Wright. Just ahead, Bernhardt saw a second gate, which swung open in response to another wave of the wand. Another bend, and the main house came into view. Like the other buildings, the DuBois residence was built to unify the earth and the trees with the panoramic view that was just visible through the trees beyond the house. To himself, Bernhardt nodded approval. With unlimited means, DuBois hadn't built another San Simeon. Instead, he'd chosen a partnership with the earth and the sky.

The graveled driveway looped around in front of the house. Once more James activated the wand.

"They'll let you in." As he spoke, James automatically moved to open his door, intending to go around and open Bernhardt's door.

"No. Please." Bernhardt tripped the latch, swung his own door open.

Impassively James nodded—and perhaps smiled.

The entry was stone walls framed by massive timbers and floored in slabs of slate. The front door was a three-dimensional sculpture fashioned of dark, weathered iron. The abstract shapes had been roughly cut with a torch and twisted into a vast interlocking whole that was unified by irregular welding seams of bright, flowing brass.

As Bernhardt was about to press the bell button set into

the rock beside the timbered door frame, the door swung slowly open. A woman stood in the doorway. She was small and middle-aged, neatly dressed in a simple shark-skin skirt, plaid blouse, and cardigan sweater. "Sensible" was the catchall word for her hair, her glasses, and her makeup. Her manner was direct, her voice brisk.

"Mr. Bernhardt. I'm Grace Campbell. I'm Mr. DuBois's secretary."

"I know." He decided to extend his hand, and was rewarded with a firm, friendly grip. Her hand was remarkably cool. She stepped back, invited him inside with the same gesture she used to touch a switch that activated the door-closing machinery. Economy of motion came naturally to Grace Campbell.

"Mr. DuBois is waiting for you." As she spoke she turned and began walking down a long, wide, high-ceilinged hallway. Up to a height of ten feet, the walls were burlap painted white. Everything else was natural wood, rich in the simplicity of its joinery. Light flooded in from clerestory windows that were continuous from the top ledge of the walls to the planked wooden ceiling. Like the porch, the floor was natural slate. The walls were hung with scores of paintings and wall sculpture.

Aware that Bernhardt was lagging as he looked from one painting to another, marveling, Grace Campbell waited for him at the far end of the entry hall that was really a gallery. When he joined her she said, "That's only a small part of it. Later I'll take you on the tour." Then, without waiting for an answer, no time for pleasantries, she turned away, opened the inner door, and led the way down a smaller, narrower hallway. The architecture of the two hallways was identical, a unity that had clearly been designed to display the works of art.

Grace Campbell passed two doors on her right, then knocked on the third door. It was a perfunctory knock, a formality before she pushed open the door. The room was a study. Floor to ceiling, bookcases covered three walls; the fourth was all glass set into oversize posts and beams in natural wood, apparently the architectural motif of the entire house. The glass wall overlooked the cityscape below and the distant ocean to the west. A sliding glass door led out to a deck fashioned of natural cypress and rough-cut redwood. A solitary figure occupied the deck: Raymond DuBois. Remarkably, the figure was deeply etched in Bernhardt's consciousness: a frail, formally dressed figure sitting lopsided in his high-tech motorized chair, restrained by straps that kept him from falling to the deck, where he would lie as helpless as a newborn baby.

Grace Campbell went to the glass door, slid it open for Bernhardt. "I'll be in the hallway when you're finished," she said.

As Bernhardt stepped through the glass wall, it was with the feeling that he and Lewis Carroll's Alice were soulmates. He was still smiling wryly at the thought when DuBois activated his wheelchair and turned to face him.

"Sit down, Mr. Bernhardt." DuBois nodded to a redwood patio chair that was placed to face the deck railing and the view across Benedict Canyon.

"Thank you." Bernhardt nodded in return and did as he was told. "Magnificent house."

"Do you know Los Angeles?"

"I lived here for two years. In Santa Monica."

"Did you like Santa Monica?"

"Yes, I did. I didn't like Hollywood, though. Or, rather, I didn't like the film industry."

"You wrote screenplays."

"I *tried* to write screenplays."

"But you wrote a play that was produced off Broadway."

Bernhardt looked away, off over the haze of the city below to the haze of the ocean beyond. "That was a long time ago." In his own voice he could hear the familiar accents of ancient regret. Could DuBois hear it, too?

Yes, DuBois had heard: "It's my understanding that you suffered a series of personal tragedies after *Victims* was produced."

"*Victims,*" he'd said. Signifying that, yes, DuBois had had him checked out.

With his gaze still cast far away, Bernhardt's reply was utterly without inflection. It was his only defense against the pain. "In one year's time, my mother died of cancer and my grandparents died in a one-car accident. Then my wife was mugged just a block from our apartment. She hit her head on the curb, and she died two days later."

"And you had to get out of New York."

"Yes."

For a moment DuBois said nothing as he, too, stared off across the city. Then, also without inflection or emotion, he said, "I've never experienced the untimely loss of anyone I loved. There are those who would say—" Something that might have been a smile touched his pale lips. "Some would say, perhaps, that I've never experienced love, and could therefore never experience loss. Looking back, I can see truth in the allegation. I equated love with vulnerability, dependency. I was wrong, of course. But realization didn't come until a small blood vessel in my brain burst. By then, it was too late. So I became dependent upon whoever I could hire. The more I paid, the more loyalty I bought. Except that it doesn't work that way. Not when greed is a factor."

"Powers, you mean."

DuBois nodded. Repeating wryly: "Powers."

"Betty, too?"

"That remains to be seen; the story is still unfolding, isn't it?"

"I suppose so, yes."

"I became psychologically dependent on Betty, you already know that. Without her, I was unable to care for the room. You understand my meaning, when I say 'the room.' "

"Yes, sir, I understand."

"There are filters to be changed, and humidifiers to service, and alarms to test. There are security devices that must also be checked."

Security devices. What, Bernhardt mused, did the words mean?

"It's been four months since Betty left."

"Four months, yes." Even though DuBois spoke softly, conserving his strength, Bernhardt could hear the sorrow in the other man's words. The sorrow and, yes, the defeat.

"Last night," DuBois said, "on the phone, you alluded to a plan—some solution to the problem."

"The man I met outside the Federal Building, the man staying at the Fairmont—he's an insurance adjuster. His company has reinsured a number of very valuable paintings, and they paid off when the paintings were stolen. Renoir's *The Three Sisters* was one." Bernhardt paused, stole a look at DuBois. But the other man's face was in profile on the paralyzed left side.

"If I were to contact him on your behalf," Bernhardt continued, "and if he paid you, say, twenty-five cents on the dollar for the paintings you have in your, ah, room, then everyone's home free. The paintings would be safe, you'd have several millions, I'm sure, and you'd also be off the hook with the feds. And I'd send you a bill for services rendered."

"This adjuster—do you trust him?"

"I've only talked to him for an hour. He seemed very straightforward. In fact, I liked him."

"And you know his company, I assume—who he represents."

"I have his card."

DuBois remained motionless for a long, silent moment. Only seeing the left side of his face, it was impossible to determine whether he was lost in thought or slipping off into exhaustion.

Bernhardt shifted in the redwood deck chair. Another long silence passed. Finally DuBois said, "You realize, of course, that I can't deal directly with this gentleman. Additionally, he can't come here, can't see the room, or the paintings, while they're in my possession."

Bernhardt nodded. It was a problem he'd already considered. With evidence of possession given by John Graham, the FBI would surely ask for an indictment.

"What's required," DuBois said, "is that you must take the paintings to neutral territory. A secure warehouse, for instance. What's this man's name?"

Without hesitation, himself surprised, Bernhardt answered, "John Graham."

"And his company?"

"I don't remember, sir. And I left his card in San Francisco."

"You're willing, I assume, to undertake the function of a mediator, a go-between."

"As long as I don't do anything illegal, and I'm paid enough." Bernhardt nodded. "Yes. I'm willing."

"There are two primary elements to the problem.

There's security, of course. But most of all there's trust. Integrity. As I told you before, I must trust a total stranger. You. And I must trust you, literally, with the only part of my life that's left, namely my good name. Through arrogance, I assumed that I was above the law. And, as long as my body functioned properly, I *was* above the law. Now, though, I face public disgrace. And I will do anything—*anything*—to avoid that. Because once the mighty have fallen, the rabble show no mercy. There are, literally, hundreds who would do whatever is necessary to see me in prison."

"Jesus . . ." In wonderment, Bernhardt shook his head.

"Do you doubt what I'm saying?"

"No, sir, I don't."

"Well, then, it's time to make plans."

Hearing the words, spoken so softly but yet so decisively, Bernhardt experienced a momentary tremor of deep, visceral excitement. Could this really be happening? To him?

"There are fourteen paintings and three ceramic pieces. At current market prices—the prices they'd bring at Sotheby's or Christie's—being very conservative, the paintings would go for a hundred fifty million. The three ceramics might bring two or three million."

"My God . . ." Bernhardt had heard a similar estimate from Betty Giles, but coming from DuBois the prices assumed the full weight of absolute reality.

"It's obvious, of course, that the art can't be insured, so long as it's here, on the premises."

Bernhardt said nothing.

"Meaning that security—complete security—will be an absolute necessity."

"Yes."

"Then there are the details. Protection against damage while in transit, for instance. The pictures will have to be

packed and crated. For this job—and others—I'd like Betty
Giles here. But, even assuming that she calls you on Tuesday, as you've planned, and even if she agrees to return to
help, there might not be time enough to wait for her.
Today's Saturday. Best case, Betty wouldn't arrive for four
more days. My political contacts estimate that an indictment might be just six days away."

"I don't see how we can get all this done in three or four
days. You talk about protection, crating for the pictures. My
God, that alone will take—"

"I have the crates here on the premises. You've only
seen a small part of this house. It's built on the downhill
slope of the canyon. We're now on the top floor. There are
four levels below us. The fifth level, the lowest, is a work-
room, where you'll find a crate for each painting, each one
labeled. A few hours' work and you'll be ready."

"And that's when the problems start."

Ignoring the remark, DuBois said, "I presume you have
facilities for checking on John Graham."

"Sure. But I doubt that I can get into the computers on
the weekend. I'll try, but I doubt it."

Thinking—calculating—DuBois sat motionless in his
chair. Suddenly unable to contain himself, no longer able to
conduct this incredible conversation without being able to
judge reactions, Bernhardt rose, paced to one side of the
small deck, then turned. From this position he could see the
right side of the other man's face. He saw another ghost of a
smile briefly animate the blood-drained face. DuBois was
amused.

"You want to see my face. The good side."

"Yes," Bernhardt answered gravely. "Yes, I want to see
your face."

"Shall I go on?"

"Please." At the railing now, Bernhardt remained standing. He was still suffused with a sense of unreality.

"As you'll see," DuBois said, "the secret gallery is actually quite small. Eight feet by fourteen feet, to be exact. So finding an off-site location to make the transfer need not be a problem. A small, unobtrusive rented house might be a possibility. Or even the right kind of hotel room. The only consideration is security. You'll be moving paintings worth more than a hundred million dollars to an unsecured location. Of course, you'll have guards with you. Certainly John Graham will have guards with him. Which, of course, could present added complexities."

"My God." As Bernhardt visualized the scene, the aura of unreality returned. Could he do it? *Should* he do it?

"The format, of course," DuBois was saying, "is familiar. Every week on TV, one sees heavily armed drug dealers exchanging millions of dollars in cash for suitcases filled with heroin. Or, if you prefer the Cold War idiom, spies being exchanged at the Brandenburg Gate, with cold-blooded professional killers from both sides of the Iron Curtain looking on." DuBois broke off. Then, with a small smile, he admitted, "I've always liked the Cold War literature. Le Carré—masterful."

"I assume," Bernhardt said, "that you'd want payment made in cash."

"Such transactions are always made in cash. There's no other way."

"Okay. So let's suppose that everything goes according to plan. Let's assume I deliver the paintings and get a suitcase filled with money. Millions. Everyone's satisfied. Graham takes the paintings and leaves with his people. I take the money and leave with my people. But instead of coming back here with the money—millions, in cash—I get on a freeway and I disappear. What then?"

One last time the ghost of a smile briefly touched the pallor of DuBois's face as he said, "Firstly, the very fact that you mention the possibility confirms my favorable evaluation of you. And secondly, there's James."

"Ah, yes. James."

"James is an interesting case, Mr. Bernhardt. He was born in El Salvador. He's an Indian. Or, more accurately, a *mestizo*—part Indian, part Spanish. He was raised in a small town. His father was a guerrilla fighting the landowners in the hills north of San Salvador. In fact, his father was a guerrilla leader, a hero to his people—something of a legend, actually. His name was Fernando Abras. James—Juan, really—lived in the hills with his father and mother. She, too, fought with the guerrillas, beside her husband. So James, you see, was born to kill.

"Some years ago, the government troops cornered Abras. They killed him and his wife, and put their heads on stakes. The whole guerrilla band was slaughtered—everyone but James, who led another teenager, a girl, to safety. At the time, I had extensive holdings in Salvador, among them a large sawmill that processed South American hardwoods—mahogany and teak. Like every sizable business enterprise in Salvador, the mill was protected by a large contingent of government troops. It was necessary to pay off the government for this protection. And doing that—acquiescing to bribery—I refuse to do. So I no longer do business in South America.

"But I digress. James, as I said, managed to escape the guerrilla slaughter, and he finally made his way to the mill, even though he was wounded. He would have died, except for the girl. Purely by chance, my Central American representative and his wife were visiting the mill at the time, and they saved the boy from being murdered by the soldiers that guarded the mill. The wife insisted on taking the boy—a late teenager, actually—to the States for medical care. At the time, I had a Guatemalan couple living here on the grounds. She helped clean the house and her husband was a gardener. They were childless, so it was a natural combination. They took James, and cared for him. Shortly thereafter, when James was about eighteen, the woman died, and the man decided to return to Guatemala. But James had no papers. If he left the States, he couldn't get back in. So he stayed, and did gardening. That's how it started. Then I began letting him ride with my bodyguard, in a second car. I won't go into the rest of it, Mr. Bernhardt. Suffice it to say that, on at least two occasions, James showed himself absolutely fearless. If there's such a thing as a dedicated killer, it's James. So far as I know, he'll do whatever—*whatever*—is required to protect me."

"And he'll be going with us when we make the exchange."

"Yes."

"And if I should succumb to temptation . . ." Amused by the theatrics of his own words, Bernhardt smiled. "James will know what to do. Is that it?"

Gravely DuBois nodded.

SIXTEEN

It was precisely in a situation like this, Andrea knew, that disaster could strike. Steal a fortune in jewels, execute a masterpiece of tactics, plan the perfect getaway, and a tire could go flat.

Or, in the present event, two ostensibly innocent weekenders, she and Harry, on a Saturday morning hike through Benedict Canyon, amiably trespassing, cameras slung, sandwiches and wine in their backpacks. But they could run afoul of a security guard, one of dozens, certainly, hired by affluent local residents. "The binoculars?" she would say. "Oh, they're for bird-watching."

"And the tape recorder?" the six-dollar-an-hour guard might inquire.

"Music while we hike," Harry would say, flashing his all-American smile.

"Yeah, but—" The guard might frown, puzzled. "What kind of a tape recorder is that, with an antenna?"

As, through the tiny Lucite earpiece, she clearly heard:

"Sit down, Mr. Bernhardt."

"Thank you," Bernhardt's voice replied. "Magnificent house."

"You'll find Grace in the hallway," she heard DuBois say. "She'll familiarize you with the house and grounds. You're free to go anywhere you like. At two P.M., we'll talk again."

"Yes, sir."

Through the binoculars, Andrea watched Bernhardt leave the deck railing and disappear through the study's sliding glass doors. She switched off the tape recorder, retracted the antenna, then ejected the cassette. She slipped it into a jacket pocket, then handed the recorder and binoculars to Harry, who put them in their knapsack. Like her, his gaze was fixed on the DuBois house, an architectural marvel built in five levels down the steep slope of the canyon. Across the quarter-mile that separated them from the house, without binoculars, the solitary figure of Raymond DuBois sitting in his battery-operated wheelchair was tiny as a doll. Harry shifted his gaze to Andrea's face, in profile. It was a perfect face. Would he ever see this face profiled as she lay beside him in bed? The answer, he knew, was no. Andrea's body was meant for barter, playing for high stakes. She didn't believe in fraternizing with the help.

The face that launched a thousand ships . . . It was a line remembered from high school English. Helen of Troy, the most beautiful woman in the world, the most precious prize in a game played only by kings.

Helen, the Grecian beauty who'd caused a war . . .

Andrea, the South American beauty who'd turned Ned Frazer into a corpse.

Andrea Lange, hardly thirty, stalking one of the richest men on earth, her next victim. Andrea Lange, who'd somehow managed to bug DuBois's study and the small deck adjoining, where DuBois conducted his most important, most highly classified business.

"How was the reception?" he asked.

"Fine. No problem." She checked the time. "Let's go."

"Right." In a crouch, he moved into a screen of trees and began slipping and sliding down the red clay soil of the hummock that had given them enough elevation to see

DuBois and the tall man over the high wall that completely surrounded the estate. The wall was at least eight feet high; six feet of brick and two feet of continuous, interlaced, black wrought iron topped with sharpened fleur-de-lis. Every ten feet, according to law, small black and white plastic placards attached to the wrought iron warned that the fence was electrified.

Off the knoll now, with the DuBois house no longer visible, they were walking erect down the canyon slope on a footpath that bordered the brick wall. This unfenced land, Andrea had said, belonged to the estate that adjoined the DuBois estate to the south. The terrain here was lightly wooded, and crisscrossed by trails like the one they now traversed: animal trails, deer and raccoon, even fox—

—and dogs, she'd said. Guard dogs, some of them.

They'd left their cars in a parking area near the bottom of the canyon, then walked up the slope to the knoll. For days Andrea had scouted the terrain while he waited in the car. The first day, he'd been angry. Taking orders—taking money—from a woman, how had it happened to him? Of all people, him? Two days ago, looking for trouble, a way out, fuck it, he'd started an argument. Her face unreadable, nothing given away, she'd listened to him. When she'd finally answered, her voice had been as cold and calm as a judge's: "You can't get out, Harry. It's too late to get out." They'd been parked in her BMW, at the bottom of Benedict Canyon. She'd been sitting behind the wheel, staring straight ahead. She'd let him think about it, about what she'd said, how she'd said it. Then, speaking very softly, her voice hardly more than a whisper, she said, "Ned—he wanted out."

A short, precisely timed pause. Then, still very softly: "You remember Ned."

And, as she'd known it would, the instant's vision had

flashed across his consciousness: the Lincoln town car, its rear windows tinted, moving slowly across Park. Ned Frazer, carrying flowers, for God's sake, flowers meant for Andrea. The rear window sliding smoothly down. Ned, halfway into the intersection. Ned's face turned toward him. Then the deafening crash of the shot, the flash of orange flame. Ned, clutching the flowers as he fell to his knees in the busy intersection.

One shot, in the center of a walking target's chest, perfect shooting. Ten thousand dollars for a thirty-second job. Twenty thousand per minute, more than a million dollars an hour, he'd once calculated.

Meaning that, if he walked away from this job, it would cost her another million dollars an hour to take him down.

Unless, pinching pennies, she did the job herself.

They were on level ground now, no longer slipping and sliding down the slope. Ahead was the tall cyclone fence that separated private land from Benedict Canyon Road and the public land along the bottom of the canyon. A heavy padlock and thick chain secured a gate set into the fence. Four days ago, early in the morning, he and Andrea had stood lookout for Frank Youmans, who'd learned about locks in prison. It had taken more than an hour, but Youmans had finally made a key that worked. Predictably, Angela had kept the key. She'd been careful not to—

From the right and behind, he heard a growl.

"Jesus." It was Andrea, close behind him. Moving slowly, with great deliberation, Harry turned to face the German shepherd squarely, at the same time gesturing gingerly for her to stand beside him. The dog was in a crouch, ready to spring. Its tail was flicking. Harry raised his left hand, index finger extended, as if the finger were a weapon in direct line of fire with the dog's yellow eyes. The growling diminished.

"Don't move," he breathed. "Stay right there." As he said it, still with his left hand raised, momentarily immobilizing the shepherd, he moved his right hand to the hip pocket of his jeans and his switchblade knife. As the dog followed the slow, deliberate movement of the right hand, its growl came from deeper in its throat. Harry finally touched the knife, cautiously working it free. The dog dug its claws into the pine needles carpeting the ground, gathering itself, ready to spring.

"Stay." It was a sharp, sibilant command. The left forefinger came up, once more an instrument of command, of domination. The dog's eyes shifted, sliding into full eye contact. As he moved forward one tentative half-step, Harry eased the knife free of his pocket. As, still, he held the dog's gaze fixed on the left forefinger that was angled forward between man and beast, a witching wand, moment-to-moment magic.

"Don't move," he whispered again to the woman. Then he coughed to cover the click as the knife blade snapped open. The dog's eyes tracked the sound, but then returned to Harry's left forefinger. Five feet separated him from the dog.

"Stay," he breathed. "Stay right there." With the knife free, in plain view, he advanced on the dog. His voice dropped to a deeper, more compelling note. Three feet separated them. Two feet. Now, for the first time uncertain, the dog blinked, then seemed to frown. The initiative had passed from animal to man.

The left hand, fingers extended, was now only a foot from the shepherd's snout. The dog blinked again—once, twice. The deep, menacing growl had changed to a low, tentative whine. Moving with infinite caution, Harry slowly extended his left hand to touch the shepherd on the right side of the head, just behind the bulge of the jaw. The dog's only response was more whining. The dog wore a leather collar. Harry touched the collar, then gripped it with two fingers and his thumb.

"Stay . . ." Then, with a smile, "Good dog."

The dog's response was another whine. The yellow eyes were shifting; the dog was puzzled.

"Good dog," Harry crooned. "*Good* dog."

As, with his right hand, Harry used the knife to lay open the dog's throat on the left side of the head, just below the ear. The dog yelped once, took two steps forward as Harry stepped quickly back. Then, whining, the dog fell heavily on its right side. The lightning-quick slash had been perfectly executed.

As Andrea watched him clean the knife on the carpet of pine needles and return it to his pocket, she spoke in a low, awed voice: "Jesus, Harry. You enjoy your work, don't you."

"You do the planning," he said. "I'll handle the killing." He turned downhill toward the cyclone fence that ran at an angle to DuBois's brick wall. "Come on. Usually guard dogs work in pairs."

As she followed him down the thickly wooded path she said, "We always had shepherds when I was growing up."

"Well, now you're grown. Aren't you?"

SEVENTEEN

"Mr. DuBois especially wants you to see the bottom floor," the secretary said. "That's the fifth level down—the workshops and the laundry, things like that."

They were standing in the large room that opened immediately off the main entry hall. Here the walls were paneled in rich natural wood. The floors were planked oak, scattered with Oriental rugs. One wall was entirely fieldstone, with a huge fireplace set into it. Hand-hewn beams were intricately joined overhead to support the lofty wooden ceiling. French doors opened on a large deck that offered a view to the northwest, a vista more heavily wooded in the foreground than the view from the smaller deck off DuBois's study. Eyeing the architecture and the massive furniture that was arranged at random, Bernhardt decided that the room could have been the lounge of a world-class hunting lodge. Compared to the art hung in the central exhibition hallway, the paintings here were less abstract, more recognizable as landscapes and cityscapes.

"I gather," Bernhardt said, "that Mr. DuBois spends a lot of his time in his study or on his deck." It was a test question. In their marathon talks before she'd fled the country, Betty Giles had often mentioned that DuBois received special visitors either in his study or out on his deck. Because, she'd explained, the study and the deck were periodically swept for listening devices. The deck in particular offered few places to conceal a bug. Therefore, in the whole establishment, it was only on the deck that DuBois felt secure enough to discuss his most profound secrets.

"Mr. DuBois also spends time with his art collection," Grace Campbell answered.

Bernhardt looked at her sharply, an involuntary reaction. Which art collection—the public collection or the art in the secret room? Was it possible that the stolen art was an open household secret, actually no secret at all? Was DuBois delusional? Without doubt there was always at least one employee present in the mansion at all times, if only to be there if DuBois collapsed. During the four months since Betty had left, how could DuBois have managed to visit the secret room without being seen? Even though entrance to the windowless secret gallery was possible only through two locked doors, certainly the servants must speculate what lay behind the first door.

Was it possible that DuBois was playing an intricate double game, creating an illusion to serve some secret agenda?

Covertly Bernhardt studied Grace Campbell as she stood quietly apart from him, as if she awaited his pleasure. In her forties or early fifties, the secretary spoke with restraint, dressed with restraint, behaved with restraint. She was a small, compact woman. Her brown hair, simply worn, was flecked with gray. Behind professorial tortoiseshell glasses her eyes were calm and watchful. Plainly Grace Campbell accepted anonymous self-effacement as the terms of her employment.

Grace Campbell runs the house, James had said. Meaning that whatever secrets the other servants knew, she would also know. But, by temperament, she would always know more than she chose to reveal.

"What else did Mr. DuBois want me to see besides the

workrooms?" As he spoke he moved to sit on a nearby sofa, gesturing for her to sit in a facing chair. She nodded as if to thank him for inviting her to be seated. She sat with her legs primly crossed, and spoke as she'd spoken before, calmly and precisely, in a cadence that was certainly the product of good schools:

"Anything you want to see, of course, you're welcome. I only meant that he especially wanted you to see the workrooms."

"Did he tell you that I might be crating up some of his paintings?"

She considered the question, then decided to say, "I assumed that would be the case."

Nodding in his turn, he sat silently, watching her. As the seconds of silence lengthened, she shifted slightly in her chair, but otherwise revealed no suggestion of discomfort. Her eyes were steady. Finally Bernhardt said, "There're a few things I need to know. And I understand you're the person to ask."

She smiled, nodded attentively, but said nothing.

"How long've you worked here?" he asked. "How many years?"

"Five years. Five and a half, really."

"And you run the house—write the checks, hire and fire."

"I do those things with Mr. DuBois's approval."

"Let's say the cook decides to quit. How would it work?"

"I'd find someone else, and check her references. We'd agree on money. If she sounded all right, she and I would talk to Mr. DuBois."

"How long would a conversation like that take, normally?"

"Five minutes. No more."

"And you'd talk—where? In Mr. DuBois's study?"

"Probably."

"Not on his deck."

Her lips twitched in a small, knowing smile. But she said only, "No, not on his deck."

The understated response, Bernhardt decided, signified that Grace Campbell was a woman who kept her own counsel, observing but not commenting. He couldn't imagine her ever raising her voice, losing control.

"You worked with Betty Giles, then."

"Oh, yes."

"Did she help run the house?"

She shook her head. "No. Betty was a curator. She and Mr. DuBois were constantly buying and selling works of art. It was a full-time job that involved a lot of travel, a lot of negotiation. Betty had her own office. It's on the fifth level down. Mr. DuBois wants you to see that, too. I gather that's where you'll be working."

"It's not settled whether I'll be working here. There're a few loose ends. We're meeting again at two o'clock."

She nodded. "I know. If you need to make any calls, Mr. DuBois would like you to use Betty's office. It's fully equipped—private phone line, intercom, computer, copier, fax machine."

"Did Betty get paid by you?"

"No."

"How was she paid?"

She shook her head. "I don't know, Mr. Bernhardt."

But the real message was that she *did* know. Or at least suspected.

Testing the thesis, he said, "I think that, technically, Betty was employed by Powers Associates. I think she was on their payroll."

Her only response was a cool, impersonal stare.

"How's the house laid out, Miss Campbell?"

"There're five levels, stepped down the side of the canyon. The first level—this level—has the main entry hall, which is really an art gallery, as you know. There's this room, which is actually very seldom used nowadays. It was intended as a kind of reception area. The house was built about twenty-five years ago. In the days when Mr. DuBois gave parties, mostly receptions for prominent artists, this is where the receptions would be held. And, of course, in the old days, a lot of very important people visited him. Oil sheikhs, secretaries of state, even royalty, they all came. And this is where he'd receive them." She spread her hands to encompass the room.

Bernhardt followed the gesture as he said, "I'm surprised. I mean, this room is informal. Rustic, almost. Wouldn't the Queen Mum be put off?"

Once more she smiled, this time indulgently. "As it happens, the Queen Mum did visit, years ago. She was disappointed, though. Her taste in paintings seems to run to flower arrangements."

"Are you kidding?" Once more, marveling, Bernhardt looked around the reception area. "Was the Queen Mother really here?"

"No kidding."

"Hmmm."

"One of Mr. DuBois's great regrets," she said, "was that he couldn't get Frank Lloyd Wright to design this place. When you have a chance to see more of it, I'm sure you'll agree that it's really quite remarkable. As an engineering feat alone, it was a triumph. And, in fact, that's why Mr. Wright refused the commission, I believe. He didn't think the building would stand up to an earthquake. Luckily, he was proven wrong. At least, so far."

"How'd the Queen Mum like the place?"

"Whatever her opinion was, I don't think it had much effect on Mr. DuBois. He has no real interest in other people's opinion of him. In the vernacular, he doesn't give a shit."

Bernhardt guffawed, nodding and smiling. He would, he was deciding, enjoy getting to know Grace Campbell.

Back in her tour guide's mode, in a detached monotone, she said, "There's a large kitchen adjoining this room." She pointed. Then, pointing again: "At the other end of this level, as you know, there's Mr. DuBois's study, where he transacts his business. I have a small office just down the hallway from his study. Normally I'm the only one to deal with Mr. DuBois. Whatever he wants—a personal letter written, something to eat, instructions for the staff, personal hygiene—whatever it is, I get the request, and act on it. If I'm not on the premises, James takes over. He and I are always in touch." She drew back her beige cardigan sweater to reveal a pager at her waist.

"Do you sleep here, too?"

She nodded. "There're two apartments on the fourth level. One of them is mine."

"So you've got a full-time job, it sounds like. Twenty-four hours a day."

"I take time off—several weekends a year, really. The truth is, Mr. DuBois is a very considerate employer, provided the employee is doing a good job. And James is very responsible, very conscientious. Monica, the nurse, lives on the grounds, and James has a bungalow on the grounds. And, of course, there's always Mr. Powers to make decisions."

"Do you and Mr. Powers work closely together?"

She thought about it, then said, "We coordinate, I'd say, on certain things. If someone calls for Mr. DuBois on business, for instance, and if it sounds legitimate, I take the number and pass it on to Mr. Powers. If it's minor, I handle it myself. It's a judgment call."

"But no one gets through to Mr. DuBois directly. They have to go through either you or Powers."

"Mr. Robbins—Albert Robbins, Mr. Du Bois's personal lawyer—he gets through to Mr. DuBois directly, on his private line."

Bernhardt took out his wallet, extracted the number he'd gotten from DuBois, recited the number. "Is that his private line?"

Amused, she said, "The only answer I can give you is yes and no. Mr. DuBois has three private lines—different levels of security, you might say. That number"—she nodded toward the slip of paper—"that's the middle number."

"The top number—who has that?"

She considered the request with obvious deliberation, then decided to say, "Only Mr. Powers, Mr. Robbins, and me, as far as I know. Three people."

"The number I have—will he always answer that one?"

"About half his calls on any of the three numbers go to his answering machine. That's because he spends about half his time resting, or being medicated or changed."

"Changed?"

"He's incontinent, Mr. Bernhardt. I thought you knew."

"Jesus, no." He shook his head. Then: "Mr. DuBois has no relatives."

She shook her head. "Two ex-wives, that's all. They've both remarried. Rich, and remarried."

"And he has no children."

She nodded. "No children."

"God." With feeling, Bernhardt shook his head. "All that money—that power. What good is it to him?"

"He has his paintings, his art. They mean a lot to him."

For the first time her voice was warm, her expression compassionate.

Bernhardt decided to probe. "When Betty left, it must've been hard for him."

"Yes," she answered, "it was." Once more, quickly, her voice had gone neutral, her manner noncommittal. Had Grace been jealous of Betty, of Betty's importance to DuBois? Would that account for her reactions?

"You started to tell me about the layout of the house. I'd like to see the grounds, too, the whole layout."

"Now?" Expectantly she moved forward in her chair.

"Please."

They were in the workshop, standing beside a head-high band saw. It was the last stop on a tour that had taken more than a half hour, a walk-through of all five levels of the mansion. On at least three occasions Grace Campbell had walked past closed doors, any one of which might have led to the secret gallery. Once, a test, Bernhardt had asked what lay behind one of the closed doors. "A bathroom," Grace had answered casually, adding, "There're thirteen bathrooms altogether."

He gestured to the workbenches, the machinery. "Who operates this stuff?"

"James," she said. "He's the only one with a key to the master switch."

Thinking back on their tour, Bernhardt said, "I'm impressed, obviously. But I guess I expected more opulence. More flash. After all, one of the world's richest men—I guess I expected more on the scale of Buckingham Palace."

"As I said earlier, Mr. DuBois isn't interested in ostentation."

"The matching Mercedes limos," Bernhardt suggested. "A *little* display, maybe?"

Her smile was amiably condescending. "Those two cars are bulletproof, designed to deal with kidnappers or assassins. Even the undersides are armored, in case some terrorist rolls a grenade under the car. And Dalimer-Benz, as it happens, offers the best deal on that kind of car."

"I guess that's my cue to say touché." He checked the time: almost noon.

"Are you hungry?" Grace asked.

"No, thanks. But if you've got time, I'd like to run a few things by you, see what you think."

Once more the small subtle smile twitched at her mouth and eyes. Yes, Bernhardt decided, the longer his exposure to Grace Campbell, the more substance he was discovering.

"Whether or not I've got the time, my orders are to accommodate you."

"Okay, then—how about Betty's office?"

"Fine." She led the way to the office and sat on the couch, leaving Bernhardt to sit behind the desk.

"You probably know," Bernhardt began, "that I'm here as a substitute for Betty Giles, who's out of the country. Mr. DuBois is going to sell some of his paintings, and he wants me to handle the transaction—crate up the paintings, and make sure they get to where they're going safely."

She made no response, either by word or shift in body language. Perfectly composed, she simply waited for him to go on.

"I know James handles security for Mr. DuBois, so I'm going to have to work with him, especially when it comes time to actually move the paintings. However, I don't find James very forthcoming." He decided to break off, wait until she answered:

"James is waiting to get instructions from Mr. DuBois. He is very closemouthed. In a security man that's a plus, I'd say."

"I'd say so, too. But if I take this job on, I've got to know that I'm getting access to all the information I need. And the truth is—" He looked at her squarely, dropped his voice. "The truth is, the deeper I get into all this, the more I get the feeling that people aren't telling me what I need to know— what I've *got* to know—if I'm going to get this job done."

"When you say 'people,' are you including me?" She spoke evenly; her manner had acquired a certain brittleness, an edge. She was eyeing him steadily, making up her mind about him. Could she trust him? How far? For how long? Finally she gestured to an outside door. "There's a rock grotto just down the hill. It's very nice." Without waiting for a response she rose, went to the door, punched a series of numbers on a small panel beside it. When a green light glowed, she stepped outside. Careful to close the door behind him, Bernhardt followed her down a slope to a wonderfully fashioned grotto, rocks and pools and ferns bowered over by low-growing branches. There were two benches made of natural rock and slabs of slate. As they sat facing each other, Bernhardt said, "Is Betty's office bugged?"

"The whole house is wired," she answered. "It's security."

"This grotto could be bugged, too."

She shrugged. "Possibly."

In her eyes he saw something stirring as she let her glance linger meaningfully with his. Did Grace Campbell have her own agenda?

"You don't care whether we're bugged?" Bernhardt asked.

Once more she shrugged. Her eyes were bolder now as she answered, "Life is a gamble, Mr. Bernhardt. Don't you think so?"

"Of course. But it's always smart to get the best odds available." His smile was a carefully calculated invitation.

After a final search of his face, she began speaking in a crisp, clipped voice. This, Bernhardt realized, could be the real Grace Campbell.

"All through school," she began, "I consistently scored about a hundred twenty-five or more on IQ tests. Which is to say that I'm no dummy."

Bernhardt smiled, nodded appreciatively.

"When I was a little girl," she continued, "my father had a lot of money. He made a couple of fortunes speculating in California real estate, mostly in the San Joaquin Valley. But he also lost a couple of fortunes. He also drank. When I was in high school—a private school—my father went broke. Then he died—cirrhosis of the liver. Then, surprise, my mother started to drink. So by the time I got out of Stanford, thirty years ago, all I had was the future."

In sympathy, Bernhardt's answering nod pantomimed heartfelt regret. They were orphans, both of them: orphans in their mid-forties. They shared the same pain, however dulled by time.

"Of course," she said, "I married a man who was my father reincarnated. Except that my husband went to Stanford, and my father didn't finish high school. Still—" She smiled, a rueful up-curving of her small, firm mouth. "Still, I had a daughter, and that helped. But then, about a year after my husband finally packed his bags and left, one jump ahead of his creditors, my daughter was killed. It was her senior prom night, from high school. Her date had just gotten his driver's license, and he—" Suddenly she broke off, began to blink. From the waistband of her skirt she took a handkerchief, which she pressed to her mouth. She held herself rigidly, giving herself no quarter. Finally, in a low, deadened monotone, she said, "You seem to be a very perceptive man, Mr. Bernhardt. I'm sure you know that I'm not in the habit of baring my soul to someone I just met."

He inclined his head gravely. Yes, he knew.

"The reason we're having this conversation," she said, "is because I'm in my fifties, and I've got nothing to show for it. I'm a servant, really—a very well-paid servant. I spend my days trying to keep a dying man alive. But when he dies, I'm out of a job. I'm not even sure whether I'm in DuBois's will."

He could think of nothing that wouldn't sound irrelevant, empty.

"Mr. DuBois has an incredible mind." Now she was speaking objectively, clinically, in what Bernhardt had come to believe was her essential manner. "He has an uncanny ability to go right to the core of things. A person, a business deal—a painting—he makes his evaluation instantly, and he's almost always right. He acts on his judgments, too. Instantly. Without hesitation. He only has one flaw—one weakness." As she said it, she looked at him expectantly.

"Am I supposed to guess?"

"If you like."

He considered, then ventured, "Arrogance?"

She nodded gravely. "Arrogance. Exactly. He's so incredibly sure of himself, his own infallibility, that he doesn't think ordinary people could possibly get the best of him, ever. It's the emperor without his clothes, that kind of thing. It's understandable, certainly. Everywhere he looks, every decision he makes, he sees proof of his own infallibility. He can't conceive that he's made a mistake."

"Except," he said, prompting her, "he *did* make a mistake. One very big mistake."

Holding his gaze, she spoke gravely: "You know, then."

Another silence drew taut between them before Bernhardt said, "Yes, I know."

EIGHTEEN

"Here." Grace Campbell handed Bernhardt a plastic ID plaque embedded with a magnetized strip. "This opens everything: the outside doors, the elevators, this door—" She swept Betty Giles's office with a wave of her hand. "There's a bathroom next door." She gestured to the desk and the telephone console. "There's all the house numbers on the index."

Bernhardt nodded, stepped behind Betty Giles' desk, tried the drawers. They all slid open; they were filled with detritus: writing paraphernalia, papers, brochures. The right-hand top drawer contained a sizable assortment of cosmetics. In the center drawer he found a corporate checkbook and ledger, together with stationery and business cards. The checkbook, letterheads, and business cards were all imprinted "E.J. Giles, Inc." Across the bottom of the business card, "Elizabeth Giles" was embossed. There were two telephone numbers, one domestic and one international, plus a fax number. The domestic phone number on the card corresponded to the number on Betty's phone. Pulling out the center drawer to its stop, he searched in vain for an address book or personal checkbook. All he found was a magnifying glass and a scattering of stamps.

"She apparently took her address book," Grace offered. "And some other things. Personal things. But the files seem pretty much intact."

"She left in a hurry, apparently."

She shrugged. "I'd say she decided to leave one day, and left the next." She pointed to the cosmetics: "She didn't want to take anything she couldn't carry in her purse."

"What about her ID plaque? Did she take that?"

"Yes. But the next day everything was reprogrammed."

"Did you see her the day before she left?"

She nodded. "Yes. Briefly."

"Did she seem agitated that last day?"

"I didn't really have a chance to form an opinion. We just exchanged a few words." She consulted her watch. "I'd better check in. Knock on my door about five minutes to two." Once more she gestured to the phone. "Anything you want, I'm zero-two."

"Will I see you after I've talked to DuBois?"

As if they shared some special secret, she smiled into his eyes. Saying: "Oh, yes, Mr. Bernhardt. You'll see me." She let the look linger, then left the office.

Bernhardt drew up an executive armchair and sat down behind the desk. He lifted the phone, but heard nothing. Neither did "0" produce anything. He debated punching out "0-2," but instead tried "9". Yes, he got a dial tone. Experimentally he touch-toned his office number. Moments later he heard his own voice on the tape. He cradled the phone, looked around the room. Designed to conform to the rest of the mansion's architecture, Betty's office was a combination of natural wood and glass. There was a leather sofa and a matching visitor's chair. One entire wall, floor to ceiling, was bookshelves. Only half the shelves were filled, primarily with art books. The desk was placed facing away from the sliding glass doors that led out to a small private deck. With each level going down the canyon wall, the view from the decks had become less dramatic, until here, on the fifth level, treetops blocked off almost everything.

Except for the phone console and the computer, the desktop held only a magnificently tooled leather folder. He sat down, pulled the folder closer, flipped it open. The single word "Pending" was inscribed inside. He went through a half-dozen letters. Each letter had been opened and paper-clipped to its envelope. Two began "Dear Betty"; the remaining four were addressed formally to "E.J. Giles, Inc." All six letters were dated during the same week in October—the week before Nick Ames was murdered.

One of the "Dear Betty" letters read:

> You said you might be in New York the second week in November. If it happens, please let me know in time so that I can arrange for you to meet Joe McCarville. Dinner at Pierre's, followed by an after-hours tour of the gallery? Joe's table manners need polishing, but I do think, at 32, he's someone you should seriously consider. Really.
>
> I'll give it a week or so, and if I haven't heard from you I'll call.
>
> Ciao,
> Randy

The letterhead read simply, "Randolph Portman, Dealer in Fine Art," followed by a 57th Street address and phone/fax numbers. The stationery was improbably thick.

The other "Dear Betty" letter, also written on expensive stationery, was a simple handwritten note.

> "Angelica" and "Shadows #8" went off today, by air. Documents follow. They're each insured for a half million. You've got a great eye, Betty. Congratulations.
> Michelle

The letter had been sent from Paris.

A cursory scan suggested that the other four letters were of a piece, all business related. Bernhardt returned them to the folder, returned the folder to its corner of the desk.

The checkbook was next. During the six months preceding Betty's sudden departure, she'd written only fourteen checks. Two were for amounts in the high six figures, one to Sotheby's and one to Christie's. Others were written to companies, for nominal amounts. None had been written for cash. He rose, went to the steel files. Most of the drawers were empty. Only two had been used to file old correspondence, auction catalogs, and articles clipped from magazines and newspapers. One of the articles, dated a year ago, was a *Time* piece on DuBois: *His Hunch Transforms a Country*. Bernhardt remembered reading the article, which described the creation of a jet-set resort mecca on the coast of Belize.

He closed the drawer, returned to the desk, sat eyeing the phone. Was it tapped? Somehow he doubted it. Was the office itself bugged? Almost certainly. Meaning that, whoever he called, he must assume that his part of the conversation would be taped.

The time was twelve-thirty.

At two o'clock, DuBois would be waiting for his decision.

His Hunch Transforms a Country . . .

Raymond DuBois, whose slightest whim could change the course of world events.

Raymond DuBois, a shrunken little man imprisoned in his wheelchair who had, incredibly, placed himself at Bernhardt's mercy.

Or so the little man said.

Two o'clock . . .

Hardly aware that he meant to do it, he was reaching for

the phone, once more touch-toning his own number in San Francisco. Three rings, and the recorded message came on. When he heard the beep, Bernhardt said, "Paula, if you're there, pick it up." When there was no response, he said, "Paula, it's about twelve-thirty Saturday. I'm at the client's. I'll be here probably until about three-thirty. Then I'll go back to my hotel. I want you to call me at the hotel between five and five-thirty. Also, I want you to contact C.B. Tell him to call me during that time, too, at my hotel. Then I want you to call John Graham, at the Fairmont. Give him the same message. Oh, and Mrs. Bonfigli, too—talk to her about Crusher. I'll talk to you soon." He broke the connection. Then, recasting in his thoughts the phone message he'd just left, he shook his head, smiling ruefully. How was it possible? How, on the one hand, could he make plans to pull off a multimillion dollar art deal while, on the other hand, he must concern himself with the welfare of an Airedale?

NINETEEN

They were, once again, on the small deck adjoining DuBois's study. Both men were at the railing, looking out at the view to the west. Clouds were gathering on the horizon as the sun began to sink. The tops of the clouds were brushed with a delicate orange; beneath them the distant ocean was purpling. Overhead, a small airplane was flying toward them. Was it possible, Bernhardt wondered, that the occupants were spying on them, perhaps taking pictures? Could it be that—

"Once we've concluded our negotiations," DuBois said, "assuming that we come to an agreement, then we will go to the gallery. It's essential, I think, that you see the paintings."

Bernhardt felt the words register, a hollow sensation, lost and lonely. Nick Ames had died because of the paintings. How many others would die—or had died?

Tentatively he cleared his throat. "I have an associate—a woman. We're, ah, involved, the two of us. I have to talk to her about this. I can't decide, make a final decision, until I talk to her."

"The grand jury meets Thursday, five days from now. According to my information it's possible that the state will ask for an indictment against me at that time. A search warrant will surely follow. Therefore, time is of the essence. By Wednesday, this matter has to be settled."

"I understand. But I can't—"

"Mr. Bernhardt, I've put my trust in you. I don't think of you as a man of action, particularly. You have no instinct for the jugular. Temperamentally, you're an artist. However, I also believe you to be a person of integrity. Therefore, I am, literally, trusting you with my reputation. Not to mention trusting you with the successful divestiture of art worth millions."

There was only one answer possible, one protest remaining: "We haven't discussed terms—haven't agreed on anything."

The reply came instantly, plainly preprogrammed: "Mr. Powers has given you a check from Powers Associates for ten thousand dollars. That's in addition to your expenses. Additionally—" DuBois produced an envelope from the folds of the blanket that covered his legs and handed it over. "That's a check for twenty-five thousand. Ostensibly you're a security consultant for Powers Associates. By mail, you'll receive the contract covering the entire thirty-five thousand. However, until our transaction is consummated, that's all the payment you'll receive from Powers. The rest of your fee—" He paused, for emphasis. "The rest will come out of the money you collect from Mr. Graham. That money, as we've discussed, will be in cash. When you deliver the money from the sale of the paintings here, in cash, you will deduct ten percent—cash. At that point, our business will be concluded."

"You'll sell the whole collection to Graham. Is that it?"

The old man nodded. "That's it. One transaction, no loose ends."

"And the price?"

"We will first invite Mr. Graham to make an offer, then we will probably counter. But for your information, your ears only, I will not accept less than twenty-five million.

That's roughly one quarter of what the collection would bring at auction."

Bernhardt swallowed, blinked, cleared his throat. Saying finally: "Twenty-five million."

"Or more. Not less, however."

"So my end would be—" Suddenly his throat closed. He couldn't pronounce the words.

"Two million five," DuBois said. "Less, of course, your expenses."

"Of course."

TWENTY

As she collapsed the antenna and put the recorder on the floor of the BMW, she realized that she was smiling. It was a broad, spontaneous burst of pleasure, something she'd never before experienced, not like this.

Raymond DuBois, one of the richest men in the world.

Raymond DuBois, a prisoner of his own misshapen body, at bay.

Raymond DuBois, vulnerable.

Cannibals, she'd once read, ate of their victim's hearts so that they might possess the fallen enemy's courage.

Was that the source of this feeling, this ultimate high? To take down Raymond DuBois—would that finally release her, free her from the need for more, always more?

"Thursday," DuBois had said. Meaning that, in five days, her whole world would change. And for that, give the devil his diabolical due, she must thank Ned Frazer. Therefore, rest in peace, Ned. With thanks for this glimpse from the heights, this breathtaking view of her future.

It had, in fact, begun with a view—the view from the rooftop bar of the Rio Hilton. She'd been sipping Glenfiddich and watching the lights come on far below as a soft dusk fell over the city. She'd been dressed in a simply styled natural linen dress, square cut at the bosom. Among all her cocktail dresses, it had been the one that pleased her most, her can't-miss dress. Except for two emerald clips at the corners of the neck and matching earrings, she'd worn no jewelry. Uncharacteristically, Wilhem had been late—and she'd been on time. Her first glimpse of Ned Frazer had caught him in a typical gesture, slipping the captain a bill for a good table. Although Ned was sophisticated enough to do it subtly, he was gauche enough to leave the bill unfolded, on display.

"Watch carefully how someone deals with a servant," her father had once admonished. *"It'll tell you a lot."*

Her father—that urbane fop, that meaningless man who'd almost succeeded in getting through life with nothing more than a gigolo's smile and manners to match.

By accident or design, the captain had given Ned a table next to hers. She'd watched him as he moved toward her. Even then she'd sensed something contradictory about him. There was a kind of watchful carelessness contradicted by an air of carefully calculated indifference, an aloofness that didn't quite come off.

Of course, once he was seated, she'd felt his eyes on her. And, of course, pretending to search for Wilhem, she allowed their eyes to meet. Ned had smiled and nodded, nothing more. But as he'd later told her, that one look had told him all he needed to know about her.

All he needed to know . . .

All he'd ever know.

In the end, her only regret was that Ned had never known why he'd died. In death as in life, Ned had probably been puzzled.

As she took the cellular phone from its cradle, she realized that the surge of euphoria had already subsided. It was time to go to work.

"Harry?"

"Yes."

"I've got everything I need for now. It's quarter to three.

I'm going to do a couple of things, then I'll go back to the apartment. Wait until five o'clock, here. If nothing develops, come to the apartment."

"Right. How're we doing?"

"We're doing fine, Harry. We're doing just fine."

"Glad to hear it." But his voice, as always, was edged with irony. Whenever she scored a point, Harry resisted. Never mind that they were on the same team.

For now, at least, on the same team.

TWENTY-ONE

"Press four," DuBois ordered.

As the elevator began to descend, Bernhardt asked, "Who else is in the house?"

"No one. Whenever I do this, visit the collection, it's Grace's job to get everyone out of the house. When she verifies that everyone's out—" He broke off as the elevator door slid open, giving access to the main fourth-level corridor. When the elevator had shut behind them, secured, DuBois continued: "When everyone is out, and Grace has verified that the house is completely secure, then she leaves. She goes to James's bungalow. When she arrives there, she notifies me." He gestured to the electronic console built into the right armrest of his chair. "When I'm finished, and I'm once again upstairs, I notify Grace to recall the staff." As he spoke, he turned his chair to the left, then stopped in a secondary corridor just beyond the elevator. He was, Bernhardt knew, waiting for the questions he knew were coming:

"How long do your visits take, usually?"

"Never more than an hour, never less than thirty minutes."

"Surely Grace must have some idea what's going on, some suspicion."

"I suspect," DuBois answered, "that you already know the answer to that question."

Bernhardt was standing on the left side of the wheelchair. It was, thank God, DuBois's blind side, preventing DuBois from seeing his face, reading his expression as he parried, "Grace says that your house is completely wired for surveillance."

"The house," DuBois answered. "But not the grounds. The rock grotto, for instance, isn't wired."

Bernhardt smiled covertly. Deciding to say, "Good. I'm glad." It was the first time he'd ventured to test DuBois.

"You're a man who enjoys innuendo," DuBois observed. "You appreciate subtlety."

"I hope so."

"I do wish we'd met before," DuBois said. "I could have used you to great advantage."

Bernhardt's smile was ironic. "Thank you."

"Since Betty left," DuBois said, "I've sensed a change in Grace. She's had an unhappy life. It's easy to miscalculate, dealing with someone who bears psychic scars. Especially when the wounds were inflicted at an early age."

"That's probably a very astute observation," Bernhardt answered. "I'll try to remember it."

"From your manner, I assume that Grace confided in you."

He'd known the question would come, and he'd decided on an answer: "She's an intelligent woman. I suspect she knows you've got a secret."

"Of course," DuBois answered. "That's to be expected. But we all have secrets. The question is, of what value are these secrets? To whom are they valuable?" He touched his console; his chair moved forward. Walking beside the wheelchair, still on DuBois's blind side, Bernhardt checked off the coordinates: out of the elevator at the fourth-level corridor, turn left, pass two doors on the right, turn left again into a small intersecting hallway. There were two identical doors in the small hallway, both closed. A panel of buttons was set into the frame beside both doors. On each panel, a tiny light glowed red. DuBois maneuvered his chair to face the door on the right, then gestured to Bernhardt, a silent command. Nodding, Bernhardt stepped back, turned to face the main corridor. In that position, DuBois could see him, making certain that he couldn't observe the numbers DuBois was punching out on the panel. He could only hear a series of four electronic cheeps and chirps. There was a pause, followed by another series of four chirps.

If he were wearing a wire, Bernhardt realized, he could have recorded the chirps, turned them into numbers.

"All right, Mr. Bernhardt."

He turned to see the door on the right sliding open. Once more, a reprise of his earlier sensation of sinking unreality, Bernhardt felt himself go hollow, suddenly overwhelmed by where he was, what he was about to do.

And all without Paula's approval. How had it happened? The answer, he knew, was greed.

As he waited for Bernhardt to approach, DuBois seemed to smile, as if to encourage a timid child. Obeying the silent invitation, Bernhardt advanced one step, then two. With each step, he could see more of an interior hallway. Like the main gallery hall on the first level, the walls of the secondary hallway had been covered with a rough fabric, then painted white.

With Bernhardt beside him on his right side, DuBois pointed to the electronic panel beside the door. "It takes a four-digit code before the red light goes off. Another four digits, and the green light comes on. Then, automatically, the door slides open. Needless to say, I'm the only one who knows the codes. Of course, I've written the numbers down, and hidden the scrap of paper."

"Betty didn't know the codes, then."

"Of course not. Whenever she entered, I was with her."

"The slip of paper—did she know about it?"

"Betty knew there was a slip of paper hidden, but she didn't know where. However, should I die, she would have received a sealed envelope from my lawyer, Mr. Robbins, with instructions for finding the paper. Needless to say, after she disappeared, the letter was destroyed."

"Then if you should die . . ."

"If I should die now, Mr. Robbins will know what to do."

"You trust Mr. Robbins."

"In legal matters—custodial matters—I trust him completely. But nothing beyond that. Compartmentalization, Mr. Bernhardt. It solves a lot of problems." With that, DuBois turned away and entered the narrow hallway. The hallway was windowless, lit by indirect cove lighting, and was, Bernhardt judged, about ten feet in length. At the far end there was another door, also with an electronic panel. Hesitantly, irrationally cautious, perhaps claustrophobic, Bernhardt followed DuBois as he approached the second door. When Bernhardt had gone halfway, he heard a mechanical whir behind him. He whirled, saw the first door sliding closed.

"You'll notice," DuBois said, "that there's an identical panel beside the door we've just come through, on this side. To get out once the door has closed, it's necessary to punch out the same two series of four numbers that is required to get in."

"So—" The wayward thought was so temptingly diabolical that Bernhardt knew he must blurt it out: "So, once you're in here, and the outer door slides shut, if you couldn't remember the numbers . . ." Sadistically he let it go unfinished.

"It would take an acetylene torch to rescue me. The first door is armor plate, an inch thick." DuBois spoke with a hint of wry fatalism, as if the thought of dying in such circumstances intrigued him. Then he turned to the second door, waited for Bernhardt to withdraw, then punched out another combination, this one only three numbers. As the door slid open, DuBois pivoted his chair to face the inner gallery. Bernhardt advanced to stand a few feet behind the other man. From that position, with the door frame blocking his view of the two side walls, only the far wall opposite the door was visible. There were only two paintings hung on the far wall.

The artist, this one artist among all others, was unmistakable.

"My God," Bernhardt breathed. "Van Goghs." Then, after a moment of helpless speechlessness, he heard himself say, "Are they real? Originals?"

It was, he knew instantly, a monumental faux pas.

"Mr. Bernhardt. Please."

"Sorry," Bernhardt whispered. Repeating inarticulately, "Sorry."

DuBois moved farther into the small room, allowing Bernhardt to step through the open doorway. Each of the two sidewalls was hung with five paintings. Except for the two large Van Goghs, the paintings were nearly of uniform size, about two by three feet, no more. The room was long and narrow, smaller than the smallest bedroom, a little larger than an outsize walk-in closet.

"Fourteen paintings," DuBois had said. Bernhardt turned again, looked at the wall space beside the inner door. Unmistakably, the remaining two paintings were Rembrandts, one a portrait of a young child, one a sketch of a forest glade.

"I've got no words," Bernhardt finally said. "Everything I think, even, is wrong. I feel—numb."

"You realize, don't you, that you're only the third person to be here. You, Betty, myself—that's all."

"I know . . ."

DuBois had been staring at the three ceramic pieces in their glass display case mounted on the far wall beneath the two Van Goghs. After a brooding moment of silence, he said something inaudible.

"I beg your pardon?"

DuBois pivoted the chair to face him. "Dust," DuBois muttered. "Dust on top of the case."

Once more, Bernhardt was unable to frame a reply.

TWENTY-TWO

Grace Campbell pushed a plain envelope across her desk. "That'll keep you walking around. Anything you charge at your hotel will be paid through Powers Associates."

The unsealed envelope was stuffed with twenty-dollar bills.

"Five hundred dollars," she said. "It's from the house's miscellaneous cash account. Beyond that, Mr. DuBois knows you'll be spending sizable sums, in cash. On short notice I can always lay my hands on five thousand dollars, in cash. More than that, I'll have to go to the bank. You might bear that in mind."

"Do you need receipts?"

She shook her head. "No. No receipts."

Bernhardt slipped the envelope into the inside pocket of his corduroy jacket. Somehow the pressure of the money snug against his rib cage activated a desire to feel his .357 Magnum exerting a similar pressure, holstered at his belt. He made a mental note to speak to Paula about the Magnum. He glanced at his watch: almost four o'clock. By five he must be at the hotel, to take Paula's call. Or, more like it, courtesy of Powers Associates, he would call Paula. And C. B. Tate, if Paula hadn't connected with him. And John Graham, at the Fairmont.

"I need another car."

"Besides the two Mercedeses, there're three other cars. Would you like a Honda Accord? It's new, very nice."

Bernhardt nodded. "Fine." He watched her open another drawer, produce a set of keys, slide them across the desk.

"You have my personal number," she said. "Unless it's vital that you talk directly to Mr. DuBois, I suggest that you call me for anything you need. The number's good day or night, and it rings through to a beeper."

"If I have to talk to Mr. DuBois directly, when's the best time?"

"Eight to ten in the morning, and two to four in the afternoon," she answered promptly. "Otherwise, it's important—vital—that he have complete rest."

"The identification plaque you gave me—does that open everything? The gate, the front door, the elevators?"

She nodded. "Everything."

"If something else should change—another defection, like Betty's—who'd be responsible for reprogramming the system?"

She thought about it, then said, "James would work it out with the security people. I'd pay the bill when it came in. With James's approval, of course. Mr. DuBois wouldn't be involved."

He pushed back his chair, rose to his feet. "I'd better get back to the hotel. Can you find me the Accord?"

"Certainly." One last time, pleasantly, she smiled.

TWENTY-THREE

"I was just going to call you," Paula said.

"I know. But I'm on an expense account, it turns out."

"That sounds," she said, "like you're going to do it."

Loud enough for her to hear, he drew a long, deep breath. "That's right, Paula. I'm going to do it. We made the deal a couple of hours ago. I've taken some money."

There was silence. Then she said gravely, "Are you sure, Alan? Are you absolutely sure?"

"No, I'm not absolutely sure. But I never am. Nothing's ever a hundred percent."

"How about seventy-five percent?"

"Paula, I've got thirty-five thousand in my pocket. And there's more. There's a hell of a lot more."

Silence.

"Paula?"

"I'm not going to badger you, Alan. And I'm not going to second-guess you, either. Not from this distance, anyhow."

"I want you to come down here. I need you down here."

"When?"

"As soon as you can get here. Tonight?"

Another silence. Then, with deep reluctance: "Okay. I'll get some things together. What should I bring?"

"Have you contacted C.B.? Is he around?"

"Yes. He's waiting for you to call."

"I'll call him, then get back to you. He can pick you up and you can go to the airport together. I'll want him to bring a couple of his guns. You give him our guns—your Chief's Special and my three-fifty-seven, plus ammunition. He'll know how to get them on the airplane."

"Alan, Jesus, this sounds like a war."

"There's a lot of money involved. We need insurance. What about Crusher?"

"It turns out that Mrs. Bonfigli is still here. She didn't go out of town after all."

"Good. Tell her to leave Crusher in my place at night. I'll feel better about the files and everything."

"How long'll we be gone?"

"A few days, I'm not sure. Not beyond Wednesday, probably."

"Jesus, that's five days."

"It could be a lot quicker. It just depends. Tell Mrs. Bonfigli I insist on paying her. A hundred dollars a day."

"She'll never accept it."

"Then I'll buy her a microwave."

"She doesn't *want* a microwave, Alan."

"If she had a microwave, she'd love it. Guaranteed. Listen, I'm going to call C.B., then I'll get back to you. Did you contact John Graham at the Fairmont?"

"He's checked out."

"*What?*"

"But he left a message on our machine. It's a phone number." There was a pause, then she read off the number.

"That's a Los Angeles number."

"I know."

"Just the number? No message?"

"No message."

COLLIN WILCOX

"Okay, I'll call C.B. and Graham, then call you back."

"Right. Love you—in spite of everything." The line clicked dead.

Warmed by her last words, smiling, Bernhardt put his electronic memo on the bed, punched in C. B. Tate, then touch-toned the number.

"Hey, Alan," came the deep, rich Afro voice. "Hey, what's happening? You hooked a big one down there, sounds like."

At the sound of Tate's voice, reassured, Bernhardt kept smiling. C. B. Tate was a big, black, bullet-headed bounty hunter, a modern-day samurai who drove a black Corvette and lived on a houseboat in the Sausalito Yacht Harbor. Born in the ghetto, Tate had run wild for his first eighteen years and then served hard time until he was thirty. He'd done some acting in San Quentin, and his parole officer had sent him to Bernhardt, anything to keep a parolee off the streets. By pure chance, Bernhardt had been about to cast *The Emperor Jones.* In the lead part, Tate had given a performance that at least one local critic had compared to Paul Robeson's performance in the same role.

"I've hooked a big one," Bernhardt said, "and I don't want to get pulled out of the boat. Which could happen."

"Ah." It was a melodic monosyllable. "Ah, he's quick with a quip, as ever. It's always a pleasure, Alan. Especially when I seem to catch a fragrance of money."

"If it works out, your end is twenty-five thousand, by Wednesday. It it doesn't work out, you get five thousand."

"By Wednesday?"

"By Wednesday."

"You've got the money in hand, sounds like."

"I've got two large checks. Very large checks."

"Checks . . ." It was a doubtful rejoinder.

"They're good, C.B. Believe it."

"So what're we talking about? What kind of job?"

"There's going to be a swap—a van full of artwork in exchange for a hell of a lot of money. In cash. The transaction'll take place in a safe house, then the cash has to be carried from the safe house to a millionaire's mansion. It'll happen in Los Angeles, in the next few days. Once the money's delivered, that's the end. After we take our slice, that is."

"So we're talking about muscle."

"Right."

"And guns?"

"Right again."

"What about expenses?"

"Covered."

"Sounds like we got a deal."

"It's five-fifteen now. Any chance you can get your stuff together and pick up Paula in the city and catch the ten o'clock shuttle down here? I'll meet you at the airport."

"Jesus, Alan. It's Saturday night. An old friend is coming over. We're going to have steaks on the barbie. And scrambled eggs and lox with champagne for breakfast tomorrow."

"C.B.—I wouldn't ask if I didn't need help."

"Hmmm . . ."

"Call her up."

There was silence. Then: "I'll call her. If I get her—if she hasn't left already—I'll see what she says. That's the best I can do. We're talking about my sex life, here."

"Let me give you my number."

"Right." Tate copied the number, repeated it, and broke the connection. Immediately, Bernhardt touch-toned the number for John Graham in Los Angeles. It was a switchboard number for a hotel, and moments later John Graham's smooth, reassuring voice came on the line.

"It's Alan Bernhardt, Mr. Graham."

"*Bernhardt!*" The single word resonated with pleasure. "Where are you?"

"I'm in Los Angeles."

"Are you here in connection with the matter we discussed in San Francisco?"

"That's right. And I'd like to talk with you. As soon as possible. I'm at the Prado, on Wilshire."

"It sounds like you're on an expense account."

"That's right."

"Can I guess whose expense account?"

"Not on the phone."

"I can be there in a half hour. Which room?"

"It's eight-oh-six."

"Are you alone?"

"Yes."

"Good. A half hour." The line went dead.

TWENTY-FOUR

"My God," Graham said, "for a mild-mannered actor, you keep busy." His eyes were speculative, cautiously intrigued.

"This whole thing came looking for me," Bernhardt answered. "I'm running to keep up."

"Yeah . . ." Graham spoke absently, plainly preoccupied with his private calculations. Then, refocusing, he leaned toward Bernhardt and began talking rapidly, intently: "I'll give you my random thoughts, in no particular order. Okay?"

"Fine."

"First, I'm thinking that it's going to be very, very difficult to raise that much money between now and Wednesday. And then, God, that much money in currency—" He shook his head. "What'll it weigh?"

"I don't think DuBois'll accept anything but cash. He doesn't want a paper trail, obviously."

"Does he know where to find a Brinks truck?" It was an ironic question. Then, more seriously: "What's the name of his front organization?"

"Powers Associates."

"Yeah. Well, during business hours, there wouldn't be any problem wiring a few million to Powers Associates, ostensibly for a concealed stock transaction. That happens routinely, sometimes unkindly called money laundering. But—"

"I'm sure DuBois knows all about—"

"But before I could begin to get authorization for that much money I'd have to see the merchandise. Plus, I'd want to have an expert look at it, too."

Bernhardt shook his head. "That'll never happen. Not until the actual moment when the deal comes down. Which will not—repeat, *not*—happen on DuBois's premises."

"Have you actually seen these paintings?"

"Yes," Bernhardt said. "I have. Today, in fact."

"How many are there?"

"Fourteen paintings and three ceramics."

"Do they look authentic to you?"

"Yes. But I'm no expert."

For a long, silent moment, once again lost in thought, Graham stared down at the carpet. Finally he said, "Rock bottom minimum, I've got to have a description of the pieces—artist, title, approximate size, date, if any. I also need pictures. Polaroids."

"No problem. At least, not getting the descriptions."

"Really?" Graham's expression was speculative, shrewd. "Can you make that decision without clearing it with DuBois?"

"No, I can't. Not really. But if he doesn't go along, then I'll probably bow out."

"And lose a lot of money."

"In my opinion, he needs me more than I need him."

"That's your opinion."

Bernhardt shrugged.

"I still think," Graham insisted, "that the money should go through Powers Associates, by wire."

"And I keep telling you, John, that it simply won't happen. The reason being that DuBois doesn't trust Justin Powers. Unless I'm badly mistaken, he's going to dissolve their relationship."

"Why?"

"It's got a lot to do with the paintings—Betty Giles. That's all I'll tell you."

Dressed Los Angeles casual in white canvas trousers, a striped boating shirt, and white designer sneakers, Graham sat slumped in an armchair, legs straight out, staring at his shoes. The shirt was short-sleeved, revealing heavily muscled forearms. At the neck, thick ginger-colored hair curled at the open collar. Watching Graham, remembering his Ivy League persona when they'd first met in front of the Federal Building in San Francisco, Bernhardt decided that Graham had acquired the gift of protective coloration, dressing and acting to blend into the background. His moods, too, were variable. In San Francisco he'd had been affable and open, quick and easy with a quip, charming and disarming. Here—now—Graham's demeanor was moody, plainly projecting a caution edged with distrust.

Finally, frowning, Graham said, "There's something wrong with all this."

Bernhardt decided to make no response.

"Here's one of the world's richest, most powerful men," Graham complained, "and he's handing over a fortune in art to a virtual stranger. Then, after the deal comes down, he trusts that same stranger to trot dutifully back to home base carrying millions of dollars."

Letting his impatience show, Bernhardt sighed, shifted irritably in his own chair. "I've already tried to explain that. He's about to be indicted by a grand jury for receiving stolen goods—among other things. He's got to move those paintings, or he's screwed. And he can't get out of his goddam wheelchair. He's got to have help."

"Has it ever occurred to you that he might be using you, Alan? Have you ever thought that—"

Bernhardt's phone warbled. Without excusing himself he went to a small desk, picked up the phone on the second ring.

"It's all set," C. B. Tate said. "I promised to buy the lady a new jogging outfit if she'll skip tonight. She's into physical fitness. Her flesh is very firm, great muscle tone."

Bernhardt glanced at his watch: seven-thirty. "Good. Have you talked to Paula?"

"Yeah. I'm picking her up in a half hour, give or take. She says not to worry about Crusher. Everything's cool."

"Great." Bernhardt turned his back on Graham, lowered his voice. "Listen, bring some, ah, muscle."

"Like guns, you mean."

"Right."

"What d'you want? My two nine-millimeter Brownings, like that?"

"Perfect. And mine. And Paula's, too."

"You got someone there with you, sounds like."

"Correct."

"So you want your three-fifty-seven and her thirty-eight. Right?"

"Right."

"Nothing else? Your sawed-off?"

"We'll get one of those here."

"This is sounding more serious all the time," Tate said.

"I know."

"I'll call you from the airport in San Francisco when I know the flight."

"Fine. Thanks. I'll pick you up in the drive-through." Bernhardt cradled the phone and turned back to face Graham.

"You were, I gather, talking about guns."

"No comment."

"Do you mind if I make a personal observation, Alan?"

"Please." Bernhardt gestured broadly.

"I think you're getting in over your head here."

"Oh?" It was a chilly monosyllable.

"Let's assume that DuBois is right about the grand jury, about getting indicted on Thursday. What's the first thing he's got to do in the next few days?"

"He's got to get the paintings out of the house before a judge issues a search warrant. He's also got to find a buyer. You, for instance. You and Consolidated."

Graham nodded judiciously. "It could happen. However, there's nothing I can do until Monday. Absolutely nothing. That's the first point." He raised one finger. "Point number two"—the second finger came up—"I can tell you right now that no matter what's in that secret gallery, no matter whether you have pictures, descriptions, everything, there's no way I can get the company to go for twenty-five million, not without a duly certified appraisal."

"That's bullshit. The Renoir alone—*The Three Sisters*—is worth twenty-five million. You said so yourself."

"If it's genuine, yes. But if it's a copy, it's maybe worth a thousand."

"But you know *The Three Sisters* is out there somewhere, in a secret collection. You told me that it—"

"Alan." It was a condescending rejoinder, tainted with smugness. "You're new at this game. Allow me to enlighten you." For the first time in the last hour, Graham's frown eased. Clearly he savored the pundit's role.

"When a major painting is stolen, and disappears for a year or two," Graham said, "as we've already discussed, the first thing an unscrupulous art fence would do would be to have it copied. That's especially true of the French Impressionists that're easily copied. Then, when the time comes, he'd—"

"I thought you said Ned Frazer was honest."

"He *was* honest. But I'm talking about—"

"He's the one who sold *The Three Sisters* to DuBois. I know that for a fact."

"Alan." Now the condescension had turned long-suffering. "I'm sure you're right. All I'm telling you is that, if DuBois won't allow an expert to look at the goods, there's no way—none—that I can go more than ten million for the whole collection." Graham shrugged, spread his hands, smiled slightly, wearily. "If the stuff is genuine, then I'm a hero. If not, I could've spent ten million of the company's money for stuff worth maybe twenty-five thousand."

"So what're you saying?" Bernhardt asked irritably. "What's the bottom line?"

"I'm saying that first thing Monday, I'll call my people in New York. I'll describe the situation to them. I've been in Los Angeles for a couple of days, and I've opened a bank account here. I'll recommend that my people wire ten million dollars into that account. If they agree, then we might have a deal."

"DuBois'll never take the ten million."

"Alan." Graham projected a world-weary sigh. "People like DuBois never say never. Never."

"He told me specifically that—"

"You talk to DuBois, and I'll talk to my people. Then, probably Monday afternoon, let's you and I talk."

"You came down here two days ago. Why?"

"I figured center stage had shifted from San Francisco to L.A. You realize, I assume, that until now you were a minor character in all this. The feds want Betty Giles, and they figured they could get to her through you. Maybe they still figure that way. But me, I decided this was where it would all come down, with or without Betty Giles."

Bernhardt made no response. When Graham left, he would phone Grace Campbell, ask her to put him in touch with Albert Robbins, DuBois's lawyer.

"If this thing comes down like you hope," Graham said, "best-case scenario, how would it go?"

Bernhardt considered carefully, then decided to say, "Best-case scenario would be that, sometime tomorrow—Sunday—I rent a modest bungalow in some place like Glendale, a house with a two-car garage and a garage door opener that works. Then I rent a van. Meanwhile, with DuBois, I catalog the paintings, and take some Polaroids. Then I get the paintings ready to travel. Tomorrow night, I and my two associates stay in the rented house, with the van and another car in the garage. That's Sunday. Monday, bright and early—five, six o'clock, because of the time difference—you're working out things with your people in New York. They agree to the twenty-five million, provided the deal looks good to you. If that comes off, you also rent a van. You should also hire an assistant, I think, considering that you'll be carrying a fortune in used bills, and then carrying the paintings.

"Then, next day—Tuesday—I'll arrive at the DuBois mansion, which is in the Hollywood Hills. My crew takes the paintings from the concealed gallery in DuBois's house into his garage, which will be vacated. We'll load up the van, which shouldn't take more than an hour. I and one man—the toughest man I've ever known—will drive the van. DuBois's chief of security, a Central American peasant named James, will follow us. We'll drive the van to the rented house, and into the garage. You'll be on the scene, and you'll follow us into the garage. We make the swap. You leave, and so do we. You go wherever you're going, and I'll go back to the mansion—with James following us. I'll deliver the money, and take my cut. Then I leave. End of story."

Graham studied Bernhardt for a long, speculative moment before he said, "Would you like some advice?"

"Sure."

"Be careful, that's my advice. Be very goddamn careful. I've been around this track a few times, and there's something that's not quite right here. It feels like you're being set up."

"Set up?"

Graham nodded. "Set up. I mean, here's Raymond DuBois, with all the resources in the world. And here's you, someone he doesn't even know. And he's relying on you—only you—to save his ass." Graham shook his head. "It doesn't add up. Something's missing. Something important."

"He's lonely," Bernhardt said. "He's a lonely old man."

"Mmmm."

TWENTY-FIVE

"There." She pointed. "That's it. That white Pontiac beside the red Japanese car." She braked the BMW and pulled to the curb just beyond the Prado's passenger loading zone. She switched off the engine, switched off the headlights, switched on the parking lights.

Beside her, Harry was reaching over the seat for the small nylon sports satchel. With the satchel on his lap, unzipped, he handed the scanner to Andrea, then inserted a new ni-cad battery in the tiny homing device. He pressed the test button, got a green light. "All set. Hit the horn once if you get the signal."

Andrea nodded, watched him get out of the car and walk into the hotel's parking lot. When he reached John Graham's rental Pontiac, he walked to the far side of the car to put the bulk of the car between them. Andrea switched on the scanner. Yes, the digital bearing read 240 degrees, about right, and all five proximity lights glowed red, indicating a target at close range. She touched the horn, and waited for him to stoop quickly and attach the magnetized homer to the inside of the Pontiac's right front fender. Then, walking easily, his own uniquely compact, arrogant stride, Harry returned to the BMW. Handing him the scanner, Andrea said, "Just find out where he's staying. If it's a hotel, see if you can get his room number. But don't take any chances."

"What about you?"

"I'm going to stay here at the Prado, at least for an hour or two."

Harry's sidelong smile was lascivious. "What's the plan, Andrea? Lay the tall guy with the glasses, see what happens? Is that the plan?"

She held his eye for a contemptuous moment, then said, "I wish you'd find a whore, Harry. Maybe then you'll keep your mind on business."

"I'm thirty-five, and I only had one whore my whole life. Anyone with my looks, my strokes, who needs a whore?"

"Was that a girl whore? Or a boy whore?"

"I imagine," he said, "that you're joking. Otherwise . . ." He let it go ominously unfinished.

The contempt in her face gave way to aloof amusement, a challenge. Because he was so vain, and so dangerous, it amused her to taunt him, effortlessly dominate him.

"What about you, Andrea? Which way do you swing?"

She decided to counterfeit a smile. Saying softly, "Another remark like that, Harry, and I'll terminate your employment."

"Big fucking deal. A few thousand, once in a while. What's that? A few thousand, and pie in the sky. Killing a dog—what's the going price for killing a dog, Andrea? Dogs have teeth, you know. Human beings, they've just got fists."

Nearby, a white-coated parking attendant suddenly materialized, trotting fast into the main parking lot. Like Harry, the attendant was blond and beautiful, a California beach bum earning money for a new surfboard. The attendant passed the Pontiac, stopped at a gleaming red Mercedes 560SL. Sticker price sixty thousand, at least. As she considered how to deal with Harry's current temper tantrum, Andrea watched the parking attendant maneuver the Mercedes out of its parking place, then come toward them. He drove with flair, a youthful elan. When the Mercedes passed, she turned again to the man sitting beside her. "I'm assuming, Harry, that this is just another one of your bouts of bad temper. As opposed to a calculated move to get out of this job." She watched him as he opened his mouth—then balefully closed it. Then he silently shook his head, scowling. It was a typical response. Hit Harry with a few big words, something he couldn't muscle out of, and he went tongue-tied. Muscle-bound and tongue-tied. It was a completely predictable response, therefore a measurable asset. Whatever she wanted from Harry, she knew precisely which button to press.

"Is that it, Harry? Do you want out?" Still studying his face, still making up her mind, she spoke calmly now, mildly.

"I don't want out," he retorted. "I want *in.* Here I am, I could've been bitten by that goddam dog, and I don't even know why."

"It's for your own protection, Harry. Remember New York? Remember Ned Frazer lying there?"

"Is that what happens to the guys you fuck, Andrea? What is it—that bug that eats its male afterwards?"

"That's a praying mantis, Harry. It's impressive, your knowledge of insects."

"I'm glad you're impressed. I'm very glad."

"If I were you, Harry, I'd forget about who's fucking who. Just forget about it. Forget about sex, and think about money."

"Oh? What money is that, exactly?"

She made no reply.

"Who's the old guy in the wheelchair? Who's the tall guy with the glasses? Who's the one with the bugged Pontiac?"

Listening to him, watching him, she realized that something had to give, to change. Harry was constantly pressing harder, the thorn that bit deeper every day.

She's discovered Harry more than a year ago. She'd been with Dominick Patroni, discussing the percentages a fence had offered for the Trombly necklace. They were having drinks at the Royalton. Across the small, elegant bar room, an improbably handsome man—Harry, it turned out—nodded respectfully to Dominick, then smiled meaningfully at her. "You ever want to have someone taken out," Dominick had said, "that's the guy you want." One drink later, their business concluded, preparing to leave, Dominick had offered her a ride; his driver would take her wherever she wanted to go. When she'd declined the offer, Dominick had looked from her to Harry, then back to her. "Go slow with that guy," he had warned. "He's first class at what he does, no nerves at all. But he enjoys it too much. You get what I mean?"

When she'd acknowledged the well-meant advice, Dominick had nodded, smiled politely, and left her with a courtly tip of his hat, a mafioso of the old school. She'd waited five minutes, making sure Dominick wouldn't return. Then she'd smiled at Harry, just that one smile, her first invitation—and her last. Harry's fantasies had taken it from there—fantasies about sex, fantasies about money, the combination that never failed. This time, though, working that particular combination, it was necessary to fine-tune Harry's fantasies. Harry lived on illusions, yet another face-saving macho-man gimmick.

Because even tough guys needed their illusions, pabulum for hungry egos.

Tough guys and psychopaths.

She turned deliberately now to face him.

"The one in the wheelchair is Raymond DuBois." She waited for a reaction, but saw nothing in his face. "DuBois is one of the world's richest men."

"Ah . . ." Pleased, he nodded broadly. Then, as the name vaguely registered, he nodded again. "Ah—yeah."

"The one with the glasses is a private eye from San Francisco. His last name is Bernhardt. He's staying here at the Prado. And him—" She nodded to the Pontiac. "His name is John Graham. He's an insurance adjuster who works both sides of the street. He's a go-between, fronts for a syndicate, mostly fencing big-ticket things—jewels and art." Projecting puzzlement, a test, she frowned. "I'm surprised you haven't heard of him."

"I mostly stick to New York."

"Graham does, too. That's the point."

"He and Ned Frazer—were they doing business together?"

"Probably."

"You and Ned, though—" He let it go meaningfully unfinished.

"That's none of your business, Harry. That was private."

"You expect me to believe that? Ten thousand dollars—you forgot that, Andrea? Ten thousand you paid me for that one. And you're telling me it was nothing."

"I can afford it. That's all you have to know."

"Ah, yeah." His smile twisted, a bad imitation of a crafty interrogator. "The word is that you're loaded. The word is that your grandfather got out of Germany after the war with a suitcase full of diamonds. He was a big-shot Nazi, that's the word."

Her smile mocked him; her gray eyes danced derisively. "You're a student of history, Harry. I had no idea."

"Whatever affects me, that's what I'm interested in. Which is why I want to know what this is all about. Now. I want to know right now, or I'm gone. I'm not kidding, Andrea. I'll tell you right out. Part of the reason I went for this, it was because of you, that body of yours. But now I'm—"

"Did you forget the five thousand I gave you up front, Harry? Did that slip your mind?"

"I been in L.A. for almost a week. I'm not impressed. Maybe that's because I hate palm trees. And I'm definitely sick of Benedict Canyon. When I was eighteen, I had poison oak so bad I was in the hospital. I've got very sensitive skin, the doctor said. So I've had it with Benedict Canyon. Finished. And I'm sick of flying blind. I get the feeling it's getting tight, this thing we're doing. So if I'm not in, then I'm gone. Now. Right now. Your people might live like kings down in South America someplace, that's what I hear. But I'm living on your goddam handouts. And I'm sick of it."

She studied his angry, determined profile, assessed the aggressive set of his muscle-bunched shoulders. This bout of temperament, she decided, was genuine. In his mind, Harry was already on the airplane to New York.

Speaking precisely, she said, "Raymond DuBois, the old man in the wheelchair, has got a houseful of paintings and art objects. Some of the stuff was stolen, and the FBI got the tip. DuBois has to get rid of the paintings, and he's hired Bernhardt to do the job."

"What about the other one?" He pointed to the Pontiac. "Graham."

"I already told you—he's the front man for some big money in New York. He's going to take the stuff off DuBois's hands."

"For how much?"

"A million dollars. At least. Maybe two million."

"Mmmm." He was, she could see, looking at the Pontiac with renewed interest. Harry was tempted.

"The plan is to wait for them to do their business, then take the money."

"Oh." He nodded derisively. "Just like that. 'Give me the money,' we say. 'Thank you very much.' "

She made no reply.

"How do you know all this? How good's your information?"

"My information is first class."

"You've got a bug planted on the deck at DuBois's. Right?"

She smiled mock-sweetly. "You wouldn't want me to tell you all my secrets, Harry, would you?"

With their eyes locked, fully engaged, she saw him mocking her in return, an unexpected subtlety, Harry's little surprise.

"All I need to know," he said softly, "is when I get my cut."

"You get yours when I get mine. Your end is twenty-five percent or ten thousand dollars, whichever is larger. Just what I promised."

"A million, you say . . ." He nodded approvingly. He was almost smiling.

"At least."

"Have you got someone on the inside of this thing?"

In complete control of her reactions, she studied him for a long, silent moment. Then she said, "Why'd you say that?"

"Because I don't think you planted that bug yourself. I figure you got somebody inside. I figure—"

In the gathering twilight, another parking attendant materialized, moving at a fast trot. They watched him angle toward the Pontiac and open the driver's door.

"I'll see you at the apartment," she said. "You follow Graham." She watched him walk to his Lincoln, parked nearby.

TWENTY-SIX

As he completed the male urination ritual and flushed the toilet and was zipping up his fly, Bernhardt heard the warble of his phone. As he walked into the suite's sitting room, he glanced reflexively at his watch: seven-thirty. In San Francisco, C. B. Tate would be in his Ford, driving from Sausalito across the Golden Gate Bridge to San Francisco. Another hour and they could be at the airport attending to the intricate business of checking a piece of specially designed luggage that contained four registered handguns.

He lifted the phone. "Yes?"

"Mr. Bernhardt." It was a statement, not a question. A woman's voice, assured, authoritative.

"Yes. Who's this?"

"It's Andrea Lange, Mr. Bernhardt."

"What's it concern?"

"It concerns Mr. Raymond DuBois."

"I don't believe I know you."

"That's true, you don't."

Amused, Bernhardt nodded to himself. Andrea Lange was quick with a quip, cool with a comeback.

"Does it concern Mr. DuBois? Or some of his property?"

"It concerns property. I'd like ten minutes of your time. I'll be in the bar downstairs. The Carnelian Room."

"How'll I know you?"

"You don't have to know me. I know you."

"That doesn't answer the question."

Her reply was amused: "I'm not quite thirty. I'm a brunette, and tall. Shoulder-length hair. I'm wearing safari slacks and a madras blue-checked shirt. I'll be the best-looking woman in the bar."

"Ten minutes."

"White wine," Bernhardt said to the waiter. "Chardonnay."

"I'm fine," Andrea said, dismissing the waiter. She raised a half-full glass of Glenfiddich on the rocks, saluted Bernhardt, sipped the Scotch appreciatively.

"I don't have much time," Bernhardt said.

She put her drink aside, leaned across the small round cocktail table, dropped her voice.

"The first thing you should know," she said, "is that you're involved in a three-sided game—at least."

"Oh?" Bernhardt studied her face. In a lifetime, he imagined, in the natural course of things, a given man met perhaps three truly beautiful women. Even during his years in the theater, and later on the fringes of Hollywood scriptwriting, he'd seldom seen anyone to match the beauty of the calm, completely assured woman he was facing. "Beautiful all over" was the phrase meant for Andrea Lange.

"You said ten minutes," she began, "so I'll get to it."

He nodded. "Good."

"I know bits and pieces about how you fit into this. But I don't—"

"Excuse me, but when you say 'this' what're we talking about, exactly?"

She smiled into his eyes, an appreciation. It was, he suspected, a moment he would long remember. When she spoke, the rich contralto of her voice matched the muted provocation in her eyes. "We're talking about art, Mr. Bernhardt. Contraband art, worth millions."

"And?" He was pleased with his response, not too coy, not too fatuous. Mr. Cool.

"And Raymond DuBois is a player. In fact, he's probably the world's most important player. But now he's old. Dying, some say. And the authorities are after him. He's got to get out. Fast. And he's hired you to help him."

The waiter arrived with a chilled glass of chardonnay, placed it before Bernhardt, smiled discreetly, withdrew.

"You said a three-cornered game. What's that mean?"

"It means that there's DuBois in one corner, with the paintings. And there's John Graham, with money from the insurance carriers. And then—" Once more she sipped her Scotch. The drink, Bernhardt could see, was almost finished. Watching her handle her cut-crystal glass, he decided that Andrea Lange understood about drinking.

"And then," she said, "there's me." The slow, subtle smile returned. "To be concise, I represent a syndicate of businessmen who, frankly, see a possibility for profit here."

"Ah." Bernhardt nodded appreciatively, returned the smile. It was an acknowledgment of Andrea Lange's nearly perfect sense of timing. Had she ever done any acting? What was the origin of her slight accent? "Yes, I see." He, too, sipped his drink. Then, trying for a casual nonchalance, he decided to say, "That accent. I can't place it."

"I grew up in Argentina."

He nodded again. "Yes, I see."

"My maternal grandfather managed to get out of Germany after the war. My mother made money—a lot of money—in export-import. She's utterly self-centered, and she has no sense of humor. She's very beautiful, though—and she collects young men. Boys, sometimes. My father is an Argentinian playboy. He's very handsome, very urbane—and utterly useless, except for drinking and playing polo. He collects women. Girls, too."

"That," he said, "is a truly remarkable thumbnail autobiography." Then, even though it was a cliché, he added, "You should write."

She smiled.

"So why're you telling me all this? What's the bottom line?"

"The bottom line is money. As always."

"This syndicate—how big is it? How much money does it have?"

"There're three men, two European, one Japanese. I'm not prepared to tell you how much money there is. However, like Mr. DuBois, all three are entrepreneurs, speculators. Each one has far-flung interests. This operation is merely one of many for them—a diversion, one could say, a little excitement, a change from buying and selling stocks and bonds and real estate. Some speculators form pools to buy racehorses. They do it purely for fun, excitement. That's the thinking of these three men, the motivation. Quite simply, they're bored."

"Are they collectors?"

Her smile suggested that she found the question amusing. "They collect money. Not art, especially. Money. Power. However, for men like that, the unique has great appeal. To possess something of great value that no one else can ever have, that's almost irresistible." She considered for a moment while she signaled their waiter for another round. Then: "At another level, however, my clients think of this as an ordinary distress sale. DuBois has to get rid of this stuff, and quickly. Therefore, he's got to sell at a loss. That creates a profit opportunity—the free market at work. Buy low, sell high." She raised her shoulders in a graceful

shrug, spreading her hands. The fingernails, Bernhardt noticed, were natural, polished but not colored. The cloth of
her madras blouse drew taut across her breasts.

"Do your people know the art we're discussing is contraband?"

"Of course. Remember, though, it's contraband according to U.S. law."

"So you intend to buy the paintings here and ship them
abroad."

She nodded. "Exactly."

"What happens if you get caught?"

"Then I've lost my gamble. But it's a gamble for which
I'm being very well paid."

"Up front?"

"Some of it." She waited for fresh drinks to be placed
before them, at the same time asking the waiter for the
check. Bernhardt thanked her, sipped chardonnay as he
looked appraisingly at her over the rim of his glass. She met
his gaze squarely, frankly appraising him. Her eyes were a
dark brown, alive with speculation—and something else.
Could the something else, Bernhardt wondered, possibly be
sexual?

Feeling his way, he said, "I'm still thinking about your
biographical sketch—on very short acquaintance. How
come?"

"I believe in knowing something about whoever I do
business with. Naturally, I assume others feel the same."

"What d'you know about me, Andrea?"

"Not much, really. I know Raymond DuBois has
enough confidence in you to give you the job of selling his
paintings. That's all I need to know, really. Of course—"
Once more her eyes shifted speculatively, boldly. "Of
course, anything you care to tell me, I'd be happy to listen."

"I figure the less I tell, the better position I'm in."

"I suppose that depends on what you might've told me."

"What d'you know about John Graham?" he asked.

"I know he's basically an ordinary insurance adjuster who happens to specialize in very expensive claims, a lot of them involving larceny. Maybe *all* of them involve larceny. I've never met the man, but I hear he's very smooth, very urbane."

"It sounds like you and Graham are working the same block, on opposite sides of the street."

"It wouldn't be the first time."

Bernhardt checked the time. In fifteen minutes, give or take, he should return to his suite and wait for C.B. and Paula to call from the airport.

"Obviously," he said, "I've got to run this past DuBois. Maybe I can get through to him tonight, maybe not. Otherwise, I'll talk to him tomorrow morning. Where can I reach you? Which hotel?"

"I've got an apartment. I'll call you."

"Ah." He nodded knowingly. "It's like that, eh?"

"I've learned to be careful."

"I'll bet." He sipped the chardonnay. Then, trying for an easy, offhand air, he said, "This apartment—do you have a garage?"

"As a matter of fact, yes."

"Is it secure?"

Her smile was playfully inscrutable. "As in secure enough to store some very valuable art? That kind of secure?"

Watchfully he waited.

"The answer is that, yes, it would probably work. But only for a few hours, until the exchange is made."

They drank in silence, each covertly assessing the other. Then, with an air of finality, he said, "If you won't give me a phone number, then you'd better give me some figures, some guidelines."

"I'd have to know which paintings we're talking about."

"And I'd have to clear that with DuBois."

"How soon does Graham expect to have an offer ready?"

"Not until Monday. Everything in New York is closed until then."

She frowned. "He told you that?"

Bernhardt decided not to answer the question. Instead, he finished his second glass of wine and shifted restlessly in his chair, a signal that he was about to leave. How would Paula react if she could see him now?

"I think," Andrea said, "that Graham is lying. If he wants to get some answers from his people over the weekend, he can."

"I'm just telling you what he told me. Hell, I basically don't have any idea what's really going on. I'm just the goddam go-between."

She regarded him quizzically for a moment, then said, "I figure you for someone who only resorts to profanity when you're frustrated. Am I right?"

Caught off balance, Bernhardt chuckled. "You might have a point there. I'll have to listen to myself."

"I also figure you for an intellectual." She pointed to his empty glass, an invitation. "One more?"

He shook his head, moved his chair back. "Sorry. I've got to get to my phone."

"If it'll help, I can come up." She said it quietly, looked directly into his eyes.

I'm not quite thirty, she'd said. Meaning that, for more than a decade, she'd been fending off sexual advances, most of which had certainly begun as this one was beginning:

with the particular eye-to-eye, woman-to-man challenge that conveyed only one possible message: the elemental urge to copulate.

Holding eye contact, she began a slow, knowing smile. The message: she knew exactly what he was thinking. And she was amused.

He realized that, without knowing that he meant to do it, he was shaking his head. Then, dropping his eyes, he said, "This isn't the time."

"I'm sorry to hear it." As, yes, the smile held between them. Signifying that the offer was still open.

"I, ah, I've got make some calls. And I've got to meet people at the airport. My, ah, colleagues."

"Ah." Now, still amused, she nodded. "I see. Or, anyhow—" Her eyes shifted obliquely. "Anyhow, I think I see."

"If you'll give me a phone number . . ."

The smile faded; the sexual game was played out, and it was once more time to do business. She shook her head. "No, no phone numbers. I'm sure Graham is handling this very differently. Exchange cards, my people'll be in touch with your people, that whole routine. But my situation is, ah, unique."

"Yes . . ." Speculatively Bernhardt nodded. "Yes, I can see that." About to leave her, give himself time to think, make plans, he decided instead to improvise, follow the random pattern of his own thoughts: "You say you want an inventory, you want guarantees. Well, I'm sure DuBois is going to want guarantees, too. These three guys you're fronting for—I'm sure DuBois'll want their names. He'll want—"

"That's no problem," she broke in. "I'll gladly give the names to Mr. DuBois. But I won't give them to you."

"Which, translated, means that you want to meet with him."

She shrugged. "You said it yourself: you're a go-between. I think it's time for principals. Don't you?"

"You're a go-between, too, Andrea." He watched her eyes, looking for shift, some hint of vulnerability. There was nothing. "*Aren't* you a go-between?" He accented the question delicately, a suggestion that he was just one step ahead of her. "Or are you in business for yourself? These three guys—what are they, Andrea? Straw men? Props?"

Suddenly her eyes went cold. Her mouth tightened, the ligatures of her face and neck drew taut. Her voice roughened, dropped to a low, angry note of accusation. "You're calling me a liar."

He considered her accusation, then decided to shake his head. He would try for a casual response, a change of pace, keep her slightly off balance: "I'm not really calling you a liar. I'm saying that you're probably a pretty good poker player. And good poker players—good gamblers—bluff." He tried a smile. It was a mistake.

"You talk about poker," she said, her voice dead level. "Well, I'll tell you this, Alan: I've got a lot invested in this game. And I'm not going to walk away with money on the table."

"But you aren't going to name your three guys."

"Not to you. I give you the names, you get on the phone, make your own deal—where's that leave me?"

"You're suggesting that these high rollers are readily accessible. That's not been my experience. If it's that easy, you'd have called DuBois."

"Honor among thieves," she quoted bitterly. "Christ, any thief I know, he's more trusting than you are."

"Now *you're* swearing."

Plainly struggling to control her anger, she looked away, said nothing.

"I'll tell DuBois what you said. Let's see what happens." He pushed back his chair. Then, on impulse, he said, "I'll tell you this, though, Andrea. If—" He broke off. Should he finish it? Should he turn up his card for her to see?

Yes, he'd do it—just this one card: "If you want to get in the game, it'll probably take about twenty-five million dollars. Very negotiable dollars. No checks accepted." He smiled, rose to his feet. "Thanks for the drinks. Keep in touch."

As he turned and walked away, making his way through the Saturday night drinkers, he began to whistle softly. Delivering the last several lines, he'd felt very good, very much in command of his performance. And the exit line had been timed perfectly. The proof had been her reaction: pure, naked fury.

TWENTY-SEVEN

At the fifth series of unanswered rings, Grace Campbell's voice materialized on a recording. It was a short message, simply her unlisted phone number repeated, followed by a request that the caller leave a brief message.

"This is Alan Bernhardt calling, Grace. It's seven forty-five Saturday evening, and I—"

"Mr. Bernhardt," her voice interrupted. "What can I do for you?"

"The, ah, job I'm doing for Mr. DuBois. I can't go any farther until I've seen him. Or at least talked to him."

"Mr. DuBois is already in bed for the night. At eight o'clock his light goes out. He never takes messages after eight."

"It isn't quite eight." He put an edge of authority on his voice. "I'd like you to tell him that—" He broke off, to order his thoughts. Then: "Tell him that I've got to have a detailed inventory of the, ah, merchandise before I can go any farther. Emphasize that. No inventory, no progress. Nothing."

"Will you hang on? Or should I call back?"

"I'll hang on."

In less than five minutes she came back on the line. "Mr. DuBois says to tell you that he understands the message. But he's tired. He'll see you tomorrow at eight A.M. That's the best I can do. Shall I send a car for you tomorrow?"

About to decline the offer, Bernhardt decided instead to say, "Please. And I'd like James to drive."

"Not Raul? He's the regular driver."

"I want James."

"Oh." A moment's pause. Then: "Fine. Consider it done. Shall he pick you up at your hotel? Seven-thirty tomorrow morning?"

"Fine. I'll be in front."

"Mr. DuBois wanted me to ask you whether your negotiations are producing results. When I get your answer, I'm to report back to Mr. DuBois. Briefly."

"So far so good, I'd say. But I won't have anything substantial until Monday midday. Assuming, that is, that I get the information I need from Mr. DuBois."

"He also wants to know whether help has arrived. Your people."

"They'll be arriving tonight, from San Francisco."

"Good. I'll go tell him." She spoke crisply, decisively. "Will I see you tomorrow after you've talked to Mr. DuBois?"

"Certainly."

"Good." The line clicked, went dead. Bernhardt cradled the phone on the nightstand, decided to stretch out on the bed, let his eyes slowly close. About eleven o'clock, he estimated, the phone would ring. It would be Paula, announcing their arrival at LAX.

A few months ago, they'd taken a trip to Santa Fe, and stayed for two nights at a luxury motel that he really couldn't afford. It was only the second time they'd slept together in a hotel or motel, and Paula had confessed that staying in motels turned her on. Then she'd proceeded to prove it—dramatically.

From the very first, he'd known they suited each other, complemented each other. Fundamentally they were both quiet people, like most actors essentially introverts. They'd both seen their brightest young dreams turn to ashes, and the experience would always mark them. Both only children, they'd both had sheltered childhoods. Much loved, Paula had grown up in Los Angeles, where both her parents taught at USC. She'd gone to Pomona, where she'd graduated with a split major in English and Drama. Almost immediately after graduation, helped by her father's connections in the USC drama program, she'd begun getting movie walk-ons. In New York, he'd started getting small parts off Broadway. Only a year out of college, they'd both gotten married—he to Jennie, she to a charismatic, deeply neurotic screenwriter who'd already been married twice before, and who drank. At that point the two stories diverged—and then cruelly converged. Paula's marriage had ended in a traumatic divorce.

His marriage—his life, for almost the next twenty years—had ended just before eleven o'clock on a beautiful spring night in the Village. He'd answered the door to find two uniformed policemen in the hallway. There'd been an accident, a mugging. Two white males, early twenties, maybe late teens, had tried for Jennie's purse. She'd resisted, and they'd knocked her down. Her head had hit the curb. She'd died.

Escaping their memories, both he and Paula had retreated to San Francisco, the last stop for a lot of people fleeing fear and defeat and loneliness, only to discover that the pain had gotten worse, not better.

Worse for him, until he'd found Paula.

And, yes, worse for her, until she'd found him.

He yawned, turned on his side, yawned again. How many thousand-dollar bills would it take to make twenty-five million dollars?

How many . . .

* * *

In the clangor, the confusion, the shrillness, he was dangling in a void, alone, surrounded by nothing, yet constrained by everything, too fearful to open his eyes. Fearful? Of what? Where? Why? Should he . . . ?

It came again: the clangor, the shrilling. But it was more melodious now. More—

The telephone. Close beside him. On the nightstand.

"Alan."

Yes, it was Paula.

"Hi. You made it." He yawned, checked the time: ten minutes after eleven.

"We're at United."

"Okay. Twenty minutes, with luck. Everything all right? Crusher?"

"Everything's fine."

"Okay, here I come."

TWENTY-EIGHT

"Ah . . ." Tate nodded approval as he surveyed his impressively furnished room. He stowed two suitcases in the closet, put another beside the bureau. "Yes. Very nice. Suddenly I'm feeling more positive about this gig." He looked at Bernhardt. "You cashed the client's checks yet?"

"As a matter of fact," Bernhardt answered, "I put them in the ATM today. By Tuesday they'll clear. Meanwhile, the client's paying for everything. Including this." His gesture swept Tate's room.

"Good." While Tate tested the bed, checked out the small wet bar, tried the TV, took note of the bathroom complete with phone extension and then went to the window and admired the view from the eleventh floor, Bernhardt moved close to Paula, took her shoulders, smiled gravely into her eyes, and kissed her meaningfully. As he felt her respond, felt her urgency, he waywardly thought of Tate's girlfriend, alone in Sausalito on a Saturday night. Or maybe not alone.

With perfect synchronization, Bernhardt stepped away from Paula at the same moment Tate turned to face them. "Anyone hungry?" Bernhardt asked. "Thirsty? Room service is included." He looked at Paula, who asked for a B and B. The request, Bernhardt knew, boded well for their night of love. The last time Paula had asked for a B and B, they'd been in Santa Fe, at the overpriced motel.

"I'll take a bottle of Dos Equis," Tate said. "And a big plate of Mexican snacks, heavy on the nacho chips, plus avocado dip. Plus lemon wedges."

Adding a glass of chardonnay for himself, and then deciding to get a plate of seafood, courtesy of Powers Associates, Bernhardt phoned in the order. Then he gestured to a small round table with four expensively upholstered chairs. "Let's talk."

"Right." Tate sat at the table, then produced a single sheet of paper torn from a spiral-bound composition book he'd taken from his luggage. Whenever they did business, the two men signed an agreement, retained by Tate. Bernhardt read the agreement, signed, returned the handwritten letter to Tate.

While they drank and nibbled at the room service food, Bernhardt told his story, beginning with the visit of the FBI men and ending with his last conversation with Grace Campbell, more than four hours ago.

"My God," Tate breathed, "you want my opinion, I say the guys that make a movie of this are the ones going to clean up. I mean, this baby's got everything."

"Including," Paula observed, "the ravishing South American beauty." She looked speculatively at Bernhardt.

"What we should start figuring out," Tate said, "is how it'll go down, step by step." He looked at Bernhardt. "Like, let's say we rent a house tomorrow, which shouldn't be a problem, according to what you hear about the economy down here. And let's say that, also tomorrow, you get the descriptions you need, and you give them to Graham, and he says okay, everything's cool. And then let's say that Monday, Graham gets the money. So everything's set for Tuesday, maybe even Monday night."

"Tuesday," Bernhardt said. "I'm figuring Tuesday at

the earliest. Don't forget, I've got to crate the pictures. That'll take most of Monday."

"We going to make the swap during the day? Or at night?"

"During the day. The earlier the better."

"Okay." Tate used the last two nacho chips to scoop up the dregs of the avocado and salsa dip. "Okay. So it's Tuesday, bright and early. So then what? How's it go? Hour by hour?"

Thinking through the time frame, improvising, Bernhardt speared a jumbo prawn, dipped it in an extraordinary white wine and capers sauce, reflectively chewed. "Monday night," he began, "we stay at the rental house, the three of us. We—"

"Goddam," Tate interrupted, "we should have Crusher here. A friend of mine, he never does a big-money dope deal without his faithful rottweiler. He says everyone likes to shoot their guns. But nobody wants to tangle with—"

"Come on, C.B.," Bernhardt interrupted irritably. Thinking to himself, *The longer you talk, the longer Paula and I have to wait.* Saying audibly: "It's one o'clock."

With easy good humor Tate looked at each of them knowingly, then amiably subsided as he gestured broadly for Bernhardt to continue.

"Let's start with Monday, best case. We have the house and the van we need, and Graham has the money from New York, converted into cash. The inventory's acceptable, no problems. So Tuesday, bright and early, Graham brings the money to the house. We'll check it out. If everything's cool, C.B. and I'll take the van and we'll drive to Benedict Canyon. We'll be buzzed inside the grounds by James, who's DuBois's security man. James is very—" Bernhardt hesitated, searching for the word. "He's very formidable.

Very quiet, very calm. And he's totally loyal to DuBois. So James takes us inside the mansion. Or, rather, he'll probably take me inside. C.B., you'll stay with the van while I talk to DuBois. Then you'll drive into the garage, and wait."

"Does the garage connect to the house?"

"I'm not sure." Bernhardt pointed to Tate's spiral-bound notebook. "Tear me off a sheet." Tate handed over two sheets of ripped-out paper and a ballpoint pen, one of several he carried in a brown plastic pocket protector. The protector was an incongruous Establishment touch, whimsically at odds with the clothing Tate had chosen for the flight to Los Angeles. He wore Birkenstock sandals, blue jeans, a flamboyant balloon-cut shirt. His neck, tree-trunk thick, was festooned with gold chains. In contrast, he wore only one ring, massive gold, custom-wrought into a "CBT" design. At almost two hundred fifty pounds, most of it muscle, head shaven, Tate was a formidable figure. He wore a close-cropped black beard, now lightly flecked with gray. His eyes were lively, characteristically perceptive, often alight with a humor that some considered quirky. Tomorrow Bernhardt would ask him to change his outfit, lower his profile. For the next few days, anonymity would serve them best.

On the paper Bernhardt wrote: *Ask G.C.:* On the next line he wrote *(1) Do garage, house connect?*

"Let's assume," he said, improvising some more, "that you can drive into the garage, and that it connects to the house. You stay in the van, with the outside garage door closed. I go into the house, probably accompanied by James, at least until I connect with DuBois. Then, maybe James will go to you in the garage. Grace Campbell, I think, will be out of the house, with orders not to come back until she gets permission from DuBois. That's the normal procedure when DuBois goes into his secret room. The nurse will be asked to leave, too. So it could be just DuBois and me inside the house, with you and James in the garage, waiting for the paintings. DuBois and I'll go to the secret gallery, and DuBois will open the two doors. Then I'll—"

"I have two questions," Paula interrupted.

One glance at her face and Bernhardt quickly smiled, a wry apology: "I already know the first question," he said. It was an attempt to finesse her irritation at not being included in the planning. "What's the second question?"

Disciplining him, she did not return the smile. Instead, speaking with chilly deliberation, she said, "My second question is how DuBois has it arranged so that he gets into the secret gallery alone, unaided."

"It's like an airlock," Bernhardt answered, grateful to be answering a factual question. "He goes to the outer door, which is steel armor plate, and he punches in a four-number code. The door slides open. When he's inside, the outer door slides closed automatically. He's in a short, windowless hallway, nothing on the walls. He goes to the inner door, which can't be opened unless the outer door is closed. He punches in a three-number combination, and the inner door, also steel, slides open. So now he's in the gallery, which isn't very big, only eight by fourteen feet."

"No windows," Tate said. "Artificially humidified. Probably with a few killer gas jets, if something goes wrong."

"Hmmm . . ." Bernhardt's eyes turned speculative.

"What's his procedure for getting out?" Paula asked, spearing a morsel of calamari, one of her favorites. She spoke crisply, remotely. Only when her first question was answered would she relent, unbend.

"He gets out the same way he gets in, a three-number

code followed by a four-number code. I imagine the exit codes are the same as the entry codes. Otherwise, he'd have to memorize fourteen numbers."

"Okay," Tate said, "so you and DuBois are in the gallery, and let's say James and I are in the garage, waiting for you. Then what?"

"Then," Bernhardt said, "I imagine I'll start moving the pictures one at a time, maybe stacking them in the hallway beside the interior door to the garage. I imagine it'll take an hour, at least. And I'm sure DuBois will be with me the whole time."

"Is he up to it?" Paula asked. "Physically?"

"If there's a problem," he answered, "there's always James standing by. He'll know what to do, how to contact Grace Campbell or Monica Gross."

"This James," Tate said, "will he be carrying a gun?"

"I'm sure of it. I'd be surprised if he didn't carry a handgun plus a Uzi, in a suitcase."

"And what about us?" Tate looked at Bernhardt, then at Paula. "What'll we be carrying?"

"I'll carry my three-fifty-seven," Bernhardt said.

"And I'll have my gun." As she said it, Paula shot Bernhardt another meaningful look.

"I'll have my two Browning nine-millimeters," Tate said. "What about a shotgun?" he asked, addressing Bernhardt. "There's nothing like a shotgun, up to fifty feet. Why don't I buy one tomorrow, and a hacksaw?"

"Fine. I'll give you some money. Don't forget to buy a ruler, too. Sixteen inches, breech to muzzle. No less. Otherwise, it's a sawed-off."

"Speaking of guns . . ." Tate rose, went to the closet, opened the foam-filled case that held the two automatics and the two revolvers, holstered, plus ammunition. He handed Bernhardt the .357 Ruger, handed Paula the .38

Chief's Special. They each verified that their weapon was unloaded, then tossed them on Tate's queen-size bed, along with two boxes of ammunition.

"So," Tate said, picking up the thread, "you've got the paintings as far as the garage. I'm inside the garage, probably with James the bodyguard, who's keeping his eye on me. So what then?"

"Then," Bernhardt said, "I imagine we'll load up the pictures. When everything is ready, James and I'll get into the van, and back out of the garage. James'll be driving. I'll be sitting beside him, with my hand on the butt of the three-fifty-seven. You'll follow us, C.B. James will open the front gate with an opener, and we'll drive out onto Benedict Canyon road. We'll drive to the house we rent, where Graham and Paula will be." He looked at her, smiled. "That's the answer to your first question. You'll be guarding the money—you and Graham. You'll also be keeping an eye on each other."

"My God," Tate said, "Paula's the one should have the goddam shotgun. For every crook wants to hijack a few paintings, there're a hundred ready to steal a few million in cash. Matter of fact, when you think about it, figuring that, let's face it: I've had more experience shooting people than Paula has"—he shot her a wide, friendly grin—"so I should stay with the money, let Paula go with you."

"Are you serious?" Bernhardt asked.

"I'm absolutely serious. Think about it."

As Bernhardt looked from one to the other, he felt the hollowness of indecision begin, a suddenly overwhelming awareness that he was in beyond his depth, foundering. How could he have committed them—committed Paula—to mortal danger without any real plan? How could—

"I've got an idea." Paula's eyes were alight as she spoke. Bernhardt knew that mannerism, knew it could compound his problem. Paula was petite. And Paula spoke softly. But Paula was determined. Very determined. And, yes, very stubborn.

"My parents," she said. "They live in Pasadena. They've got a couple of German Shepherds. And they're *very* intimidating. The dogs, I mean."

"Ah." Tate smiled, nodded deeply. "That could be the edge."

"*Wait* a minute." Exasperated, Bernhardt raised both hands, turned to Tate. "First you halfway convince me that Paula should go with me. And now you—"

"Remember what I said about rottweilers and drug deals," Tate retorted. "Okay, a shepherd isn't as heavy-duty as a rottweiler. But *two* shepherds—" Once more, sagely, he nodded. "Two shepherds, one goes for the legs, one goes for the throat. That's very big medicine."

"He's right, Alan. I'll call my folks first thing tomorrow." As if the matter were settled, Paula consulted her watch with an air of finality.

"Oh, Jesus." Bernhardt shook his head, drank the last of his wine, rose to his feet. "Come on." He clipped his revolver to his belt, left his shirttail out, to conceal the gun. "Come on, let's go to bed. I've got to leave here at seven-thirty in the morning."

Exchanging a knowing smile with Tate, Paula retrieved her own revolver, put it in her shoulder bag. Now the smile changed intimately as she grasped Bernhardt's shirttail and tugged him toward the door of Tate's room.

TWENTY-NINE

"Now Bernhardt's got a couple of people with him," Harry said. "A big black guy wearing a loud shirt, looks like he can really take care of himself. And a woman. Small, brunette, early thirties, I'd say. Great little body, looks like class. Bernhardt picked them up at the airport, and the black guy checked in. When I got that far, I decided to split, quit while I was winning. Midnight, one o'clock, hanging around a hotel lobby—" He shook his head. "Next thing you know, there's a security guy leaning on you."

They sat in the living room of the apartment Andrea had rented. The April night was soft and warm; drapes drawn over open windows billowed gently. Waiting for Harry to return, Andrea had taken a long, hot shower. Now, wearing a white terry-cloth robe, her hair in a matching towel, she sipped Glenfiddich over ice, watched Harry drink Jim Beam and water. It had been a successful night; Harry had done his job, no questions asked. He'd followed Graham and a young, dark-haired woman as they'd driven to a four-star restaurant. At eleven o'clock they'd returned to the Beverly Hilton, and gone upstairs. Later, when Harry had called on her car phone, reporting in, she'd ordered him to break off the surveillance at the Hilton and take over from her at the Prado.

"So what's next?" he asked, sipping more whiskey.

"I'm wondering whether we could use two more people, for what I'm thinking now."

"What's that mean?" he demanded. "What is it you're thinking now?"

Her smile was gently patronizing. "Don't worry, Harry. What I'm thinking, it'll be a lot bigger pie, more in it for both of us. But . . ." She let it go unfinished. Tomorrow morning, Sunday, could she make some calls, find two reliable hands, fly them out from New York the same day, time enough to brief them, get the job done by Tuesday? It was, she knew, a doubtful prospect. And yet . . .

"If this was New York," Harry was saying, "I know a dozen guys'd take a thousand each to shoot their way in, at Benedict Canyon, wherever. And they'd supply their own guns, too. But here, this place, Christ, we don't know anyone." Moodily now, he drank more bourbon, then said, "You should've planned ahead better, Andrea. What've we got? A couple of handguns?" He shook his head grimly, finished his drink with another long, noisy gulp.

"You're overlooking something, Harry."

"Oh, yeah? What's that?"

"I never intended that we shoot our way in."

He poured more bourbon, went to the kitchen for water and ice, returned to sit slumped in the threadbare chair, picked fretfully at the frayed fabric of the arm. He'd wanted to rent a place in a good neighborhood, one the police didn't have on their list. But Andrea had decided on a small furnished apartment in a run-down neighborhood, not too tough but not too fancy.

"I suppose," he said acidly, "that you're eventually going to give me a hint what it is we're going to do, this new idea, whatever."

"DuBois is a virtual invalid. We go shooting our way in, and he'll probably die right in his wheelchair."

"So? What's wrong with that?"

"I'm almost certain that he's got the paintings locked up somewhere in his house. And certainly he'd be the only one with the key, or the combination, whatever. So all we've got to do is get inside the house and find him. We make him take us to the paintings, all very quiet, no fuss. He'll be a hostage. One of us keeps an eye on DuBois while the other loads a panel truck. If we have to cope with some of his people—James, for instance, his security man—we'll disarm them, and handcuff them, whatever works. If they don't go along, we'll tell them the old man's going to suffer. We'll disable their cars, disable their communications. We'll throw roofing nails behind us when we leave. When everything's done, no problems, we'll leave DuBois somewhere. Anywhere. Then, once we're back here, with the van in the garage, everything safe, we'll call the police, tell them where to find DuBois."

Harry sat slumped in the lumpy chair, drinking steadily, eyeing her over the rim of his highball glass. After she'd finished, as if he were depressed, utterly baffled by what he'd just heard, he began to slowly, solemnly, shake his head. Now, more in sadness than in rancor, an aspect of his persona that Andrea had never seen revealed, he said, "Before we got into all this—before we made our deal—I checked you out, Andrea, in New York. And the word I got was that you were one of the smartest operators around. You had it all, everyone said—looks, brains, plenty of nerve. You were even rich. Not rich because of what you stole, the deals you put together, but rich all your life. The word was that the life turned you on—living on the edge, the guns, everything. And, Jesus, I saw your face after I pulled the trigger on Ned Frazer. I saw your face, and I figured you wanted to pull the trigger yourself, that's the way it looked to me. But most of all, I figured you for smart. And I figured you for tough, too, making a deal. 'Andrea gets the last dollar,' that's the word in New York. But now, Jesus, here we are—'' He gulped the bourbon, waved an exasperated hand around the small, dingy, dimly lit living room as they faced each other across a cheap, badly chipped white Formica coffee table. "Here we are, and you're sitting there telling me how the two of us are going to pull off the biggest art heist ever. We've got—what—three guns between us? *Three?* And you're telling me we're going to get into that goddam place of his that looks like—'' He searched for the word, finally said, "It looks like the fucking Pentagon, the way it goes on, all those levels. And once we're in, we're going to tap DuBois on the shoulder, and tell him, hey, he's got to get us into the place where he's got this art, wherever that is, and we're going to tell him he's got to let us take all these priceless paintings, and load them in a goddam truck and drive away. And we're going to do all this, plan everything, the most complicated job I ever heard about, in just a couple of days. Plus, Christ, we can't even raise our voices to the guy we're robbing, for fear he might die on us. And furthermore, after we get the paintings, then what? Are we going to—''

"Do you have a better plan, Harry?'' She spoke softly, dreamily. Her gaze was fixed on the half-full bottle of Glenfiddich on the coffee table. An hour ago, the bottle had been almost full. It was, she realized, a mistake to be matching Harry drink for drink, a no-win contest, winner take nothing, loser could die.

"You're goddam right I got a better plan—*your* plan, for Christ's sake. I say, first of all, we buy an Uzi, or a Mac Ten, whatever. Christ, in this town you can buy a goddam bazooka for a few hundred bucks. And then we go after the goddam money, just like you said first. Forget about the paintings. You got DuBois's place bugged, I'm not so dumb I can't figure that out. So we find out when the buy's going to come down, and we scoop up the money, however many millions it is, and we split. DuBois loves his paintings so much, let him keep them. Let—"

"Anyone can steal money, Harry." She spoke quietly, even delicately, as if she were instructing him in some intricate rite of initiation. "But to steal paintings worth a fortune, that requires talent. Imagination and talent. It requires—"

"Oh. So you want to be famous, is that it? You want every one to know how clever you are. Ego, that's what it's all about, isn't it? You—"

"Have you any idea how much that art is worth, Harry? Fourteen paintings, by some of the world's greatest masters—do you know what they'd bring at auction?"

"No, I don't. But I know you're going to tell me, Andrea."

"One painting alone—Renoir's *The Three Sisters*—would bring at least twenty million at Christie's. Add that to a couple of Van Goghs, and at least one major Picasso, well . . ." She poured some Glenfiddich, went to the kitchen for ice. Was the bottle really that empty? Was she, therefore, talking too much? She returned to the rump-sprung couch, placed the drink untasted on the Formica coffee table. It was time to let Harry talk.

"How d'you know so much about the stuff DuBois's got?" His voice was slightly slurred, his eyes slightly blurred.

"I know because of Ned. He knew about every stolen painting in the world. He knew where it was, and he knew how much it'd bring at auction."

As she said it she saw a faint, knowing gleam kindle in

his clear blue eyes. "After Ned went down," he said, "you went to his place. I stayed in the car, and you went upstairs. You were wearing surgical gloves."

She let him see the calculation in her eyes. How much did Harry know—really know? How dangerous could he be?

"There was a list." He nodded deeply, a drunk's bleary omniscience. "A goddam list of those paintings. And that's what you killed him for. You and him, you were living together once. But you killed him for the list."

Surrendering to the pure pleasure of complete contempt, she began to smile. What would she do without Harry to bait, to manipulate—to eventually discard?

"I'll tell you a secret, Harry. You won't tell, will you? You wouldn't do that."

In the distorted twist of his answering smile, she could see her own contempt reflected. At one level, then—the most elemental, one-syllable level—they understood each other.

"Ned died because he did something very stupid a couple of years ago." Casually, patronizingly, she smiled at him. "Would you like to hear about it, Harry? You might find the story enlightening."

He shrugged, waved for her to go on, drank more bourbon.

"It was in Mazatlán. Ned was dealing a set of jeweled Cellini goblets to a Kuwaiti sheikh, one of the royal family. We were all staying in the same hotel, the Coronado. The sheikh didn't drink, but he was a goddam cokehead, and he decided to give a party for Ned, to celebrate their deal. It was the most lavish spread I've ever seen. There were even dancing girls—thirty dancing girls, especially flown in for the party on the sheikh's seven-twenty-seven. There was a Hungarian woman, a countess, she said, and after a few drinks and a snort of coke, Ned started staring down her dress. I said something to him, but he still kept staring— and smiling. It was a new experience for me, a first." Reflectively, she sipped the Glenfiddich. "I decided to leave the party, go to our room. I gave Harry exactly an hour, then I called a friend in the *policía*. I told the friend where to find the goblets—and where to find Ned. The goblets eventually disappeared, of course—and so did Ned."

"Jesus." Harry blinked, sat up straighter. "You're telling me you turned Ned in because he looked at some other woman? Is that what you're telling me?"

"Beautiful people have their problems, too, you know. If you're plain, you let it pass if a man's eyes wander. You can't afford to do otherwise, sometimes. But if you're beautiful, and you're rejected, especially in public, the pain can be unbearable. The only solace possible is revenge."

"So you stuck Ned in a Mexican jail."

She made no reply. Her expression revealed nothing.

"So what happened? How'd he get out of jail?"

"He made a deal with the FBI."

"The FBI? In Mexico?"

"Pay the Mexican police enough, you get anything you want."

"What was the deal?"

"The deal," she said, "was illicit art—and illicit collectors."

"DuBois."

She nodded. "DuBois. The feds want him. Badly."

"So—what—they got Ned sprung, and he came ringing your bell? Is that it?"

"That's it." She drained the highball glass for the last time, set it resolutely aside. She'd had enough.

"He didn't know you turned him in?"

"I was never sure." She spoke reflectively.

"So then what?"

"The word was out that Ned had copped, so no one would do business with him when he tried to set up shop again. And Ned had expensive tastes."

"So you gave him money, and . . ." He let it go unsaid.

"He gave me a name. That's all I needed. A name."

"DuBois."

She made no reply.

"So then you didn't need Ned anymore. Good-bye Ned."

Her smile was almost playful, almost a coquette's smile.

"That party, with the dancing girls—that was Ned's big mistake, I guess."

Her smile widened almost imperceptibly.

THIRTY

As he always did afterwards, he kissed Paula gently on her forehead, lightly caressed her, all passion spent.

"Just think." he whispered, "What if you'd decided to move to Cleveland instead of San Francisco?"

"Hmmm . . ." She stirred, snuggled, sighed.

"There never would've been the last five minutes. They never would've happened."

"Hotels," she murmured. "What is it about hotels? Fresh sheets. That must be part of it. The anonymity, and fresh sheets."

"Then there's also the guy you came with." He kissed her again.

"Hmmm."

He raised himself on one elbow, looked over her shoulder at the travel alarm he'd put on the nightstand.

"What time is it?"

"Almost one-thirty."

"What time will it go off?"

"Six-thirty."

She sighed again. Paula was not an early riser. Neither was she a night person.

"You don't have to get up."

"Let's see what happens. How long'll it take tomorrow, with DuBois?"

"It shouldn't take long. After an hour or two, he runs out of energy."

"Will you come back here afterwards?"

"I haven't decided. A lot depends on how it goes with DuBois. If I get the inventory, I'll want to take it to Graham, at the Hilton."

"So—what—do C.B. and I wait here until you come back?" With the question, the pillow-talk muzziness in her voice cleared. Paula was thinking ahead. Questions would soon follow.

"I think one of you should stay close to a phone. Basically I've got no idea how tomorrow's going to play out. Minimum, though, we've got to rent a house. And we've got to rent a van, too. Plus another car. The Accord Grace Campbell gave me is fine. But the Lincoln Powers rented for me is too conspicuous. I don't want to drive that on Tuesday."

For a long, reflective moment they lay silently side by side, both of them staring up at the ceiling. Finally Paula ventured, "There's a sense of"—she broke off until she found the word—"of unreality about all this."

"I know exactly what you mean."

"It's the money—all that money. It's like astronomy. Light-years. Who can really comprehend a light-year? My God, the distance a beam of light travels in a year, going a hundred eighty-six thousand miles a second. That's astounding enough in itself. But then the sun is—what—two hundred million light-years from the earth."

"I don't think so. I think that's the most distant star. The sun is closer."

She chuckled. "Here we are, talking about astronomy."

He chuckled, too.

"Alan?"

He knew this new shading in her voice, this subtle shift of inflection. They were about to get serious.

"What?"

"It can't be as simple as it sounds. Those paintings, worth all that money. It sounds like it's an open secret that DuBois has the paintings."

"I'm beginning to think so, too."

"So if it's an open secret, then who else knows? How many?"

"That's not the point. The point is that—"

"Alan, for God's sake. That's the *whole* point. Here we are, you and C.B. and me. You're one of the nicest, smartest, most sensitive men in the whole wide world. And C.B. is a big, black, overstuffed lamb, even though I'm sure he's very tough, and very streetwise. And then there's me. I—Christ—I still feel like I'm a little girl sometimes, being overprotected by my parents. We're innocents abroad, Alan. Amateurs. And we're playing at the same table with one of the world's richest men."

"But that's DuBois's problem. He's got so much money that he can't trust anyone. He's got two divorced wives and no children. He hires Powers to front for him in business, and he hires Grace Campbell to run his house. But he doesn't really trust either one of them. I think he trusts James, his bodyguard. But James can't deal with these paintings. Which leaves me. For some reason, DuBois trusts me."

"That's because you're the nicest, smartest, most—"

He kissed her, laughed with her, said good night to her.

THIRTY-ONE

As he'd done the previous day, James got out of the town car and walked around to open the rear passenger's door. And, another repeat of yesterday, Bernhardt shook his head, opened the front right-hand door, got into the car. As soon as they were under way, Bernhardt said, "The reason I wanted you to pick me up, I want to talk to you." As he'd done yesterday, he tried to project an aura of authority, of command.

With his eyes on the road ahead, James nodded. "Yes, I was sure that was what you wanted."

"In a couple of days we're going to be working together, you and me. Has Mr. DuBois told you about what we'll be doing?"

"He's told me that he's selling some of his paintings, and you're going to deliver them to the buyer."

"Did he say who the buyer is?"

The other man shook his head. "No, sir. All Mr. DuBois said was that the paintings will have to be guarded, because of their value."

"Have you ever done this before, guarded paintings on their way to customers?"

"No, sir. Never."

"Why do you suppose you'll be doing it now?"

"Because Betty Giles isn't here, that was my thought."

"Mr. DuBois buys and sells paintings frequently. How're they usually handled? How're they shipped?"

"Usually by United Parcel. Sometimes by Federal Express, or an ordinary truck line."

"You said yesterday that you've been with Mr. DuBois for three years. What'd you do before that, James?"

"I worked for Carla Jeffries."

"The movie star?"

"Yes, sir."

"As her bodyguard?"

He nodded.

"How do you get a job like that?"

"I worked for a security agency. You know, rent-a-cop. I was assigned to Miss Jeffries after her bodyguard quit, and then she hired me permanently."

"How was she to work for?"

"She was very—" He searched for the word. "Very unpredictable. And—" He glanced at Bernhardt before he decided to say, "She could be unpleasant when she drank. One night she threw a glass at me. After that, I quit."

"How's Mr. DuBois to work for?"

"Very fine. Very—" Once more, he hesitated, then said, "He's very fair."

"And very predictable, I imagine."

"Oh, yes."

"Do you carry a gun?"

"Yes, sir."

"All the time?"

"Only when I'm on duty."

"Are you carrying a gun now?" Bernhardt looked at the navy-blue blazer the other man wore. There was no apparent bulge of a shoulder holster.

Aware of Bernhardt's appraisal, James answered, "I have a Colt Cobra in a holster at my belt."

"That's not a very serious gun."

"I also have two nine-millimeter semiautomatic pistols and a forty-four-caliber Magnum."

"That," Bernhardt admitted, "is a serious gun."

"Yes."

"What about a fully automatic weapon?"

James hesitated, looked appraisingly at Bernhardt. Finally, with obvious reluctance, he said, "I have—we have—two machine pistols."

"You say 'we.' Who else do you mean?"

"They belong to Mr. DuBois, really. But they're registered to me."

"Do you have a permit to carry them concealed?"

James shook his head. "No, sir. No private party has that kind of a permit."

"Friday, when we were at the Huntington, did you have a machine pistol then?"

"Yes, sir. In the car. It's an Uzi."

"Have you ever shot the Uzi?"

"Two or three times, on a private range."

"Are you any good with it?"

"I think so."

Having passed through Beverly Hills, making good time in the early Sunday morning traffic, they were on the Canyon Drive, beginning the climb up the narrow, winding road that would lead to Benedict Canyon. In ten minutes, perhaps less, they would arrive at the DuBois estate.

"You grew up in Central America, Mr. DuBois told me."

"Yes, sir. I was born in San Salvador."

"But you spent your boyhood in the mountains. Your parents were guerrilla leaders."

This time James made no reply. Neither did he look at

Bernhardt. Impassively, expertly, he guided the Lincoln into a series of esses, with the thickly wooded canyon dropping away sharply on their downhill side.

"When we move these paintings, probably on Tuesday, I'll want you to be armed. Fully armed, probably including the Uzi."

"Are you expecting trouble?"

"No. But I'm *preparing* for trouble. We'll be transporting art that's worth a lot of money. Millions."

"How far will we be taking it?"

"Not more than ten miles, probably. We'll be taking the stuff to a private home, and meeting the customers. We'll give them the paintings, and they'll give us a suitcase full of money. Maybe two suitcases. We'll take the money back to Mr. DuBois. And that's it. The whole thing shouldn't take more than an hour, once the paintings are crated."

"You'll need a van, I expect." As he said it, James allowed the Lincoln to slow on the uphill grade, reached for an electronic wand clipped to the sun visor. Ahead, Bernhardt saw the gates to the DuBois estate. He looked at his watch: seven forty-five.

"I'll have a van," Bernhardt answered.

Nodding, James waited for the gate to open, then drove slowly ahead.

"You say you worked three years for Mr. DuBois. How long've you lived in the States?"

"About ten years." James was guiding the big car through the gates.

"Is that your house?" Bernhardt pointed to a small bungalow on their right.

"Yes, sir. I'm closest to the gate, you see."

"Stop here for a minute." Bernhardt waited for the car to come to a stop, explaining, "We're a little early, and I've got a few more questions."

The other man made no comment. He simply sat as before, both hands on the steering wheel, eyes forward, as if he were still driving.

"There's a woman named Andrea, very beautiful, from South America. Argentina, I think. She's about thirty, tall, dark hair. Have you seen anyone like that recently? She'd be trying to contact Mr. DuBois about the paintings we're selling."

James frowned. "How recently?"

"During the last week."

"No, sir. No one like that." Pointedly the other man consulted his watch.

"Okay. Let's go. Thanks, James."

"You're welcome." James put the car in gear, drove slowly ahead. As the main house came into view, Bernhardt saw a black Jaguar sedan parked at the door.

"Visitors? At eight o'clock on a Sunday morning?"

"That's Mr. Robbins's car." James pulled up behind the Jaguar.

"He's Mr. DuBois's lawyer. Right?"

"Right." James reached for his door latch.

"Don't bother. Please." Bernhardt got out of the car, thanked his companion, strode across the flagstone entryway to the massive metal-sculptured door. As he was about to press the button, the door slowly, ponderously opened, revealing Grace Campbell. She greeted him briefly, gestured down the short hallway to DuBois's study and the deck adjoining it.

"Mr. Robbins is with him," she said as the door swung closed. "They're on the deck. You're to join them."

"Thanks. I'll talk to you later."

She nodded, at the same time gesturing again. The message: at three minutes after eight o'clock, he'd already wasted three minutes of the great man's precious time.

* * *

Two white plastic chairs had been drawn up to DuBois's mechanical wheelchair, which was placed to face the view to the west, where the morning fog still lingered off the ocean. As Bernhardt stepped through the sliding glass door connecting the study to the deck, Albert Robbins rose to his feet and extended his hand as they exchanged names. Dressed for the golf course, Robbins was a tall, spare man in his mid-fifties. He was almost totally bald. His face was long and lean, his lips permanently pursed, his expression permanently pinched. Conforming to the dry, precise cast of his face, he wore small rimless glasses that might have come from an earlier era. After they'd shaken hands, with a proprietary air Robbins gestured Bernhardt to one of the white deck chairs while he took the other.

When they were seated, DuBois spoke first to Bernhardt: "I wanted you to meet Mr. Robbins. He is, as you know, my personal lawyer. Albert knows, in broad outline, of our, ah, negotiations with respect to the paintings. Therefore, I wanted you two to meet." He turned to Robbins, saying, "Mr. Bernhardt has my personal trust, Albert. You understand."

Robbins nodded somberly. "I understand."

"Good." The pale ghost of a smile touched DuBois's lips. "With that in mind, then, having graven Mr. Bernhardt's face on your consciousness, you are now free to join your foursome."

Robbins's answering smile was prim. Plainly he disdained any irony directed at him. He rose, said his good-byes, and left them.

"I'd like to ask a question," Bernhardt said.

With a nod, DuBois granted permission.

"What does 'broad outline' mean?"

DuBois smiled benignly as he said, "It means that Albert knows enough to be of help in a crisis—but no more."

"Does Mr. Robbins know about the gallery?"

"No. No one knows but you."

"I'm flattered, Mr. DuBois. And curious, too. Why do you think you can trust me? I'd like to know."

"After you saved Betty Giles from certain death it appeared for a time that Justin Powers might be accused of hiring the man who killed Nick Ames and tried to kill Betty. In that event, I thought it prudent to have you checked out. You seemed to me a remarkable man, an intriguing man—and probably an honest man. My face-to-face evaluation seemed to confirm the impression I got from the background check. I don't think you're greedy, Mr. Bernhardt. And the absence of greed is the single most important prerequisite of honesty. Don't you agree?"

Bernhardt made no reply, and after a moment DuBois said, "In my desk in the study, you'll find paper in the left-hand drawer and pens on top of the desk. If you'll get them, I'll dictate the descriptions Mr. Graham requires."

Bernhardt went into the study, found pen and paper. After a moment's deliberation he selected an outsize book on Etruscan art to write on. Fifteen minutes later, on two sheets of paper, the descriptions of the paintings and ceramics were complete. Clearly the effort required to dictate the descriptions had tired DuBois. Bernhardt returned the book to its place on the shelf, then returned to the deck. Sitting on the other man's right, with DuBois's un-numbed face in profile, Bernhardt ventured, "Graham also wanted pictures of the paintings. Polaroids."

"No. No pictures."

"I'd like to know why not. I told Graham I'd provide pictures."

"There will be no pictures. When you make the exchange, you will offer to uncrate one painting that Graham may select at random. That's all."

"But, my God, the others could be fakes."

"Think of Russian roulette, Mr. Bernhardt." The other man considered, then said, "Two paintings, chosen at random by Mr. Graham. No more."

Reluctantly Bernhardt agreed to the compromise. Whereupon, matter-of-factly, DuBois said, "When I die, my will provides for disposition of all my works of art, including those in the concealed gallery. My net worth is almost five billion dollars, as you know if you read the newspapers. Most of that goes to establish two art museums, one in California, one in New York, where I was born. I fully intend that they will be the best museums in America, if not the world. Mr. Robbins will be my executor. He's very capable. And if something happens to him, his law firm will provide oversight for the museum."

"Mr. Robbins strikes me as very dependable. Very honest."

"Mr. Robbins has a very handsome income, with or without the money I pay him. Aside from a first-class collection of classic cars, including a 1954 Ferrari Testarossa and a 1927 Bugatti, his only vice is golf."

"Powers, though . . ." Bernhardt let it go elliptically unfinished.

"We've already discussed Powers. In the capacity for which he was intended, he served admirably. True, he's a coward. But in my experience, cowards don't often steal from those who're in a position to ruin them." He paused, then added, "In fairness, Powers's failure of the spirit was my fault. I never should have involved him in, ah, the matter of Nick Ames. He just wasn't up to the job. I should've made other arrangements, difficult though that would have been." DuBois allowed his eyes to close as he spoke with a note of finality: "Anything else, Mr. Bernhardt?"

"Well, yes, there's the question of money—of John Graham's people, and their demands."

"Ah—Graham. Yes. He has, I assume, made additional demands beyond those we've already conceded."

"It's not a demand, exactly. He says, though, that he's absolutely certain his company won't pay more than ten million for the whole collection. He says twenty-five is out of the question."

"From which I infer that he knows about the grand jury."

"I think he does, yes."

"Well . . ." DuBois touched a button on the arm of his mechanical chair, which buzzed as it slowly rotated in a half circle to face the study. "Do the best you can, Mr. Bernhardt. Keep in mind, though, that your share will be ten percent of whatever I get." With a soft mechanical whirring, the chair moved across the deck and through the sliding glass doors leading to the study.

THIRTY-TWO

Parked in her car on Benedict Canyon Drive, she smiled as she switched off the radio receiver and removed the lightweight headset, then finger-fluffed her hair.

Never before had she experienced this particular sensation, this feeling of elation, of separation, this utter triumph, this ultimate possession of power.

A fortune, literally a king's ransom, soon to be neatly packed in fourteen crates. Current owner, Raymond DuBois. Future owner, Andrea Lange.

To excel, her grandfather had often said, that was the one true gift life offered. The triumph of supremacy, of looking down on the hordes of others. Now, for the first time, she could sense what her grandfather must have felt, standing on the reviewing stand just behind the Fuehrer.

THIRTY-THREE

Once more, slowly, Graham read the list of paintings. Each with a cup of coffee before him, Graham and Bernhardt were sitting across from each other at a glass-topped patio table beside the pool of the Beverly Hilton. Across the poolside lanai, C. B. Tate and Paula toyed with tall drinks as they stole covert glances at John Graham.

"Can I keep this?" Graham asked.

Bernhardt shook his head, extending his hand for the two sheets of paper. "Sorry."

"Ah." Graham nodded approval. "Right. Nothing in your own handwriting. Very prudent." As he spoke, he took a sheet of paper from his own pocket, raised his head to accommodate his bifocals, and studied the paper, periodically comparing Bernhardt's list with a sheet of paper he drew from an inside pocket.

"What's that?" Bernhardt asked. "A list of stolen paintings?"

Still reading, Graham nodded. Finally he refolded his paper and returned it to the pocket of his natural linen jacket. When he met Bernhardt's gaze fully, his expression was thoughtful, speculative. He said nothing.

"And?" Bernhardt asked. It was an impatient question. With half the Sunday gone, he had yet to rent a house and a van.

With seeming nonchalance, Graham shrugged. "As far

as I can see, our two lists correspond. Every painting on your list has been stolen within the last ten years, and none of them have surfaced. Of course, as the poet says, what's in a name? I'd much rather see Polaroids before I talk to my people."

"Suppose they were forgeries? From pictures, how could you know?"

"That's true," Graham admitted.

"Earlier today," Bernhardt said, "I talked to Mr. DuBois. I told him you probably won't offer more than ten million for the whole lot."

"I said I didn't think my *people* would go any higher."

Waving the distinction aside, Bernhardt said, "Let's assume that all the paintings are authentic. At a guess, according to your list"—he pointed to Graham's jacket pocket— "how much would you say the paintings would bring at Sotheby's? A hundred million? Two hundred? More?"

"The answer, probably, is 'more.' However—" Graham smiled, a subtle, quizzical smile. "However, this is distressed merchandise."

Expecting the gambit, Bernhardt was able to keep his expression bland, revealing nothing.

"I'm referring, of course," Graham said, "to the government's case against DuBois for receiving stolen property. Then there's the state of California, which is looking to collect property taxes. Not to mention the fun *Sixty Minutes* would have at DuBois's expense."

"That's not my concern. I'm selling art for Mr. DuBois. Period. And if we take two hundred million as fair market value, then ten million is only five percent of the total. That's bullshit, and you know it."

Graham's expression hardened—then turned ironic. "When we first talked, it was pretty obvious that you were awed by the numbers those paintings represent. Now you're pooh-poohing a mere ten million dollars."

"I'm a quick study, John. Didn't you know?"

"What you are," Graham answered, "is a middleman. And a middleman has a thankless job. You'd save yourself a lot of trouble if you got DuBois and me together tomorrow, let us do the bargaining."

"I'd save *you* a lot of trouble. But you aren't the one who's paying me."

"Indirectly, though, I *am* paying you."

Bernhardt shook his head. "Wrong. Your company's paying. Which makes you a middleman, too."

Once more Graham's smile crooked affably. "We're wasting time. I'll call New York at six tomorrow morning, California time. By noon, I should know something. Shall I call you at the Prado?"

"I'm going to find a more secure location. I'll call you. Noon."

"Fine."

"What about security? You said your people will wire money to your bank, with an authorization that'd let you turn it into cash. You certainly don't plan to walk around with that much money without protection."

"I'm working on it." Graham pushed back his chair. "Don't worry. You tell me where to be, and I'll have the money there on Tuesday. Assuming, that is, that my people authorize ten million."

Bernhardt rose, waited for the other man to rise. Then he smiled, extended his hand. "Twenty million. Not a quarter less."

"Let's see what my people say."

"I'm surprised you can't talk to someone you work with on weekends. Don't you have home numbers, for something as big as this?"

"Actually," Graham said, "I've got calls in to two of the three people that'll have to approve this. But they haven't called back. The third one—the big boss—is actually in the air as we speak. He's been in Rome for three days."

"What if this were a billion-dollar loss? A natural disaster?"

"Natural disasters get on the TV news, and everyone drops their golf clubs or their mistresses, whatever, and flocks to the office. This deal, the last thing we need is publicity." Graham smiled, flipped his hand. "I'll talk to you at noon tomorrow." He turned away, walked across the poolside patio and into the cabana that led to the hotel's main lobby. Head-high indoor plantings flanked the entrance to the cabana. Graham stepped behind the screen of plants and looked back at the poolside scene. Bernhardt had left the table, doubtless gone to collect his car. And, yes, the big black man wearing the Ralph Lauren polo shirt and the small, attractive brunette, certainly C. B. Tate and Paula Brett, were preparing to leave. Graham smiled to himself. Amateurs were so predictable, so careless, essentially so trusting. He turned away, entered the lobby, and crossed to the bank of telephones next to the check room. He deposited a quarter in the first phone in the row, and waited through the required four ring bursts before Powers came on the line.

"Can you talk?"

"To a degree," Powers answered.

"I think it'll take twenty."

"But you said ten, maybe fifteen. Now you say twenty."

In the words Graham could hear the other man's petulance and, therefore, his fear. Clearly Justin Powers had come to the end of his inner resources.

"Originally they said twenty-five, remember."

"I know. But—"

"Tomorrow afternoon, that's the cutoff. You understand."

"Yes."

"I'll call you tomorrow, at one o'clock in the afternoon."

"Yes."

"Tuesday, that's when it all comes together. So by Monday, we've got to be ready. Completely ready."

"Yes."

"Twenty."

There was no response.

THIRTY-FOUR

Standing in front of the meticulously clean fireplace, Tate nodded approval as he surveyed the spacious living room. "Very nice, considering it's basically a tract house. What's the rent?"

"Twelve hundred a month." Bernhardt picked up the telephone and put it to his ear. Nothing. He flipped a nearby light switch. Yes, there was electricity.

"So," Tate said, "twelve hundred plus deposit. Does that come out of your front money?"

"I already told you, C.B. No. All I do is send the receipt to Powers. Quit worrying."

"You already said this Powers is a flake. So it figures that—"

"He's not a flake. He's a—a lightweight."

"There's a difference?"

"Come on." Bernhardt hefted his suitcase in one hand and Paula's in the other. "Let's put our stuff away and—"

"The stove works," Paula called from the ranch-style kitchen. "The gas is on. And the water, too."

In the hallway leading back to the bedrooms, Bernhardt pushed open a bathroom door. Two sets of mismatched washcloths and towels were hung neatly on chromium racks. The ad had read "Lightly Furnished."

"I'm going to stow our suitcases," Bernhardt called

back. "Then let's get something to eat. It's almost six, and there's still lots to do."

"I'll take this one." Tate pushed open the door to one of the three bedrooms. "Leave you guys with the master bedroom." He raised the case containing the guns. "Let's take these with us. I don't want to leave them here."

"Right." Bernhardt went down the hallway to the master bedroom. There were linens on the bed, and the room smelled fresh and clean. He put their suitcases on the floor beside one of two bureaus, and went to the sliding glass door that opened on a small private patio surrounded on three sides by a head-high cinder-block wall. The patio was furnished with a low white plastic table and two matching chairs. The chairs, Bernhardt saw, were identical to the two chairs on DuBois's deck.

In the hallway, both Paula and Tate were going toward the living room, Tate carrying the gun case. Bernhardt quickened his pace, came up behind Paula, patted her bottom. She gave him a quick, bright, over-the-shoulder smile. How would she feel, Bernhardt wondered, making love tonight with Tate sleeping just down the hallway?

"Well," Tate admitted, pushing his plate away and signaling the waitress for a second bottle of beer. "For a greasy-spoon Mexican restaurant, those were pretty good tacos."

"You must've liked them," Bernhardt said. "You ate four."

"I want to try my folks again." Paula slid out of the red Naugahyde booth.

"Do you want coffee?" Bernhardt asked.

"No, thanks." She walked to the rear of the restaurant, where a pay phone hung on the wall. Bernhardt saw her dial, then saw her smile as she began to talk. Good; she'd connected with her parents. He'd always known that Paula was especially fond of her parents, especially proud of them. Just as, for as long as she'd lived, he'd been especially proud of his mother. Was it because they were both only children, the entire focus of their parents' love?

"I've been thinking. You sure we want to get involved with dogs?" Tate asked.

Bernhardt shrugged. "Why not?"

"How do we know they'll get the game plan right? How do we know they won't tear the throat out of the wrong party? Me, for instance?"

"Because you're on Paula's side. Besides, Paula's going to ask whether she can bring them to stay with us tonight and tomorrow night. By Tuesday we'll all be buddies."

Tate shook his big, shaven head, doubtfully stroked his close-cropped, gray-flecked beard. "I don't know about this. I've never been real fond of dogs. They sense these things, you know."

"I thought you were touting a rottweiler yesterday."

"That was hypothetical. This is the real thing."

"Crusher thinks you're great."

"Crusher and I go way back. Besides, Crusher's an Airedale. I trust Airedales. I don't trust German shepherds."

"You don't know anything about dogs, C.B. You already admitted it. Don't worry. We'll get some meat. Steak. You can feed them. That's a very big deal with dogs. They like whoever feeds them. By Tuesday they'll be willing to die for you. Trust me."

"Hmmm."

Smiling, Paula was back at their booth, sliding in beside Bernhardt, her thigh warm against his. "It's all set. When we get back to the house, I'll take the van and pick them up. It'll take twenty minutes to Pasadena, and I'll have to spend an hour, at least, with my folks. But I think we should get the dogs as soon as possible, so we can all get acquainted."

Bernhardt nodded agreement. "I was saying the same thing to C.B. Be sure and bring some dog food, and steak. Lots of steak for C.B. and me to feed them." Then, after a moment's appraising silence, he asked, "Do you want me to come with you?"

She first looked apologetically at Tate, then seriously at Bernhardt. "I don't think this is the time for you to meet my folks. I think we should come down especially for you to meet them. It should be dinner, with a white tablecloth and the best silver. And then we should sleep in the guest room. That's what I think."

Conscious of the relief the words brought, a surge of appreciation, of gratitude, he nodded agreement. In Paula he'd found a winner, a class act. "I feel the same way. Exactly." He looked at Tate, whose bottle of beer was still half full. Reading the look, Tate said, "You want to go, I'm ready. How about if I ask the waitress where there's a supermarket. We should lay in some provisions, seems to me."

Bernhardt nodded agreement, and laid his credit card on the dinner check.

THIRTY-FIVE

"What we gotta do," Tate said, "is write it down. The whole thing, day by day, hour by hour. Which is why I bought these at the supermarket." He gestured to a Big Five tablet and two ballpoint pens arrayed on the dining room table.

Sitting across the table, Bernhardt nodded. "Good idea." He headed the first page *Monday*. "First thing, we've got to call Consolidated Insurance in New York, and make sure John Graham is who he says he is." He wrote *8 A.M., check out Graham.* "I want you to do that, C.B."

"Aw, man, that'll be an hour in a phone booth, at least. More like two hours. Plus, I might sound too Afro to those New York suits. How about Paula?"

Bernhardt shook his head firmly. "I've decided to take Paula out to DuBois's place. I'll tell DuBois I want to crate up the paintings, and I'll need Paula to—"

"What about me going with you, and Paula doing the phoning? If there's heavy lifting, I'd be better than—"

"There's no heavy lifting. Besides, you're too big and too black and too tough-looking. I don't want DuBois to feel intimidated." He wrote *8–12, talk to DuBois, crate pix.*

"I want to be finished by noon, so that people can come back into the house to take care of DuBois. Then, at twelve-thirty, we'll meet here." He wrote *12:30, home base.* "Hopefully, C.B., you'll've checked Graham out in New York. If he's okay, I'll call him by noon at the Hilton. That'll be three o'clock in New York. By that time, we'll know whether we've got a deal, whether Graham can get the money."

"If he can't get the money, all your work crating will be wasted."

"Not necessarily. Don't forget, DuBois has to get rid of those paintings before the grand jury meets on Wednesday. That's nonnegotiable."

"Ah . . ." Tate nodded thoughtfully. "Yeah, I see."

"Assuming that Graham gets the money, he'll have to have it converted into cash. That'll take time—an afternoon, at least. While he's doing that, we'll rent another car, a sedan. We'll go buy a shotgun and some shells and a hacksaw." He wrote *12–3, gun, car.*

"Will Graham have someone with him? A guard or two?"

"I'm not sure. Why? You want the job?"

"No, man. At this point, I'm not into changing anything. I'm just wondering, is all. I mean, all that money, it just isn't logical that he wouldn't have some backup."

"I don't expect him to tell me his game plan. He's interested in getting the paintings to a safe place in good shape. I'm interested in collecting the money, taking it to DuBois, and taking our cut. Then I want to get out of town as soon as possible."

"Okay." Tate pointed to the tablet. "So go on. What's next?"

"By, say, three o'clock tomorrow, five at the latest, it'll be either a go or a no-go for Tuesday. Assuming it's a go, then I'll probably go back to talk to DuBois and Grace Campbell and James one last time, make sure there's no loose ends. Then—"

A sudden metallic rumbling began, somewhere in the house. Tate's head jerked up, his whole body tensed, muscles taut.

"It's Paula," Bernhardt said. "The overhead door opener."

"Ah." Tate sank back in his chair, instantly relaxed, half smiling. The door mechanism growled again; moments later an interior door opened and closed.

"Hello," Paula called out to the accompaniment of toenails clicking on the hallway floor and restive canine whining. Then, flanked by the two German shepherds, one on either side, she stood framed in the kitchen. "This is Duke," she said, ruffling the dog's neck and ears. The dog moved appreciatively closer to her—but kept his eyes fixed on Tate.

"And this is Duchess." She stooped, grasped the smaller dog behind the front legs, and hoisted the animal up to stand on its rear legs. "They're brother and sister."

"What about meat?" Tate asked. "Did you bring the meat?"

"I left it in the car." She dropped the female dog to all fours as she said, "Stand up, Alan." As he obeyed, she stepped close, gave him a big robust hug. Both dogs watched intently.

"Pat me on the tush," she ordered. "Not too hard. Medium hard."

Eyeing the dogs, he obeyed.

"Okay." All business, she pulled away. "Now pet them. First Duke. Otherwise he gets jealous. Maybe you should get down on your knees. Duke responds to that."

Moving slowly, Bernhardt sank to his knees, stared into the unblinking yellow eyes.

"Call him by name."

"Hi, Duke. I'm Alan. I hope we'll be great friends."

"Now pet him."

Gingerly Bernhardt touched the dog's ruff, just below the ear. The dog remained motionless, staring fixedly into his eyes. Still on his knees, digging into the thick brown fur with his fingers, he inched forward until his face was a little less than a foot from the dog's face.

"He likes that," Paula coached. "Keep going."

Now the dog began to softly whine. Then, suddenly, he leaned forward, licked Bernhardt's cheek and nose with a large, thick, rough tongue.

"*Excellent.*" Now Paula turned to Tate. "Okay, C.B. Your turn. You can pat me on the back, instead of the tush, gentleman that you are. Alan, you start petting Duchess."

As Bernhardt turned to the female, Tate said, "Listen, Paula, how about that steak first? You know my ancestors were slaves, and sometimes they'd get a notion to run away. So the massa, he hunted them down with dogs. So there's an imprint on dogs' genes and black folks' genes that—"

"Oh, come on, C.B. That's bullshit and you know it. Genetic imprints are eye color. They're—"

"That's not true. They're just discovering that, over a few generations, learned behavior can be inherited. I read it in the *New York Times* just a couple of—"

"Listen, you two." Bernhardt gave Duchess a final pat on the head, then rose to his feet. "Genetics can wait." He pointed to an empty chair at the table, then pointed to the Big Five tablet. "Sit down, Paula. Let the dogs check out the house while we go over the plan. We're doing a timetable, and we're already to tomorrow evening."

"But it'll just take a few minutes for C.B. to—"

"It's after ten," Bernhardt said firmly. "The schedule's more important than petting the dogs. Besides, I want your input, run everything by you, see what you think."

As he'd known it would, the last argument prevailed. Most of all, Paula wanted in on the action.

* * *

"So," Bernhardt said, speaking to Paula as he pointed to the tablet. "What d'you think?"

"As I understand it," she said thoughtfully, "whenever DuBois visits his secret collection, everybody—*everybody*—has to be out of the house. Even the trusted secretary and the chief of security and the indispensable nurse. It's routine."

Bernhardt nodded. "Right."

"And yet he made an exception in your case."

"He didn't have a choice. I thought I already explained that."

"You did explain. And I realize he didn't have a choice. But what makes you think he'll let me inside?"

"The same reason he's letting me inside. He doesn't have a choice. A couple of those paintings are big, three by four feet, at least. I'll need help just taking them down from the wall, not to mention taking them down to the workshop and crating them and hauling them back to the gallery."

"Is that where they'll be Monday? In the gallery?"

"Yes."

"What're the odds," Tate asked, "that the people who work for DuBois—the secretary, for instance—know all about the secret gallery?"

"The odds're very good. But knowing is one thing; acting on the knowledge, doing damage to the master, that's something else. Think back to the old English families, with their faithful retainers. Belowstairs, all they talked about was who the master was screwing, or how many plates the mistress threw at the master. But that's belowstairs. They'd never think of repeating the gossip outside the manor house."

"That's merry old England," Tate said. "We're talking the Hollywood Hills, USA."

"Let's get back to the plan." Bernhardt tapped the tablet.

"It's Monday evening. We've got the van, we've got the Taurus I rented. We've got the shotgun, and we've sawed off the barrel and the stock. New York says Graham is everything he says he is. I've talked to Graham at the Hilton, and he's sure he'll have the money by Tuesday morning. Meanwhile, C.B. and the dogs have become fast friends."

As Tate grimaced, Bernhardt wrote *6 P.M. everything set.* Then he wrote *Tuesday* on a fresh sheet of paper. "So now it's Tuesday morning. First thing, I go to a pay phone and call Grace, who'll put me through to James. I'll tell James that we'll be picking up the paintings sometime in the next few hours. Then I'll call Graham, and confirm that he's got the money." He wrote *Call Grace, James, Graham, et al.* "We'll take the van and the Taurus, and we'll go to DuBois's place. Paula and I'll be in the van. C.B., you'll be driving the Taurus. James will open the gate for us, and both cars will enter the compound. James will open the garage, which will be empty. We'll drive the van inside. C.B., you'll stay outside in the Taurus, on guard. You'll park the Taurus so it blocks the driveway to the garage. James will close the garage door, with Paula and me inside. Paula will wait in the van, inside the garage, while I enter the house through an inner service door." He looked inquiringly at Paula, who nodded to signify that, so far, the logistics seemed reasonable.

"I'll check in with Grace, and tell her to get everyone out of the house, including herself. When that's done, I'll let Paula into the main house." He looked at her and smiled. As he did, the two dogs entered the dining room and began meticulously sniffing him. He put out his hand, which the male dog perfunctorily sniffed, then ignored. Turning to Tate, the male repeated the ritual while the female began sniffing Bernhardt.

"Put out your hand, C.B.," Paula urged. "Like Alan did."

Warily Tate obliged. Just as warily the dog sniffed—and sniffed. Then, finally satisfied, Duke rounded the table and lay down beside Paula. "Ah." Pleased, she smiled broadly. "Good. I think he likes you."

"Think?" Tate asked dubiously. "Is that the best you can do? Think?"

Declining the gambit, she turned to Bernhardt. "So it's Tuesday morning, and we're inside the mansion, alone with DuBois. So then what?"

"We take the crated-up pictures up to the first level from the fourth level down, and we put them in the van. You'll stay with the paintings, Paula, while I get Grace Campbell back inside the house. Monica Gross, too. She's the nurse. Then I'll contact James. At that point I'll give him the plan." He wrote: *Noon, caravan ready.* "What'll happen, C.B.'ll move the Taurus out of the driveway, and James will open the garage door with his opener. I'll back the van out onto the turnaround in front of the house. You'll get out of the van, Paula, and trade places with C.B., who'll get out of the Taurus and get into the van. At that point, we're ready. Paula, you'll go first, in the Taurus. Obviously, you'll keep us in sight, in the mirror. If there's any trouble, anyone tries to hijack us, they'll probably try to block our way in front, then come up on us from the rear." He broke off, looked full at Paula. "That'll be up to you, if someone tries to block us."

She blinked, then gravely nodded. She didn't return his smile. Neither did she flinch, ask for clarification. For months, ever since she'd pestered him until he'd finally taken her into the business, she'd been pressing him for more responsibility. Therefore, Bernhardt allowed himself a moment's secret amusement as he still held her gaze. Now he saw her smile. Signifying that, yes, she knew exactly what he was thinking.

He turned to Tate. "We'll stow the shotgun in the van

when we leave here, so we'll have it when we start out. I'll tell James to bring up the rear. He'll have at least one handgun, and I'll ask him to bring his Uzi."

"Ah." Tate nodded. "Good. That was my next question. Firepower."

"Paula has a handgun, I have my three-fifty-seven, you'll have your two nine-millimeters plus the shotgun. All that plus whatever James brings. We should be all right."

"For what's involved, the amount of money those paintings represent, Christ, someone could hire a half-track."

"That's assuming the paintings're genuine," Bernhardt answered. "If they're fakes, the whole collection is probably worth ten thousand dollars."

"Hmmm." As he spoke, Tate looked at Duke. The dog yawned. Then, looking up at Tate, he licked his chops.

"So we're in the cars," Paula said, "and we drive here, no problem. Then what?"

"Then we drive the van into the garage, and leave the Taurus and James's car in the driveway. I leave you and C.B. inside the garage. I take the Taurus, and I go to a pay phone. I call Graham, and tell him we're ready. Only then will he have this address. He'll get his own van, or whatever, and he'll drive here, probably with a guard or two."

"What about James?" Tate asked. "Does he stay outside, parked in the driveway?"

Bernhardt nodded. "That's what I'll tell him to do. But I don't see myself giving orders to James."

"Why's that?"

"For one thing, he'll certainly be representing DuBois. Also, he's very, very tough."

"Maybe he'll take orders from me." Tate spoke with a certain stillness, a quiet anticipation. This part—the possibility of confrontation—would be Tate's call.

"When Graham arrives," Bernhardt said, "We'll move

one of our cars, and let Graham drive inside the garage. Then we'll block the drive again. He'll want to look at two of the paintings, his choice. While I'm uncrating them, the two of you will check out the money. I have no idea how much twenty million in cash weighs, but it's probably hundreds of pounds."

"What about Duke and Duchess?" Paula asked.

Bernhardt smiled. "That's up to you. You're our canine commander."

"We probably should leave them here in the house while we make the trip to DuBois."

"Fine."

"So let's say everything's done," Tate said. "You're satisfied, and so is Graham. So then what?"

"We let Graham go first, get him out of the way. Then we load the money in the van, and we caravan back to DuBois, the same sequence as before. Except that I think we should take the dogs in the van with us."

Tate cleared his throat, looked down at Duke. "You and me and the dogs and the money? Is that it?"

"That's it," Bernhardt answered.

"Hmmm."

"We deliver the money, and we take our cut. And that's all. We're out of there." Bernhardt spread his hands reassuringly. "We come back here, close up the house. We take back the dogs and return the two cars. Or maybe we keep the sedan. We drive back to San Francisco, instead of flying, if it means checking our two million dollars."

"Jesus . . ." In wonderment, Tate shook his head. "I have to tell you, I get goose bumps when you talk like that."

"Like what?"

"Like it's just part of the day's work, hauling that much money around. I mean—two *million?*"

At the sharp exclamation, both dogs snapped to avid attention.

"C.B.—" Paula took a small sack of dog biscuits from her shoulder satchel. "Here." She handed over the sack. "Give them each a dog biscuit."

"What about steak?" he asked, looking down dubiously at the dogs. "Wouldn't that make more of a statement?"

"Biscuits are for training," she answered. "Steak is for rewards, after they've learned who's boss."

"I think," Tate answered ruefully, "that they already know who's boss. Them."

"C.B." Sternly, she pointed again. "Now. Do it."

THIRTY-SIX

"There." She dropped the bundle of hundred-dollar bills on the coffee table. "Ten thousand, to demonstrate good faith. And ten thousand more, win or lose, Tuesday night. If we win, your end should be a hundred thousand, depending on how it goes, which way they jump, Tuesday."

Smiling slightly, Harry set his highball aside, scooped up the bills, squared off the stack, divided it, slipped the money into his trouser pockets. He decided not to thank her.

"Between now and Tuesday," she said, "we've got to find out where Bernhardt and his crew went after he checked out of the Prado. Graham, I'm assuming, will stay at the Hilton until the deal comes down. Out at the DuBois place, so far, there're no surprises. But we've got to find Bernhardt. And the only way is to keep track of Graham. It's almost a certainty that they've got to meet again, make their arrangements. When that happens, we'll tail Bernhardt. Or the woman. Or the black man."

"You missed your chance today, Andrea. They were all at the Hilton. You should've followed Bernhardt after he talked to Graham."

"I had to choose, and I wanted to keep track of Graham, see who he contacts. The money that's involved, he's got to have help."

"He's got a woman with him."

She shrugged, then said, "As long as that beeper on Graham's car keeps working, we'll work it out."

Harry went to the sideboard, replenished his drink. Then, mockingly playful: "Why do I get the feeling there's something you aren't telling me, Andrea?"

"Because, Harry, there *are* things I'm not telling you. That's because I'm the employer, and you're an employee."

"Big deal," he muttered. "Big fucking deal."

"You're drinking too much, Harry. Much too much."

He decided to burp. Noisily.

THIRTY-SEVEN

As Bernhardt flipped the van's turn signal he checked the mirror to verify that Paula in the rented Taurus was close behind. He drove the van across the broad concrete apron of the Shell station and drew to a stop beside the two phone booths as Tate said, "What we should've done is stayed at the Prado and *visited* the house, to set things up. That way, we'd have a communications base. I mean, shit, a *phone* booth, when I'm trying to deal with some goddam bureaucrats in New York? A *gas* station?"

"Jesus, C.B., give it a rest, will you?" Bernhardt switched off the van's engine. "So I made a mistake—maybe. Suppose someone's following us, trying to set us up? If we had a phone in the house, they might be able to trace us through the phone company. As for the Prado, hotels are like fishbowls."

"Hotels also have security."

Aggrieved, Bernhardt sighed, swung his driver's door open as he asked, "Have you got my calling card number?"

"I've got it memorized." Still registering displeasure, Tate's broad brown face was impassive.

"It's already eleven o'clock, you know, in New York. See if you can get something by noon, our time. We've got to know about Graham before we commit ourselves. He could be a con man, for all we know. All the data I've got on him is a business card."

"Hmmm."

"Come on, C.B. Let's *do* it." Bernhardt got out of the van, went to one of the phone booths, and put his notebook on the booth's tiny shelf. As he touch-toned Grace Campbell's number, he saw Paula handing over the Taurus keys to Tate. As, yes, Tate was smiling, affably nodding. Between Paula and Tate, there had always been a special understanding.

"This is it." Bernhardt swung the van into the short driveway that led to the massive iron gates.

"I have to admit," Paula said, "that I've got butterflies. To actually see someone, talk to someone, who's so rich and so powerful and so famous, it's—" She shook her head. "It's awesome. For as long as I can remember, I've known about Raymond DuBois. He's an institution."

"He's also pitiful," Bernhardt said. "A husk. He can move his right arm from the elbow, but beyond that he's helpless. And lonely, too—he's utterly alone, except for the people he pays to take care of him."

"Ah . . ." It was a soft, compassionate response. "All that money, and no one to give it to." She looked at him, then said softly, "Everyone needs someone."

He returned the look—and said nothing in return. This wasn't the time, or the place. As if on cue, he saw James walking toward them on the other side of the gate. The bodyguard wore pressed blue trousers, black loafers, and a white shirt and tie. A beeper and tiny surveillance radio were clipped to his belt. Add a loose-fitting blue blazer worn over a nine-millimeter slung in a shoulder holster, and James would be ready to go to work.

"I want you to stay with James," Bernhardt said, speaking rapidly. "In his car, his bungalow, wherever. I'll talk to DuBois, probably just for a few minutes. Then he'll tell

Grace to clear out the house. I'll let you in the house. You and I'll talk to DuBois. Then, hopefully, he'll let us start crating up the pictures. Got it?"

"Got it."

"So." He smiled, delicately caressed her cheek, "So here we go. Ready or not."

As, slowly, the gates began to swing open.

"You and Paula Brett," DuBois said. "Are you lovers, as well as partners? Is that what I perceive?"

"Yes, sir, that's correct."

"Are you also in love? Really in love?"

"Yes, sir, we are."

On DuBois's deck once again, they had taken their previous positions: DuBois in his mechanical chair, positioned to face the west, Bernhardt sitting beside him, both of them overlooking the fog-shrouded ocean.

"It is, of course, the ultimate cliché," DuBois said, "but I would trade everything for someone I could love."

"Yes . . . I know."

"*Do* you know, Mr. Bernhardt? Do you really know?"

"My father died in World War Two. When I was in my early twenties, my mother died of cancer. That same year, my grandparents died in a single-car accident, probably because my grandfather had a heart attack. Then my wife—her name was Jennie—she was killed during a mugging. She was twenty-three."

"Children?"

Bernhardt shook his head. "No children."

"So now you have Paula."

"Yes. Now I have Paula." He resolved to say no more, reveal no more of himself. He had, after all, come on business. Potentially larcenous business.

Murderous business?

As if he were reading Bernhardt's thoughts, DuBois spoke quietly, concisely: "When will you hear from Graham?"

"Noon, our time, at the earliest."

"If he offers twenty million, that will do."

"I understand."

"Do you agree? Your percentage will remain unchanged."

"Yes," Bernhardt answered, "I agree."

"No less than twenty million, though. If we must, we'll make other arrangements."

"I think you're right. But what other arrangements can we make, on short notice?"

"I have instructed Powers to arrange for a secure warehouse. You and your crew can remain with the paintings, in the warehouse, until we make other arrangements. Is that satisfactory?"

"I suppose, if negotiations break down, we won't have a choice."

"You agree, then."

"Yes."

"Good." DuBois bobbed his pale, narrow, bony head. "And now, you may tell Grace to clear the house. Then Paula can come in."

"Shall I bring her here? To you?"

"Of course, to me."

He touched a button on the arm, felt the chair pivot until he was facing the glass doors leading into the study. He released the button, glanced at the clock built into the chair's left arm. Time, eight-twenty A.M. In Japan the Nikeí had closed, off four hundred points. In London, shares were fractionally higher. Gold was marginally higher, silver unchanged. In New York, the Dow was holding steady; trading was brisk. In three days' time, the Saudis would announce a three-percent production restriction, yet another attempt to solidify oil prices.

And in London, at Sotheby's, his agents were authorized to offer no more than two million for an early Utrillo street scene, untitled.

While, in Benedict Canyon, he waited.

"The kindness of strangers" was the line from *A Streetcar Named Desire.*

Blanche DuBois, his namesake, that pitiful figure who'd lost control of her life.

Just as he, too, had lost control of his life. At seventy-eight, with eternity beckoning, the institution known as Raymond DuBois must depend on the kindness of strangers.

Put love aside. Put children aside. Acknowledge the loss, acknowledge the yearning. Then affirm, again and yet again, that autonomy was the fountainhead of his transcendent power. Because he was so exquisitely attuned to every financial nuance, his perception as delicate as a spider tending its web, and because he could react instantly, without consultation, therefore without delay, he existed at a level unimagined by lesser men. Let the mark drop a pfennig, and he could make millions in less than an hour. Or, if his timing were faulty, he could lose millions. If he chose to destroy an enemy, one phone call sufficed. Dial the phone again, and a friend was rewarded, set for life.

Friend?

No, not friend. There were only trusted associates, a few of them. Satraps, really, most of them. Petitioners. Inferiors.

Yet he called them friends. It was essential that he call them friends. How else could he reward them? Servants—croupiers—maître d's, one tipped. But friends, perforce, were equals. Therefore CEOs. Or divas, bought and paid for.

Or artists who acknowledged their fealty to him, and who were therefore made whole, emergent, finally famous.

And then, in seconds, had come the fall. In the brain that *Fortune* had once called a center of financial power unto itself, a blood vessel had burst. Leaving him with his fortune still intact, multiplying hourly, compounding exponentially—

—but leaving him the helpless hostage to his one mistake from which there was no salvation: the sin of pride, of arrogance.

When it became necessary, without a second thought, he'd often operated beyond the law, above the law. Three times he'd ordered assassinations, one of them a minister of trade. Therefore, almost on a whim, knowing full well that it had been stolen, he'd acquired *Seascape at Trouville.* He'd been sixty years old. Experience had immunized him to most temptations. But, from the very beginning, contemplating *Seascape at Trouville,* he'd been aware of the age-old lure of forbidden pleasures. Alone with *Seascape At Trouville,* he somehow felt himself in touch with the essence of himself. Finally he'd found a possession that fully engaged him, confirmed his own true power, his own transcendent mastery. And, with each surreptitious acquisition of stolen art, the fatal attraction had taken a stronger hold on whatever wayward tendril of his psyche had somehow escaped the domination of his rigid self-discipline. In his seventh decade, he'd been hooked. The concealed chamber was the logical result of the fixation—and ultimately his undoing. The concealed chamber, the symbol of his addiction, had—

In the doorway a small, trim, dark-haired woman materialized, and behind her Alan Bernhardt. With an effort DuBois nodded, at the same time willing the unparalyzed half of his face to lift in a smile of welcome.

"Come, sit beside me," he said. Then, lifting his right

arm in a gesture to Bernhardt: "You may wait in Grace's office."

Bernhardt nodded, smiled, turned away. DuBois watched the woman as she came toward him across the deck. Ready for work, she was dressed in blue jeans, a light poplin jacket, white running shoes, and a plaid madras blouse under the jacket. Her dark eyes moved calmly, perceptively; her stride was confident and controlled, her manner composed. Her smile was cordial, neither too sympathetic to his plight nor too aloof, uncaring.

He raised his arm again, gesturing her to a deck chair as he maneuvered his motorized chair to face her.

"Miss Brett."

"Mr. DuBois." Like her manner, the modulation of her voice suggested both intelligence and a certain gravity, an inherent reserve.

"You know about the concealed room, and the paintings."

She answered without hesitation: "Yes, sir, I do."

"Mr. Bernhardt trusts you, then."

"Yes, sir, he does."

"You're—what—in your middle thirties?"

Her smile widened; amusement warmed the depths of her dark eyes. "I'm thirty-four."

"You and Alan—you're in love."

"Yes, sir." She spoke gravely, without smiling, sans coquetry.

"You're a fortunate woman, I think. And Alan is a very fortunate man."

"Thank you." She inclined her head, a measured acknowledgment.

"You and Alan—you both went to college."

This time she'd been caught by surprise. Her quick, spontaneous rejoinder was quizzical: "Yes, we did."

"I did not graduate from high school. My parents were poor, and my mother was always frail. When I was sixteen, I went to work. I carried messages on Wall Street."

"I know that."

For a long moment he regarded her in silence. Then: "In a very real sense, I'm trusting you and Alan with everything of my life that matters. You understand that, I think."

"Yes, sir, I do."

"If things go wrong tomorrow, I would be ruined. Not ruined financially. Money has nothing to do with this. But ruined spiritually. Do you understand that?"

"It's your place in history—your good name."

"My good name, yes . . ." As he said it, he experienced a sudden sag of fatigue. His reserves were ebbing, running low. He must keep in reserve the strength to take them to the paintings, let them into the concealed chamber—

—and let the final act begin. "The Divestment" was the phrase he'd chosen. Himself divested from himself, signifying that at last, death must be all that remained.

Following behind the frail old man in his high-tech wheelchair, Bernhardt touched Paula's shoulder, signaling that they should fall back until DuBois had punched the four numbers that opened the sliding steel door. As she slowed her steps she moved close, whispering, "I'm getting butterflies again."

He smiled, said nothing.

Fifteen feet down the narrow, unadorned corridor, DuBois was maneuvering the mechanized chair so that he could reach the control panel with his good right hand.

"My God," Paula breathed, "look at him, that poor old man."

Amused, Bernhardt whispered, "Poor?"

With a soft whir, the door slid open to reveal the short,

windowless second corridor. DuBois touched a button, propelled his chair into the second corridor.

"Come on." Bernhardt stepped forward, followed closely by Paula. Once inside the second corridor, the first door slid closed behind them. As Bernhardt watched DuBois maneuver to reach the second control panel, he felt Paula's fingers tighten on his forearm. Whenever they went to a scary movie, she would always grasp him like this. For all her measured intelligence, Paula was deeply impressionable.

The second door slid open. As if he were alone, DuBois repositioned his chair, moved slowly into the gallery. The only sound was the quiet whir of the mechanized wheelchair. With Paula following a hesitant half-step behind, moving as if he were part of a solemn ritual, Bernhardt entered the gallery. He felt Paula close behind him. For a moment the three of them remained motionless, transfixed.

"My God," Paula whispered. "Oh, my God."

"That's it." Bernhardt laid the hammer aside, checked the time. Almost noon. For more than four hours, he'd been out of touch with Tate and Graham.

Paula drew the back of her hand across her forehead, stevedore style. Then she pointed to the three ceramic pieces, still uncrated. "What about those?"

"When I went upstairs with DuBois and put him into bed, he said he wanted to keep the ceramic pieces."

They were in the fifth-level workshop. Paula was standing beside a band saw, one hand resting on the saw's cast-iron table. She was visibly tired. Her face was smudged, and her hair was in casual, finger-combed disarray. It had been five hours, at least, since they'd had an Egg McMuffin and coffee.

"Are the ceramics stolen?" Paula asked.

Bernhardt shrugged. "Probably. But they aren't nearly as valuable as the paintings. Plus, they aren't part of the deal. Graham's just interested in the paintings."

"But if DuBois is afraid of the grand jury . . ."

Impatiently he shook his head. "I don't know what he's thinking. And it's not our concern once we get our money.

"God . . ." Once more she pushed back a lock of her dark hair, stroked her forehead again. "God, San Francisco suddenly sounds great."

"I know."

THIRTY-EIGHT

"Is it your understanding," Bernhardt asked, "that between now and tomorrow, whenever the exchange takes place, you're to take orders from me? Are those your instructions from Mr. DuBois?"

"Yes, sir, they are." As always, James spoke slowly, in measured cadence. "Anything you want, I'm to do."

"Without checking with Mr. DuBois?"

"That's correct, sir." James carefully guided their car into the Saturday afternoon traffic flow. In less than ten minutes they would arrive at the Prado. Sitting beside the driver, Bernhardt produced a notebook and pen. "Give me your phone," he ordered. When the other man had recited the numbers, Bernhardt said, "I've got to make a few calls after you drop us at the hotel, then I'll call you this afternoon or evening, with instructions. Will you be home?"

As if he were surprised, James glanced at Bernhardt. The possibility that the trusted bodyguard would not be on constant call was plainly unprecedented.

"Yes, sir, I'll be home. Or if I'm out doing errands, the call goes to my pager."

"Ah." Impressed, Bernhardt nodded. "Good."

"Will you need to be picked up at the Prado tomorrow?"

"No. We have two cars—a van and a sedan."

They drove for a time in silence. Then Bernhardt asked, "How old is Mr. DuBois?"

"He's seventy-eight. Almost seventy-nine."

"Do you feel sorry for him?"

Puzzled, James frowned thoughtfully before he said, "Mr. DuBois is not someone to feel sorry for. He's too— too—" His voice faded to silence as he struggled vainly to complete the thought. Then, with obvious relief, he drove the car to the inside lane, signaled for the turn into the Prado's entrance. Paula was following them in the van. When James was out of sight, Bernhardt would get into the van, and they would drive to the house they'd rented.

Paula used her key to open the front door. Instantly, squirming with delight, barking wildly, the two shepherds were whirling frantically around her, jumping so high that their paws reached shoulder height, yet never quite touching her. Finally, with Bernhardt on the porch and Tate looming in the open door, she broke off. Speaking authoritatively, in an unnaturally deep voice: "Okay! That's all."

Whereupon the dogs checked to make sure she meant what she said, then began sniffing Bernhardt, wagging their tails. He knelt, scratching each of them with both hands until he heard Tate say, "Now that we're all reunited at— what—one o'clock in the afternoon of the day before we all get rich, maybe you guys might be interested in a little late-breaking news."

Bernhardt gave each dog a final pat, straightened, followed Tate and Paula into the living room. Close on Paula's heels, the two dogs followed.

"So?" Bernhardt sat on one end of the brown plastic sleeper sofa. Paula took the other end as the two dogs settled themselves at her feet.

"First of all," Tate said, "I'll warn you that your phone bill'll probably be a record breaker. Also, I intend to put in a six-dollar chit for Gatorade. That's because I was getting dehydrated, baking in that gas station phone booth."

"Why didn't you find a booth in the shade?"

"Because," Tate shot back, "when I made the first call to Consolidated at approximately ten minutes after eight, the ocean fog was still in. It was quite pleasant in the booth. So I made the mistake of giving one of the people at Consolidated the number of the goddam booth, to call me back. So I was stuck. Oh, how I was stuck. Especially was I stuck when people kept showing up to use the phone, and I had to pretend I was talking, to hang on to the phone. That's including three wiseass teenage punks who made some pretty nasty remarks concerning my racial heritage. So, after I decked the biggest one, which is always the best strategy, and they dispersed, I decided it'd be a good idea to give the station manager a couple of twenties. Which was fine, except that he went off duty at ten o'clock. Which'll explain why there's eighty dollars on the chit for bribes. Plus the Gatorade."

"Jesus, C.B., never mind about teenagers. What about Consolidated? What about Graham?"

Seated in a plastic armchair that matched the couch, Tate flung a muscular leg over the arm as he said, "You want the play-by-play, or would you rather cut right to my opinion?"

"How about a condensed play-by-play? In New York it's already four-thirty."

"Yeah, well, moving on from my adventures in the phone booth, I started out with Graham's business card, as you'd imagine. And I got 'This is Mr. Graham's office,' from a lady sounded like she just graduated from Vassar. I identified myself, said I worked for you, and said I'd lost contact with Graham, but that I knew he was in Los Angeles, and could she give me a local number. Well, the first thing she did, naturally, was put me on hold for about ten minutes. Then a guy named Forster came on the line. He obviously was a Yale man, maybe even Harvard. Anyhow, he started pumping me. What was I doing with Graham? When was the last time I'd seen him? When did I expect to see him again?''

''In other words,'' Paula said, ''you guys were pumping each other.''

Tate nodded his shaven bullet head. ''Exactly.''

''So?'' Bernhardt urged.

''So the more I talked to Forster, the more obvious it became that he had absolutely no idea where to find Graham. It also became obvious that they badly want to find him.''

''All this,'' Paula said, ''during the exact time Graham was supposedly in contact with *them*, getting the money wired into his account out here.''

''Except,'' Bernhardt said, ''that Graham has always operated pretty autonomously. He reports directly to the head man at Consolidated. And Forster doesn't sound like the head man.''

''No argument,'' Tate answered. ''But then another guy came on the line, and he sounded like he could've been the head man, or very close to it. His name was Blair. So he and I danced each other around for a while—that's after they'd had me on hold for another twenty minutes—and finally Blair says he's going to level with me. He says that, a couple of weeks ago, Graham announced that he had a big deal simmering, and that he'd be going undercover for a while, all that hush-hush shit. So Blair says fine, good luck. That was two weeks ago, like I said. So then, a week later, Graham's confidential secretary drops out of sight. Without telling anyone, apparently. She just didn't show up at her desk one morning. Her name is Helen Grant."

"The first time I talked to Graham," Bernhardt said, "he told me about his glamorous secretary, implied she was his mistress. But I didn't take it seriously."

For a long, thoughtful moment no one spoke. Finally Bernhardt asked, "So how'd you leave it with Blair?"

"He gave me the number of his private line," Tate said. "He told me to tell you to keep in touch. He implied that maybe we could do each other some good. Moneywise."

"Did you mention the paintings?"

"Not in so many words. But it was one of those, you know, peekaboo conversations. Like, we each knew what we were talking about, but neither one of us wanted to put words to it, say it out loud."

"Hmmm."

Another moment of silence settled upon them as, reflectively, Paula scratched Duke's ears. The dog whined appreciatively as Duchess whined in protest. Then, suddenly, Bernhardt stood up, spoke urgently to Tate: "Give me Blair's private number. Maybe I can still catch him at the office."

"Do I understand," Blair said, "that you're in more or less constant contact with John Graham?"

"When we finish talking," Bernhardt answered, "I'm going to call him at his hotel."

"Will you please describe John Graham for me?"

"He's about forty-five, about a hundred seventy-five pounds. Light brown hair. Stylish dresser, but not flashy. He talks like an Ivy Leaguer, and acts like one, too. Divorced. Says he's screwing his secretary, whose name is Helen Grant. A good-looking, quick-thinking man, obviously intelligent. He wears designer glasses, gold-framed, aviator style."

"Yes, that's John. You're very good at descriptions, Mr. Bernhardt."

"Thank you," he answered dryly.

"I would like you to give me the name of his hotel."

Bernhardt sighed, glanced at his watch. For more than a half hour, on his calling card, they'd been fencing, probing, maneuvering for advantage. Fruitlessly.

"Do I understand," Bernhardt said, "that you haven't been in contact with Graham for about two weeks?"

"That's true."

"But that's not unusual, for him to drop out of sight. He could, in fact, be working on something big. Correct?"

"Yes . . ." It was a reluctant admission.

"Could it be," Bernhardt said, "that, in fact, Graham could have gotten ten or twenty million dollars together and had it wired to him in Los Angeles without your knowledge?"

"That," Blair said stiffly, "would be very unlikely."

"But it could happen. It's possible," he pressed.

"Yes," Blair admitted reluctantly. "It could happen."

"You're—what—a vice president?"

"I fail to see what—"

"Answer the question, Mr. Blair. I've been very forthcoming. Now it's your turn. What's your position with Consolidated?"

"Assistant vice president," Blair admitted.

"And how many vice presidents are there?"

"Four."

Bernhardt let a long moment pass before he said, "I've got to hang up now, and try to contact Graham."

"If you won't give me Graham's hotel, won't you at least

tell me how to contact you?" With the question, Blair's manner had turned discreetly plaintive.

"I'm sorry. I've rented a house. And there's no phone. I'm calling from a pay phone."

"A pay phone? Really?"

"Really."

THIRTY-NINE

The efficacy of clichés had always intrigued him. Birds of a feather *did* flock together. The early bird *did* get the worm.

And then there was *From the first moment I saw her.*

She'd stood in the open doorway of his office, one hand on the knob. She'd been wearing basic black: a sheath dress with a small white collar, white buttons down the front, a single strand of pearls, black pumps. Her smile had been just right: cordial but not flirtatious. Her dark, glossy hair fell to her shoulders. Her quick brown eyes had been wonderfully alive, even then sensitive to his every nuance. She'd been the third applicant Personnel had sent in less than a week.

Helen Grant . . .

She was twenty-three when she came to work. Her twenty-three to his forty-three—for them the numbers had been a perfect fit. He'd just been divorced, and was trying to fit the fragments of his life back together. She'd been looking for excitement, the kind of excitement money could buy. She'd never denied it, never equivocated. She wanted clothes and jewels and cars. But, most of all, Helen wanted excitement. She'd just broken off her first serious, live-in relationship, a passionate affair with an abstract expressionist painter who worked on "the high steel."

The high steel . . .

The phrase had become a constant goad. Women, he

knew, were often jealous of past lovers. But he'd never thought it could happen to him. Not until he fell in love with Helen.

Three weeks after she'd begun working for him, they made love. It had been meticulously scripted, perfectly executed. He'd explained that his most sensitive work was, in fact, conducted outside the office. Bars, hotel rooms, street corners, the rear seats of limos, the cabins of Lear jets, these were his venue. "The glitzy surface of the dark underside," he'd said, watching her eyes come alive. Then, reeling in the line, he'd apologized for being unable to say more—not until he knew he could trust her completely.

And so, that Tuesday night, she'd come to his apartment. She was there, he'd said, to witness a conversation that could involve a fortune in stolen art. At midnight, after sharing a bottle of chardonnay, pretending frustration, he'd announced that something had gone wrong. He was sorry, but that was the game he played—the high-stakes game with no rules, no limits. Remembering that night, critiquing his own performance, he'd realized that, yes, everything he'd said had been perfectly calculated to turn Helen on.

At the door of his apartment, he'd helped her with her coat—and then he'd kissed her. Minutes later they were in bed, making wild, wonderful love.

Wonderful until, in the afterglow, she'd told him about William, whose outsize paintings, she'd said, were primitive but powerful. And his body, she said, had been incredibly muscular. *My high-steel man*, she'd said. And then she'd begun to sob. William had been so exciting, she'd burbled, so wonderfully impetuous, so unpredictable. Graham held her naked body close, comforting her. And then they'd made love again. Afterwards, he'd whispered that, if she wanted excitement, then she was in bed with the right man.

Bringing him, incredibly, to this place, at this time,

shacked up in a suite on the top floor of the Hilton with a woman whose touch was like fire, whose eyes were like—

The phone rang. Quickly Graham crossed to the imitation French Provincial desk, a reasonably good copy. Across the living room, Helen closed a fashion magazine on her finger, smiled at him as he answered the phone on the second ring.

"It's Alan Bernhardt, John. Can you talk?"

"Yes. No problem." He turned the hotel notepad to a fresh sheet, sat down at the desk, pen poised.

"Are you ready? The money—is everything ready?"

"It's in my account," Graham answered. "I plan to leave it overnight, for safety's sake. Tomorrow morning, anytime after nine, I can get it. I'm told I have to allow an hour after I make the withdrawal request, if I want cash. Meaning that ten o'clock is the earliest I can be ready."

"I was hoping to be all finished by ten o'clock." Bernhardt's voice was peevish. Was it an attack of nerves? Graham speculated. A ploy, establishing who gave the orders, who took orders?

"Well, it can't be done," he answered. "Not unless I want to take the money to bed with me tonight. Which, definitely, I don't."

"What about security tomorrow?"

"No problem. I hired two guards from the best security service in Los Angeles. They'll meet me at the bank whenever I say. Ten o'clock, if that's what you and I decide."

"These guards—will they be in uniform?"

"If that's what I want. I haven't decided yet."

"Will they be armed?"

"Of course."

"Heavily armed?"

"Heavily enough. The way it'll work, they provide an armored van. So the transfer of money will be handled like a Brinks pickup and delivery. One man stays inside the van. He'll have an assault weapon. The other one, packing a revolver, will transfer the sacks of money from the bank to the van. And, of course, I'll be there. And I'll be armed." As he said it, his eyes met Helen's. She was on her feet now, and was standing with her whole body tightened. Her hands were clenched, rigid at her sides. Her lips were parted, her dark eyes smoldered. As if she were sexually aroused, her breathing had quickened. In this pose, her breasts were perfection.

"I've been talking to Forster," Bernhardt was saying. "And Blair, too."

"That's as high as you got?" Pleased, Graham smiled into the telephone. "Blair?"

Bernhardt made no reply.

"I knew, of course, that you'd be checking my back trail," Graham said. "But I'm not going to help you."

"Why not?"

"Company policy. The more people know about transactions like this, the greater the risk."

During the silence that followed, Graham smiled at Helen, beckoned for her to come to him, stand beside him, let him touch her. Obeying, her eyes now dusky with the languor of desire, she obeyed. Holding the phone with his left hand, he drew her close, dropped his right hand to the swell of her buttocks. With her head in the hollow of his shoulder, he felt her hands caressing him as he caressed her, both of them deeply aroused.

"Where can I reach you tomorrow?" Bernhardt was asking.

Pantomiming deep reluctance, first things first, Graham pulled away from the woman, smiled at her, stroked her buttocks one last time, then slid open the desk drawer, took out the sheet of plain paper that contained the numbers essential to the operation. He read off the number of the pay phone he'd selected. Adding to Bernhardt: "I'll be there as soon after ten o'clock as possible. I assume you plan to take the paintings to some place other than their present location."

"That's true."

"Is the place large enough to accommodate two vans— assuming you'll have a van?"

"Yes."

"How many people and vehicles will you have?"

"I'll have two sedans and a van. I'll probably have three people with me. Armed."

"Good," Graham answered cheerfully. "That'd be a precise balance of forces."

"You're sounding very—" Bernhardt hesitated, searching for the word. Finally: "Very upbeat."

"That's not surprising. I'm having the time of my life."

"Does that mean you've got your secretary with you?"

"Ah . . . you're a sly one, Alan. It's always a pleasure doing business with someone who has an active imagination."

"*Is* she with you?"

Graham dropped his voice to a more brittle register. "Let's not belabor the point, Alan. The money's come, and the arrangements are complete. Tomorrow at this time, the paintings'll be on their way to New York in a chartered airplane. You'll have a pocketful of money, and I'll be in line for a handsome bonus. End of the story."

"Why do I get the feeling there's more? A kicker."

"If I may say so," Graham answered, "that's a very common feeling in matters like this. You're doubtless unable to believe that all that money will really materialize. Not to worry, though. Twenty million is fine." As he spoke, Graham looked through the open bedroom door. Helen was sitting on the edge of the bed. She'd taken his revolver from the nightstand, and was fondling it, caressing it. Her dark eyes were musky.

"You're very smooth, John. Very persuasive."

"Thank you."

"I'll call you tomorrow, ten o'clock."

"If we miss connections, I'll come back here to the hotel. I'll wait for your call."

"Yes."

"Until tomorrow, then." Graham broke the connection. After smiling once more at Helen, erotic promises yet to be kept, he turned his back on her, consulted the list of telephone numbers. As he punched out the number he wanted he glanced at his watch. Almost three o'clock. So far, so good. On the fourth series of rings, the now-familiar voice came on the line:

"Yes?"

"Everything's set here. Are you ready?"

"I'm ready. Have you got the airplane? The clearances for customs? Are the pilots reliable? Did you check them out? Did you—"

"Don't worry about it. This is my business, remember."

"I know. But—"

"I'll pick up the package between nine and ten tomorrow, as we agreed. You probably should be there when I get it. But then, afterwards, you should go to your office, keep a very high profile."

"Yes, but—" Powers broke off. His voice had sunk to a low, cowed monotone.

"But you want to be there when I trade the package for the merchandise. Is that it?"

"Well, it's a simple matter of—of equity." Now Powers's voice rose peevishly. "I'm the one that's taking the risk, you know. I'm the one who—"

"If you want to tag along, fine. You should bear in mind, though, that our friend from San Francisco knows you. If he sees you, connects you with this, you're screwed."

"But I don't have any protection. I turn over the package to you, and you trade it for the merchandise, and an hour later you're in the air, out of the country. All I've got is your word that—"

"Listen, asshole. I don't have time to wipe your nose, so I'll lay it out for you. Right now, I've got at least three people waiting to buy some of that merchandise. A week after I arrive at an unnamed South American country I'll have raised two million dollars, minimum, for the least valuable piece of merchandise. As per our agreement, you'll get half that amount, which will be delivered to you by my own private courier." As he said it, Graham smiled at the designated courier: Helen, still sitting on the bed, fondling the revolver. "You will continue to get half as, over the space of perhaps two years, the items of merchandise are sold. If at any time you feel like you've been cheated, all you have to do is make a deal with the authorities. You'll be a hero."

No response; only the sound of irregular breathing.

"If I don't get the package from you tomorrow, as we've planned, then I'm out of it. I'll have hopped the fence," Graham said.

"I—I don't understand."

"I'll be back on the sunny side of the law, asshole. I'll be back in my corner office at Consolidated. And the first thing I'll do is blow the whistle on you." Graham hung up the phone, took a moment to regain his composure, then went into the bedroom. He took the revolver, put it in the drawer of the nightstand. Then, standing before her as she still sat on the edge of the bed, he put both hands on her shoulders, drew her close—and waited for the rush.

FORTY

Gently, delicately, Powers replaced the phone in its cradle, glanced at his watch: five minutes after four, Monday, the twelfth of April. Three more days until taxes were due. At the thought, he was aware that he was smiling slightly. Was it predictable, that, facing a crisis, the instinct was to find a verity and cling to it? *April fifteenth . . .* the time of reckoning, of secular atonement, the dread date graven into the consciousness of the affluent. And yet how comforting the April fifteenth preoccupation was now, something eternal to occupy the mind, blessed relief from the prospect of doom approaching.

It had begun on a Sunday, in itself unprecedented. They'd gone out on the deck adjoining DuBois's study, another departure from conventional protocol. Dubois had propelled himself to the railing where, in silence, he'd contemplated the view. The silence had stretched time unbearably, almost a physical pain. So that, when DuBois finally began to speak, whatever he said would have been a relief. In the months that followed, hardly an hour passed that he hadn't thought of that incredible conversation. Or, rather, DuBois's monologue. The monologue had been delivered in a dry, clogged voice, the result of a slight cold. The cold had been given the kind of medical oversight normally accorded a head of state.

The pronouncement had been a miracle of both brevity

and understated monstrosity. Betty Giles had been privy to certain secrets—vital secrets—that, if made public, could prove "acutely embarrassing." That, in itself, presented no problem. Betty, DuBois was confident, could be trusted. But Nick Ames, her live-in boyfriend, had discovered the secrets. And that was a problem. A major problem, compounded by DuBois's infirmity. Could Powers "neutralize" the problem?

His assent, delivered almost casually, a low-keyed conditioned reflex, had committed him to hiring a murderer. Too late, he realized that he was vulnerable, that the authorities could backtrack from Borrego Springs to Santa Rosa to San Francisco to Los Angeles—to him. Except for a five-minute conversation on DuBois's deck, there was nothing to connect Raymond DuBois with the murder of Nick Ames and the attempted murder of Betty Giles.

Therefore, his bondage to Raymond DuBois was complete.

Until five days ago, complete.

He'd just returned to his office from a late lunch at Le Cirque. It had been an exploratory lunch, suggesting the possibility of advantageous start-up positions in Russian food packaging and distribution. On a fifty-million initial position, returns of twenty-five percent were possible.

The lunch had gone badly. The two Russians had drunk too much, and the two men from Wall Street had been reluctant to commit themselves, even in principle. The reason, Powers suspected, was that DuBois had passed the word: Powers no longer had the power to act unilaterally. Therefore, after less than an hour at the table, in itself an affront, the men from Wall Street had suggested that they meet again in a week's time, when "the situation was clarified."

Afterwards, deep in thought, brooding about the dark portents of the lunch, he'd driven into his building's underground garage and parked his car, all without conscious perception of his surroundings. He'd just activated the electronic door locks on the Lexus and was peevishly examining a parking-lot nick on the driver's door when he realized that a man was standing beside the car's rear bumper. The stranger was well dressed and well barbered. He projected an aura of affable affluence and easygoing authority. John Graham had entered his life.

It had started with a warm, cordial smile, followed by a hearty handshake as Graham introduced himself. Everything had been perfectly orchestrated: two men of the world, each instantly recognizable to the other. Their cars had cost at least forty thousand, their golf was acceptable, their choice of wines impeccable. Their children had never spent a day in public schools.

After introducing himself, Graham had wasted no time. He'd just come out from New York, and was staying at the Beverly Hilton. His business was confidential, but involved extremely valuable objects of art that had been reinsured by his company. The objects of art, worth millions, had been stolen. Graham had followed the trail to Los Angeles, where he believed he could recover the stolen property.

Why, Powers asked, was Graham telling him this?

In reply, Graham had smiled engagingly. He was telling Powers, he'd said, because he believed Powers would be of assistance in the recovery of the stolen property. He also believed—was quite sure, in fact—that Powers might profit, personally, if Graham's efforts were successful. Of course— once more, the engaging smile—this was not something that could be discussed in a parking garage. Could they meet for drinks, anytime after five? Graham had suggested Roland's, a small, unobtrusive bar. He'd explained that a low profile might be wise.

At Roland's, after the briefest of preliminaries, in a calm, conversational voice, Graham had laid it out. If he could raise twenty million dollars, he could purchase a clandestine collection of art from Raymond DuBois that was worth at least a hundred fifty million. The transaction was being brokered by a private detective from San Francisco named Alan Bernhardt. The paintings had been stolen, and if DuBois didn't divest himself of them immediately he would be indicted for receiving stolen property. Of course, Graham could handle the transaction through normal channels, getting the money from his employer, who would then return the paintings to "ordinary public commerce."

However, Graham said, if he could raise the twenty million privately, he could take the paintings to a foreign country, where he would return them, one by one, to the underground art market.

Graham had come to Powers, he'd said, because he thought Powers might be interested in "recycling" the twenty million from Powers Associates to DuBois to Graham. Meaning that DuBois would actually buy the paintings from himself. In exchange for arranging the transaction, Powers would receive twenty million as the paintings were sold. Specifically, as Graham sold the paintings, he would pay Powers fifty percent of the proceeds until the twenty million was paid in full. Everything that was left would belong to Graham.

Instantly Powers had recognized the genius of the scheme. It would be a crime without victims, leaving Graham with a fortune in art.

And leaving Powers with a promissory note for twenty million dollars.

It had taken Graham less than ten minutes to lay out the plan—and less than a minute for Powers to decline. Where was his protection? Graham had obviously expected the objection, and had been ready. His plan, he'd said, was to transport the paintings—twelve, at least—directly from the spot where the transaction would take place to a waiting corporate jet, duly chartered and documented for foreign travel. There would be the pilot, and Graham, and Graham's mistress, who was also his courier. With the crated paintings secured in the airplane, there would still be room for one more passenger: Powers. With customs clearances, everything legal, they would fly down into Mexico, then into Guatemala, where Graham had rented a house in Indigo with the monies he'd taken from his expense account. Already Graham was in contact with people who would gladly pay millions for the DuBois collection, in whole or in part. Within two weeks, Graham had said, call it a vacation with pay, Powers could have his twenty million, and could be back in Los Angeles, or anywhere else, rich and free, independent of Raymond DuBois.

Instantly the doubts had surfaced. Citing DuBois's global reach, Powers had protested that it would be easier to flee Mafia vengeance than to escape the cold, calculated wrath of Raymond DuBois. Airily Graham had dismissed Powers's misgivings. Not only was DuBois old and infirm, but he was also vulnerable. As long as they could connect DuBois to the stolen art, they had him at their mercy. Powers's response had been a grunt of dismissal, repeating that he'd rather have the Mafia after him than DuBois.

Leaving Roland's, Graham had invited Powers to sleep on it. Graham would be at the Beverly Hilton; if he didn't hear from Powers during the next twenty-four hours, he would begin collecting the money through "regular channels." Meaning, he'd said, that if Powers wasn't interested in "freelancing," Graham would "hop back over the fence," return to the executive suite.

Powers had pretended an amusement he didn't feel. Suppose it was a trap? During the months since the death of

Nick Ames, DuBois had begun edging him slowly out of the top spot, had begun moving Albert Robbins, DuBois's chief counsel, into his place. Until two months ago, DuBois had decreed that, in his absence or "indisposition," Powers was to take orders from Robbins.

Graham's proposition had focused Powers's misgivings, forced him to finally face the fact that he was being phased out, Robbins was being phased in. Therefore, at approximately three-thirty in the morning following the meeting at Roland's, at first tentatively, mere speculation, he began to toy with Graham's proposition. Could it be done? Could he pull it off, make twenty million disappear until the next audit?

The answer, he knew, was "Easily." First set up a twenty-five-million-dollar account dedicated to a position in futures. Soybeans would be a possibility. South American coffee. Or cocoa, or foreign copper. The account would be flagged top-secret, "PP," for "Powers Personal." It would be given a name: Prospects International. The following day, with a draft for five million and his own impeccable personal credit, he would open a bank account for Prospects International. During the next few days, using instantaneous wire transfers, ostensibly moving quickly to catch a market swing, he would churn the accounts. Large cash deposits would be made, then withdrawn. Until, in perhaps four days, he would be in a position to deliver twenty million in cash on a day's notice. No problem.

No problem, but no protection. He couldn't be present at the exchange of the paintings for the twenty million, or Bernhardt would expose him. He could take one or two paintings immediately following the exchange, but then he would be in possession of stolen property, with no idea how to dispose of it on the black market.

And then, with dawn turning his bedroom window a

milky white, the solution had come full blown, as the elements clicked into place: *protection—guarantees—a chartered jet—a fortune in art.* Followed in reprise by *futures—coffee—Guatemala.*

Followed by *Indigo.*

Indigo, where coffee futures were brokered.

Indigo, where Graham had rented a house.

God, it was so simple, so symmetrical, so perfect. Laying out the parameters for Prospects International, he would let it casually drop that he saw unprecedented short-term prospects in coffee. In fact, the profit potential was so dramatic that he might actually fly down to Indigo, to establish an "advance command post." And then, smiling, he'd tell his personal assistant that, if Prospects International fulfilled expectations, he would allow himself the pleasure of taking a week to explore the ruins in Guatemala, something that had always fascinated him. Of course, he would be in daily contact with his assistant. But it would be discreet contact. Because, naturally, no one must know he was in Indigo, or coffee futures would soar prematurely. In fact, negotiations were so delicately balanced that he'd chosen only to tell his wife that he had to be out of town for a few days on business.

It had been five o'clock before he'd finally fallen asleep. But it had been a sleep enhanced by images of affluent expatriates, white sand beaches, and long nights of love.

FORTY-ONE

"The way it'll work," Andrea said, "is that I'm going to drive my car, and you're going to follow me in your car." She gestured to the two walkie-talkies lying on the floor beside an electrical outlet. Each radio's charger was plugged into the outlet. "I want you to lie back. If you lose sight of me, use the radio. Don't speed up. I just drove past the Hilton, and Graham's bug is still putting out, loud and clear. So tomorrow morning, early, we'll go to the Hilton and wait for Graham to make a move. When he does, I'll follow him, two or three blocks behind, assuming the bug's still transmitting. You'll be the same distance behind me. Got it?"

"Sure," Harry answered. "So far, so good. But then what? We follow Graham, then what?"

"Nothing happens without the money. So as long as Graham has the money, all we need to do is follow him."

"But suppose he doesn't have the money?"

"He'll have it. But not until tomorrow."

"I guess you aren't going to tell me how you know he'll have it."

"I guess not."

"So, okay, maybe you'd like to give me the plan."

"The plan is very simple, Harry. We've been over it a dozen times, and it hasn't changed." She spoke didactically, with exaggerated patience. "We go to the Hilton in two cars. We get there early, and we make sure the homer works. We—"

"What if Graham switches cars? He'll need a van to carry the paintings. What if—"

"Don't worry, I've got it covered."

He grunted skeptically.

"We follow Graham, and he leads us to the place where the exchange'll take place. Without doubt it'll be in a garage or a warehouse. Bernhardt'll be there with the paintings. We give them time enough to make the exchange. Then it's your turn, Harry. However it comes down, either they put their hands up or they decide to shoot it out, you take care of it. If they decide to put their hands up, we handcuff them." She pointed to a dozen plastic handcuffs lying on the coffee table. "If necessary—" She pointed to a small stack of newly purchased handkerchiefs and two rolls of duct tape. "If necessary, we gag them. But only if it's absolutely necessary, because of the situation. I don't want anyone suffocating."

Impatiently he nodded. "All right, so they're handcuffed and they're gagged, whatever. So what happens next?"

"What happens next," she said, "is that we take their two vans outside the warehouse, and we put our cars inside. Then we drive the vans here, put them in our garage."

"Oh." He nodded mockingly. "Oh. Good. We tie these people up, and we drive off with millions in cash and paintings that're worth a fortune, all very neat, no sweat."

Because she knew what was coming, she made no reply. Instead she examined her fingernails. She must remember to file them. Tomorrow heavy lifting was a distinct possibility.

"Either you're dreaming," Harry said, "or you're running a con. Christ, we'll need another four people, at least, to do what you're talking about. And you damn well know it."

Still examining her nails, she shook her head. "Not four people. Just one more."

FORTY-TWO

Bernhardt felt the bed shift, heard the irregularity of her breathing. Yes, Paula was awake in the darkness. They both lay on their backs, staring up at the ceiling. The time, he knew, was almost midnight; he'd set his travel alarm for six o'clock. By six-thirty tomorrow morning they should be loaded and ready. He'd allowed a half hour to eat breakfast at McDonald's. By eight o'clock, they should be at the DuBois mansion.

For an hour after they'd gone to bed, they'd talked about it: about what could happen tomorrow. Even though they lay close together, Paula in the nightgown she'd packed, he in his shorts, there had somehow been no question of sex. Instead, they'd talked about what might happen with a kind of hushed innocence, as two children might talk on the night before Christmas, visions of sugar plums, of streets paved with gold, of sidewalks in childhood dreams scattered with coins.

A million dollars . . . two million dollars . . .

Drowsily, the sleep-blurred words were combining with visions of scattered coins, images from childhood, fading into the forgetfulness of past innocence: he and his mother, living in the partitioned-off rear half of the huge Greenwich Village loft. In the front half, his mother had taught modern dance and held left-wing political meetings. When there were no dance classes, or meetings, he'd flown model airplanes in the front half of the loft.

It was at times like this, with sleep beckoning, remembering how his mother had helped him build his model planes, that he missed her so much.

Paula felt him stir, heard him draw a fitful breath.

Tomorrow . . .

Certainly he was thinking about tomorrow, planning, calculating the odds, thinking and rethinking. Was he apprehensive about tomorrow? Was he scared? Had she ever seen him scared? C.B.—had C.B. ever been scared?

The three of them—had there ever been a more improbable combination? Alan, the Jewish intellectual. C.B., with a heart of gold, born in the ghetto. And her, the pampered daughter of two college professors.

The three of them and Raymond DuBois, his body emaciated, hardly more than sallow flesh sagging on an inert skeleton, his face a death's head. Raymond DuBois, one of the world's richest men.

And the others: James, the impassive bodyguard who could be a killer. Grace Campbell, the enigmatic presence who might have been a Daphne DuMaurier creation. Powers, the frightened financier. And John Graham, that urbane manipulator.

Only hours ago, with the tip of her forefinger, delicately, she'd actually touched a Picasso painting. Decades ago, the master had put brush to palette, put paint to canvas—the same paint she'd touched today. The sensation had been indescribable, as if she were in psychic contact with the great stream of human aspiration that ran through both Picasso and her.

As she felt her eyes close, let sleep take her, she realized that what she felt, that magic, must surely have possessed Raymond DuBois, perhaps consumed him.

As if he were blind, DuBois ran the tips of his fingers over the buttons of the electronic pad that was always placed close beside his right hand, easily within reach. With his forefinger he depressed the correct button, heard the silky voice say, "The time is two twenty-one A.M."

Meaning that, in thirty-nine minutes, the nurse would tap on his door. Carrying a glass of water and three pills, she would switch on the bedside lamp and help him with the pills. Then, murmuring amiable encouragement, she would attend to the elementals: his bodily waste that had fallen through the circular cutout in his mattress to dribble into the chemical vat below. Then she would clean him, reposition him, say a few words. Finally she would switch out the light and bid him a peaceful rest.

Now I lay me down to sleep . . .

Yes, he could clearly remember reciting the words to his mother as she knelt beside his bed. And yes, he could clearly remember his mother in her coffin, her narrow, wasted head pillowed on white satin, her hands crossed at her breast.

The hands that had cleaned him and diapered him . . .

. . . the breasts that had nurtured him.

He'd been four when she died. After her death, his most vivid recollections had been the gloom of drawn window shades that turned the brightness of sunshine into oblongs of ochre. His father had worked in a tailor shop, sewing piecework. The shop had been in the Bronx, on the ground floor of a tall redbrick building. Every day, his father took him to the shop, and told him to play in the small yard behind the building. There was no grass, only dirt. His only toys had been discarded saucepans and broken cooking utensils that he used to dig in the hard ground.

His mother had died in 1910. By 1920 he'd saved enough money delivering newspapers to buy a wagon with high stake sides, enabling him to deliver substantially more newspapers. At age fifteen, with more than a hundred customers, he was earning more money than his father. A year later, wearing a suit his father had sewn, he'd gotten the job as a Wall Street messenger. Four years later, on his twentieth birthday, he was worth more than a million dollars. He'd seen the 1929 crash coming for more than a year, time enough to convert paper profits into cash. By 1930, at age twenty-four, worth more than ten million, he'd begun buying real estate for pennies on the dollar, and the rest had been play, no longer work: a one-winner game.

But the prize for winning had only been more winnings: merely numbers, nothing more. So, like Faust, like Candide, he'd begun his search. He'd found sybarites who fawned over him and his checkbook, women who would reward his attentions by welcoming him inside their bodies. The women, and eventually the wives. To be followed, nature decreed, by offspring. But a secret visit to a doctor had confirmed his suspicion that, for him, children were impossible.

Leaving him, finally, with his paintings.

In school, he'd once been required to write a composition titled "Tomorrow." For days he'd thought about the subject, almost for the first time intrigued, stimulated by an abstract concept. Finally, the night before the composition was due, he'd written: *Without tomorrow, there is nothing. Today is only the preparation for tomorrow. The successful see only tomorrow. The unsuccessful see only yesterday.*

For him, after tomorrow, there could only be yesterday. Until, finally, the clock ran down.

FORTY-THREE

"Here." Bernhardt gave one of the three walkie-talkies to Tate, another to Paula. "Let's use channel two." He set his channel selector, ordered Tate and Paula to go into the house at opposite ends and test the radios. That done, they reassembled in the garage. The two men wore jackets that concealed their weapons: Bernhardt's .357 Magnum, holstered at his belt on the left side, Tate's two nine-millimeter Browning automatics, one in a shoulder holster, one thrust into his belt. Paula carried her Colt .38 Chief's Special in the saddle leather shoulder bag that Bernhardt had given her after she'd completed her first stakeout assignment. They stood beside the big Dodge van with its two front doors open. The van was windowless; the seats had been removed. Tate had put the sawed-off on the floor of the van, along with a plastic Baggie containing six twelve-gauge shotgun shells. As always, the two dogs were close to Paula. Reacting to the heightened activity, the dogs stood with their heads high, eyes sharp-focused, alert.

"I think," Paula said, "that the dogs should go with me in the Taurus."

Bernhardt looked at Tate, who shrugged, saying, "Why not?" When Bernhardt agreed, Paula stepped to the Taurus, opened the rear door, snapped her fingers. Eagerly the two dogs leaped into the car's back seat.

"They love to ride," Paula explained. Then she smiled at

Bernhardt. It was a complex smile, almost whimsical. Recognizing it as a sign of encouragement, Bernhardt realized that his answering smile was rueful. He'd suddenly understood that he was an innocent abroad, a neophyte playing a no-limit game he'd never before played and didn't fully understand.

They stood together between the Taurus and the van, a final moment of shared irresolution, a mute acknowledgment that, really, they'd suddenly realized that they'd rather not be there. Until finally Tate flipped his hand, gave them a broad, what-the-hell smile. "Come on," he said. "A couple of Egg McMuffins and it'll all fall into place." He reached into the van, used the remote control wand to open the big double garage door.

Riding in the van's passenger seat, Bernhardt keyed the walkie-talkie, saying, "Slow down, Paula. This is a thirty-five-mile zone. We're doing forty."

"Sorry."

"Rodeo Drive's next. Then it's left on Benedict Canyon."

"I know, Alan." Even though her voice was static-blurred, Bernhardt could hear her impatience. This would be their third trip over the route.

A moment later the Taurus's left-turn signal came on. Tate checked the mirrors, eased the van into the inside lane on Santa Monica Boulevard.

"We should've had more breakfast," Tate said. "This could be a long day."

"I always taste plastic in McDonald's food."

"Then how come we didn't go to Jack in the Box?"

"Because I taste plastic in their food, too."

"Hmmm."

"Slow down," Bernhardt ordered. "Let a car get between us."

Allowing the van to slow, Tate said, "What we should've done, you should've drawn me a map of the DuBois layout. I always like to know the lay of the land."

"You're right," Bernhardt admitted. "Why didn't you say something?"

Tate made no reply, asking instead: "So we get inside the DuBois place. I get into the Taurus, and Paula gets in here. I wait outside while the two of you drive into the garage. Is that it?"

"That's it. Then, when we're inside, you block the garage with the Taurus. You stay in the car, with your walkie-talkie."

"How long'll it take you to load the stuff?"

"At least an hour. First Grace Campbell clears the house of servants. Then we start moving the paintings. There're fourteen of them in the secret gallery. We've got to take them in the elevator from the fourth level up to the first level, then into the garage."

"What about James? Where's he while you're doing that?"

"He'll be outside, with you. He'll be in his own car."

"Waiting and watching, is that it?"

Bernhardt smiled. "That's it, I think. We're riding shotgun on the paintings, and James is riding shotgun on us."

"With an Uzi."

"I think so, but I'm not sure." And into the walkie-talkie: "Benedict Canyon's about a mile ahead, on the left."

"Right."

"How're you doing?"

"I'm doing fine," Paula answered. And, yes, he could hear the assurance in her voice. Paula was up for this job.

"Look at this," Tate said, his gesture sweeping the shops they were passing as he shook his head appreciatively. "Rodeo Drive. This job works out, maybe I'll come back this way. A lady I know, she's got a thing about Rodeo Drive. She collects charms for her bracelet. Fish. She has a thing about fish. Solid gold, of course.''

Bernhardt made no reply.

"Paula," Tate said, "she sounds fine."

"I know."

"She's all right."

"I know."

"The two of you, you should get married, have a couple of kids."

"I know."

She switched on the scanner, waited for the crystals to warm up, read the digital bearing: 320 degrees magnetic. A check of the compass verified that the angle would be right for the Hilton's parking lot.

"Is it okay?" Harry asked.

"Yes. You'd better get back to your car. It's almost eight o'clock. Give me a call on your walkie-talkie, to check."

"Graham—will he be alone?"

"I've no idea." She spoke calmly yet impatiently.

Harry smiled derisively. "I've got to hand it to you, Andrea. You're cool. You're a cool customer." He watched her face for some hint of a reaction, but saw nothing. In profile, her features were perfectly formed, a Hollywood beauty.

When they were finished with the job, with his share stuffed in the black nylon athletic satchel he'd bought just yesterday, when they were about to split, get out of town, he would take her by surprise. He would slap her so hard, so often, that she would fall to her knees, semiconscious. He would throw her to the floor, and rip off the safari pants she was wearing, and he would have her. Again and again, he would have her, cruel, merciless thrusts, tearing into her until she whimpered, begged for mercy. Then he would—

"*Come on*, Harry. Let's *do* it."

"Ah, yeah." The derisive smile widened meaningfully. "Yeah, we got to do it, Andrea. We've really got to do it . . ."

Graham clipped the holstered Beretta to his belt, verified that his golfing jacket covered the pistol. In the bathroom, with the door open, Helen was spraying her short, dark hair. She wore designer blue jeans that clung provocatively to her buttocks and thighs. But here, now, on this make-or-break morning, with a fortune so close, the erotic images were a distraction.

"Helen. Please. You're beautiful. But we've got to eat something. And I've got to make some calls."

"So make some calls," she retorted impatiently. "Ten minutes, I'll be. No more."

As he stifled an impatient response, he realized that she'd never before spoken to him so sharply. Neither had he heard so clearly the abrasive twang of New Yorkese in her speech.

Bernhardt spoke into the walkie-talkie: "You'd better slow down. It's just around the next curve."

"I know."

As, two cars ahead, he saw the Taurus's stop lights blink.

"You can drive right up to the gate," he said. "It opens inward. There's a light beam that'll tell them we're here."

"Right."

Bernhardt clicked off the radio. Tate let the van slow as the Taurus turned into the short driveway leading to the massive iron gates. The pickup that had been between the van and the Taurus continued up Benedict Canyon. Tate braked the van, then turned into the driveway close behind the Taurus. As Tate nudged the gearshift into neutral, Bernhardt saw the gate begin to swing inward. Twenty-five feet beyond the gates, James was standing in the driveway. Recognizing Paula behind the wheel of the Taurus, he stepped aside, gestured for her to drive past him.

"You'll turn right, into the circular drive," Bernhardt said, speaking into the walkie-talkie. "Then stop, like we did yesterday. Get out of the car. Take the keys with you." As he spoke, the van began moving slowly forward; James stepped back into the center of the graveled driveway to stand facing them. He wore a loose-fitting blue blazer, gray flannel slacks, and black shoes. His shirt was white, but he wore no tie.

"That," Tate said, "has got to be James."

Amused, Bernhardt looked at Tate as, behind them, the iron gates swung closed.

"What is he? Samoan? Jumbo Mexican?"

"Jesus, C.B. That's a racist remark."

"If you said it, maybe. If I say it, no. Call it vocational screening. This guy's on our team. I'd like to know something about him. He could be behind me with a gun, let's not forget. Behind you, too."

"He's Indian, I think. Or mestizo, more like it. Central American Indian mixed with Spanish."

"But he's *big*. South of the border they're small."

"I'm just telling you what I was told." As he spoke, Bernhardt waved to James through the big windshield of the van, then pointed left, toward the compound's main garage that connected directly with the house.

"As I understand it," Bernhardt said, "his parents were guerrilla leaders in South America. James was still a kid when his parents were wiped out in a government ambush. He escaped, and lived with the guerrillas until he was older, maybe a teenager."

As the van moved slowly forward, Tate said, "James looks like he can really take care of himself. Those eyes— they make you think."

"Stop beside him," Bernhardt ordered. "We'll get out." Across the circular driveway, he saw Paula getting out of the Taurus, then walking toward them. As they gathered in front of the van, Bernhardt introduced Tate to James. The two big, watchful men exchanged guarded monosyllables.

"Paula and I'll go into the garage, in the van," Bernhardt explained, addressing James. "Tate will stay in the Taurus, parked so as to block the garage door. We have walkie-talkies. When we've got the van loaded, we'll give Tate a call, and he'll move the Taurus." As Bernhardt said it, Paula gave Tate the keys to the Taurus.

"Yes." James nodded gravely, then handed Bernhardt an electronic wand. "This opens the garage door."

"Thanks." Bernhardt took the wand. "When we're ready—loaded, with the garage door open—Paula will get into the Taurus. She'll go first, the lead car. Tate and I'll go next, in the van. You'll follow us. When we get out on Benedict Canyon, Paula will turn left, down the hill. She'll—"

"Excuse me," James interrupted. As always, he spoke softly, precisely. Repeating: "Excuse me, but I'm supposed to stay with the paintings until we have the money and we return here. Those are my instructions."

"Do you mean in the van?" Tate, too, spoke softly. "You want to ride in the van?"

James nodded. "In the van. Yes. With the paintings."

Tate looked at Bernhardt, who looked at Paula—who frowned, then looked carefully at James. Finally Bernhardt said, "We talked yesterday, James. We agreed that you were to take orders from me. And I want Paula in front, then the van, then you, in your car, trailing us. I want to—"

"But we could get separated."

Decisively Bernhardt shook his head. "No. We've got a walkie-talkie for you, tuned to the right channel. You can—"

"Mr. DuBois was very clear. Where the paintings go, I go. Where the money goes, until it gets here, I go. Those are my orders."

Once more Bernhardt exchanged glances with Paula and Tate. Finally he said, "I'll speak to Mr. DuBois. Meanwhile, get a car ready. I'm not leaving with the paintings unless I'm covered front and back. Is that clear?"

James nodded. "Perfectly."

"You've got an Accord. Get it ready. I don't want a limo."

"The Accord is ready."

"You're armed?"

"Yes, sir. I have a Glock nine-millimeter semiautomatic pistol and a machine pistol. The machine pistol is in my house." He gestured. "It's in a satchel, with two spare clips."

"If DuBois wants him to stay with the paintings," Tate said, speaking to Bernhardt, "then it should be the three of us in the van."

Bernhardt shook his head vehemently. "No. I want James behind us, in the Accord." He turned to James. "You go back to your house. Take a walkie-talkie with you, and stay put until you hear from me. I'm going to talk with Mr. DuBois about this."

For a long, impassive moment, the two men stared hard at each other, a grim, silent contest. Then, moving with measured deliberation, James accepted a radio from Paula, and began walking across the circle of the driveway to his bungalow, sheltered in a grove of eucalyptus.

"This doesn't feel right," Tate said. "That guy, he's got his own game going."

"What about you?" Bernhardt asked, looking at Paula. "What'd you think?"

She was thoughtfully studying James as he walked away from them. Finally she said, "He seems very straightforward, a very simple person. I guess it'll depend on what DuBois says." She turned to Bernhardt. "What'd you think?"

"Either I'm running this or I'm not. I want you in front, and I want C.B. with me, in the van. I also want someone behind us. If I don't get that, then it's off. For what we've done so far, we've been well paid. So the hell with it."

Tate frowned ponderously. "That's the way to go, no question. It don't feel good, we're out, that's the only way to handle it. Still . . ." He let a judicious beat pass. "Still, let's not lose sight of all that money we could be splitting."

"What I'm trying to do," Bernhardt said, "is cover all the bases. I don't want any surprises."

Tate smiled tolerantly, and spread his big, muscular hands. They'd had this conversation before.

"Come on—let's do it," Bernhardt said. "Let's do it, and get back to San Francisco."

FORTY-FOUR

Graham drained his coffee cup, glanced at the check, tossed two ten-dollar bills on the table. He looked at at his watch, then at Helen's coffee cup, still half full. Her croissant was only half eaten. As he suppressed an impatient sigh, it occurred to him that Helen did everything slowly. She was a slow, languid person. And, yes, a self-indulgent person.

"I've got to make a couple more phone calls." He gestured toward the lobby. "I want to use a pay phone. You finish your breakfast, and then go upstairs. If anyone calls for me, get a number and say I'll call back. Okay?"

She nodded agreement, then said, "You look worried. Is anything wrong?"

He drew a deep breath. Then, with exaggerated patience: "There's nothing wrong, Helen. However, as you might imagine, considering the situation, I've got a lot on my mind."

"Mmmm." She smiled—a slow, erotic smile. They'd made love an hour and a half ago, and now she was ready to do it again. The situation, she said—all that money—it excited her, stimulated her.

"As soon as you can," he said, "go upstairs." He smiled at her, turned away, and walked the length of the coffee shop, then out into the lobby. As he walked, he verified that he had a pocketful of quarters. He chose a phone in an alcove adjoining the registration area. He consulted a sheet of paper and dialed Powers at home. Powers answered on the second ring.

"Is everything okay? Everything's ready here."

"Y-yes. All ready."

"Will you be coming alone?"

"Yes. I'll be in a camper—a big brown and white camper."

"Is the camper registered to you?"

"No. I rented it. I had trouble, but I—"

"Can you pick up the bundle and be at the corner of Sepulveda and Vine by nine-thirty?"

"I—yes, I'm sure I can. Sepulveda and Vine, you say?"

Graham nodded impatiently. "Right. Nine-thirty. Stay in your camper until I come for you. Even if you see me, stay in your camper."

"Sepulveda and Vine . . ." There was a puzzled moment of silence. "That seems like a—"

"It's very busy. For something like this, you want lots of people around."

"I—I understand. Yes."

"The merchandise is crated. Will the camper be big enough?"

"It's big. Very big."

"Good. Then we're all—"

"I wanted to tell you, I've decided to go with you. In the airplane, I mean."

"*What?*"

"I—there're a lot of reasons."

"Is this a trick?" Graham asked.

"N-no. You offered, don't forget. You told me I could come along. I thought about it all night. And I want to go."

"Just you?"

"Just me."

* * *

In the study, DuBois pivoted his wheelchair to face the master control panel set into the wall close beside his desk. He waited for the signal verifying that the house had been vacated, then turned to face Bernhardt and Paula, who stood side by side in front of the desk.

"Are we ready?" the old man asked.

"We're ready," Bernhardt said. "And I've talked to Graham. He's ready. The only problem is James. I want him to follow us to the meeting place in one of your cars. But he wants to ride in the van, with the paintings. He said that's your wish."

DuBois frowned, then shook his head. "Sometimes James misunderstands me. Or sometimes I suspect he *pretends* to misunderstand me." He turned to the panel again, punched in a sequence. Moments later James's voice came over the loudspeaker.

"James, I want you to follow Mr. Bernhardt in our car. I want you to do exactly as he wishes. Is that clear?"

"Yes, sir, that's clear."

"Good. Thank you." DuBois turned back to Bernhardt, asking, "Is that satisfactory?"

"Perfectly."

"Then we're ready to proceed."

"Will you be with us, to open the gallery?"

"Oh, yes." Dubois nodded as he began maneuvering the wheelchair. Repeating: "Oh, yes, I'll be with you."

They'd left the largest for the last: the Picasso, almost four feet wide. The other thirteen paintings were already stacked on edge against the far wall of the garage.

"Here." Holding one end of the crate, walking backward, Bernhardt moved toward the van. "Let's put this in first."

Paula nodded, took a fresh grip on the crate. Painstakingly they maneuvered the crate between the open rear doors of the van and the closed door of the garage. Bernhardt set the crate on the floor of the van, got into the van, and slid the crate across the steel floor to rest on edge against the sidewall. That done, Paula was able to hand the other paintings up to him while he remained in the van, carefully stacking the crates. Fifteen minutes later the precious cargo was compactly loaded and securely roped. With all the paintings stowed, there would still be room for at least one person, plus the driver and passenger, in front. Bernhardt jumped down from the van, closed and locked the two rear doors. Paula had come to stand beside him as he tested the doors. She carried her saddle leather shoulder bag, with her revolver inside. Her expression was solemn. Bernhardt glanced at his watch.

"Ten minutes after nine," he said. "I'm supposed to call Graham at ten. He'll be in a phone booth, so I've got to be on time."

"Before we leave," Paula said, "I've got to go pee. Sorry."

Bernhardt smiled, turned toward the door that led to the house. "Come on. I'll show you where it is. I'll tell DuBois we're going, and I'll meet you back here."

As Bernhardt walked across the deck, the solitary figure in the wheelchair remained motionless, staring out across the city west toward the ocean. Yet, certainly, DuBois was aware of Bernhardt's presence. If the body was infirm, the old man's senses were still acute.

When Bernhardt was standing beside him, DuBois said, "Tell me, please, the exact chronology. Be very precise."

"We've got the van loaded. We're ready to go. After you and I talk, I'll use my walkie-talkie to contact C.B. Tate."

"He's your enforcer. Your muscle."

Amused by the other man's attempt at street jargon, Bernhardt smiled. "Yes, sir. He's waiting in my car. The Ford Taurus with the two guard dogs in back. In fact, the car is blocking the garage. When Tate hears my order, he'll move away from the garage door, and signal James to open the door. Then—"

"Excuse me, but you must give that order to James. He won't take it from a stranger."

Bernhardt nodded assent. Then, resuming: "We'll travel in a caravan. Paula'll go first, in the Taurus. Tate and I, in the van with the paintings, will be next. James will follow us, in your Accord. He'll use his remote control to open the gate for us and close it behind us. We'll drive to Santa Monica, where I've rented a house with a large double garage. Tate and Paula will take the van inside, and close the door. They'll have the dogs. James and I, in our separate cars, will stay outside, and wait until Graham arrives. He'll—"

"How will Graham know where to find you?"

"I'll call him between ten and ten-fifteen from a phone booth. I'll tell him the location of the house I rented. When he arrives, I'll let him drive into the garage."

"You'll all be armed, I assume."

"Yes, sir, we will."

DuBois nodded, gestured for Bernhardt to continue.

"Graham is concerned about the possibility of forgery, so I've told him he could open two crates and check the paintings. While he's doing that, we'll check the money. Then—"

"That's nonsense. Graham can't possibly know whether a given painting is a forgery. Authenticating a painting requires an expert. And it takes time. Weeks, sometimes."

"Nevertheless, I felt it was a legitimate request."

For a moment DuBois remained silent. Then: "You'll need tools to open the crates."

"I took a hammer and crowbar from your workshop. They're in the van."

DuBois nodded silent assent, waved for Bernhardt to continue.

"If we're all satisfied," he said, "we'll make the actual swap—the paintings for the money. That should be about noon. At that time I'll open the garage door and tell James to unblock the driveway. Graham and his people, whoever they are, will leave first, with the paintings."

"Where will he go?"

"I've no idea. He's been staying at the Beverly Hilton, but I wouldn't expect him to go back there. I'm sure his company—Consolidated—will take over once Graham has the paintings. If I were planning their operation, I'd have Graham drive under guard directly to the Santa Monica airport, where there'd be a chartered jet waiting. They'd transfer the paintings to the jet. A few hours later, they'd be in New York."

"The critical time," DuBois said, "is after Graham learns the location of your house. The negotiations have taken several days. Quite possibly, during that time, Consolidated could have assembled a task force. Once they know the location of the house, they could simply overwhelm you, take the money, take the paintings, all of it."

Impatiently Bernhardt sighed. "In the first place, that would make Consolidated criminals. Secondly, there's no such thing as a perfect plan." As he spoke, he consulted his watch. In less than an an hour, Graham would expect his call.

"After the exchange is made," DuBois said, "and Graham has taken the paintings, you'll return here, with the money."

"Yes, sir." Bernhardt smiled. "I imagine James will see to that."

The ghost of a smile touched DuBois's pallid mouth. "Yes, I imagine he will."

"The money'll be in my van. James will open the gates for us. We'll drive inside your compound, drive into the main garage, which James will open for us. Paula and I will go inside, and count the money. I'll leave Tate outside, on guard. I'll take my ten percent, which I assume'll be two million dollars. And that's the end. Once we're outside your compound, on Benedict Canyon Road, our business is concluded." As he said it, he searched Dubois's face for a reaction. There was nothing.

Finally DuBois said, "After our business is concluded, as you say, what are your plans?"

"My plans are to get back to San Francisco as quickly as possible." He hesitated, then ventured, "What about you, sir? What're your plans?"

Once more the pale mouth stirred with the suggestion of a smile. "I plan to put the proceeds of the sale into Treasury notes. You might consider T-Notes yourself. Wait for the rates to go down about four points, and sell them on the open market. At today's rates, you should do very well. But you must act quickly."

"I, ah, wasn't thinking so much financially. I was just thinking—" Searching for the phrase, he paused, began again: "I was thinking about you—about what you'll have to, ah, replace the paintings. For, ah, psychic satisfaction." Then he frowned. He'd said it badly, phrased it awkwardly.

DuBois let a moment pass before he said, "If all goes as we hope today, I plan to let matters settle, perhaps for two months. Then, Mr. Bernhardt, you'll hear from me."

"I—I will?" Bernhardt was aware of the foreboding the other man's words produced.

The narrow head with its waxen flesh and prominent bones bobbed once, in wan assent. "I'll be retaining you to find Betty Giles. I'll want you to go to Europe, and deliver a personal message from me."

"*What?*"

"With the illicit paintings gone, there's no reason Betty and I can't continue operating as we did before, buying and selling paintings by contemporary artists. I'm especially interested in Jean Mooney and Casper Grenville. I've been watching them, and I think Betty and I could develop them, providing they'll agree to limit their production in exchange for a performance contract. That's the key, you see—limiting production to drive up the price."

Bemused, Bernhardt could only shake his head.

"There." Helen pointed. "Is that him?"

Following her gesture, Graham saw a big brown and white camper drawing to a stop southbound on Sepulveda, then maneuvering to park behind a yellow pickup. Behind the camper's steering wheel, improbably wearing a Dodgers cap and dark wraparound sunglasses, Powers was backing and filling, struggling to get the outsize camper closer to the curb.

"That's him." Parked across the street on Sepulveda, south of Vine, Graham watched while Powers finally succeeded in parking the camper. He checked the time: almost ten o'clock.

"This Powers drives like a klutz," Helen said.

Graham turned to briefly study her face. Then, elliptically, he said, "Powers is worth many millions. I'm sure he can park his Porsche, or his Jag, with great aplomb."

In turn she studied him before she said, "Ever since last

night, when this thing started to take hold, you've been talking down to me. You know that? 'Great aplomb.' What's that mean?''

"It means that—"

"I *know* what it means. The point is, Johnny, you've changed. Just since last night, you've changed."

Once more he studied her face before he spoke softly, wryly: "I can't remember the last time someone called me Johnny."

"Oh. Well. Excuse *me.''*

He drew a deep, long-suffering breath. "There's a lot at stake here, Helen. We're anxious, uptight. So let's—"

"Speaking about what's at stake, where's that armored van? You said—"

"There's no armored van. That was my little joke."

"Oh, yeah?" She frowned. "No kidding?"

"No kidding. Armored cars attract attention." He swung open the driver's door. "You stay here. Keep your eyes open." He buttoned his golf jacket across the bulge of the Beretta thrust into his belt and got out of the white Pontiac. He walked to the corner, and waited for the traffic light to change. Hands thrust into custom-cut cavalry twill slacks, he crossed Sepulveda, crossed Vine, and walked casually toward the camper. As he drew even with the cab, he glanced at Powers, who sat rigidly behind the steering wheel, staring straight ahead. His Adam's apple, Graham noticed, was moving spasmodically. Still walking slowly, Graham transferred his gaze from Powers's face to the interior of the camper. In the dull light filtered through tinted side windows, Graham saw a large army-style duffel bag on the floor. Yesterday he'd been informed by the public relations department of the U.S. Mint that twenty million dollars in thousand-dollar bills would weigh about forty-nine pounds.

* * *

"So far, so good." Andrea switched off the scanner and settled down behind the steering wheel. Across Vine, she saw Graham strolling north on Sepulveda. She glanced at her watch; the time was ten A.M.

"He's waiting for someone," Harry said.

Andrea made no reply.

"That woman in Graham's car," Harry said. "What about her? How's she fit in?"

"I think Graham's waiting for someone to come with the money. And—" She broke off, her eyes suddenly sharp-focused on a pair of outdoor phone booths set into the front wall of a large sporting goods store. With apparent indifference, Graham had passed the booths. But now, still casually, he was turning, strolling back the way he'd come.

"Those phone booths," she said. "That's what it's about. He's waiting for a call."

"Have you got a pencil and paper?" Bernhardt asked, speaking into the pay phone.

"Of course," Graham answered.

"The money, it's all ready?"

"All ready."

"We're in three cars," Bernhardt said. "There's a big brown Dodge van, with no windows. There's a black Taurus, with a woman driving. And a blue Accord, with a man driving. Four people, total. Plus two dogs, in the Taurus."

"Two dogs?"

"Correct." Savoring the moment, Bernhardt smiled to himself.

"And the paintings are all in the van."

"Yes."

"Where's the meeting place?"

"First," Bernhardt said, "give me a rundown on your people."

"There're three of us. A woman, myself, and a man. We'll be in two vehicles. One's a big white and brown camper. The windows are tinted in back, so it's impossible to see inside, except through the front windows. The money's there, in a big duffel bag. I'll be driving the camper, and the woman will be with me. The third person is a man. He'll be following us, driving a white Pontiac."

"What's your location?"

"We're on the north edge of Culver City."

Bernhardt took a long moment to visualize the geography before he said, "It should take you about twenty minutes. The address is Forty-one Seventy-four Twenty-sixth Street. That's near Santa Monica. It's a bungalow, beige and charcoal, with pink trim. There're two small palm trees in the front yard that seem to be dying."

Graham chuckled. "There're two small palm trees dying in front of every bungalow in Los Angeles. The smog, no doubt."

"The two people who're with you," Bernhardt said. "Are they pros?"

"Of course. Cold-blooded killers, both of them. I'll see you in twenty minutes." The line clicked, went dead.

Parked on Sepulveda, Andrea held the walkie-talkie in two hands, a fond caress. Yes, the tempo was quickening. At the prospect of imminent action, winner take all, her eyes came alive, her breathing had quickened. "The ducks are on the pond," her grandfather would have said. Yes, the players were beginning to move, take their places on stage. The script would read, *Fortyish man wearing an incongruous Dodgers cap and shades, obviously a disguise, gets out of the camper. Graham and the dark-haired woman are getting out of the white Pontiac, a rental car. Quick, urgent exchange of keys, hurried instructions. Then, moving smoothly, confidentially, Graham swings up into the van, behind the wheel. The other man, probably an enforcer, gets into the Pontiac; the woman, after a revealing moment of hesitation, steps up into the camper.*

In the camper, certainly, the money was hidden. Twenty million dollars.

Andrea started her car, keyed the walkie-talkie. "Harry."

"Right here. Is this it?"

Ignoring the question, she said, "If they split up, I'll take the camper, you take the guy in the Pontiac, and we'll keep in touch by radio. The one in the Pontiac, he's the enforcer. We'll take him out first. He's the one we have to worry about."

"All right. But—"

"Just do it, Harry. This is payday. So let's just do it the way it should be done." She released the "transmit" button, put the car in gear, checked traffic, pulled out into Sepulveda. Already the camper and the Pontiac were a block ahead. The homing device was transmitting perfectly.

Sitting in the front seat of the Accord, across Twenty-sixth Street from the beige bungalow with its two stunted palm trees, the two men watched as a large silver-colored camper approached from the south.

"Wrong color," Bernhardt said.

"Unless they told you wrong," James replied.

"Yes, there's that."

But, moments later, the camper passed them and continued sedately up the street. The driver was an elderly, gray-haired man.

"What I want," Bernhardt said, "is for you to stay outside the whole time. Whatever happens in the garage with the money, Tate and Paula and I can handle it. The three of us and the dogs. I'm confident of that. It's outside the garage, then going back to Dubois's with the money, that worries me. Do you understand?"

"Of course I understand. I am, after all, a professional."

"Is the walkie-talkie I gave you working?"

"Yes, sir."

"Channel two. Right?"

Impassively James nodded. Repeating dutifully: "Channel two."

"They'll be coming in two cars, a white and brown camper and a white Pontiac. We'll let the camper inside the garage. There'll be a man and a woman inside. I know Graham, and I'll signal if he's okay."

James nodded.

"The man in the white Pontiac is the muscle. He'll be guarding Graham's back, just like you're guarding my back. So he's your responsibility. He's wearing a Dodgers baseball cap and dark wraparound sunglasses, according to Graham."

"You've not seen this man in the Dodgers cap."

"No. But he's the muscle, Graham says."

"Then I will watch the one in the baseball cap. You can watch Mr. Graham. Is that satisfactory?"

"Perfectly."

"So." Tate leaned against the sidewall of the garage and eyed the two dogs standing beside Paula, one on either side. "Here we are—you, me, a hundred million or so in bootleg art, plus Rin Tin Tin and his mate."

"I think," Paula said, "that Rin Tin Tin was a female."

"Whatever." Tate pushed away from the wall, went to the van, which stood with its four doors open, and took the sawed-off shotgun from the floor on the passenger's side.

He went to the workbench that had been built against the back wall, and placed the sawed-off on the workbench. "How about your jacket?" he asked. "Can I use it?"

"Sure." Paula took off the bright orange windbreaker and handed it to her companion.

Careful to leave the trigger guard exposed, Tate draped the jacket over the shotgun. Then, glancing at his watch, he said, "What's keeping them?" As he spoke, he drew a nine-millimeter Browning from his belt, verified that there was a round in the chamber, verified that the safety was set, thrust the pistol back into his belt. "This waiting. I'm no good at waiting."

Paula patted the dogs on the head. "Twenty minutes from Sepulveda and Vine, that's my guess."

With his gaze fixed on the closed garage door, standing with fists clenched at his sides, thick brown forearms muscle-corded, Tate made no reply.

In the rearview mirror Andrea saw the white Pontiac slowing sharply, moving to the right lane. The Pontiac was close enough for her to see the driver, still wearing the shades and baseball cap. Ahead, the camper with Graham and the woman in the cab was also slowing, but not moving to the right lane. Driving with one hand, she quickly picked up the walkie-talkie that connected her to Harry.

"Have you got the guy in the Pontiac?"

"Got him. He's parking."

"I think we're close. I think he'll walk to the meet. You follow him. He's yours. If you go on foot, take the walkie-talkie with you."

"I can't hide it, though. Not really. It's too damn big."

"Try, Harry. Try. This is the part you like best. So try."

" 'Try Harry,' " he mimicked caustically. Then he switched his walkie-talkie to "standby."

Ahead, the camper's stop lights came on. Andrea used a key to open the BMW's glove compartment. She took out a palm-size surveillance radio. With her eyes on the camper, she quickly inserted a clear plastic earpiece, switched on the radio, tuned it to "transmit." She placed the radio on the seat beside the walkie-talkie. Now the camper had stopped, signaling for a left turn into the driveway of one of the tract houses that lined the quiet residential street. Ahead, she saw Bernhardt getting into a parked Taurus. James, too, was in motion, getting into a blue Accord. As soon as Bernhardt's car moved, unblocking the garage door of the beige bungalow with the two dying palms, Andrea switched on the surveillance radio, held the tiny microphone close to her mouth: "Is the camper going inside the garage?"

"Yes."

"Are you going inside?"

"No."

"All right. If you can, keep listening to the radio."

"Yes."

Now the Accord, too, was moving, unblocking the driveway. Bernhardt was out of the Taurus. He produced an electronic wand, aimed it at the garage door. Immediately the door rose, rolling up in segments. Graham, driving the camper, looked cautiously in all directions. As the segmented door rolled up overhead, the camper moved forward, following directions from Bernhardt. In the gloom of the garage she saw a dark panel van. While the camper was still moving slowly, cautiously forward, Bernhardt stepped quickly into the garage as the door began to come down, just clearing the rear of the camper.

Andrea's rush of exultation came slowly, but finally erupted in an inarticulate exclamation, a wordless groan of pleasure more profound than any orgasm. It was as if her will had been transformed into invisible threads that were moving men and machines according to a plan that, even for her, was still unfolding.

By carefully calculated prearrangement, Tate stood against the garage wall, close beside the workbench, on guard. A flick of Paula's jacket, and the sawed-off would be in his hands. He watched Bernhardt brace himself and lift the fifty-pound duffel bag from the camper and carry it to the rear of the van, where he eased it to the garage floor. Graham and the dark-haired woman had emptied the van of the crated paintings. Working quickly, they'd propped two of the crates against one wall of the garage. Using the hammer and crowbar, Graham had opened the crates and put them flat on the floor between the camper and the garage door. He and the woman were painstakingly sliding one of the two paintings out of its crate.

"My God," Graham breathed. "It's *The Three Sisters.*" Minutes later, working just as carefully, with almost reverent care, they exposed another painting. "It's a Utrillo." Graham's voice was hushed. "It's called *Number Eighty-seven.* It was stolen years ago. Ten years, at least."

Bernhardt came around the corner of the van. "You're satisfied?"

Graham's expression was unreadable. Signifying, Tate sensed, that his hole card had not been turned over. Finally, impassively, Graham nodded, exchanged a long, searching look with Bernhardt, then with Tate. Then he turned and moved around the corner of the camper. As soon as he was out of sight, Bernhardt came close, whispering to Tate, "What d'you think?"

"He's got someone outside," Tate said. "Just like we do. He thinks he's got a kicker." As he spoke, Tate moved to his right, positioning himself so that he could see Graham loading the camper. The insurance man said something sharp to the woman, who frowned, said something sharp in return, took a fresh grip on the crate they were lifting. As they lifted it high enough to clear the camper's desk, Graham's golf jacket rose enough to reveal an automatic thrust into his belt. Tate considered a moment, then decided to draw Paula's jacket aside and pick up the sawed-off shotgun, which he held cradled across his chest, pointing away from Graham. On the far side of the van, Bernhardt was bending over the duffel bag, still on the garage floor. Thick white nylon rope secured the earth-colored duffel. Bernhardt drew a pocket knife, cut the rope. The bag gaped open as a cascade of bank notes banded into packets spilled out on the floor.

Sitting behind the steering wheel of the BMW, both radios on the seat beside her, Andrea's gaze was fixed on the mirror. A block behind, the white Pontiac was still parked; a half-block behind the Pontiac, she could see Harry's Lincoln, also parked. She keyed the walkie-talkie.

"What's happening, Harry?"

"He's still sitting with his Dodgers cap on. Just sitting. What the fuck's happening up there?"

"There's a van inside the garage. That's got to be the paintings. And the camper's in there. That's got to be the money. There're two cars blocking the driveway. One car—a Taurus—is empty. Bernhardt drove it, and now he's inside the garage. There's a guy in the second car, a blue Accord. He works for DuBois."

"The big dark-skinned guy."

"Right."

"So?"

"I want you to take the one in the baseball cap. Got it?"

"Stick my gun in his ribs, is that it?"

"That's it. But no shooting."

"If he tries to shoot me, I'm sure going to—"

"*No shooting,* I said. Not now. You'll blow everything." She clicked off the walkie-talkie, switched on the surveillance radio, spoke into the tiny microphone. "Harry's going to disarm Graham's backup. He'll hold him in the Pontiac. So that's the two of them, together."

"Yes."

"Bernhardt and Graham should be finished soon."

He made no response.

"In a few minutes it'll be over."

"Yes." In the single word, she heard it all: the quiet, utterly implacable determination, the single-minded, rock-solid commitment . . . his life and hers, inextricably joined.

James switched off the surveillance radio. Leaving the transparent earpiece in place, he dropped the tiny radio into his jacket pocket. In the mirror he could see her BMW, but not the white Pontiac; his view was blocked by a parked truck. On the Accord's floor, on the passenger side, the Uzi lay loaded and cocked, ready.

A few minutes, she'd said.

Andrea . . .

He would always remember the first time he'd seen her; the moment was graven forever on his memory. He'd been fourteen years old, she'd been twelve. There'd been a fire-fight, a carefully planned ambush on the narrow mountain road that connected Cusco and Huanto. The targets had been a convoy of two pickups mounting heavy machine guns and two Toyota Land Cruisers. His parents had led the assault; he'd been told to watch the road to Huanto. He'd had a radio then, too: a hand-held military radio captured in a recent raid on a government armory. The radio was so heavy that two hands were required to manage it. Using missiles just received from the Soviets, they'd knocked out the machine guns on the first assault. One of the two Land Cruisers had gone off the road, tumbling down the mountainside, then struck an outcropping of rock and wedged itself into a crevice. Instantly the vehicle had been engulfed in flames. Moments later, three figures had emerged: a woman, a girl, and a man, with their clothing ablaze. The man stumbled, fell, and burned to death where he lay. The woman, screaming, her own clothing ablaze, had rolled her child on the ground, beat at the flames with her hands, finally succeeded in extinguishing them. She had fallen to her knees, head bowed, as if in penance. Andrea had tried to help, but her mother had blindly pushed her away.

James's father had been the first to reach the woman. Her hair was ablaze, and her screams were growing weaker. He had scooped up the child to keep her from her mother, whose clothing and hair still burned. Then he had drawn his revolver, taken careful aim, and put a bullet in the woman's brain.

Andrea had been twelve when her parents had died, and she'd stayed with the guerrilla band for almost three years. Then, in the predawn hours of the second Sunday in May, the government troops had found them. The night before the government attack, for the first time, he and Andrea had made love. As they lay side by side afterward, he'd realized with perfect clarity that he'd just experienced the most important moment of his life.

In the government attack, his parents had died in the first fusillade. He'd been almost seventeen, already a leader in their band. It was expected, he knew, that he must stand and fight beside the bodies of his parents.

Instead, he'd taken his father's favorite weapon, an M-16, and he'd found Andrea, and they'd escaped. They'd—

On the seat beside him, the walkie-talkie beeped. It was Bernhardt speaking from inside the garage:

"It'll be another few minutes—fifteen, probably. Are you still in the driveway?"

"Yes, sir."

"All right. I'll call you before I raise the door."

"Yes."

"Is everything all right on the street?"

"Yes, sir," James answered. "Everything's fine. Just fine."

FORTY-FIVE

"What I want you to do, asshole, is just what you're doing. You sit behind the wheel. You keep both hands on the wheel. That's how you might live through the next ten minutes—you keep your hands on the fucking wheel. You understand?"

"I—yes, I—"

"And look straight ahead. Got it?"

"But I—I—"

"First, though, tell me where the gun is. The trunk? Is that where it is?"

"There's no gun. My God, you—you don't *understand.* I—I'm trying to *tell* you. I'm an important person. Millions, I'm worth millions. I'm president of my own company. I—"

"Is this your car?"

"My car?" Asking the question, desperately puzzled, Powers involuntarily half turned his head, trying to see the man in the back seat.

"Hey!" Harry struck the other man on the side of the head with his nine-millimeter Walther. *"Hey.* Eyes front. Remember?" Once more he struck, felt cold steel bite into warm flesh. Now the Dodgers cap was tilted. Beneath the cap, a trickle of blood began. *"Hey.* I said eyes front, didn't I? Didn't you hear me say that, asshole?"

"I—yes, yes, I heard. But I've got to tell you, got to make you see, I'm not a—a hoodlum. I'm just here to—"

"*Is* this your car?"

"No. It—it belongs to Graham. John Graham. He's—he loaned it to me. He's got my camper. He—they—" Powers broke off, began to shake his head in a slow, helpless arc.

"Yeah? You were saying?" He dug the pistol into Powers's shoulder.

"I was saying that—"

"Your camper. What's it doing here?"

"It—it's—" Suddenly Powers began to sob.

"You carried the money to Sepulveda. In the camper. *Didn't* you?"

"Yes. But—" With great effort, Powers choked back a sob. "But now I—I've changed my mind. I'm not going with them. I don't want—"

Beside Harry, the walkie-talkie sounded.

"Have you got him?" Andrea asked.

"Oh, yeah, I've got him. Want to hear him cry? This guy, he's just about the—"

"Are you in the back seat? And he's in front?"

"Right."

"All right. Stay there. Right there. Understand?"

"Sure. But I can't see what's happening. That truck, it—"

"Stay right there," she repeated. "I'll be with you in a minute. Just a minute."

Andrea put the walkie-talkie on the seat of the BMW, opened the canvas satchel she'd put on the floor in front, and took out the Woodsman and the silencer. The Woodsman's front sight had been filed off and the outside of the barrel threaded to receive the silencer. She screwed on the silencer, tightened it, checked the breech. Yes, there was a cartridge in the chamber. In the clip there were ten more rounds, all jacketed high-speed hollow points, .22 caliber. At close range, the .22 hollow point was more destructive than a .38. She put the gun on the floor, started the BMW, then spoke into the surveillance radio: "I've got to do Harry. And the other one—I've got to do him before he does us."

She guided the BMW out of its parking place, drove slowly to the corner, made a U-turn in the intersection. In the tiny Lucite earphone she heard James say, "Be careful. Be very careful."

"Yes." She switched off the radio, looked in the mirror. In the quiet residential street, only one car was behind her, an orange pickup. She let it pass, then stopped beside the Pontiac, double-parked. She touched the button that lowered the side window, then clambered over the floor console. As the Pontiac's rear window came down, she grasped the Woodsman, clicked off the safety. As she expected he would, Harry kept his eyes on his prisoner in the front seat, presenting her with a perfect target. She raised the pistol, sighted quickly but carefully, and shot him between his left ear and the temple. The force of the impact drove Harry down across the rear seat. Moving with a predator's smooth ferocity, she swung the BMW's passenger door open, got out. In the Pontiac's front seat, his red Dodgers cap askew, clinging desperately to the steering wheel with both hands, the man wearing the wraparound sunglasses was shouting incoherently. She drove the silencer into his neck just below the skull, and fired. In the back seat, Harry was moving, his whole body twitching spasmodically. She shot him twice through the neck and once through the left eye. Number of shots fired: Harry, four, the other man, one. Total, five. In the front seat, the other man was slumped over the steering wheel, his right cheek resting against the rim. Blood was pumping from his neck; the bullet had struck a large artery. She put the silencer to his left temple, squeezed the trigger. Now his body, too, began to twitch. The sunglasses fell on the floor, but the baseball cap, askew, was still on his head. She reached across the seat back and adjusted the cap. Then she carefully examined her fingers for blood.

"Close enough." Bernhardt dropped the last bundle of bills into the duffel bag, drew the white nylon cord tight, and knotted it. Mindful of the strain fifty pounds would put on his back, he flexed his knees, squatted, gripped the brown canvas bag with both hands, and heaved it into the van. Then, one last time, transfixed, he stood staring at the amorphous shape resting now inside the van: incredibly, twenty million dollars in thousand-dollar bills, no more than fifty pounds of paper, another pound or two of canvas.

He closed the van's rear doors, carefully locked them, tested them. He dropped the keys in the pocket of his jacket, buttoned the flap. Graham, too, had finished loading. Standing less than fifteen feet apart, both were acutely aware of the position of the others: the shrill-talking woman who'd come with Graham, sitting in the camper; Paula, flanked by the two dogs, standing between the van and the camper; and Tate, impassive as a sphinx. Cradling the sawed-off in both thick brown arms, Tate had positioned himself so that he could either shoot Graham or shoot out through the garage doors.

"Ready?" Bernhardt asked, directing the question to Graham.

Graham lifted his chin slightly, cleared his throat, finally nodded. "Ready."

"You've got a man outside, in the white Pontiac," Bernhardt said.

"That's correct."

"I've got one man outside, and two cars." He gestured to the walkie-talkie that lay on the cement floor close by; the garage door opener lay beside it. "A man named James is in the blue Accord, blocking the driveway. The Taurus, which is also blocking the driveway, is empty. When I give the word to James, he'll back the Accord clear of the driveway. At that point, when he tells me he's clear, I'll open the garage door with the opener. I'll go outside and—"

"I think," Tate interrupted, "that I should be the one to go out." He spoke very quietly, his broad, muscle-bunched face impassive. Bernhardt knew that look. Tate was making a nonnegotiable demand.

"I'm not sure we should—"

"Al-*an*." If Tate were an enemy, the single word would resonate with menace.

Bernhardt shrugged, then nodded reluctant agreement. "All right. But hide that sawed-off. There're neighbors, you know, middle-class America." He gave Tate the keys to the Taurus, then turned to Paula. "Hold the dogs."

She took a fresh grip on the dogs' collars. Bernhardt turned to Graham. "You're carrying a gun."

"I'm not *carrying* it; I just put it in the camper, on the floor in front. It's an automatic."

Bernhardt nodded, then said, "I want you to get into your camper. Now. When I raise the garage door, you're to back out and then take off. You'll drive, the woman sits beside you. Satisfactory?"

Graham's small smile was strained, plainly forced. His voice was tight: "Perfectly satisfactory." Then, after a brief, quizzical moment he said, "Next time you're in New York, give me a call."

Bernhardt's answering smile, too, was forced. Then: "Ready?" He looked at each of them in turn. Almost in unison, they all nodded. He keyed the radio, saying, "James?"

"Yes, sir?"

"We're all set, and the camper's coming out. Tell me when you're clear of the driveway, and I'll raise the door."

"Yes, sir." And, only moments later: "I'm clear."

"Okay, then. Here we go." Bernhardt aimed the electronic wand. As the big double door began to roll up, one segment at a time, the camper's engine came to life.

With the sawed-off held inconspicuously at his side, waiting for the garage door to rise high enough, Tate was standing in a half-crouched position just inside the door. The bottom of the door reached his waist level, then shoulder level. The Taurus was parked at the curb, across the right side of the driveway. Also parked at the curb, James's Accord was clear of the driveway on the left side. Sitting behind the wheel, James was nodding. So far, so good.

Quickly Tate covered the distance to the Taurus. Keys in hand, he rounded the rear of the car, pulled the driver's door open. He tossed the sawed-off on the passenger's seat and thrust the ignition key home. The engine began to grind, slow to catch. He floorboarded the accelerator; the engine began to fire, but raggedly. He'd flooded it. He pumped the accelerator. Now, finally, the engine was catching, beginning to run smoothly. As he tugged at the gear selector, he caught a flash of movement over his left shoulder. It was a white BMW, coming slowly, with a young woman at the wheel.

Suddenly the BMW's brakes squealed; the car was bouncing to a stop, double-parked beside him, blocking him. Instantly Tate jammed the gear selector into "park." He grabbed for the sawed-off as he threw himself flat across the seat, groped for the door handle on the passenger's side. He heard car doors slam, heard a woman's voice. The door handle—he'd found the handle. He tripped it, threw himself against the passenger's door, tumbled out on the sidewalk, rolled to a crouch, came up with the sawed-off, released the safety. With the Taurus between him and the other two cars, Tate looked back at Bernhardt, who was crouched for combat in the open doorway of the garage. Bernhardt's .357 Magnum was trained on the camper, with Graham and the woman inside.

The camper was blocked by the BMW, unable to escape. Tate raised his head above the roofline of the Taurus, looked again at James and the woman. She was out of the BMW on the far side, with the car protecting her. James was out of the Accord on the street side. Crouched down beside the Accord's engine compartment, the big man held a machine pistol. The large, squared-off pistol, probably an Uzi, was aimed squarely at Tate.

"*Shit!*" Tate dropped to his knees, back pressed against the Taurus's door, as he turned again to face Bernhardt, who had jerked open the camper's door. With his left hand, swearing loudly, Bernhardt was dragging Graham out of the camper; in his right hand Bernhardt held his .357 jammed against Graham's chest. Graham was holding his hands up at shoulder height, palms out, surrendering; simultaneously he was speaking softly, urgently begging Bernhardt to back off, calm down. At Bernhardt's waist, thrust into his belt, Tate saw Graham's Beretta. Tate stole a quick look at James and the woman in the BMW. The woman, too, had a gun—an outsize automatic that she handled expertly. With their weapons trained on Tate, their positions hadn't changed. They were waiting for him to make a move, commit himself.

Tate turned back to face the interior of the garage. Sotto voce, urgently gesturing, he ordered Paula to get the door opener from Bernhardt, lower the garage door. Paula nodded, sharply commanded the dogs to stay, and took the wand from Bernhardt, who was now holding Graham and the woman against the camper, their arms raised. The woman was protesting, sniffling loudly. Her makeup was running, a touch of the bizarre. Graham, his composure re-

gained, was frowning as he looked thoughtfully at Bernhardt. Clearly Graham was planning his next move, calculating the odds.

With the wand in hand, Paula looked urgently at Tate.
When should she lower the door? Tate looked one last time
at James and the woman behind the BMW. With their
weapons trained on him, they had not changed positions.
Tate nodded to Paula. Immediately the garage door mechanism began to grind. Crouched low, clutching the sawed-
off, he eyed the angles, eyed the rate the door was coming
down, calculated the remaining seconds.

When the door was half closed, he sprang forward,
threw himself full length on the driveway, rolled, came up
into a crouch inside the garage as the door thudded closed
behind him. At the same instant, splinters flew from the
door; two bullets from the woman's gun ricocheted, whining close by.

On his feet now, Tate moved immediately to the plain
panel door that connected the garage to the house. He tried
the door: it was locked. "The key—" He turned to Paula
and Bernhardt. "Gimme the *key*." Trailed by the dogs,
Paula strode to her jacket, still on the workbench. In the
pocket she found the keys to the house and garage. She
tossed them to Tate. Both dogs came sharply to attention,
following with their yellow eyes the keys as they tumbled
through the air. Tate caught the keys, went to the service
door, opened it. As he expected, the door could only be
locked from the interior of the house. Anyone coming
through the house had only to turn the knob to enter the
garage.

He turned to Paula. "Where's your gun?"

"In the van—in my bag."

"Get it and hold it on those two." He gestured to Graham and the woman, then beckoned for Bernhardt. Moving

quickly, smoothly, Paula went to the van, took her revolver from her shoulder bag, checked it, then took Bernhardt's place, her gun trained on Graham.

"Hey," the dark-haired woman jeered. "Look at her. She's a regular lady cowboy."

Paula's only response was a contemptuously curled lip. Instantly sensing the animosity between the two women, both dogs growled ominously as they eyed Helen Grant. She eyed them in return, saying angrily, "Oh, shut up."

Immediately both dogs subsided.

Bernhardt and Tate moved to a far corner of the garage, spoke in urgent, apprehensive whispers.

"What the hell's *happening?*" Bernhardt hissed.

"You're asking me? All I know, your buddy James has got an Uzi, and it was aimed right at me."

"That woman—she's the one came to my hotel."

"Yeah, well, looks like she and James made a deal. Least, their guns're pointing the same direction. At me."

"Jesus . . ."

"You think they're in it with Graham?" Tate asked. "That the feeling you get from Graham?"

"Hell, with Graham, who can tell?"

"That woman—what's her name?"

"Andrea, she said. Andrea Lange."

"Well, she's got a gun with a silencer, and she knows how to use it. Reason I say that, there's a couple of holes in the garage door, right where I was."

"James . . ." Baffled, Bernhardt shook his head. "Jesus, I thought he was rock solid."

"Looks like to me they're fixing to hijack the whole shipment. Everything. And with that Uzi, they can do it." Urgently Tate gestured to the interior service door. "I'm going to take a look inside the house, see if I can spot any more of them out there. Also check the doors and windows. Last thing we want is James behind us, with that goddam Uzi."

Bernhardt's gaze was fixed on Graham. Was this Graham's try for the brass ring, a once-in-a-lifetime gamble? In Graham's face, nothing was revealed.

"What d'you think about calling the police?"

"Shit, man, the neighbors, they saved us the trouble, probably. A big brown-skinned guy with a Uzi taking cover behind his car, like in the movies. A foxy-looking lady with a silencer and a fancy car—wouldn't you call the police?"

"That's not what I asked."

"Well, first place, we got no phone, if you remember. And then, shit, we're handling stolen property here. This thing, those paintings, all that money, first thing they'll do is put us in the slammer. *Then* they'll sort it all out. Meaning that DuBois's lawyers would dump it all on us, sure as hell."

Bernhardt gestured to the interior door. "Check out the house. I think you can see the driveway from the living room. See if they're still there. We—Christ—we're blind in this goddam garage."

"Right."

"Right."

Tate unlocked the door, pushed it open, entered the house, closed the door.

Bernhardt remained motionless for a moment, frozen in thought. Then he called out, "Graham. Get over here." He raised the .357, trained it on Graham as the insurance man came striding toward him. Graham's expression was watchful, revealing nothing.

"What's happening, John? You've got thirty seconds."

"Oh? And then? Are you going to shoot me, Alan?" He

shook his head. "I don't think so." The smile twisted ironically. Graham had recovered his composure.

"You bought James off."

"James? Is that his name?"

Bernhardt made no reply. Instead, ominously, he moved the barrel of the .357 closer to Graham's chin.

"Listen, Alan, you'd better come up with something, and fast. Odds are, somebody's called the police."

"Does that worry you, someone calling the police?"

"Definitely, it worries me. Then there's Powers, out there somewhere. He's wearing a red Dodgers cap and shades, and he's pissing his pants, he's so scared. He worries me, too. He's—"

"Powers?" Bernhardt blinked, involuntarily lowered the revolver. "*Justin* Powers?"

Graham sighed deeply, regretfully. "Powers and I are partners, you might say. Newly minted."

Bernhardt stared incredulously. Then, furious, he grabbed the other man, felt the fabric of Graham's shirt tear between his fingers. "You're lying."

"No, Alan, I'm not lying. Time is too short to lie." Then: "This is a Brooks Brothers shirt. So if you would kindly—"

"I know Powers. He doesn't have the balls for this."

Graham shrugged. "I agree. But he's running scared. Very, very scared. At the moment he's running my way. Of course, he thinks I'm running his way."

"That woman out there—is she with you?"

"No."

Bernhardt searched Graham's face, tested the steadiness of the other man's gaze. At that moment the interior door clicked, swung open. Tate entered the garage, closed the door. With his eyes on Graham, Bernhardt spoke to Tate: "Could you see them from the living room?"

Also eyeing Graham, Tate nodded impassively. The message: his information wasn't for Graham's ears.

"Oh, shit." Suddenly overwhelmed by an unreasoning anger that transcended caution, Bernhardt shook his head sharply. "Graham's all right. At least, I *think* he's all right."

"Hmmm." Reflectively Tate stroked the blued-steel breech of the shotgun as he stared suspiciously at Graham.

"Come *on*, C.B. *Talk*."

With deep reluctance, Tate shrugged. "Looks like it's a standoff. What they're doing, they're both inside their cars, and the cars block the driveway. They're hunkered down, keeping a real low profile. Looks like they're waiting for us to come out."

"So if the police come," Graham mused, "then what?"

"They're either going to shoot it out," Tate said, "or they'll run."

"If the police come," Bernhardt said, "we're all screwed."

"Some more than others," Graham said. "You'll have to answer for weapons possession plus possession of stolen property."

"This whole thing started with you," Bernhardt shot back. "You did the planning, the manipulating."

"Ah, but that's my job, you see. Recovering items that we've reinsured. So if the police—"

"The longer you guys talk," Tate said, "the worse it could be getting."

Bernhardt's gaze shifted to the two women, visible through the side windows on the far side of the camper. With Paula's revolver between them, they were eyeing each other with profound hostility. The dogs, though, were lying down, no longer on alert. The male dog was yawning, lowering his head to rest between his paws.

"Your lady friend," Bernhardt said. "What's her name?"

"It's Helen. Helen Grant. Except that—" Graham cautiously dropped his voice, stole a look at the women, still on the far side of the camper. "Except that I'm ah, rethinking my, ah, relationship with Helen. In New York, in bed, she's great. These last few days, though—" He shook his head ruefully.

"What's her part in all this?"

"Down the line, she's supposed to be a courier—and bed partner, of course. But, as I said—" Enigmatically he spread his hands.

"I think," Bernhardt said, "that I'm going to give you about one minute to tell me exactly where you stand in all this, what game you're playing. If I like what I hear, then you can play on our team. Otherwise—" He nodded in the direction of the garage door. "Otherwise, as they say, we're going to throw you outside the wagons."

"In that case," Graham came back, "I'd simply join their team."

"That," Tate said, "might be a big mistake."

"One minute," Bernhardt said. "Maybe two, if I like what I hear."

Graham shrugged. Then, in his easy, urbane voice, he said, "The truth is that shortly after we first talked, in San Francisco, I decided to go into business for myself. At first, it started as a fantasy. How would it work? How could I pull it off on my own, with no backing? I suppose it became an obsession, figuring all the angles. I had everything I needed—the connections, and the expertise. What I didn't have was the money. There was no way I was going to dip into the company till, even if it would've been possible.

"And then, by accident, almost, I discovered Powers. As

you know, he regularly deals in tens of millions—DuBois's millions. If I do say so—" In fond memory of his own manipulating, Graham smiled gently. "If I do say so, I played him brilliantly."

"You're looking to buy the stuff with DuBois's own money." As he said it, Tate smiled appreciatively. "Smooth. Very smooth."

Graham's smile widened. "Thank you. What's your name again?"

"Tate. C.B. Tate."

In acknowledgment, Graham nodded genially.

"Where's Powers now?" Bernhardt asked.

"He should be a block from here, hiding out. He's driving a rental Pontiac. White. Helen and I are supposed to pick him up when we leave."

Bernhardt studied Graham for a long moment before he said, "You and Helen get inside your camper. Roll up the windows." He waited for them to obey, then gestured Tate and Paula to a far corner of the garage. With their eyes on Graham and Helen Grant, they spoke in low voices.

"This is my fault," Bernhardt said. "We should've done this in some remote place. Not a goddam residential neighborhood."

"I don't agree," Paula said. "Some remote place, there'd be shooting by now."

"If there's only Graham and Helen Grant," Tate said, "then we could go for it, winner take all. We got them outnumbered."

"But whoever's outside has got us outgunned," Bernhardt said.

"Yeah, well—"

"What about Graham?" Bernhardt asked. "His story—does it add up?" He looked at each of them in turn.

"I think it does," Paula said. "As much as I heard."

"Likewise," Tate said. "Plus, he's got a sense of humor. Bad guys, they don't smile much."

"The woman outside," Bernhardt mused. "She must be calling the shots, pulling James's strings. Somehow she turned James."

"God." Incredulously Paula shook her head. "This is unbelievable. Here we are, theorizing, while some guy out there has an Uzi."

"And millions—tens of millions—in here," Tate said.

"What about the police?" Paula asked. "I could go through to the back of the house, hop a couple of fences, use a neighbor's phone."

"The police could save our lives," Bernhardt answered. "But they could also send us to prison. Besides, James and the woman could have the back covered. We're assuming there's just the two of them plus Powers. But that could be wrong."

"On the other hand," Tate offered, "maybe they'd like to see us escape out the back. That'd leave them to take the van and the camper out the front."

A speculative silence fell. Then Tate said, "That guy—James. We take him and his Uzi out, all we got to worry about is the woman." He gestured to the interior door. "Why don't I go back into the living room, see if I can get a shot at him?"

Thinking it over, their eyes locked together, frowning, Bernhardt and Paula exchanged a long, complicated look. In her eyes, Bernhardt saw no trace of fear, only sharp-focused intensity. Finally he shook his head. "We start shooting, it's a goddam war. This is suburbia, not South Central. There'd be police here in two minutes. The goddam SWAT team." He spoke reflectively, almost pensively. Then his gaze shifted speculatively; his eyes began to wander away. Watching him, Paula drew a deep breath. She knew this look.

"What we need," Bernhardt said softly, "is a diversion."

"A diversion?" Paula asked.

"Right." He holstered the .357 at his belt, zipped up his jacket to cover it, and turned toward the interior door. "A diversion."

FORTY-SIX

They stood together in the open doorway, both of them looking out at the vista of Middle America, a cross-hatched pattern of backyards defined by endless fences, most of them head high. In a tract that had probably been planned less than twenty years ago, there were few trees, none of them mature. Some of the backyards featured small swimming pools; others, large wading pools. In the relative quiet of a weekday morning, the sounds, too, were Middle American: dogs barking, children crying, children laughing, stereos playing too loudly. On a warm April day, many of the surrounding houses had their rear windows open. In this setting, there was no place for a gunman to hide.

The backyard at 4174 Twenty-sixth Street was brown and bare, neglected. A patio was attached to the house, shaded by green corrugated plastic roofing. There was a cheap three-legged barbecue, a round white plastic table, and four white plastic chairs.

"Shall I let the dogs out?" Paula asked.

"No," Bernhardt answered. "They might start barking when they see me hopping the fence."

Her answering nod was tentative, tremulous. Paula was frightened for him—for them. Requiring that he kiss her soundly, broaden the smile reassuringly before he went to the patio, took a chair, and walked the length of the yard. As he walked, he verified that his revolver was secure in its holster, verified that his address book was safely buttoned in the pocket of his jacket. Then, with his back to Paula, who had gone inside and was watching him through a rear window of the house, he put the chair against the high redwood fence, tested it, then gingerly stepped up on the chair. The neighboring backyard was grassy, and was crowded with children's playthings, even a full-size jungle gym. With his hands spread on top of the fence, he remained motionless, watching the house for some sign of life. To discipline himself, enforce patience, he began slowly counting.

At forty-seven he saw movement behind one of the rear windows. A moment later the back door swung inward. A young girl was standing in the doorway, facing him. Without moving he smiled at her. Like a small, skittish animal, she began advancing toward him. When she'd covered half the distance, something moved in the house behind her. It was the door, again swinging inward. Waddling slightly as he walked, an outsize Weimaraner was in the yard, trotting toward the girl. Moments later, both the girl and the dog stood together, looking up at Bernhardt.

"What—ah—" Bernhardt cleared his throat. "What's your dog's name?"

"It's Bentley," the little girl said. "That's a car, really."

At the sound of his name, the dog blinked, then reflectively gazed at Bernhardt as he licked his chops.

"And what's your name?"

"It's Susan. I'm eight and a half."

"Ah." Bernhardt nodded genially. "Susan. My name is Alan. Alan Bernhardt. I'm your new neighbor." Then, on speculation, he added, "We have dogs, too. My, ah, wife and I. Two dogs."

She nodded gravely. Then: "Are they boy dogs? Or girl dogs?"

"One of each. They're named Duke and Duchess."

"Is Duchess a girl dog?"

"That's right." Broadly encouraging, he nodded again. "A girl dog. Yes."

"Well, Bentley might like Duchess. But he'd start a fight with Duke. He always does with boy dogs."

"Listen, Susan—is your mother home?"

"She's ironing a tablecloth. She and my dad are having a party tonight."

"Well, could you ask your mother to come out for just a minute? See, we just had a phone put in—just yesterday. But it quit working, and there's a call I have to make. So I—"

Once more the door opened, this time to reveal a small, chubby woman wearing an incongruous ruffled gingham apron over stretch blue jeans. Her head was covered with pink plastic curlers.

"Hi." Putting everything into it, affability personified, Bernhardt smiled at the woman, who coolly nodded in return. But, minutes later, with the Weimaraner's muzzle never more than a few inches from Bernhardt's legs, they were walking toward the house. Once inside, the woman pointed into the kitchen. "Use that phone," she said. "See, on the wall beside the refrigerator."

"Ah." Once more Bernhardt summoned his most ingratiating smile. "Yes. Thanks." He put his address book on a counter, found the P's, and touch-toned the number he wanted. When a woman answered, he identified himself and stated his business. The woman sounded young and bored and distant. "Cool," in contemporary jargon.

"I'll see if I can locate Mr. Penziner," she said. "I think he—"

"Tell Mr. Penziner this is very, very important. Tell him he's got to talk to me. Now. Right now."

"Well, I'll see whether he's available."

Bernhardt lowered his voice, brought the phone very close. "If you don't put him on," he grated, "you'll regret it. I promise you."

"Mr. Bernhardt, did you say?" The question dripped with malice. She was, Bernhardt suspected, an aspiring actress. Penziner always hired actresses for his front office. Young, willing actresses.

"*Alan* Bernhardt. And Bernie and I—"

"Just a moment, please." The line clicked, abruptly cutting him off. Waiting, Bernhardt looked over his shoulder. The little girl and the big dog stood in the doorway, staring steadily at him. Bernhardt smiled at the girl, then shifted his gaze to the kitchen window. He was high enough to see into the backyard at 4174 Twenty-sixth Street. There was no movement, no sign of life. Paula was watching him, he knew, but she was able to conceal herself. She—

"*Alan.*" It was Penziner's voice, warm and hearty. During Bernhardt's marginal two years in Hollywood, both of them struggling, they'd been good friends. For several months, they'd dated sisters. Penziner had married his; Bernhardt had decided to move to San Francisco. "Jesus, I've been meaning to call you for months. I heard you—"

"Listen, Bernie, I've got a problem. A big problem."

"Oh?" The inflection of the single word was complex—concerned, but cautious. Plainly Penziner was wondering whether Bernhardt's problem was financial.

"What I need," Bernhardt said, "is a unit. Four, five people, plus equipment. But I need it now. Right now. They've got to roll in fifteen minutes, no more."

"Oh?" This response was also cautious. There remained an essential element, still not addressed.

"It'll be thirty minutes on-site, no more. I'll pay five

thousand on the spot, win or lose. If it's a win, tomorrow I'll pay another five thousand."

"Ah . . ." This time, the response was warm. And, yes, relieved.

FORTY-SEVEN

Andrea heard a high-pitched voice behind her, certainly a child's. She was standing close beside the BMW, exposing only her head above the car's roof as she watched the house. Now, with the Woodsman pressed to her torso, concealed, she turned in the direction of the voice. Two young boys were riding their bicycles in the center of the street, coming toward her. She glanced at James, who stood, like her, close to his car. The driver's window of his Accord was open; James was holding the Uzi inside the car, resting on the driver's seat. The transparent earpiece of his surveillance radio was almost invisible. Knowing that she would track the newcomers, he looked steadily toward the house.

As they drew closer, the two boys, no more than twelve, fell silent. Both of them were coasting now, eyeing her with open curiosity. One of them said something to the other, and they laughed together, then looked at her again, broadly lascivious. Unable to face them without exposing the Woodsman she held between her body and the car, she decided to ignore them. When they'd disappeared around the nearest corner, Andrea spoke into the surveillance radio: "This is no good."

"The police," James answered. "They could be a problem."

Eyeing the house and garage, she made no reply. The house was detached, with at least twenty feet of grass separating it from its neighbors on either side. High redwood fences bisected the lot lines. The house at 4174 had no service door offering outside access to the garage. Therefore, if the big double door was down, it was necessary to enter the garage from inside the house.

"Harry and the other one," James was saying. "The enforcer. If someone finds them, calls the police . . ."

"I pushed both of them down across the seats. They can't be seen from the street. I made sure."

He made no reply, but she could sense his uneasiness. Because they were so close, had always been so close, he'd agreed to take this risk. For her. Only for her, this once-in-a-lifetime risk. But now he—

"*Cariña*," James was saying. "What is this coming?"

She turned. Rounding the corner, a bright orange sedan was coming toward them. A large panel truck was following the sedan. The truck, too, was bright orange. A rack atop the truck mounted searchlights, booms, loudspeaker cones, ladders, and large metal equipment boxes. Everything was painted the same bright orange. As the van drew abreast of them, stopping, she saw the gilt lettering on its side:

COVERAGE, INC.

From the living room, Paula called out, "They're here, Alan."

With Tate at his side, Bernhardt turned to Graham and Helen Grant, sitting in their camper. In Graham's face Bernhardt saw a kind of detached, well-bred curiosity: a spectator's interest in what would happen next. In the woman's face he saw sullen resentment compounded by fear.

"You two stay in the camper." Bernhardt spoke softly, urgently. "I'm going to raise the door." He gestured with

338

the wand. "I'm going to go outside. Now. Right now. I'm going to go right to the camera crew. I'm going to tell them we've got to clear the entrance to the garage. That puts it up to James and the woman—move the BMW and the Accord to let us out, or start shooting. If they start shooting, everything's up for grabs. But if they decide to move their cars, because of all the attention they're getting, then that's our chance. You go first—back the camper out, and go wherever you're going. You've got your paintings, and we've got the money. So now you're on your own. Understood?"

Graham nodded. "Perfectly. Would you mind giving me my Beretta?"

Bernhardt looked at Tate, who shrugged. Bernhardt considered, took the pistol from his belt, dropped the clip. He gave the empty pistol to Graham, gave the clip to Helen Grant. She looked down at the clip in her hand, then closed her fingers over it. Her expression was unreadable. Watching her, Graham smiled appreciatively, thrust the empty revolver in his belt.

"Start the engine," Bernhardt ordered. "Now. Right now. Get ready." But then, irresistibly, he had to ask "Where're you going from here?"

"We're going to the airport," Graham said.

"And then?"

"And then back to New York. The hell with larceny. Suddenly my corner office looks pretty good." Seeing Bernhardt smile, Graham said, "If everything works out, let's do that lunch."

"Fine." Bernhardt waited for the camper's engine to catch, then activated the door opener. As the big double door began to rise, he heard the door chimes: the camera people were at the living room door, ready to go to work. He arrested the door's progress halfway up and called out to Paula, "Tell them to meet me outside." When he heard her acknowledgment, he started the garage door again, waiting for it to roll up.

"Stay inside your car," Andrea ordered. "Keep the guns out of sight. Keep your eye on me." As she spoke, she slipped quickly into the BMW, put the Woodsman with its silencer on the floor, nudged it under the driver's seat. From under the passenger seat she took a 7.65 Walther. She jacked a cartridge into the chamber, lowered the hammer, managed to slip the pistol into the soft leather shoulder holster she wore under the loose-fitting safari jacket without being observed. She opened the driver's door, got out, dropped the tiny surveillance earpiece and microphone into the pocket of her jacket. As she stepped away from the car and turned to her left, she saw the garage door rolling up. To her right, men and women were getting out of the orange van and car— five people altogether. While some of the newcomers began unloading their equipment, one of the men was walking toward Alan Bernhardt, who stood in the open doorway of the garage. There were two cars inside the garage—the camper and the van. One of them, the camper, had transported the money. The other vehicle, a Dodge van, had most certainly transported the paintings. She realized that her entire attention, her entire being, was focused on the two vehicles inside the garage. Here, now—incongruously—she stood within a few feet of her goal: treasures beyond calculation, hers for the taking.

Or the losing.

"I'm Alec Duncan. Are you Alan Bernhardt?" The newcomer was short and stocky. He wore a wide-brimmed Stetson with a snakeskin band. His manner was brusque, all business.

"That's right."

Standing in front of the open garage door, they shook hands perfunctorily. Then Duncan looked at his surroundings with a professional air. "What you've got, Bernie says, it's time-sensitive. He also says you're an actor. Director, too. So tell me what you want."

"First there's an exterior shot of the house and garage." Falling into the familiar patterns, once his stock-in-trade, Bernhardt began gesturing, blocking it out, improvising. "One exterior camera'll probably be enough. Setting up on the sidewalk, that should work. A short pan to get the whole house, that's the opening shot."

"What about the action angles?"

"The action is just two people in a convertible Jag with the top down coming down the street"—Bernhardt pointed—"then going into the garage, which automatically opens as they approach. The people are very upscale, very with it—the beautiful people. Obviously they don't belong here. That's the sense of the opening shot. "Ugh,' the girl says, looking at the house. 'Tacky.' She's dressed in shorts and a tank top, really built. That's the opening."

Duncan frowned, quickly surveyed his surroundings. "Where's the Jag and the couple?"

"They're around the corner, waiting." Bernhardt raised his walkie-talkie. "There're all set to go, once I tell them."

"It sounds a little sketchy."

"Don't worry. You get set up. Then, when you're ready, I want you to put one of your vehicles in the garage, once we get the camper out. Maybe you should figure two cameras, come to think about it, one for the interiors, in the garage. See, the entire action takes place in the garage."

"Hmmm." Plainly, Duncan was doubtful.

"First thing," Bernhardt said, "we've got to clear the driveway, then move the camper out into the street. That's first."

"Whatever." Clearly disenchanted, Duncan turned, walked back to his sound truck.

Bernhardt turned back to the open doorway of the garage. Yes, Tate and Paula had stepped back deep into the garage, one on either side of the van, in position to reach inside for their weapons. Bernhardt nodded to them both, gestured for them to stay put. Now he turned to face the growing cluster of vehicles and people spilling out into the street. Then, with a sense of heaviness, an unexplained reluctance, he exchanged a long, searching look with the woman he knew as Andrea.

Of course, she *would* be driving a BMW, leaning easily against it, eyeing him inscrutably. And, yes, she wore her khaki safari clothing with unparalleled flair. Her dark, vivid eyes were incredibly alive.

Slowly, with deliberation, he began walking toward her. He watched her shift her stance as he approached, squaring off against him.

"Who are you?" he asked. "Who are you really?"

"Nobody you know, Mr. Bernhardt."

"You and James—you're in this together."

She made no response. Her eyes were dark and calm and calculating. She was, Bernhardt realized, a formidable adversary. Formidable and incredibly desirable.

"There's someone else. There has to be."

She made no response.

They were standing close together on the driver's side of the BMW. Ostensibly, Bernhardt knew, they looked like a companionable couple, deep in discussion. Leading to her right ear, from the pocket of her stylishly cut khaki jacket, he saw a thin, transparent wire that disappeared into her dark, close-cut hair. She was wearing a wire. Or was it a tiny radio, to communicate with James? He looked at her hands, her wrists. Yes, a companion wire led from the pocket to her right hand. It was a miniature surveillance radio, her edge. The radio connected the three of them: the woman, James, and the Uzi.

"We plan to leave with the paintings," she said. "You take the money. And let us leave. Unblock the driveway. Get these people out of here."

"If I don't?"

"James starts shooting."

"That's bullshit. There're a dozen witnesses."

"All unarmed. The first shot and they'll all be flat on their bellies."

"My people are armed. Heavily armed."

"Your people are in the garage. When it's time, James will kill them all." She mocked him with a smile. "Bad tactics, Mr. Bernhardt, keeping them in the garage. They're sitting ducks."

"While James is killing them—" He discreetly drew back his jacket to reveal the .357, holstered at his belt. "I shoot you. Then James."

She made no reply. Instead, her eyes locked with his, she drew back her own jacket to revel a small automatic in a shoulder holster. As she let her jacket fall together, he glanced covertly back over her shoulder. The camera crew was completely set up. Alec Duncan, standing beside the camera, was plainly impatient, looking to Bernhardt for instructions. Duncan tapped his watch. Except for an almost imperceptible shake of his head, Bernhardt did not respond.

But the woman had caught Bernhardt's covert look, and involuntarily moved her head to follow his glance. Instantly Bernhardt stepped forward. With one short, quick sweep of his hand he hooked the wire leading into her right hand. A sharp tug, and the wire came free, snaked through the air. Following through, he grasped her right wrist, twisted, wrestled with her, threw his full weight into a hammerlock. The silent struggle was fierce; the pain forced her to turn with him, come hard against him, her back to his front. Her body bucked wildly, but she couldn't break the hammerlock. With her left hand she was trying for the shoulder holster. He switched his grip on her right wrist to his left hand, used his right hand to reach across her body, grasp the butt of her Walther. With possession of the gun, he thrust it into his belt, then put increased pressure on the hammerlock. Even while she writhed in pain, she still fought him, kicking for his shins. As he drew her body tight against his, feeling her struggle, unconquered, as wild and defiant as a trapped animal, he realized that he was sexually aroused. If they were alone, in some elemental descent into the final brutality, he might have raped her.

They struggled silently, secretly, both realizing that witnesses would endanger them both. A last cruel twist of her arm lifted her on her toes; the pain finally wrung from her a gasp of pain. He looked at the nearby faces. Only one face—a boy's—was watching them; everyone else, curious, was watching the film crew. Breathing hard, Bernhardt bent over her shoulder, whispered into her ear from behind: "Walk over to James."

"Ah . . ." It was an inarticulate refusal, another animal response.

"*Walk*, or the arm comes out of the socket." He shifted his grip again, increased the pressure, felt her body's involuntary response, heard her gasp, heard her curse him, a vicious string of obscenities.

"*Walk*."

One step. Two. In the blue Accord, seated behind the wheel, James was motionless, his obsidian eyes revealing nothing as he watched them come closer. With her back to him, their bodies pressed together, they covered the last few feet to the Accord.

Once more Bernhardt shifted his grip on her arm, grasping her right wrist with his left hand. With his right hand he surreptitiously drew the .357. He rested it flat on the woman's right shoulder, so that James could see the muzzle aimed at her neck.

As, from Bernhardt's right, where the second camera was now set up, he saw Alec Duncan. Making no effort to conceal his mounting impatience, Duncan once more advanced on Bernhardt. As he drew close, frowning, Duncan said, "Alan, I just talked to Bernie. Maybe he didn't tell you, but—" Seeing the gun, realizing that Bernhardt held the woman helpless, Duncan broke off, stopped dead in his tracks. Bernhardt saw his eyes widen, saw him swallow hard.

"Hey." Duncan blinked. "Hey, what—"

"We're rehearsing. I decided to scrub the Jag. Tell Bernie it'll be another few minutes. Tell him I'll pay. I'll double my original offer. Tell Bernie that."

"But—"

"*Tell* him, goddammit. Go back to the cameras, and call Bernie. *Now.*"

"Well, Jesus, sure." Duncan stepped one long stride backward, then turned, began walking fast to the camera truck. Bernhardt watched him take a cellular phone from the truck's dash, watched him punch out a number, saw him begin to talk. Was it Bernie Penziner, Duncan was talking to—or the police? If it was the police, seconds counted.

Bernhardt shifted his gaze to the open garage. Both Tate and Paula, their handguns concealed, the sawed-off out of sight, had left the shelter of the van, and had advanced almost to the sidewalk, both of them with their eyes fixed intently on him. It was as if they were restrained only by the force of some invisible barrier that had replaced the garage door. As he watched, he saw Paula say something to Tate, who nodded grimly. Still in the camper, Graham and Helen Grant had not moved. They simply sat motionless, eyes front. Graham, then, was out of it, now no more than a spectator, one potential danger neutralized, their rear secured. When the driveway was clear, Graham would take the paintings and leave.

Bernhardt was about to speak to James when he caught a flicker of movement through the van's rear window. It was one of the dogs. Assessing the variables, Paula had decided to confine the dogs in the van—with the money. He smiled, looked at Paula, looked back at the van, then nodded to her. She'd converted the dogs, wild cards, into assets. In this delicate situation, she'd positioned them perfectly.

Slowly, cautiously, he slightly relaxed the hammerlock, breathing into the woman's ear: "We've got to get out of this. Both of us—we've got to get out, or we're screwed. If that director calls the cops, we've had it. Understand?"

She made no reply. But, still holding her close, he could feel her fury subside. Yes, she understood. Still cautiously, he backed off his grip. Lowering the .357, his finger on the trigger, he slipped the pistol inside his open jacket, pointed at the woman.

She stepped away, then turned to face him. Her eyes blazed, her lips were drawn back from tightly clenched teeth. Distorted by fury, her face was no longer beautiful. Still holding the .357 under his jacket, he turned with her so that the concealed pistol remained trained on her.

"You see this gun inside my jacket?"

She dropped her eyes contemptuously down at the bulging jacket, but made no reply. James's eyes were fixed on her: the hired gun, waiting. Whatever the woman ordered, James would do. Whatever power she held over him, it was absolute.

Ignoring James—but keeping him always in his peripheral vision—Bernhardt spoke to the woman: "James is carrying a nine-millimeter Glock, plus the Uzi. What I want him to do is leave the guns on the floor of the car." He gestured to the Accord. "Then I want the two of you to go to the BMW and get in. Both of you. Then"—he pointed—"move the BMW about ten feet ahead, so the camper can back out of the garage. You're to drive very slowly. I'll be walking beside you—with my gun. When you're clear of the driveway, I'll take your keys. The two of you will stay in the BMW. At that point, the camper backs out of the driveway, and leaves the scene. You'll—"

"The paintings," she said. "They'll have the paintings in the camper?"

Bernhardt's smile was rapacious. "Does that bother you?"

She made no reply. Her eyes said it all. Never, Bernhardt knew, would he face hatred like this.

"Next," Bernhardt said, "I'll tell the camera crew to leave. You're to stay in your car during the time it takes them to pack up and leave. When they're gone, we'll leave in our van. We'll have the Uzi and the Glock. As we pass you, I'll toss your keys out in the street. And that'll be the end of it. If you can get away, fine. So far as I know—whatever I could testify to—you're clean. What problems you have with the law, that's no concern of mine."

The woman said nothing. But James, still inside the Accord, said, "You have the money in the van, Mr. Bernhardt?" As always, he spoke quietly, respectfully.

For a long, thoughtful moment Bernhardt studied the big man. Then: "Why, James. Tell me why."

"I have nothing but good feelings for you, Mr. Bernhardt. And Mr. DuBois, too. I would not harm him."

"That's not what I asked."

"I am aware of that, sir." James allowed his dark, opaque eyes to rest for a moment upon Bernhardt. Then, solemnly, he shifted his gaze to the woman. His meaning was clear.

Bernhardt's smile was reflective now as he nodded once to James. Yes, one male animal to another, Bernhardt understood. The woman possessed him.

For a long, final moment neither of them spoke or looked directly at each other. Then, in response to some secret sign from the woman, moving with great deliberation, James put his pistol and Uzi on the floor of the Accord. In a companionable group, as they walked to the BMW, Bernhardt looked at Tate and nodded. So far, so good.

When they were clear of the garage, Bernhardt stopped the van, got out, activated the electronic wand. As the door came down, he tossed the wand and house keys inside the garage. Then he got back in the van, behind the wheel. He and Paula sat in the front seat, the Uzi on the floor between them. Tate followed in the Taurus with the sawed-off. As the tension subsided, the dogs dozed, their heads pillowed on the duffel bag filled with thousand-dollar bills. Bernhardt drew a deep breath, smiled at Paula.

"Last lap."

"Thank God. I'm a wreck."

They were still parked in the driveway, engine running. Bernhardt surveyed the scene: the Accord, empty, parked at the curb to his left; the BMW, also parked, to their right. In the BMW, the woman who called herself Andrea sat with both hands on the steering wheel. James sat beside her, his hands concealed. It was possible, Bernhardt knew, that there were more weapons inside the BMW; he'd decided not to check when he escorted them to the car. They might have pistols, but he had the Uzi, along with the keys to their car. He'd decided to discount the possibility that they traveled with a second set of keys, a negligible risk.

"I'm turning left," Bernhardt said, speaking to Tate. "You can watch them as we drive away."

"Right."

Bernhardt released the parking brake, waited for a car to pass, backed the van out of the driveway. As he turned left, away from the BMW, Paula said, "Didn't you tell them you were going to toss them the keys when it was all over?"

"That's true, I did. But I lied."

FORTY-EIGHT

"It wasn't the money," DuBois said. "James would never do it for the money."

"Whatever the woman told him to do," Bernhardt said, "he did. I had the impression of an automaton."

"Before I hired him, I commissioned a background check, of course. I was told there was a woman. Her grandfather was a high-ranking Nazi who fled to Argentina during the last days of the war. When she was very young, her parents were killed by the guerrilla band that James's parents led. Afterwards, she went with the band—with James. By all reports she was remarkable, even at a very young age. She was beautiful, ruthless, acutely intelligent. And, like her grandfather, utterly amoral."

Bernhardt nodded decisively. "That's her. Do you have a name?"

DuBois waved to the filing cabinets built into the wall beside his desk. "It's in James's file. If you care to read the file, you're welcome."

With thanks, Bernhardt nodded, then shook his head. Not now.

"If you've made an enemy of this woman," DuBois said, "you should be careful."

"What about you, sir?" Bernhardt gestured to the bagful of thousand-dollar bills he'd carried from the garage, where

Paula and Tate now waited. "This money—what about security, with James gone?"

"When you left with the paintings I called my lawyer.
Mr. Robbins. He has arranged for a Brinks truck to take the
money from here to Powers and Associates at my command. Whereupon I'd planned to contact Mr. Powers, with
instructions to deposit the money in a trading account.
However, I'm somehow unable to contact Mr. Powers.
He—"

"From something Graham said," Bernhardt interrupted, "I have the feeling that Powers, ah, defected."

"You mean—" The old man let it go unfinished.

"It looks like both James and Powers betrayed you, Mr.
Dubois. All that money . . ." Heavily, Bernhardt shook his
head, dropped his eyes to the large earth-brown duffel bag
and the small red nylon flight bag resting against the it. The
duffel bag contained eighteen million dollars. The flight bag
contained Bernhardt's commission: two million dollars.

"But the paintings," DuBois said. "You believe, do you
not, that Graham will deliver the paintings to his people in
New York."

"Yes, sir, I do. I believe that he intended to steal them.
But then I believe he lost his nerve. Or came to his senses,
take your pick."

"Ah." DuBois nodded. "If that is true, then it is all that
matters." DuBois nodded again, an expression of philosophical resignation to betrayal. If anyone understood the
mechanics of greed, it was surely Raymond DuBois.

"Mr. DuBois . . ." This time Bernhardt pointed to the
bags filled with thousand-dollar bills. "James must know
I'd bring the money here. And he's out there somewhere,
with that woman. He's got all your security codes. Everything. Christ, you—you're defenseless."

351

DuBois nodded calmly. "I know."

"But I—I can't leave you like this."

Once more the old man nodded. Then, faintly, he smiled. "I know, Mr. Bernhardt. I know."